THE
CALL
OF
FIRE

A
NATURA
ELEMENTALS
NOVEL

SLOANE
CALDER

Published by Pretty Dynamite Press, LLC, Austin, Texas

ISBN: 9781733379458 (paperback)
LCCN: 2020920692

Cover Design by Hang Le
Editing by Holly Ingraham and Joyce Lamb
Formatting by Champagne Book Design

To my husband and children
Thank you for supporting my dream

Of living things, some are made friends with Fire and some with Water,
Some with Air and some with Earth, and some with two of these,
Though a rare few with all.

From the Greek text Kore Kosmou, 510 BC

THE
CALL
OF
FIRE

CHAPTER
ONE

Savannah, GA

Twenty paces, and the wait would be over.

Aleron Foussé gripped the gate's black spires. His Fire element rose, and beneath his hands, the iron glowed red. He killed the heat and bowed his head to open his senses, casting his power through streets canopied by moss-draped Spanish oaks.

Might as well dull his Fire element now of his own accord. The moment he walked through the gate, the inhibitors would render him neutered. He'd be a double-mantled Fire reduced to a weak-ass warlock, if only temporarily.

He'd hate every second of it as much as he hated Seanair Lennox, so he'd get in, get his orders, and get out.

He reined in his energy. Now was not the time to risk a human catching a glimpse of his hands lighting up like glowsticks. Humankind had to be kept ignorant of the elemental powers inherent to the Natura race, powers that had been battering and rocking the earth since the dawn of Homo sapiens.

His need to remain concealed from humans didn't have his Fire in a fury. Truth was, hiding his power had become habit. What he needed was to kill Seanair, and he'd do it in the streets like a blazin' Wild West showdown if he could get away with it.

But he couldn't.

Besides, acting rashly on his revenge—and without the

Goddess's help—wouldn't get him anything but dead. Both brutal and power mad, Seanair wasn't reckless. He hadn't killed his way to the top of the North American Naturas by using the "light" version of his powers, and Aleron wouldn't be able to catch him unaware.

What Aleron needed still seemed impossible. He had to get their leader alone in one of the Goddess's chapels. Those were the only places on the planet where Seanair let down his guard, but in the twelve years Aleron had been in the monster's servitude, he'd never seen an opportunity.

He looked at the mansion, squinting against the sunlight and the pain lancing through his head. The spear in his temples struck when he snuffed out the simmering siren call to obliterate the man who'd killed Bill Foussé, the greatest man who'd ever lived.

His father.

He took a long, slow, Fire-dampening breath. It didn't matter if it took twelve more years. Twenty. Fifty. He'd long given up on miracles, so today, he'd remain muzzled and leashed.

And patient.

He hitched the duffel bag higher on his shoulder and strode up the red brick sidewalk. The magnolia at the house's corner drew him up short. He looked to the windows hidden by branches and remembered the view from the guest room on the first anniversary of his father's death. Seanair had declared an end to Aleron's mourning. Clear as yesterday. The Christmas that had forever changed him.

The problem with having an unrelenting memory for details meant he could picture the monstrous, ornamented fir dominating the foyer. Red bows had dotted the window wreaths and fence posts. Atop it all had been his recommitment. A star of determination.

To finish what his father had started.

And fix his own fuckup.

He inhaled and concentrated on keeping his steps steady as he passed through the first damper barrier, his power now blunted embers barely smoldering inside him. Thanks to his mother, he had a touch of Air, the ability latent, but that secret weapon was also scrambled by the inhibitors. The cravings within him clawed to restore his element power. Earths liked dirt, Waters their mist. Airs adored stirring the atmosphere, from brutal gusts to petite puffs.

And Fires? The hotter, the better. The place inside him where his power lived yearned for blue. A brilliant, scorching blue.

Eyes trained on the stained-glass door, he walked up the steps and stood before the doorbell camera. Why waste the energy to ring the damned thing? Seanair had sensed his arrival the second his taxi crossed into the city limits, for Goddess's sake.

He laughed to himself. The Goddess. Yeah. Some divine being She was. He didn't understand why She hadn't punished Seanair for his abomination. How had he gotten away with blaspheming Her temple with murder? Aleron had been sure, before that horrific moment, Mother Nature was real. Then—

He gave his head a hard shake to stop the memory, the smell, the horror. Yet, he remembered Her voice as he'd stared at his father's ash pile. Her voice had been gentle, but firm. Telling him, *I'm here.*

Their Goddess/Mother Nature/Creator might have shown up, but She hadn't done jack to intervene.

Tired of waiting, he moved to ring the doorbell, and pain speared him in the temples. Fuck. Now was not the time. He closed his eyes, his pulse kicking, his headache throbbing. Goddess, he needed to commune with his element. Badly. He also needed time to connect with his Fire, surround himself with flame, and bask in its all-consuming strength.

Not today, though.

Best he could do was toss back a handful of ibuprofen to take the punch out of the pounding thing, but—what do you know?—he was flat out of pain relievers.

The door opened.

"Mr. Foussé, it's so good—" The butler faltered, his I-didn't-see-anything face returning in a blink.

Ah, his scar. A slashing reminder of who and what he was.

"Follow me." The butler strode across the foyer.

Dropping his bag by the door, Aleron took a deep, open-mouthed breath to try to dull the throbbing. He walked past the double staircases into the hallway, a bit stunned the Beta-level butler was still around. Naturas lived a little longer than humans, but this geezer had more than a toe in the grave.

He steeled his gut and ignored the archway to the dining room where he'd sat long ago on the one-year anniversary of his father's death.

As they approached the end of the long hall, Aleron felt stunted stabs of power bounce off his shields. Fire energy wavered against his insides like clothes strung on a line. A heavily lacquered door fanned open to reveal a team of men standing in a line, facing Seanair.

Aleron stood at the threshold and scanned the wilted heat signatures of eight Alpha Fires he didn't recognize.

Assassins, like him, also temporarily castrated.

His dad would be so proud of that résumé bullet.

An A-plus killer.

The unmistakable odor of burnt flesh hung in the room in an acrid, smoky haze. He stepped inside and kept the wall at his back, swallowing waves of nausea. For a moment, he thought he was going to hurl all over the shiny wood floors.

"Unlatch the door, if you would." Seanair looked to the butler, his baritone as polished as his suit.

Oh, Goddess. Whatever the reason for today's meeting, it wasn't just to get his orders.

The man obeyed quickly, as all in Seanair's orbit did, and opened the French doors.

Seanair began to speak, his words low and in Latin. Not the full prayer, but the equivalent of burying a body without the casket or the service. Aleron made the mistake of looking down and caught sight of the mound of gray dust. A breeze whipped through the room and whirled the small pile into a cyclone, a tiny tornadic reminder of what struck his dreams every night. The bits spun, moving through the billowing curtains and out into the late afternoon haze.

A man reduced to ash.

Gone. *Poof.*

Memory slashed him again, intensifying the nausea. He hadn't been here for the crackling of burning skin that he'd once mistaken for a candy wrapper being opened, but death had a taste. One of loss, of nothing. A permanent dehydration no amount of liquor would sate.

"I was clear on the ramifications of failure. Do not disappoint me again. Whoever's starting those wildfires must be caught and brought to me. Santa Barbara, on fire, best not happen again." Seanair's words were ominous, his tone unchanged.

The men bowed and turned in unison to file out of the room, their custom suits making them appear like a band of bankers. To a nosy neighbor, this was nothing more than a business meeting.

Poor humans. If they only had a clue what controlled their small, sheltered world.

"Aleron." Seanair held out his arms like Christ the Redeemer.

Time to pretend.

"I apologize for the delay in my arrival, sir." He took a knee, biting the inside of his cheek to stuff down a remark about the demeaning tradition that every other element Magnus had dropped.

"I was informed. Please, join me."

Aleron got to his feet, his fingers tingling, his Fire flopping like he'd been Water-doused. Twelve years. And their leader still wore the same smug-ass expression.

Seanair's phone chimed. He pulled his cell from inside his jacket, reading like Aleron's time and existence were of no consequence.

At the moment, his temper wouldn't serve him, so he did a mental refresh on his goals. Get the man alone in a sacred place, kill the self-serving tyrant while his powers were down, take the Goddess-forsaken cuff off the bastard's wrist, and search for the rightful wearer so the planet's Fire energy would equalize.

He might as well have wished to be Father Time, Mother Nature's absent lover and the Naturas' rumored deadbeat dad.

"You're going to New York." Seanair continued to scroll his thumb over the phone screen. "My granddaughter's getting married and requires elite security."

He was pulled off an intelligence mission to diva-sit? Goddess save him from shopaholic socialites.

"Congratulations, sir," he managed, thinking of the man's six grandchildren and realizing he'd met only the four males.

"It'll be quite the event." The old man tucked the phone back inside his pocket and toyed with the intricate gold cuff on his wrist. "She's marrying Yuri Burkov in a month. There's chatter, but no one's going to stop this union."

Odd. The Russian factions usually kept to themselves. Always had. And yeah, the other continents for sure wouldn't want an alliance between two of the wealthiest Natura groups. Moreover, King Mikhail equaled Seanair in the savagery department. No one sane wanted an alliance of their sociopathies. The girl was marrying the heir apparent, but Yuri would take power eventually. Aleron had a feeling Seanair had grand visions of controlling the thrones of both North America and Russia.

"She's promised to the Burkovs?" Aleron had ignored the engagement rumors, mostly because he could give a shit about the Lennox women who were, no doubt, as obnoxious as the men. He gave even less of a shit about the Lennoxes' adherence to the old-school tradition of arranged unions, always for maximum power. But the Russians? Who would marry their granddaughter into the throngs of that batshit conglomerate?

Who was he kidding? Seanair Lennox would marry his granddaughter to exponential batshit if it bought him something he wanted.

"I need her safe, but I also need her visible." Seanair walked over to the credenza and poured a whisky. "Get to Manhattan, get her out of the apartment and into public view. I want the others to see what their defiance has cost them."

He stood at perfect attention and bit back the crude suggestion that would get him melted on the spot. Seanair was a Dual, and though most feared his Fire energy, the subtlety of his Air was the true danger. When inhaled, the potent combination of oxygen and power weaved through a person's body and revealed their inner thoughts when they exhaled.

Not a good sitch when his power hovered at a tenth of normal levels and Seanair had a full freakin' tank.

To most, Seanair Lennox looked the quintessential Southern gentleman, ready for lunch at the club. But his genteel exterior disguised a ruthless tyrant who'd singlehandedly controlled the Natura families in North America for fifty years and who clearly intended to use his grandchildren to every advantage.

"She'll be safe with me, sir. It's an honor to be asked to protect her."

"Your work of late has been exemplary. I commend your thoroughness." Seanair took a small sip from his glass and tipped the rim in Aleron's direction. "You'll receive a file complete with her photo, places she frequents, and a profile of her best friend, who's an incorrigible Water. Keep an eye on Kazumi Fukada. She attempts to lead Elspeth astray at every turn. Your role will be to get Elspeth safely to the altar and guard her until the ceremony's completed."

Aleron's cell phone vibrated in his pocket, likely signaling the arrival of Elspeth Lennox's file. If she was anything like her brother Lach, no doubt she was a hundred percent high maintenance and guaranteed to be a pain in the ass until she got shipped to the land of snow and cagey assholes.

"I'll head to the airport immediately." Good thing he traveled light and often. Everything he owned was in the duffel bag he'd left at the front door.

"One thing regarding my granddaughter." Seanair's draw on his whisky was meant as misdirection, but Aleron hadn't survived this long by dropping his guard. "If she complains about you in any way, there will be repercussions."

The skin along his scar itched. Heated. Burned. He should purge the mark Seanair had given him, but why eliminate the visual reminder of his only goal? He kept his gaze on the wall and rode out the pain. Savored it, actually. Pain brought clarity. Pain meant he was still alive and could exact his revenge when the time was right.

"I guarantee her safety, sir." Aleron's fingers tensed, the hand wanting to fist, to counter the sizzle on his face and neck.

Seanair's eyebrows rose in an appreciative arc. Power and strength were the only things he respected.

"Barring me, there's no stronger Fire than you. I wish I had ten of you." He set the tumbler on his desk. "Of course, no one else but your father gives up his mantle to protect his son, now do they? It's too bad we Naturas normally have only one mantle, a worse shame your father's level of generosity's so rare. An army of invincible two-mantled warriors at my *disposal* would make me unstoppable."

The logical portion of Aleron's brain knew he was being tested. Seanair enjoyed tossing out the occasional reminder of that fateful day. Aleron didn't dignify the provocation with the response Seanair wanted, focusing instead on his choice of words. He often liked to think of himself as a *garbage* disposal, with Seanair as the next scrap he'd destroy.

"Lach's in New York as well, keeping his ever-watchful eye on his sister. If you detect any disintegration in his Dual energies, alert me immediately."

Ah, hell. Not that terminal douche. "Yes, sir."

All Naturas had one or two complementary powers, max. Rumor had it Lach was tripowered. Those thankfully rare individuals were usually dead before their twenty-fifth birthday. Their slide into madness triggered weird shit. Hail in Mexico. Triple-digit temperatures in San Francisco and Paris. The global warming humans loved to debate.

It was real, all right, but not manmade in the way people believed. The Industrial Age had both started the end-of-the-world party and sickened the Natura, the earth's keepers.

"Lach's my most skilled interrogator. You might learn from him while you're there."

Hell no. Aleron killed for a living, but he had *some* standards.

"Sadly, he won't be around much longer, but my grandson isn't the only problem. He's the reason for this marriage, as I have to do something to get this situation under control. Naturas are taking ill in greater numbers. People are starting to be overly bold in suggesting I should bring back the Tribunal." Seanair's gaze shifted to Aleron's. "This isn't a democracy."

He hid his surprise at this rare disclosure of Seanair's reasoning. The man didn't share. He demanded, and you didn't want one of his explanations.

Aleron kept quiet in disbelief. He didn't dare say, *Hell yes. Bring back the Tribunal. Justice belongs to the people, not a party of one.* Such a remark would guarantee him chargrilled skin.

"Another thing." Seanair turned the glass on its coaster with his fingertips. "She can't protect herself, and you can't sense her, so you need to be on 24/7. I've not grasped the logic of why Mother Nature doesn't alert us to the absence of a power seed until a child's twelfth birthday. Duds should be announced at birth so families have options. How a weak link polluted my bloodline I'll never know, but she is mine, and I protect what's mine."

He'd forgotten the woman was Passive. If he'd been born without power, he'd be the world's biggest flaming asshole. Goddess help him. The woman had to be a total raging bitch, but her status further explained the marriage. Seanair's granddaughter was a genetic gold mine. Not an ounce of power except for the supercharged babies she'd produce. Poor girl.

Still, the Russians? Some lines he wouldn't even approach, much less cross.

Seanair took two stacks of hundreds from the desk drawer and slid them toward Aleron.

"Your ticket's already booked. The flight leaves in three hours." Seanair tossed back the last of his whisky.

"Her name is Elspeth?" Aleron stood in the doorway and tried not to scorch the money clenched in his hand. He'd have to be nice to a Lennox.

He didn't do nice. He did death.

"Yes, but you will call her Miss Lennox. Handle the situation however you see fit, but make sure she's out and about. I have a message to send. Are we clear?"

Hell yeah, he'd handle the situation. He could be cordial for a month.

"Yes, sir."

He grabbed his duffel on the way out the front door, strode down the steps and out the gate, the metal clanging shut behind him. Fire energy flooded him, blowing and burning inside him like someone had cranked open a gas line and tossed a match. A breeze teased across his face, and the truth smacked him so hard he nearly stumbled.

He had to get Seanair's granddaughter to the altar.

Altars were in chapels.

Chapels were sacred spaces where the use of power in the presence of the Goddess was considered an abomination. Seanair had committed the ultimate sin before, right in front of Aleron, but he would never commit such sacrilege in the midst of hundreds of Naturas attending a wedding.

The truth struck him twice. A miracle, maybe, this lightning bolt in his brain vivid and white-hot. No wonder the Goddess had talked to him all those years ago instead of striking Seanair down. Aleron saw now, understood he'd been…chosen.

The Goddess was charging him with taking Seanair out.

The plan cemented in his brain. His energy crackled over his skin like static.

After more than a decade, he'd found the weak link. The way in. The one shot to exact both his and the Goddess's revenge.

Elspeth Lennox.

The poor Passive who had no idea how much her world was about to tilt.

CHAPTER
TWO

Hell's Kitchen, New York City

Elspeth stared at the signature line, her fingers poised to type, her heart sure to stop. Lightning flashed, followed by a clap of thunder. Shadows moved over her desk and the rest of her office as the storm lit up the night sky. Her gaze shifted to her business-card holder, and the thought occurred she soon wouldn't have to worry about refilling it. Or arranging any more introductions. Or negotiating marital mergers between powerful families. In the years since she'd graduated from NYU, she'd helped arrange hundreds of Natura marriages.

So why was she hesitating on her own?

There were worse things than marrying a Russian prince.

She looked at her computer screen and the document awaiting her signature.

Contract of Marriage.

Everything slowed. Her breath. The air. Time. The words *death warrant* whispered in her mind. Or maybe that's what dying dreams did as they fizzled. A last struggle for reality. A final plea. Then... gone.

Their treatment's the only one that works. Do it. Sign it. Buy him time.

The truth killed the last of her hesitation. The tripowered disease claimed most of its victims soon after their power arrived on their twenty-fourth birthday. Not Lach. He'd somehow made it past thirty, and she wasn't giving up on her big brother.

The Russians' treatment was his last hope, and it was something money couldn't buy. They wanted a trade: her for the treatment. Take it or leave it. She'd presumed her grandfather would have given the Russians the royal middle finger, as Seanair Lennox took shit from no one. The fact he'd granted King Mikhail's demand had given her pause, but then, her grandfather considered her to be worth less than nothing, so maybe the cost of the treatment wasn't all that exorbitant after all.

Another flash and a second crack of thunder rattled the glass in the turn-of-the-century building, too close this time. She swiveled her desk chair and took in the show of forked light. Tonight, the sky's drama wasn't natural. Goddess, what Air element families were feuding now and why?

Knowing her grandfather's people would address the situation, she forced her gaze to her favorite picture. The photographer had caught the closed-eyed smiles of her parents on the dance floor. One of her mother's hands rested on her father's shoulder, the other clasped in his. The side of her face was close to her father's neck, her nose right below his ear.

Two people she couldn't remember, whose fairy tale had ended in brake failure and a tree when she was two. She wondered what it'd be like to do a father-daughter dance with the man who shared her vivid green eyes and dark hair. What would a man who'd married his college sweetheart say about her arranged marriage? What would he tell her as they stood together behind closed chapel doors, the aisle and guests waiting on the other side?

Would he be proud of her for trying to save Lach? Would he admire her sacrifice? Or would he tell her she didn't have to go through with the wedding, say he'd protect her, love her, no matter what?

What would a father's love feel like?

Her grandfather's came with terms.

She returned to the keyboard, typed *Elspeth Andrea Lennox*, and plunked the enter key with her pinkie. Before she could stall any longer, she emailed the contract.

Her gaze went out of focus. Numbness settled over her, heavy and dense like the thunderclouds. Shouldn't she should feel something? Six weeks of negotiating was done. She'd checked off the top task on her to-do list. *Buy Lach time.*

With herself.

At least I'm not marrying Karl, she consoled herself. Or any of the other conniving charmers who'd tried to slither their way into her life and her bed.

"I'm doing the right thing." Her words earned a head turn from one of her guards stationed in the hallway outside the open door.

Maybe marrying the Russian would get her some damn privacy, or at least a little control over her security detail, her schedule, her life. Her low, bitter laugh earned her a second glance. Who was she kidding? Her superpower was making superpowered babies, and her status as a Passive had landed her this marital gig. Well, that *and* her last name. Every Natura wanted to sidle up to a Lennox.

Still, she couldn't shake that she'd been traded like an athlete, her all-star sport…incubating heirs.

It didn't make sense to dwell. The deed was done. Still, there was a tiny squeal deep inside, a yelp of yearning for so much more than her "at least" life.

For one moment, she let herself imagine her dream husband and the true love she'd longed for, a love her parents had supposedly shared. Her groom would be tall, with dark hair and eyes, and Goddess bless, he'd be a Fire. There was something about men of that element. Their intensity. Their drive. Fires could be a tad…focused. Passionate. Even though she wouldn't actually be able to feel a Fire's elemental touch, when she considered the idea of a rest-of-her-life lover, the thought of being the sole focus of a Fire's sizzling scrutiny stoked her in places too long untended.

"Hey. Need to talk for a sec." Egan, assistant extraordinaire to both her and her cousin Ross, strode in and shut her office door.

"What's up?" She dug deep for a smile, letting the idea of true love go as quickly as her emailed contract.

Egan put a finger to his lips, heading straight for her desk, his expression dark with concern. "Is your cell dead?"

Ah, crap. She picked up her phone, certain she'd missed some dating debacle. Or maybe someone had died. In addition to the dating app, she also maintained a database of Natura births and deaths for Kindred, one of her grandfather's companies. As the continent leader of North America and the Fire Magnus, Seanair demanded meticulous recordkeeping and a smooth online experience to support his pledge to all Naturas of full transparency. She loved her grandfather, but she also knew that promise was a load of crap. Kindred was his way of keeping tabs on his people.

"I needed a half hour of privacy and forgot to turn off airplane mode. The contract's signed and sent, so your daily emails from the Russians should slow." She eyed the warlock her cousin had hired as their secret weapon for all things administrative. "You and Ross can start wedding planning."

"Later. Pick up line one." His gaze cut to the landline phone on her desk. "Kazumi's on hold. Says it's urgent."

She jerked the receiver from its cradle and punched the button. "Zum? Sorry, I—"

"*Listen*," came a voice so low that she plugged a finger in her other ear. "Ditch your guards. Come get me in your car. Don't text until you're at the corner of 27th and 10th. Hurry."

The line went dead.

An ominous sense of doom closed her throat. Kazumi Fukada feared nothing. Even with her power only eight months old, nothing held back the petite Water.

She reconnected her cell phone. Three unanswered calls. Twelve missed texts. All from Zum. Shit.

"I need a favor." Her gaze locked with Egan's. "A big one."

"Granter of wishes." He looked over his shoulder toward the door, then back at her. "Lay it on me."

"Get the guards away so I can sneak out." She kept her voice low, thankful Naturas didn't have advanced hearing.

His expression crumpled. "Ross will kill me."

"No, he won't. You make him look good with my grandfather. That's lifelong job security."

"I need to keep said job. Night school's not cheap."

"Zum's in trouble, so her security detail must not be with her." Her heart echoed her worry, its beats frantic.

"Then, definitely no."

"She wouldn't ask me to come unless it's a true emergency. She must need me because no one can sense me."

One perk of having no power? No element signature for other Naturas to read. Which was why her guards were posted at all entrances and exits or within sight distance.

Gotta protect the poor, powerless Passive.

She stood and braced her hands on the desk, giving him the glare that had worked on her brothers for years. "I'll owe you one. No matter what it is. You need something from me? Consider it done."

He stepped closer to the desk. "If anything happens to you, I'm a dead man."

"I close my office door all the time to work. The guards won't even know I'm gone. I just need a distraction."

Egan scowled. "Fine. Give me two minutes to burst the hot water line to the coffeemaker."

"Thank you."

He gave her a nod and left, saying something in the hall to the guards about wanting coffee. Goddess, Egan was awesome. She had no clue why most Naturas treated the coven classes like dirt. With lower Gamma- and Delta-level power, witches and warlocks had no innate energy, but they could call their given element through incantation. Still, the Alphas and Betas viewed the coven classes as little more than rechargeable element batteries with short shelf lives and not "real" Naturas.

She slipped off her heels beneath the desk and swapped them for the tennis shoes she kept for rainy days. From the top drawer, she pulled out her car's key fob and slid it into one pocket. Took her license from her wallet and stashed it in her bra, along with her phone. At the door, she turned the dial on the wall, increasing the in-house music's volume. Realizing a guard might open the door to check on her while she was gone, she hurried back to her desk and took a new pack of gum out of the center drawer. If she got busted when she returned, she could say she'd been visiting the vending machine three floors down.

She took a deep breath and let it out slowly.

Slip out. Get Zum. Slink back.

No problem.

A shout sounded. The scramble of feet and commotion filtered from the kitchen. She put her hand on the knob. Now or never.

She poked her head out the door, looked both ways, and side-stepped into the hallway. Tiptoed past Ross's office. The main conference room. Supply closet.

Hello, fire escape.

She winced at the snick of the push bar, but crept into the concrete stairwell and ensured a silent escape. Round and round she went. One flight of stairs. Two. She cut through the human travel agency three floors down and took its direct elevator to the parking garage. A strange sensation came over her, her instincts sharp and prickly.

At this time of night, she could get to the meeting spot in five minutes if luck and the traffic lights held.

She started the Mini Cooper and cranked up the heat, hauled ass out of the garage, and zipped the turbocharged car up Ninth Avenue. Her hands shook. MIA blasted from the speakers, singing about borders. Goddess, if Lach was her rock, Zum was the riptide in her sedate life. She loved her best friend like a sister—a sister who courted trouble a little too often. She pulled up behind a taxi, its exhaust swirling gray in the frigid January air.

Come on, light. Turn. Green.

The cars around her moved, and she gunned it, zigging around the taxi, zagging in front of a bus, and making record time to 25th Street. She hooked a right on 10th, blasted through a yellow light, and screeched to a hard stop at the curb in front of a fire hydrant.

She fished her phone from her bra and typed.

Here

She tried not to worry as she waited for a response. The phone chimed, and she fumbled to keep from dropping it.

1 Sec

She leaned forward, glancing through the windshield down the sidewalk. Was Zum at the McKittrick Hotel? A short figure dressed in black sweats and a hoodie jogged toward the car. She unlocked her doors seconds before Zum plopped into the passenger seat.

"Go!" A hand with black-painted fingernails tap-tapped the dashboard.

She pulled from the curb, the tires squealing as she got ahead of oncoming traffic.

"What the hell, Zum? Are you okay?"

Goddess, being powerless sucked. She couldn't sense Zum's element or assess if she was hurt.

"I'm fine. Head to the pier." Zum pushed back the hood, revealing her hair was slicked back into a sprig ponytail. "I don't think they fully sensed me, but a beady-eyed bat-faced witch knew something was amiss. I felt her skank power skulking around, and that's not me slinging racist BS. That's me saying that power was not divine. It was dark and dirty, and it scared the *fuck* out of me."

Elspeth looked from the road and caught the swirl in Zum's blue eyes. If her bestie couldn't keep her Water contained, she was truly frazzled.

"Keep talking, or I'm pulling over." She caught the shake of Zum's hands.

"I ditched my guards so I could spy on my mom at a meeting with the New York covens."

Goddess on the subway. *WHAT?*

She gripped the wheel tighter, the leather wrap creaking beneath her hands. "Do you have a death wish?"

"No, and I'm never crashing another coven sit-down. Every detail of that meeting was orchestrated to send a message, right down to the location. Gallow Green—a rooftop bar named after an execution site for witches." She leaned forward, burying her face in her hands. "Serious shit's coming. I feel it."

"Define 'serious shit.'" She stopped at a light.

"I need a minute, or the inside of your car's going to get washed."

She cut a quick glance at Zum and pulled forward as she considered what she knew about the class divide.

Naturas and witches didn't mix. Period. Her cousin Ross hiring Egan without her grandfather knowing had been a major coup. Ross had vetted the young warlock over a month before hiring him, and if perfection did exist in administrative assistants, Egan was it. Although, maybe her grandfather did know about Egan and was letting them think he didn't.

Zum placed her hands on the dash and blew out a long breath. "I think there's going to be a war. Seanair's ignored the covens' existence for too long, and my mom tried a secret mediation. It didn't go well."

"How the hell did you prevent your mom from detecting you?" As the global Water Magnus, Zum's mom wasn't a Water. She was *the* Water.

"Black-market witch charm."

Of. Course.

She pulled into the Pier 66 parking lot and, since it was eight p.m., easily snagged a space.

Killing the engine, she shifted in her seat. "Are you sure you're okay? If I can see your power, then humans can, too, and we can't chalk up those swirly blue eyes to contact lenses."

"I'm good. I just haven't used that much power before, not even close. I need to regen, and—" She took Elspeth's hand and squeezed. "Goddess, now I know why they harp in Natura 101 about not letting your element levels get too low. I need to have sex for a solid week."

Zum hooked up on the regular to stay at the top of her element game. She must have let her energy drain dangerously low. Her heart pounded as she tried to remember the Natura 101 classes from boarding school. In addition to normal classes, she'd been allowed to attend the early training so she'd know the basics and could raise Natura children. Even at beginner level, the instructors had been clear. If a Natura's innate power levels dipped too low, they died.

Which was why the upper-level classes included regeneration

seminars so they learned how to cycle energy and refuel via the energy produced by sex.

"Why would you take such a risk?" She leaned over the center console, got in Zum's face, and caught the subtle scent of sea-salted air.

"Ever since I caught wind about this meeting, I've been having dreams about my mom dying. Drowning. Natura Waters couldn't hurt her, but I'm not sure about the covens. I know we're technically all Natura, but witch and warlock power feels different." Her gaze locked with Elspeth's. "I thought if someone tried to harm my mother, I could help or be her secret weapon. What I felt tonight? Those witches aren't toting around kiddie power." A soft smile pulled across Zum's face. "I'll be all right. I'm just completely tidal right now. You always make me feel better. I need to ditch this charm, then I need a drink. There's a Natura-run dive two blocks up."

They got out of the car. Elspeth folded her arms across her silk blouse, but she might as well have been wearing nothing with the wind coming off the Hudson River.

"Where's your coat? This ain't Georgia, girl." Zum pulled her hood back up.

Thank goodness a thread of teasing had returned to her best friend's tone. Zum's true first language wasn't Japanese, but sarcasm.

"Don't you think my coat would have screamed, 'Hey, guards, I'm giving you the slip'?"

She laughed. "Yeah, probably. How did you manage your escape?"

"Egan helped."

Zum put a hand over her heart and quickened her stride. "Goddess love that hot, sweater-vested warlock. I'm not sure who's better looking, Egan or Ross. Wait. What am I saying? It's Ross. Now, that's an Earth I'd have a regen marathon with."

Poor Zum. She'd had a crush on Ross since the first time she met him.

"He's married to his job. I never see him date or even go out, so his power levels may be in the shitter too."

"With him? Low flare, don't care. When an Earth of his level regens with a Water of equal ability such as myself, the orgasms are freakin' *planetary*. I now understand the saying 'land and sea's the one for me.'"

They stopped at the edge of the pier. Zum placed the charm she'd used to gain access to the coven meeting on the pavement and stomped it beneath her black high-top.

She didn't put much thought into her cousin's personal life. Ross had a fiercely guarded public persona, understandable given his high-profile role as Seanair's event planner. Maybe that's why he didn't date anyone seriously. Maybe, like her, he'd made a fortress of his heart.

Zum picked up the flattened feathery disk between her thumb and forefinger and flung it into the dark river. "Drown."

The word floated over the murky depths, a white stream in the icy air. Light surrounded where the charm plunked into the water, the blue-lit orb racing down, down, down until it disappeared.

"I'd have been better off lighting that two grand on fire. Wacky damn charm. The thing masked my signature, but I could see one of the Earth witch's energy. It was a tangle of light, all shades of green, but black and smoky at the edges. Not normal and nothing like ours." She wrapped her arms around her middle and bounced to warm herself. "Let's get out of this wicked weather. I'll never get used to this kind of cold."

They headed into the large parking lot. Her grandfather had few hot buttons, but the subject of witches about sent him into orbit. Oddly enough, she had more in common with the coven classes than she did with the most powerful Naturas, since witches had no power, like her. They could call it to them, though, and contain it in a vessel inside them.

Unlike her.

"We're all Mother Nature's children. I wish Seanair would acknowledge the existence of the covens. A few evil witches don't make them all bad." She looped her arm around Zum's and huddled close.

Although her grandfather couldn't prove anything, all signs

pointed to witches as the perpetrators behind her parents' car accident, which was the only evidence Seanair needed.

"Yeah, well, good luck with changing Grandpa Corleone's mind."

She smiled at the only Natura who'd dare compare their North American leader to a fictional mobster. She should probably get back to her office. Still, trouble now, or trouble later—it didn't matter.

She was having a cocktail with her bestie to break the news. "I need that drink now."

So I can make your night worse.

"That's why you're my bestie. You drive like a hell bat, and you never say no to a cocktail." They jaywalked across the street. "Be glad you don't have power and no one can sense you. You have a level of freedom you don't realize."

"Four guards isn't freedom." A shiver went through her, and she wondered if her bones could freeze-dry. "Let's hope I can sneak back in undetected, or I won't even be able to pee by myself."

"With luck and liquid courage, you'll be fine. If you get caught, go the guards-with-benefits route. I've seen how those dudes look at you."

"Zum."

They turned the corner, thankfully getting out of the Goddess-forsaken wind.

"What's worse? Sex with a hot dude, or pissing off Seanair?"

She'd not given any of her guards a second glance. Hell, most of them stared at the wall all the time and acknowledged her *good mornings* with a classic clipped response.

"No guard sex." Her throat tightened at her reality. There'd be no sex at all until she was married.

They made a right and came to a beat-up door with a green neon sign that read Freddy's.

Zum looked her up and down. "You're not getting any because you're dressing so... Are you running for the school board?"

She didn't bother to tell her friend she was trying to look the part so her grandfather would take her seriously. If he ever decided to show his face at the office again.

She followed Zum into the dark, earthy-scented bar. A bell clanged overhead, and as her eyes adjusted to the dim light, she wondered if she'd walked into a florist's shop.

"What is this place?"

Green surrounded them. Trees. Houseplants. Planters filled with petunias. Violets. Buckets of…dirt? An old-school jukebox stood in the corner, the lights flashing as the strange white noise changed from crashing waves to chirping birds and intermittent breezes.

If she closed her eyes, she'd swear she was about to have a cocktail in the woods.

"Freddy's an old, hippie Earth who smokes a lot of weed and tends a massive garden out on Long Island. If it's an exotic plant, he grows it to perfection and sells it to the highest bidder. You'd be surprised how much someone's willing to pay for roses that last. His peonies are incredible too. He sends them regularly to my mother so she'll overlook his bootleg-liquor business."

They wandered farther into the bar. Her senses filled with the rich scent of rose and jasmine and the peaty froth of freshly turned soil. They decided on a two-person table in the back. Before she could sit, Zum pulled her into a hug, nearly squeezing the life out of her.

"Thank you for coming to get me. You always have my back."

Her heart sank faster than the dead witch charm.

In her head, she'd rehearsed this conversation a gazillion times, but she'd never have the right words. The marriage would change their friendship. She'd consoled herself that it was just distance and a time difference. Saint Petersburg was only seven hours ahead of Manhattan.

"You know I'd do anything for you." She savored the warmth of her best friend's arms.

Pressure crept behind her eyes. Their relationship had started as roommates in boarding school at twelve, followed by four years at NYU. After college, Zum had moved back in with her parents, mainly so she could begin her training for when she took over as Water Magnus from her mother.

Still, the idea of any real distance between them burned like she'd been stabbed with a hot poker. Goddess, how could she go from emergency ice cream runs, girls' night out, and the occasional shopping and lunch-athon to…video chats and texts?

"About that." She pulled back and took a seat, noting most of the other tables were filled. "We need to talk. I signed the contract."

Zum's expression dropped, and she flagged down a waiter. "We'll take two rosewater lightnings. Make them doubles." Her gaze locked with Elspeth's. "You're joking, right?"

"A treatment for Lach isn't a joke. It's the only option left."

"We talked about this. Over and over." Zum hunched over the table, her voice low. "My mother knows of no viable treatment, and if anyone would know, it would be the *Water Magnus*. And if there really is one, just buy the damn thing."

"Seanair offered twenty million. They said no."

The waiter placed two glasses on the table. No ice. Just a pale pink liquid that glowed like the bartender had sprinkled it with silver glitter.

"One each is all you get." The guy shot them a stink eye. "Freddy's taking no chances with that one." He tilted his head toward Elspeth.

Great. She'd been recognized, in a dive bar, on a Tuesday night.

"One's all we need." Zum's gaze moved, slow and easy, over the waiter.

The guy gave Elspeth a last look and walked away.

They earned a few more looks from other patrons. Maybe she should be frightened, but she wasn't. In the shadows of her grandfather and Lach and her cousins, she went largely unnoticed. Hell, her other brother, Graham, landed in the gossip columns more than she did.

Oddly, a sense of lightness settled over her. She was in a bar. With her best friend. About to enjoy a neon cocktail. Without her entourage.

"No one goes to Russia, E." Zum raised her glass. "They don't hold meetings there. All four elements have little to no communication with the Russians. You don't know enough about what you're getting into, but I'm going to investigate fully on your behalf. Cheers."

They clinked glasses.

"Yuri's been to the States several times and has met with Seanair." Her fiancé's name tasted sour against the cocktail's subtle floral sweetness. "I haven't met him, but Seanair says he's worthy of me."

"You decide who's worthy of you." Zum's eyes closed, a pleased smile pulling her lips tight as she savored the drink.

Elspeth took another sip, and a bloom of warmth spread in her stomach, chasing away the chill. "My marriage will be no different than the hundreds of power-couples I've joined at Kindred. Come on, you know the situation will be the same for you."

Zum's eyes popped open. "The hell it will. I'll swear off men for the rest of my life before I let you marry into that disaster. Seanair's up to something." She took a long slug, and her eyes widened. "Goddess, I love this drink. Freddy knows his moonshine and flowers."

She'd probably have a hella hangover tomorrow, as she tasted zero alcohol in the cocktail. For once, maybe she'd call in sick and spend the day in bed, dreaming of being a Jones or Smith or Williams.

Not a Lennox.

Not a Natura.

Not a godfather's granddaughter.

And damn sure not a Burkov.

She took in the pure pleasure on her best friend's face, thinking about all the times they'd split a bottle of wine in a dorm room. Or shared a piece of pie at their favorite dessert spot.

I love you, and I'm not sure I can watch our friendship change.

Pressure built in her head and chest. The memories and sentiment rose like floodwaters, guilt threatening to choke her. Zum had become as close a confidant as Lach, and she'd gone behind both their backs to work the deal with the Russians and Seanair.

Zum leaned closer. "I know you don't want to hear this, but think about it. Who'd withhold a treatment with a potential benefit to many people? This disease affects Naturas everywhere. This is a power play. The Russians want superbabies, but what's your grandfather getting?"

"Rid of me." She caught the ripple in the pale pink liquid of her drink, courtesy of Zum's ire, and held up a hand. "Hear me out. I'm the first Passive in my family, and my parents were especially powerful. Seanair expected great things from me. For so long, I've felt like the nugget of fool's gold in a twenty-four-karat family. Lach's the reason I'm okay with both who I am and what I'm not. If I can help him hang on while we search for a cure, there's no other choice for me."

Kazumi stared at the bar's front windows like she wanted to blow out the glass. "Do you know anything about this so-called treatment?"

"They've sent preliminary data to Seanair. His people have looked at the trials and say they're promising. I even looked through the information, and though I'm no medical expert, it seemed legit. The Russians have been able to stop the disease's progression."

"It's not a cure." Zum tossed back the rest of her drink.

"No, but it's time, and I'm buying it."

"You in exchange for this supposed treatment is a shit trade."

Kazumi was an only child. She didn't get sibling loyalty.

"Lach was still there for me when the rest of my family turned away." She folded her hand over Zum's. "He's my brother, and I love him. He'd do it for me in a heartbeat."

Zum's eyes filled with tears. "What about your options? Your life?"

"I haven't had options since my twelfth birthday, and because of the family I was born into, my future has never been my own." She'd majored in business to prove to Seanair she could get a "worthy" degree. But honestly? She had no clue what she wanted to do, knew even less about who she was meant to be, and wondered why she'd been born in the first place. Naturas were supposed to tend the earth, but as a Passive, she could do little more than water her store-bought plants and hope she didn't kill them. "If I don't go through with the wedding, Lach's dead. End of story."

"Say you buy him five years, then what? I need the rest

of your drink, or the Hudson will crest its banks." Zum took Elspeth's half-consumed cocktail and downed it in one chug. "All it is is a little more time for Lach in exchange for a future of misery for you. But I get it." Understanding weighted her finally calm blue eyes. "If I had a brother like Lach, I'd try to save his ass too. Have you told him?"

"No." Her vision wavered, her body toasty and relaxed. "What was in that thing?"

"Psychedelic flowers. The effect lasts about an hour. It's only dangerous if you drink too much." Zum's head lolled toward her. "Take Lach out of town when you break the news, or he'll burn down Manhattan and blow the rubble into the Atlantic."

She couldn't picture Lach destroying anything without purpose, as he was a master of control. He was the Dual-powered brother who'd let her play with the Fire energy dancing between his fingertips and used his Air power to tangle the hair of catty high school girls who'd been mean to her. He'd shot mini flames over her marshmallows so they were the perfect golden brown for their s'mores on the deck.

A wave of peace rolled through her, the subtle rose scent burying the stress. "Why haven't you brought me here before?"

Zum laughed through an easy smile. "This bar's packed with powerful Earths. They won't mess with me now that I have power and am stronger than them. I'd never put my bestie in danger." Another laugh escaped. "Goddess, I wish Freddy sold liquor to go. When does Yuri get here?"

"Ten days. He's coming in a day before the couple's shower to see if we're compatible."

"My cat and I are compatible." Zum leaned back in the chair and rested her head against the wall. "Before you buy the bottle, you need to taste the wine."

"I know." The wedding would be a big enough deal. She wasn't going to make the first night as a couple any more awkward. "Actually, the Russians have been surprisingly easy to deal with. Their main problem is with my current security."

"Seriously? Four guards aren't enough?"

She thought about the details of the straightforward contract.

"They've ordered my grandfather to assign some kind of *elite* guard." She laughed at the absurdity of the situation. Goddess bless Freddy and his flower-power lightning. "Who knows what I'll get if Seanair gets wind that I snuck out?"

"We'd better go." Zum sat forward, widening her eyes as if to try to sober herself. "Give me the fob for your car. We'll both catch cabs, and I'll have one of my guys come down tonight and get the Mini. I'll drive it to your place tomorrow. Tell your detail I borrowed it."

She was likely in all kinds of trouble. At the moment, she wanted nothing more than an XXL jug of that pink sparkly elixir.

"That won't work. I never loan my car." She pulled out her phone. No one had texted or called.

Maybe the toast was fear…coast was clear. She blinked, recognizing liquor and her thoughts weren't meshing well.

"Tell them I stole it," Zum said, her voice scratchy.

That, her guards would believe.

The waiter came over. "Freddy ordered cabs for you."

"Tell Freddy we love him." Zum damn near giggled, a laugh attack imminent.

Both of them enjoying the timeout from their worry, they chilled out in silence for a few minutes, the white-noise music changing to the trickle of a babbling brook. Once they'd made their way to the front, they hugged one last time inside the toasty bar.

"This isn't over." Zum's hands rested on Elspeth's shoulders, her expression that of a coach giving a pep talk. "I'm going to learn everything my mom knows about the Russians. And then I'll come up with a plan to stop my best friend from making the biggest mistake of her life. We'll talk more when I bring over your dress for the gala. I'm almost done, and it is *fabulous*."

"I'm sure it is. I can't wait to see it." She pulled Zum in for a hug and wondered how many more they had left before her life changed.

Two taxis pulled up, and they stepped out into the cold. She gave a last wave and got in the first one. As it pulled away from the curb, her phone buzzed in her bra. Once. Twice. She reached into her pocket and pulled out the pack of gum, for once not caring about pissing off her grandfather. Or her guards. Or anyone.

She'd been a good little girl for so long, and where had it gotten her?

Married off to a Russian guy she'd never even met. In a month. And if she wanted to have a damn drink with her best friend?

She. Would.

And that lame new *elite* guard would just have to deal.

CHAPTER THREE

Elspeth came awake slowly. A low voice pushed through the fog in her brain, something about two seconds and *going in*, followed by clipped replies.

Several knocks sounded, harder than usual.

She tore back the covers.

"One second," she yelled, struggling to get her bearings.

Light streamed through the windows. She looked to the clock. Noon? Good Goddess, she'd missed two conference calls, but oddly, she didn't care. She'd call Egan and have him reschedule, if the warlock extraordinaire hadn't already handled the issue.

She got out of bed, her head a little spinny, her stomach a tad angry. It all came back, blaring like the sunlight through her windows. Rosewater lightning.

Blessed nectar of the universe. With a morning after sucker punch.

Heading for the door, she swiped a hand across her face, caught a whiff of hangover breath, and did her best at finger combing the mass of tangles in her hair. Nothing her guards hadn't seen before.

Another series of knocks, less patient this time. She thought briefly of the lie she'd spun—and her guards had bought. Well, not *bought*, but hadn't been able to prove otherwise. *I went to get gum* had somehow worked.

And she'd had a fantastic night out with the one person tied with Lach for Most Awesome Person Ever.

More pounding. Goddess, maybe she should take her entire detail to Freddy's so they could chill the hell out.

She yanked on the handle.

Looked up.

Big. Unknown. Badass.

She flinched before calling on years of never-let-'em-see-you-sweat self-training.

"Can I help you?"

His gaze drew down her, holding at her legs, and he swallowed hard.

"I'm Aleron Foussé, your new guard from Elite One." His attention shifted to something behind her.

She looked down at her thighs. Her *thighs*. Crap.

The sweatshirt barely covered her. Her thoughts spiraled, trying to recall last night when she'd undressed and gotten into bed. The previous evening seemed to end right after she'd given her guards the "I went to buy gum" line. She dared not look down again, so she concentrated on detecting what was beneath the sweatshirt. No bra, but yes! A scrap of material had crept into the wedgie zone.

"Ms. Lennox, the clause in your marriage contract calls for increased security. I need to begin my safety checks and go over your new protocol. It would be best if we begin immediately."

She locked gazes with the rock-wall man in front of her, wondering why her skin felt like static electricity filled the room. None of the four guards in her regular safety rotation, all of whom had been dealt from the deck of badassery, straight-lined her hackles or launched her pulse into orbit.

"It would be best, Mr. Foussé, if you waited in the hallway until I'm ready."

Big frown, and a scowl that threatened to singe her.

"Are you not alone?" He leaned to look behind her.

Great Goddess above, she had so little privacy. He could do his job without digging into her personal life.

"That's none of your business."

"It's most definitely my business. Your safety's my responsibility, even if it includes your own reckless behavior."

The door smacked the wall, and he barged in, moving past her with speed and stealth a man his size shouldn't be capable of.

She followed, hell hot on his biker boot heels as he stormed into the living room, stopping at the entrance to her bedroom. "If you're not powerful enough to sense another Natura, then I question my grandfather's use of *elite* in reference to your guarding capabilities."

He turned, and something flashed in his eyes. If she'd had element energy, she'd know for sure whether it was anger or reluctant admiration at her challenging him. The moment was too brief, and she didn't want to dwell on her powerlessness.

"There's not a Natura within five miles of here," he scoffed. "I'd suspected a *human* male."

Judgmental jerk. So sleeping with humans was frowned upon and viewed as a waste of time since they couldn't recharge Naturas. She couldn't either so—

"You're not going to dictate who's in my bed. If I had a human male tucked away in my room, it's definitely not your business."

She looked to the fireplace, swearing she'd heard a crackle, but the logs weren't lit. Maybe his arrogance had fried the last of her patience.

"Just so we're clear, any guests have to be approved by me."

"I'll let you know who's stopping by, but they don't require your approval." *And they never will.*

He folded his arms behind him. "If you want to make this difficult, that's your choice."

The. Nerve. Of. This. Man.

"You just accused me of having someone in my apartment." She closed the distance between them, standing just off his boots. "There's no one here, big boy. Satisfied?"

His gaze locked with hers, challenge ablaze in his eyes. "You need to get dressed so we can get started."

"Was there a 'please' in there somewhere?" She shot him her super-saccharine smile. "I think I missed it."

He didn't bite, but he also didn't budge.

For her part, she wasn't remotely impressed. Concrete Column

Foussé didn't realize she'd spent her entire life refusing to be intimidated by arrogant Naturas. But she also hadn't gotten to where she was by being unreasonable.

"I didn't think anyone would be assigned this fast." She'd give him that much. "I'll be ready in ten minutes."

He moved an inch closer, and she realized her mistake. He intended to take a mile.

"Just so we're clear, I didn't think I'd have to worry about a sneaking-out problem. You certainly don't want the Russians getting wind of it, or you won't be dealing with just *one* extra guard."

Her stomach did an oh-shit dip.

He reached inside his leather jacket and held out a large, shrink-wrapped package of…gum. "I'll order a case, for both here and the office. That way, you won't need to go on any more unsanctioned scavenger hunts for vending machines."

So. Busted.

Sure, she was down, but not out, and he wasn't going to tarnish one of the best nights out she could remember.

"That won't be necessary. I'll just make sure to get your approval before I go on a candy run. Sometimes, I need a little *sugar*."

If she hadn't been looking straight at him, she'd have missed the spark of surprise. Heat flushed up her back at her own innuendo. Since when did she drop those?

He stood there, giving her an any-day-now expression.

Her stomach roiled. She needed a cheeseburger, a pot of coffee, and a toothbrush. "Get settled in. I'll get back to you this afternoon."

"It is after noon."

Her smile should have frozen him solid. "Regardless, my regular detail can brief you on my schedule, and I'll come get you later."

His gaze raked over her and hung a second too long on her legs.

She sensed the sweatshirt's hem hitting her just below her butt. Surely, it covered her.

"One second. Let me check something." He pulled out his phone, and as he communed with it, she took the moment to give Mr. Pushy a thorough once-over.

Wavy hair cut tight framed a forehead anchored by hard eyes and an even darker glare. He wasn't at all pretty. Given the slight bump on his nose and his scowl, he could pass for an MMA fighter who'd suffered a few punches to the face. Gym rat, for sure, with that lumberjack build.

Deep lines scored the skin between his brows, as if he'd been born pissed off. Then there was the scar.

Straight-on, the mark wasn't visible, but he'd turned his head ever so slightly as he read his phone. Like he wanted her to see the slash about the width of a finger creeping down his slightly stubbled jawline like a mudslide plowing through grass.

"Yep. Exactly as I remembered." He shoved the phone in his back pocket. "You'll need to review Section 7, Clause 4. I'll let you get to that while I map the access points in your apartment and walk the building's perimeter. I'll give you thirty minutes instead of ten."

The urge to tell him exactly where he could shove his thirty minutes nearly had her careening off the high road. If she'd learned anything at Kindred, it was the most powerful Naturas were usually the biggest assholes.

Unfortunately, her job required her to hone a nearly eidetic memory. She'd read Section 7 three times. The words ticked off in her mind.

Intended shall have additional security from date of signing until conclusion of Binding Ceremony, which shall include, but is not limited to, an Elite-level guardian in personal attendance at all times.

Her stomach fell. With her signature, she'd agreed to shitty Section 7 and received a supersized, muscled timekeeper to satisfy the clause.

She stepped so her bare toes bumped the tips of his black boots. "Let's get something straight, Mr. Foussé." Her heart kicked up at being this close to him. "You might be my guard, but you are not my boss. You will not be barging in again and acting as a stopwatch. Are we clear?"

The barest hint of grudging respect flashed in his eyes again, and then Captain Concrete returned.

"I've detected an uptick in energy in the city. In addition, your alert level has been upgraded to sight distance. The rest of your team will stay on entry and exit points, but I'll be inside your apartment." He glared down the crooked slope of his nose like she should swoon that his cavalry of one had arrived. "If you need any more sugar, *I'll* handle it."

He likely knew about the whole Freddy's rendezvous. Maybe they all did. Too bad, not sad. Or flustered. Or scared. No one could take away from her the few moments of wild, thrilling freedom she'd had with Zum, especially not Mr. Elite One.

The guy had balls and nerve, but she'd grown up with brothers, which gave her steel to his brass. In truth, he seemed sort of…different. Solid. Controlled. He had attitude, but not like Lach. More stubborn, like Ross. Was this guy an Earth? He was unusual. Something more. Why couldn't Mother Nature have at least allowed Passives to sense element energy?

Her brain snapped to something itching at her from the moment she'd heard his name.

"Why don't I know you?" She cut a glance to his left hand. No wedding band, and no way would she have missed this guy in Kindred.

"Because my job is to be invisible, and Naturas like you don't look past your invited guests at your galas and get-togethers."

"Naturas like me? Mr.—"

"Ms. Lennox, we're wasting time. Surely you own a pair of pants."

Her sweatshirt covered a good bit of her, but she may as well have been naked before him. "You act like you've never seen a woman's legs before."

"I have. It's been awhile since I've gotten a glimpse of green lace."

She should slap the self-satisfied smirk right off of his face. Goddess, he was aggravating and terrifying and…exhilarating. No way was she hightailing it to the bedroom and covering up. He'd barged in, he could deal with the result.

He was also bigger than Lach, which was saying something, and clearly used to instant obedience of his every word. Yet, he waited, his *game on* stare locked with hers, determined to win.

Hmm…what was he?

She tallied her clues. Cold. Rigid. Angry. He tried to hide the last one, but his intensity gave away his buried ire. It made sense. Placid mountain exterior. Lava core. Good thing she'd mastered her Guess the Element game.

She had two Earth cousins, and Aleron's whole immovable-object vibe totally meshed with their heel-digging stubbornness. "You're an Earth."

His head jerked back. "I am *not* a dirt digger."

Had an "oh, shit" come from the hallway?

But he'd given himself away with the temper flare, although she had to give him credit. Most Fires failed miserably at hiding their feelings.

"Interesting. I'm rarely wrong." She decided to take his lead with giving orders. "If you'll excuse me, I need coffee." She shouldn't, but she couldn't resist. "And while you're out on your perimeter check, grab a pack of spearmint from the market next door."

She called up her Southern roots and pasted on her best bless-your-heart smile. Something flared deep in his eyes. The slightest flicker, swiftly snuffed. She'd spent most of her life surrounded by Fires and Airs, but a pissed off Fire was like those trick birthday candles that couldn't be blown out.

"Yeager," he barked, and the tall redhead, a captain if she remembered, stepped inside her apartment.

"Yes, sir." The woman shot him a clear you're-an-asshole glare.

"Please verify my identity and rank for Ms. Lennox."

Yeager looked to her. "Mr. Foussé is a senior officer in your grandfather's elite squad. He's a Dual-mantled Alpha Fire of unequaled strength, ma'am."

Her contract had called for top-tier security. No surprise there. Seanair had personnel he preferred to use, but she knew of no elite *squad*.

"Thank you." He looked to Yeager, giving her a curt nod and receiving one in return.

He turned back toward her and Yeager left, shutting the door behind her.

"Ms. Lennox, while I commend your reluctance to adhere to my rules, let me be clear. There are many who want to stop your upcoming wedding by whatever means." He leaned so his face was level with hers. "I don't get paid to be polite, which is why your grandfather sent me. I'm...*recognized* in my field, and your Russian groom will approve."

There it was. The real reason he was here. Not to protect her so much as to guarantee her grandfather's master plan went off without a hitch. No doubt Aleron had been sent a file on her. The same kind of file she prepared for every Natura she matched.

He'd have scrolled through the bullet points—name, address, hair color, eye color, height...weight.

Whatever. She had no problem with weighing one-sixty, eating dessert, and giving the finger to diet days. Life was meant to be lived. Her breath caught as she thought of the next line in every folio, hers revealing the shame haunting her.

Element status and power level: Passive. No element power. No latent ability. No element-detection ability. Defenseless.

Pressure built behind her eyes. She'd accepted what her people deemed as weakness. Still, sweatshirt or not, she'd been stripped bare before this man, though she didn't know why she'd give a rat's ass about a guard's opinion of her.

Something deflated in her chest. Likely the last of her hope her grandfather would one day see her worth, her accomplishments, or just see...her. Like he had when she was little. Before the terrible birthday when she'd been revealed as a null.

This scintillating little conversation reminded her of how invisible Elspeth Lennox, the woman, was in this game.

"I'll get to my perimeter check." His voice warmed a few degrees. He stepped back and his take-no-prisoners facade returned. "From now on, no one is allowed in this apartment if I'm not with you."

The door clicked shut. It was a good five minutes before she dragged herself to her room and managed to get into yoga pants and a cashmere hoodie. She tamed her attacked-by-Airs hair and pinned one side back with her favorite faux-ivory barrette.

When a knock came again, she was ready. She opened the door and shoved her hand into the space between them, determined not to let him see her falter.

"Let's start again. Elspeth Lennox." She didn't need his approval, but she'd be damned if she'd allow him to add another line item to her file, like *doesn't play well with others*.

She was so done with guards, so done with lists, so done with being *a Lennox*.

He took her offered hand, his massive one folding around hers. Warmth spread up her arm like her sleeve had turned into an electric blanket. The heat swirled, danced, expanded into the empty space inside her she'd tried to patch with hard work and loyalty and enthusiasm.

"I'm surprised your apartment is so small. I'd presumed the dimensions incorrect on the floor plan." He followed her inside, his presence at her back feeling like being tailed by a predator.

"My bedroom's right there." She swept her hand to the left. "Feel free to scan inside. Nothing's in there but furniture and dust."

Without a word, he went in and returned seconds later. "So, two bedrooms, two baths, a living room and a kitchen. Nothing else?" He looked around, his brow wrinkling.

Great. He seemed to have the layout of her whole life.

"I prefer a smaller unit." She rubbed her arms as she moved toward the mantel to get the matches. "Cozy spaces aren't so hard to heat."

"You're cold?" He seemed offended by the idea.

"It's impossible to get warm in New York in winter." Last night at the pier had been like walking around inside a giant freezer. Goddess, how would she survive Saint Petersburg?

Flames ignited in the fireplace, the match still cold in her hand. Warmth circled her, an invisible rope of heat shooting out and wrapping her in a luscious coil. She stopped, turned.

"Better?" The word was low, determined.

Something lit up inside her. Calling it a spark sounded cliché, but it was a flash. There, then gone. She been powerless her whole life, but the question occasionally surfaced. What would it feel like to have power? To exchange it? To move elements with the flick of a wrist, the bat of an eye, or with a thought?

Maybe a Fire could warm her and thaw places long frostbitten?

"Yes, thank you." She folded her arms to further stem the remaining chill that chased her year-round. "With opening courtesies out of the way, we need to iron out the details of your short stay."

His lips twitched at the words, and she kind of liked how her mouth pulled into a soft smile in response.

"I'm surrounded by enough protection. I don't need an in-house babysitter." She would hold on to some shred of privacy.

His eyes moved over her, and her face flushed. There wasn't anything lascivious in his expression. A sexist once-over could be dismissed. No, his look had been much more disconcerting. Thorough. Making her feel...*seen.*

"I'm sure we can create something workable."

She stepped closer to the grate and held out her hands. As a kid, she'd predicted she would be a Fire. Flames soothed her, their warmth blanketing her body and soul. Right now, the heat pressing into her thighs was physical, but she had the oddest sense the warmth came from him, not the logs behind the grate. But what did she know? She'd already flubbed guessing his power.

She needed to shut down the ill-timed question of what it would feel like to be surrounded by an Alpha Fire.

"I can't deal with this today." She kept focus on the flames. "Bunk with the others for now, and we'll get this worked out tomorrow."

Flickers of sensation, like a dying lightbulb, scattered over her. As her file spelled out, and she'd been reminded for years, Passives sensed nothing, so maybe Mother Nature was messing with her and providing a lovely reminder of her incapability. She went over to him, noting his carefully stoic glare. He saw her like everyone else. Helpless. Scared. Pathetic. Given the unyielding set of his mouth, he'd deemed her vulnerable, but valuable.

Well, forget that. And forget him. It was one thing to have a living, breathing superiority complex camped outside her door. No way was she going to share her apartment with someone who saw her as inferior and kept a file filled with her damned flaws.

Aleron's expression didn't change, but his vibe did. "I should remind you that your safety is vital for political stability."

Swear to the Goddess, she sensed his Fire energy grazing over her, searching for weakness.

Bring it, Fire man.

"You think I need reminding of my role as a Lennox? I'm getting married. It's personal, and it's *private.*" So what if her tone had bite? She knew there was nothing private, nothing intimate, about what was coming. Luckily, there were no clauses in the contract requiring witnesses of her wedding bed. But just as she wasn't going to discuss her feelings about the contract, other than Section 7, with this stranger, she wasn't about to discuss Lach's illness with him or acknowledge the flush-turned-inferno beneath her hoodie.

"True. Marriage is personal and shouldn't be taken lightly." Judgment poured off of him, from his carefully blank expression to the rigid set of his shoulders. "I'll be with you right up to the altar. The email I checked confirmed I'll be a groomsman."

Good Goddess, her grandfather was going to turn her wedding into the spectacle of the century.

It's not a wedding. It's a merger.

She gave him her evilest eye. "Don't presume to comment on my life."

His shoulders pulled back. "I wouldn't dream of forgetting my place."

She'd learned the hard way with Lach. A Fire would argue until they got the last, smokin' word.

"Excellent. Then it's settled. The team outside will get you set up in the adjacent apartment. They're using it as a barracks of sorts."

She wanted to tell him she had value other than her last name and her uterus. But that would mean she cared about his opinion. She thought of her favorite quote, Eleanor Roosevelt's lovely mantra Lach had told her early on, and one she repeated daily.

No one can make you feel inferior without your consent.

And she sure as hell wasn't consenting to Aleron Foussé.

She normally didn't challenge Seanair, but as it appeared her grandfather had a whole squad of elite whatevers, she'd order up another one who at least had a pulse.

"This isn't going to work. I'll call Seanair and have you replaced."

She hooked her gaze on his, and her breath caught. A strange attraction. Irritation. His hair, his face, his voice, his intensity. The culmination called to her, a collection of her favorite features of the men in her dreams. Except for the cold glare. She couldn't stomach his indifference.

Her one hope with her future groom was she and Yuri would burn bright together. She'd find common ground with her Earth husband, and they'd grow to be friends, lovers, partners. Maybe they'd never be soul mates, but they could build something special.

The Fire before her took a loose strand of hair that had escaped from her barrette and tucked it behind her ear. "There is no better person to protect you than me."

His hair was as dark as his smile. No teeth, just ego and something even darker.

A shiver ran down her body, followed by a push of the same warm energy. It *was* him. She should be horrified by the intimacy, offended at the bold strokes of his power, but *holy shit*, she *felt* him. The force of him. The strength. The sheer breadth of him.

And he was pure toasty bliss.

She couldn't explain the sensation and didn't want to analyze the feeling further. She was not, however, into self-torture. No way would she spend her last month with a big-ass reminder of all she wasn't. She ignored the delicious swirl of heat inside her and whirled around.

"I need my phone." She mentally retraced her steps, unable to remember where she'd likely flung it last night, but determined to find it fast.

"I'll put my things in your spare bedroom, and we'll get started."

She let out a frustrated huff. "Have you heard a word I've said?"

"I've heard them all, but in the end, this is happening, Ms. Lennox. I will protect you, and I will do it here."

She went into the kitchen, checked the breakfast table, the countertops.

Why hadn't she picked a hot pink, blinged cell phone case? She proceeded across the hall to her bedroom, but it wasn't in its usual spot on the side table.

His footfalls, which should have been thunderous and heavy, came up quietly behind her. She turned and saw that his irises burned a bright red. Rule number one for Naturas was to hide their power and avoid human detection. Was he trying to scare her or show off? Or was he that powerful? Or had she managed to make him lose control?

Her insides smiled at the notion of having power over him. To her irritation, he handed her the black case with her phone tucked inside.

She took it, biting back the thank-you he deserved but her piqued pride wouldn't allow.

She should dial her grandfather.

Right. Now.

She dropped her hand to her side. Why bother? Through the years, she hadn't changed her grandfather's mind on much. She'd be a fool to think she could change any of this to what she wanted, what she needed.

Resigned to her mountain-guard fate, she returned to the living room, Mount Aleron in tow.

Moving to the alcove she'd turned into her home office, she steeled her resolve and faced him. "For future reference, I'm a Passive, not a pushover."

A smile pulled across his face, hard to read. Part mocking. Part… friendly.

"Duly noted." His eyes glowed. "There's something else you should know."

"What's that?" She disregarded his intentional flex of strength as the yellow in his irises turned orange. The glow became a fierce red again, the edges a powerful Alpha blue. Not one ring, but *two*.

"I was assigned this job because nothing—and no one—escapes me. You can relax now and focus on your wedding. Your days of sneaking out are over."

CHAPTER
FOUR

E lspeth closed her bedroom door, needing space between her and that infuriating…*Aleron*.

She glanced around at the explosion of dirty clothes across her white carpet. White walls. White bedding. She'd even had the fireplace brick painted white. Color was provided by the view out her windows of Central Park. Green treetops. Blue sky. Puffy clouds. The people walking the sidewalks were her favorite. She liked to imagine where they were going, what plans they had, what their lives were like.

She went to her bed, sat on the end, and texted Zum.

My new guard showed. He's an elite asshole.

A gray text bubble popped up, the dots undulating.

But is he hot?

She considered the man likely putting his things away in the guest room. In the sanctity of the only private space she had left, she'd admit he was fantastic looking. Not pretty. Not preppy. Ruggedly hot. A man with a dark gaze radiating experience, determination, and…focus.

Yes, he's hot. He's even got a bad-boy sexy scar.

More dots.

GUARDS. WITH. BENEFITS. Hopefully big. ☺

He's not staying. He's too bossy.

Is he a Fire?

Yes.

Dots.

She stood and went to one of the three bays of windows, thankful she didn't live in one of Manhattan's many steel-and-glass megatowers. Her eighth-floor apartment in a ten-floor building had once been a servant's residence for the two-story penthouse Lach occupied. The sidewalks were scarce of people, the bitter cold keeping them inside. Needing to move, she paced over to the fireplace, trying to form a plan. With luck, Mr. Elite would be out the door by dinner.

Words to live by: You'll never tire of a night with a Fire. Carpé the flames!

She shook her head, a laugh escaping. Her gaze went to the treadmill doubling as a clothes rack, and her jaw quivered. Tears brimmed. She'd agreed to marry, not have her life turned upside down by some domineering, brutish guard. None of this was funny. Reality came roaring back. Would she laugh in Russia? Would she make a friend she could crack up with like Zum? She typed a response before Zum's friendship-distress radar went off and she FaceTimed.

No pokers. No stoking flames. You are not helping.

I am the most helpful help. Gotta run. Russians to investigate!

Goddess, her best friend had been a cyclone of energy even before she'd had power. But Zum could search all she wanted. The Russians' treatment worked, and the deal was done.

Raised voices came from the hallway, followed by the doorbell. Several chimes. What now?

"Coming." She opened her bedroom door and walked smack into a hot, hard wall. Thick, warm arms slid around her, steadying her.

"You got two seconds before I blow this motherfucker down," a voice bellowed from the hallway outside her apartment.

Her hands rose to his chest. She met Aleron's narrowed gaze and reminded herself to breathe.

"It's my brother." Her gaze cut to his jaw and the barest hint of stubble surrounding his scar and back to his brown, brown eyes.

"I know. I answer all doors." His gaze hopped from her hair to her eyes to her mouth.

"Not this time. I can't risk him getting mad." Her pulse pounded, her body furnace hot, especially in places it shouldn't be. She should back away. Back away now. Except he hadn't loosened his hold.

"I'll introduce myself." He stepped aside, and disgust flashed across his face.

Vines of embarrassment grew, threading through her and tightening around her throat. She still hadn't brushed her teeth. She had tumbleweed hair for sure. Why did she care?

She watched him walk away to answer Lach's increasingly irate summons. His jeans fit him perfectly. Loose enough not to be baggy, but tight enough to highlight what lay beneath the denim was big, muscled and firm. Wide body. The kind she dreamed of covering hers.

The door opened, and she stood there, like a car-stunned squirrel.

"Good afternoon, Mr. Lennox. I'm Aleron Foussé, the new head of your sister's detail."

"Yeah, yeah. Let me in."

"Hey." She rushed up behind Aleron, placing a hand on his back and peeking around him. She looked from Lach to Aleron, the two men staring like they wanted to chicken-fry each other. "Let's all go inside."

Aleron made the first move, holding his glare but making space in the entryway. He assumed the same position as her regular detail. Ramrod straight. Eyes on the wall.

"I've missed you." She grabbed Lach's hand and pulled him inside. "What's going on?"

"I'll tell you what's *not* going on." Lach stormed across the apartment, straight to the fireplace, bracing his hands on the mantel. "Help me with something, E. I can't decide." His head swiveled toward her. "Should I blow something up or rip something to shreds to cool down my pissed-off ass?"

Aleron had taken up residence at the wall near one end of the L-shaped sofa, right beside her bedroom door.

She studied her badly-in-need-of-a-pedicure toes for a second, but when she looked up, she wiped all uncertainty from her face.

"I was going to tell you about the marriage, but you haven't answered my calls for three days."

"Been a little busy."

"Okay, but you can't come in here and rage at me when I wanted to let you know before you heard through the grapevine."

"Grapevine? I'm at a sit-down in Tribeca with the Irish, having a good ol' time. Folks are getting along for a change since we cut them in on two building contracts. Then the head short shit pipes up to ask me why they weren't offered first dibs on marrying you. That they'd been bypassed for the Russians, had taken offense, and will be filing a grievance with the continent council." He folded his arms and pinned her with his brown eyes—now flecked with orange. "Of course, I had no idea what they're talking about, but I tell myself, 'Lach, don't be an ass and assume your sister went behind your back. Go get the truth straight from the source and ask if she's really hell-bent on screwing up her life.'" He plopped down on the long end of the sofa and folded his arms. "So." He cleared his throat. "Are you really *hell-bent* on screwing up your life?"

He kicked off his shoes and reached toward the coffee table, pulling the crystal dish into his lap. He shoved a lemon drop into his mouth and chewed the hard candy, loud crunches splitting the quiet.

She turned to Aleron. "Can we have some privacy, please?"

"No. Sight distance at all times." Aleron looked to Lach. "She has a sneaking-out problem."

"I know." Lach popped in a few more pieces. "Freddy's. Rosewater lightning. Excellent choice, by the way." His gaze shifted to hers. "If Zum had taken you anywhere else, she and I would be having words. Of all those crusty old Earths, Freddy's solid. He called me before you even walked inside."

The air thinned. Her hands shook. "You're spying on me?"

"I am the eyes and ears of this city. Nothing happens here without me knowing about it. That's why Seanair lets me run it. It's his biggest pain in the ass because there are so many Naturas, and the peace holds because the people like me. Well, except for that dustup between two Air families the other night. It's handled now." He arched a brow. "They probably don't like me."

"I have guards. I don't need you following me around or spies reporting my whereabouts." She gripped the back of the sofa. "How could you keep tabs on me like that and not tell me?"

"Since your power-reveal party, your safety has been my top priority. You only got the basics in Natura 101. Sorry, E, but you don't know shit about what we can really do, and if I have my way, you won't find out." Lach's glare shifted behind her. "I can take a vacay now that he's here."

She looked over her shoulder, then back to her brother. "You know him?"

"I know every Fire of his caliber. The fact he's here explains why Seanair's in a dither." A Southern twang stole into Lach's words, which happened when he was pissed. "Now, back to the matter at hand. You know why I'm here, so out with it."

Only a fool would try to bullshit her brother, so she dove straight in with the truth.

"The Russians have a promising treatment for your disease, and I'm marrying their future king to get it." She held up a hand as the contents of the glass bowl melted into a yellow pool. "Keep a lid on it." She widened her eyes, hoping Lach got the message to cool it in front of Aleron.

"Don't worry, I'm not gonna pick a fight with your new watchdog." Lach didn't break his stare at her. "I'm fine. I don't need a fucking treatment. I have it handled."

"Lach."

"E."

She moved to take a seat on the floor at his socked feet.

"Yuri Burkov is the best match I could have hoped for." She held up her hand at his deepened frown. "Seriously. No family has made an offer for me. I'd considered committing to a human nunnery."

"Great idea." Lach chewed what was left of his candy. "I'm fine with the convent. Then I won't have to kill anyone for having sex with you."

"Too late for that."

"If you're trying to distract me, stop. Don't bother with excuses either. You're not marrying that Russian."

She looked to Aleron and wished she could burst him into flames. He had no business listening to their private conversation. Goddess, what little privacy she'd had was gone, but maybe she'd never had any. Lach had spied on her. For years. And now...now this gargantuan man she didn't know had a prime seat to their family secret.

"If you breathe a word of what we're talking about, you will pay for it. Dearly." She probably shouldn't taunt the guy, but logic had left the building the moment he'd knocked.

Aleron gave a dismissive grunt. "Discretion is part of the job."

"Hey." Lach's hand covered hers. "Seanair's elite dogs have seen it all. They know the drill. They run their mouths, they're ash."

A flare of discomfort pinched Lach's expression. She gave Aleron a last glare. Screw him. If he blabbed to anyone about what he heard, she'd destroy him. How, she didn't know, but she'd find a way.

"Do you have a headache?" She turned her fingers in Lach's and lightly squeezed. He must be having one of his head-splitters since he was so agitated. Human medicines did little to soothe the side effects of not properly tending an element but could be a stopgap in an emergency. She'd nursed one too many torturous migraines and had spotted the dullness in his eyes. Clearly, he wasn't even tossing back an aspirin. "I'd be happy to rub your temples like I always do, but please tell me you're not neglecting your elements again."

The last thing he could afford was weakened primary powers.

"You're my mama and my doctor tonight? I don't need either, thanks."

"Lach."

He folded his arms across his CrossFit body. "I'm shutting this BS convo down on all points. I'm having plenty of sex and honing my element chi on the regular, Dr. Elspeth, but get this through your thick skull. You're not marrying the Russian. It will not happen."

She thanked the Goddess for the gift of the steel shell she'd developed by having two older, arrogant, stubborn-as-hell brothers. She'd also acquired a treasure trove of battle tactics. He was in a mood, so there'd be no reasoning with him. To most, Lach was a cocky, brash, temperamental bastard. On the inside, he had the heart of an artist, a man who noticed too much.

"Do you remember the night we learned I'm a null?" She launched her sneak attack past his hardened exterior, aiming straight for his innate kindness.

"Worst birthday party ever? Yep, but Mother Nature did you a solid that night."

"Two hundred sets of eyes on me and no shooting star is not a *solid*. It was a shit moment, and you know it."

The clock had chimed. Everything had gone quiet, the world either holding its breath or averting its gaze. She remembered one movement, of mouths dropping open, and the whispers that followed.

A dud? There's some justice, she'd heard on the wind.

"I'll admit Mother N bitch-slapped you good, but that's the night you learned what's important." Lach moved the dish from his lap back to the table. "You're brilliant, E. Smart. Funny. Kind. If our family has any hope of redeeming itself, you'll be the one to do it. It won't be Graham, our wannabe Bill-Nye-the-science-guy brother, or any of our misfit cousins. Ross has promise and Flora's kickass, but Kerr's a d-bag. Goddess help us if he grows a spine to go with his snivel."

"There's other benefits to this marriage." She focused on the redemption part of his comment. "I can open a dialogue with a regime shut off from the world." She put a hand on his ankle when he moved to sit up straighter. "Without you, I would have lost myself. The night I became a disappointment to Seanair was the night you promised me everything would be fine. Even without power, I was still a person to you. A person who mattered. I felt it in here." She tapped a finger over her heart. "On my worst night ever, you became my backstop, the wall where every doubt I had bounced off into the dirt. I never felt second-rate, because you believed in me." She met his reddened gaze with her watery one. "It's my turn to be *your* wall."

"The Russians are lying, maybe not straight up, but there's a catch." He pulled his feet toward him and crossed his legs. "I appreciate you stepping up for me. Sure as shit, no one else would, but it's done, E. Seanair's ticking off the days until he'll take me out. No worries. I'll save him the trouble."

The truth coiled its claws around her throat. She couldn't think about the unspeakable, about what Natura families had to do with their diseased before the person lost control of their powers.

"*No*. Promise me you won't do anything without talking to me first."

"You're not going to be there if I have to ghost out."

"Yes, I am. I won't let you be alone when you—" The word wouldn't form. She stood and moved away from him, unable to even consider his words. "All the morbid talk's a waste. I'm going ahead with this, and there's nothing you can do to stop me." She grabbed a throw pillow from the other end of the couch and turned her back on Lach, holding it as a barricade against her heart.

Aleron's black boots crept into the edge of her peripheral vision. Damn his intruding ass for being in her private business. Damn her grandfather for sending him. Damn—she would not cry. She would not.

The leather creaked, and she knew Lach was coming to her. Like he always did, figuratively or literally, ready to defend, argue, protect, or support her.

"Look at me, sis. And listen to your wise elder." Humor forever his shield, he rested his hands on her shoulders and turned her, lowering his head to meet her gaze. "There's no cure. If there were, Seanair would already have it, as he'd never miss an opportunity to be a savior. If he could save me, he would, but only because he wants the glory and I'm useful to him. He's about to lose one of the best hammers in his supernatural mob boss toolbox."

Lach's official role was in business development for Seanair's investment firm. She understood he had a darker role, but he wouldn't speak to the rumors, and quite frankly, she didn't believe them. How could a man who produced paintings that she loved so much she'd adorned her walls with them possibly be an assassin for their grandfather?

"Seanair's not warm and fuzzy with his words, but he loves you." Maybe she cut their grandfather too much slack, but she remembered the old Seanair, before his beloved wife, Mathair, passed. "I've seen the Russians' data. Our scientists are encouraged."

"Are the researchers encouraged by actual science or because Seanair's encouraged their encouragement?" He pulled away, jamming his fists on his hips. "Has Graham seen the data?"

Graham. Superscientist. Terrible brother.

"I don't know, but getting him involved is a good idea. Seanair wouldn't lie about something like this." She mirrored Lach's battle pose.

"E, our grandfather's a professional liar. He's made sure you only see his *less-bad* side. I shouldn't have sheltered you from who he really is." Lach's eyes flared blood red, and he backed away from her, putting the sofa between them. "The only reason he hasn't killed me yet is because of you, which is maybe why I didn't tell you the bad things. When you're around Seanair, he has non-asshole moments, and I remember when I was a twinkle in his eye, rather than a problem."

She bit her lip and blinked hard. Lach was the only one who didn't treat her as someone powerless and, worse, invisible. Kindred's clients dealt with her because they had to, not because she gave each union the same attentive care and detail as she would her own wedding. She'd sought to prove herself worthy of her people by using her brain and organizational skills, by insisting each couple go through counseling before they walked down the aisle, by showing them power wasn't every damn thing.

She was Lach's only chance, his last option, and she would per-fucking-sist until she found a cure.

"It's my decision, not yours." She locked her gaze with his. "I'm marrying into the Burkov clan, and there's jack all you can do about it."

"Listen up, Ms. Jack All." Lach braced his hands on the sofa back. "The Burkovs are dangerous. You're not even going to meet them."

Wrong. She was meeting them in three weeks. The wedding was coming up too quickly for an engagement party, so Ross had already preplanned a couple's shower complete with exclusive coverage by *The New York Times*.

Sauna-like heat wrapped around her.

"Don't you dare melt my sofa." Changing tactics, she placed a hand over her belly, focusing on one of two things Lach couldn't resist. "Being a power amplifier's a Passive's only advantage, and I'm using it. My fertility's not guaranteed past thirty, and I want children. Lots of them."

Lach loved babies second only to his spoiled-rotten English bulldog.

"There's so much wrong with what you just said. Shame on you for wielding tiny Naturas against me. No man's good enough for you, and I'm not going to be around to teach your little tater tots everything they need to survive." A breeze ruffled the magazines on the coffee table. "Listen hard. Seanair's up to his usual tricks, and I can hear him cackling from here. This is all about him. Not me—or you. Even Graham will back me up on this one. Better get your trunk packed for the convent, Sister, 'cause the humans' Jesus has a cold bed and bad clothes waiting for you."

Irritation skittered over her like fleeing ants. Lach was so damned, nerve-frying stubborn.

"You were there for me when no one else was, and I'll be there for you." She'd show him nothing but strength. "You aren't dying. Not if I can do something about it. I sit around, day after day, arranging everyone else's happily-ever-afters, and I'm giving you a shot at yours. It's done, and you can't undo it, so you might as well go huff and puff somewhere else."

Lach cocked a brow, but she caught the sheen of a drying tear on his cheek.

"Great idea. I'll go tell the big, bad Grandpa Wolf this marriage gig ain't happening."

She shrugged. "Go ahead. He's the one who arranged it."

"Well, he didn't consult with me."

"Because he knew you wouldn't go for it, and he knows you need that treatment to survive. We don't want to lose you, Lach."

His gaze softened. "Again, for little sisters who don't listen: I. Am. Fine. And lucky for you, I always get my way, so cancel the wedding-dress shopping."

His dismissal of his disease and what she was trying to do meant one thing: He was getting worse.

"You'll get married one day because you love the guy." He held up his hands. "Assuming I approve of him, of course. Actually, the convent's the perfect place for you until then."

Her gaze snagged on several faint lines spreading from his wrists to his palms. "What's that?" She moved toward him.

"Tattoos. I'm just getting started."

"You don't have tattoos."

"How do you know? Private parts are *private*."

She didn't buy his attempted shutdown. Lach feared one thing—needles. There wasn't enough liquor in Manhattan to get him into a tattoo parlor, but black and vine-like scrolls marked his palms, almost like henna work.

"Gotta run. Asses to kick. Names to take." He headed out.

She let him go, watching the door close. A sense of rightness came over her. Maybe she was exactly where she was supposed to be, powerless but yet...powerful.

If she could save Lach, she didn't need Earth, Air, Water, or Fire.

She closed her eyes and thanked the Goddess for giving her... nothing.

Nothing but unbreakable determination.

———•———

Aleron held Elspeth's gaze as she stormed toward him, her gaze full of fury. "Not a word." She held up a shaking finger. "My family's private business needs to stay private."

She clipped his elbow as she blew past him and slammed her bedroom door.

Holy. Shit.

His Fire crackled and shoved against his skin, wanting O-U-T. He'd need hours to pry his teeth apart after grinding down the overwhelming desire to melt Elspeth's dickhead brother into a sticky red puddle. Lach was everything Aleron expected from a Lennox. And killing him would save Aleron some grief down the road.

He suspected Seanair would be ordering said death soon enough.

Sheer wrongness had poured from Lach's body. His element energy had been deformed into some weird hybrid Aleron had never felt before, his powers in a knot, bouncing around in a shockingly organized jumble of energy that indicated he still had control. Single and Dual Naturas were the norm. But added to Lach's dominant Fire and Air energies was a trickle of Water. That third element caused an imbalance in his powers that Lach would eventually be unable to manage.

Unfortunately, Aleron sensed Elspeth's brother didn't have long before dementia began to knock. Most families handled such situations before they became a problem, and so far death had been the only solution. Lach being a Lennox complicated matters, though, but at least an Elite One unit monitored his every move.

Which was the only reason he was still alive.

Still, Aleron's main goal was to gain Elspeth's trust. Promising to keep her secrets could score him some much-needed points. Besides, he'd already done her a solid. When he'd gotten the report on her sneaking out with the Fukada woman, he'd logged in to the Elite database and expunged the violation before the daily report had gone out to Seanair.

The fewer guards, the better, and Miss Goody Bedhead's new rebellious streak would have earned her a security battalion. Ah, being one of Seanair's top Dobermans certainly had its privileges.

He heard her soft sniffles through the wall, and a weird feeling crept over him. When Lach had blazed in, he'd expected drama like in the soap operas his mother used to watch. Without power, Elspeth didn't emit emotion he could read, but Lach? Dead man walking or not, the dude had some fierce love for his sister. Take-a-bullet love.

And fuck, what Elspeth was giving up? She clearly had no idea what she'd agreed to and didn't seem to care. Lach was all she saw, and he sure as hell hadn't expected that kind of sacrifice and commitment from a Lennox.

He scrubbed a hand up his face, needing some sleep and some answers. The Irish getting their knickers in a knot wasn't good. With the pending Russian alliance, certain Natura families would be gunning for Elspeth, and they wouldn't be filing formal grievances. The Russians would be here soon, too, which would bring another unknown into this snowballing clusterfuck.

Goddess, he hated surprises, and having to deal with Lach was a bad one. Aleron was going to have a talk with his new charge, as her brother was a danger she couldn't afford, and one he didn't want to waste time on.

But one thing was clear.

Lach couldn't escape his fate, and if he didn't take himself out, he'd eventually turn on his loving sister without remorse, when the dementia transformed him into a conscienceless, violent monster that destroyed everything in his path.

CHAPTER
FIVE

Aleron leaned against the headboard in Elspeth's guest room, letting his head *thunk* against the wall, and savored the thrill coursing through him. After she'd slammed her bedroom door yesterday afternoon and not come out, he'd plastered the walls, doors, and windows with Fire energy, sealing the apartment from elemental intrusion, and ordered in the best damned spaghetti he'd ever had. He'd nodded off sometime after midnight.

He checked the clock beside the bed. Eight a.m.

Holding out a hand, he turned it over, freeing the victory burning inside him. Threads of orange arced and raced between his fingers. The wedding bells were faint, and Seanair wasn't dead yet, but he'd gotten his foot in the first door—literally—and he was still in her apartment. Energy crackled over his hand.

Elspeth hadn't tossed him out or had him removed.

He'd won round one.

But *damn*, what a hard sell. He'd had to put his Fire on lockdown and persuade her. He didn't negotiate. Didn't make deals. He didn't need to. He was an enforcer and, when necessary, an assassin. Whatever got the job done. He gave orders. And people followed them.

Or they got their asses fried.

He retracted his Fire energy, the light and heat reabsorbing into his skin, and looked around the room. Comfy bed. Nice furniture.

Cool mirror above the dresser. Not a palace by any stretch, but sterile compared to her bedroom. Clothes on the floor. Empty water bottles on the bedside table. Browned flowers in a vase beside the bottles. He'd expected an extension of Seanair's pristine palace.

Elspeth Lennox was one helluva surprise.

Chicks like her wore pricey, silky things to bed, not ratty, threadbare sweats. Goddess, she seemed clueless to the ramifications of marrying into a Russian dynasty. She probably didn't know the French had fired off a letter of protest about the wedding, and the word coming out of the Ukraine? Well, they wouldn't be sending a scathing email containing their feelings on the Lennox family's alliance with the Russians.

There'd been chatter among his other connections. A lot worse waited out there, especially from those who didn't advertise their plans on the internet.

Something was off about Elspeth, though. Something he didn't like.

She…derailed him, made him hesitate, had him considering something he'd never have, like dreaming of buying a Lamborghini when all you could afford was a beat-up Honda.

So she was beautiful? He also liked the way she came back at him, how she didn't take his shit. It'd been a long time since he'd heard back talk, and coming out of her pouty pink mouth…

Goddess. The next month was gonna be ball-chafing rather than tingling.

His gaze shifted to the bedroom door, his stare taking him back to the moment yesterday when he'd seen her for the first time. He'd…faltered. Not on the outside. Hell no. Inside, though, he'd been jabbed, his instinct elbowed with a strange heads-up vibe he'd never experienced.

A warning, but not necessarily bad.

The worst part had been her eyes, the color he'd forever label as *irritated green*. A shade he hoped to see again, not on the diva he'd expected, but on the mussed-up bombshell with a glare that clocked him right in the common sense.

He grabbed his phone from the bedside table and pulled up her picture and thought to…what?

She couldn't recharge him, and sex was his sole interaction with women. Best be straight with himself and call his side glances what they were—pent-up lust. He needed to get laid, get his element recharged, and focus on what mattered.

Which was keeping Elspeth Lennox nice and safe until he tossed her into the arms of her Russian groom and got on with his real mission.

He checked the Elite One app to see what had been cooking while he was out. He read the daily report. Read it again. Fourteen Airs had been eliminated for spawning a tornado in Arkansas, an entire family wiped out by Elite Two. Promotions expected.

Holy shit. His heart damn near gave out. He hadn't even been gone twenty-four hours, and Seanair had settled another score. No trial either. Just the judgment of one person and the sentence handled brutally. Another reason their leader had to go.

He attaboy'd himself on deleting her little sneak-out session from the archives. He'd play that card with her today, how he'd already "saved" her so she'd think he was on her side. It was too bad Lach had known, but Aleron had to give the guy points for kickass sister surveillance. If Aleron had had a sister who looked like Elspeth and had no power, he'd have had her LoJacked and bugged so he knew her every move.

Her voice filtered through the wall. Naturas didn't have enhanced senses, no more so than the automatic draw to pay attention inherent in their genetics, but Elspeth wasn't exactly keeping her voice down.

"Yes, I've seen Lach, and he's fine. He's unchanged. I see him the most. I'd *know*."

Hmm. Lying to Granddaddy? Her brother had obviously been on the Getting Worse Express.

"This guard's not staying inside."

Wait. She hadn't called Seanair yesterday like she'd threatened. Why had she hesitated? Even though his gut was on high alert, since he remembered Seanair's not-subtle warning about any complaints from her, he had to smile at her shrill tone. He'd never heard anyone get disrespectful with Seanair and live.

"Four guards are more than enough."

The idea came to him.

Four guards were *four too many*.

She hated having all those guards around, and he needed her to be more agreeable to his constant presence. And, lucky him, he was *in charge* of her security detail for the next four weeks. Relieving all those extra guards would make his plan to take out Seanair come together much easier. No other guards around would mean no one to get suspicious. And based on what he was hearing through the wall, she'd agree in a heartbeat to having only one protector—him.

He got up, unzipped his bag, which held everything he owned, and pulled clothes from each stack. Jeans. Sweater. Undershirt. Skivs. Socks.

He grabbed his toiletry bag, walked into the small bathroom, and took a quick shower. After toweling off, he threw on his clothes and leaned toward the mirror, opting to skip his shave. Manhattan was ass-freezing cold, and his cheeks would appreciate the scruff.

Finishing up, he brushed his teeth and turned his head to get a good look at the ropey mark stretching from his ear along his jaw, ending below the corner of his mouth. At first, he'd hated the sad-ass reminder of the day his entire world went to shit. Now, the mark served as his North Star, the imperfection a continual reminder of his mission.

He drew a finger down the scar, and pain lanced through his brain like he'd been struck by lightning.

"Mother...*shit*," he choked out, his head tilting back. "Not now, damn it."

Clutching his temples, he tried to send a focused shot of heat to relax the knotted muscle threatening to cut off the blood to his head. It would be a hell of a lot easier if he could find a Fire to regen and get himself back in order.

As to the whole communing with his element to honor the

Goddess, he had over a decade of spiritual neglect behind him. He had no honor. He had no gratitude for his so-called gift. Getting ultrapious and going metaphysical to become one with the Goddess was a coven thing. He could pray all day. When he completed his mission and died, She wasn't taking his energy back. Once something spoiled, there was no recycling it.

And his elemental soul goddamn reeked.

For the moment, all he needed to focus on was getting this migraine under control before he found himself laid out on the bathroom tile.

"I'm hungry. We're going out." Elspeth's voice filtered through the walls, a knock sounding at the door of the guest room.

Footsteps sounded. Keys jangled.

What the hell? She'd best not set one mussed strand of hair outside the apartment...

He bolted out of the bathroom, one hand pressed against his pounding skull, catching her as she strung a purse across her body. His gut gave a something's-wrong wrench. He flung a precautionary wave of Fire energy and blanketed the walls, protecting them in what equated to an impenetrable oven.

He raked his gaze over her and struggled to sense why his instincts flared. Jeans. Hair shiny and straight. A smile of pure mischief pulled her unglossed mouth.

Yep. Definitely up to something.

"I'm ready." She stopped a few feet from him and frowned. "What's wrong?"

A couple of things. Her sweater. Red. Fuzzy. Definitely showcasing his new favorite features. So he was a tits man? Sue him. They were the ultimate ode to femininity. Warm. Weighted. If he got lucky, they filled his hands.

"Nothing." He struggled to keep his gaze on hers. "Where are we going?"

"Nowhere yet." Her full bottom lip slipped between her teeth. "I'll bet my grandfather ordered you up here before you had a chance to commune."

Point to her for nailing the problem.

"I'm fine."

"You're not." She folded her arms beneath her mouthwatering breasts. "I know a Fire migraine when I see one. I've tended my brother's for years. He excels on the regeneration part, not so much on the prayer."

Hmm. He and Lach had something in common.

"Do you have any Advil, Tylenol—"

"They don't work." She cut her gaze to the sofa. "Go lie down, and I'll fix it."

He reared back, his mind going straight to sex.

"Not like that. Afraid I can't help on the refuel."

Shit. "I didn't think you meant—"

"I saw the look on your face." She glanced down toward his firming dick and met his gaze. "I'm Passive, but I know how the process works. I got Natura 101 basics in boarding school."

Holy shit, he was fifteen again and back in Algebra II with uncontrollable hard-ons.

"I'm fine."

"Do you make it a habit of going out when you're not at full strength? Kinda takes the 'elite' out of Elite One, don't you think?"

"I'll take the pain relievers. They work for me." He wasn't about to admit she was right and that he hadn't had a chance to stop by a pharmacy.

"I don't have any."

Of course not. He sighed, certain it'd be one of those days where the universe would flip him off repeatedly. Seanair's orders had been to make Elspeth visible, which he couldn't do standing in her apartment.

"What's this miracle treatment you have?"

As a high-and-mighty Lennox, she probably had access to some herbal tonic he'd never heard of. As long as it worked, he didn't care. He'd been so busy fielding Seanair's barrage of orders, he could sit his ass in a volcano for a week and not heal the fractures in his Fire.

"Take off your boots, lie down with your head at this end." She pointed to the longer part of the sectional.

"No—"

"Look, I know my grandfather. You arrived far earlier than I expected, which means he barely gave you time to pack a bag. I've seen my wickedly powerful brother brought to his knees by a so-called headache. If you're sick, I can call Seanair and have him send someone else. I won't let you suffer on my behalf."

Fuck.

"Fine."

"I'll be right back." She dashed into her bedroom.

Maybe she had adapted an Earth remedy, as they were always burning sage or some other bullshit. He unlaced his combat boots and stretched out along the sofa. His feet hung a few inches off the armrest so his head would lie flat on the cushion.

"This works every time for Lach, and he's the worst. I swear he goes to the Goddess like humans go to church only on Easter and Christmas." She set a candle on the coffee table. "Can you light it?"

Duh. He'd get his head in the game as soon as someone pulled the skewer out of his temples. He lit the wick, a task nearly automatic for someone of his strength. She went to her knees beside his head.

"What I do for Lach is I take an oil and massage it into his temples, scalp, and face. He's back to rights pretty fast." She acted like being close to him was no big deal. "Lie still."

A smartass remark sat ready behind his teeth. Something about regenning being fast and furious, maybe, but never still. He squashed the asinine thought of saying something crass to her. Last thing he needed to do was drop sexual innuendos with a Passive. A Lennox Passive.

Like he traded sexual innuendos with anyone.

"How long will it take?" He looked to the small bottle in her hand. After Seanair's teach-him-a-lesson beatdowns in his teens, he'd sworn to never let a Lennox touch him ever again. But if he didn't parade Elspeth around like Seanair had ordered, he would be ash on the ground.

"Fifteen minutes, maybe? Lach says the relief starts almost immediately."

A wave of nausea hit him, and he swore his blood had drained to his feet.

"Okay." Some woo-woo scalp massage wasn't going to work.

She stood, grabbed a pillow off a side chair, and handed it to him. "Put this under your head. I stole this treatment from Ayurveda. What we are doesn't completely align with their holistic healing system, but it works for Lach, so I don't question it."

He got comfortable, or as comfortable as he could get being this close to her.

"Close your eyes and don't talk."

Easy. He didn't talk. He received orders and executed them with no chatting required. Folding his hands over his stomach, he found a tarnished silver lining when his errant, embarrassing dick backed off. Wasn't hard getting his eyes to shut. He needed about a year of solid sleep.

Rustling sounded behind his hand. The wrench of a cork from a bottle sounded, followed by a clink on the coffee table. A soft swishing sound stopped, and then a decadent scent filled his nose.

"What is that?" He sensed the heat of her hands over his face.

"Shh. It's sandalwood oil, vanilla, and ylang-ylang. I tried several dosha healing oil blends, but this combo works best for my brother."

He didn't know half of what she'd said, but the more the scent pushed into his lungs, he didn't care.

"I'm going to do your temples first. Let me know if it's too much." Her fingertips settled on his skin with the barest touch, moving in gentle circles, the pressure increasing slowly when he didn't object. "Your pulse is practically punching my fingers. I'm sorry you didn't get a chance to prepare," she whispered.

Her voice stroked over his senses like the gentlest rain, the pain easing a hair off of punishing. A slow huff of breath escaped his mouth. Her hands flattened against the sides of his face, holding his head, which felt like it was sinking into the couch.

"This isn't proper." He tried to find the strength to move.

He shouldn't have agreed. Seanair would fry him instantly. He wanted to hate what she was doing, didn't know how she was damn doing it either, her medicine nothing more than human quackery.

"How can easing a person's pain be improper?" Her hands started in the same circular motion, massaging his face, her thumbs hooking inside his ears.

He wanted to tell her to stop, that he didn't deserve this, but warmth fanned out over his scalp like she'd wrapped his head in a heating pad.

"Any better?" she whispered, and he wondered if he was dying. He'd heard stories of pain receding at the end of life, peace coming over you like a blanket so your last moments were gentle relief. Assuming you died naturally and not incinerated by a madman, as his father had.

"Yeah," he breathed, in awe at the ribbons of agony twirling away from him. He tried to open his eyes, but it was as if his mind had fallen into a well, taking his logic and objections with it.

Her hands stroked down his face and back up. All the while, the sandalwood feathered like sweet smoke into the pain. An odd thought struck. He felt…cared for. But no one had concern for him anymore, other than him getting his job done.

She moved to his hair, her fingers in a soft curve around his skull, pressing and holding on these amazing points. The throbbing lessened, like she'd tenderly poked holes in his head so the pain could seep out like sand from a torn bag.

Soon, too soon, the soothing kneading stopped. She clasped the sides of his face, her warm palms like soft, firm pillows.

"I'm going to grab a towel to wipe up the excess oil. Focus on your breathing for a few minutes. I'll hand you the candle, and I want you to hold it over your heart." Her warm breath brushed the side of his face. "It's weird, but it works. I'll be back."

She gave his shoulder a delicate squeeze. He cupped the candle she placed on his chest, the heat seeping deep, and swore he felt her hands on every part of him. As her soft footfalls crept away, he exhaled a harsh breath, the last claw of the headache retracting. He wasn't sure what to do with the sting in his eyes or the sluggish, fragrant fog filling his head from those oils. Something tightened around his Fire, an Ace bandage wrap of pressure, reinforcing his splintered energy.

He hadn't felt this whole in months. Years.

He heard her knees pop and sensed her sinking to the floor beside him again. A soft towel stroked up one side of his face and down the other. Several soft presses later, she stopped, and a tentative hand landed on his shoulder. He opened his eyes.

"Are you better now?" Her soft smile read as genuine.

"Why did you do that?" Better yet, why did he care?

She let out a small laugh. "You were in pain. How could I not help when I know how to fix the problem?"

He funneled a touch of Air toward her face to try to sense the Lennox lie. Her family helped no one but themselves. He caught a strange scent. Rose and smoke? It left, the oils overpowering anything else, his element completely…fixed. Not forever, but it was a damn solid patch.

He turned his head and watched her fold the cloth and recap the oil. Her fingers were long, elegant, her movements graceful and sure.

She turned her head, and a closemouthed smile pushed up her rosy cheeks. "Go on and say it."

What? That he'd sign her up for nurse duty any day of the week? He didn't know what to make of her simple, yet kind solution. Didn't know what to make of any of the non-Lennox-y vibes she gave off.

There. He'd identified what this weirdness with her was. He'd had his first encounter with a unicorn.

"Thank you." He closed his mouth since he didn't trust himself not to say something he shouldn't. Having been in the care of a gorgeous, giving woman, his gut tensed at the tender flame waving inside him.

"In a bit, if you feel up to it, we'll go to the best restaurant in a ten-mile radius. I grew up in Savannah until I went to boarding school. Southern cooking is my favorite. Believe it or not, there's fantastic fried chicken here."

"Give me a few minutes." Certain she had some hidden motive

for helping him, he waited to read the intent in her exhalations, noting the thick fall of her hair over her shoulders stopping right above—nope.

Look away.

He would give her credit for not glamming herself up and wearing a two-grand outfit, like the rest of her family would, to go eat fried food. Still, liars came in all flavors.

He called back his Air energy, inhaling and tasting her desire, something she wanted with mouthwatering fervor. Chicken. How could a mobster's granddaughter want cheap chicken? He'd bet his left nut it'd be served on china.

He caught a second thread in her exhalations, one she was trying to suppress about…Lach. Illness. Worry. And she had every right to be concerned. They would be perfect buttons for him to push, as the dude's Natura clock was one click from midnight.

"Thank you again." He stuffed down the flare of gratitude encouraging him to fall at her feet. "Before my headache issue, I'd planned to make you an offer, one you might like."

"I'm listening." She rubbed the excess oil into her hands.

"I can get rid of the other guards," he said, lightening his tone as if he didn't care.

She eyed him like she was trying to figure out the catch. "Why would you do that? My marriage contract calls for more protection, not less."

Goddess, how could she marry into a Natura family more screwed up than her own?

"Think of me as twenty guards in one."

She pinned him with those killer green eyes. "I won't jeopardize my arrangement with the Russians by violating a clause in the contract."

She kept her sharp gaze locked with his, obviously measuring him.

"Your grandfather instructed me to handle the situation as I see fit. The Russians know who I am and won't see the departure of the other guards as an issue. You'll be safest with me and only me."

She reached toward him, and everything slowed. Her fingertips grazed his shoulder, the brief contact feeling like he'd taken a bolt of electricity. She pulled a long brown hair from his sweater, and his heart skipped every few beats.

"Sorry. My hair goes everywhere. I vacuum every day." A blush crept over her cheeks, and she moved away quickly.

"You don't have a housekeeper?" He realized he hadn't seen any household help listed in her file.

"No. I like my privacy, and it's always been weird to me to have someone else folding my laundry. I don't like a spotless house. I have enough pressure to be perfect everywhere else. Clutter is life."

Well, that explained the clothes on the floor.

"Are you serious about getting rid of my other guards?" She eyed him like he had to be kidding.

"Yes."

Human hell to the yes.

"We have a deal, then. Get rid of those guys. They're driving me bonkers."

Bonkers? Who still used that word?

"Give me a second, and we'll go." He sat up slowly and rested his forehead in his hands. Other than a bit of fogginess, he felt ready to take on the world. After a few deep breaths, he stood and moved to the front door, stepping into the hall and thanking the Goddess that Seanair had given him free rein on handling the situation. "Yeager, your team's dismissed. Report to scheduling and have them reassign you." The not-too-shabby Beta-level captain opened her mouth to speak, closed it, and gave a nod.

The four guards went down the hall and into the neighboring apartment.

Win No. 2!

He poked his head back into the apartment. The warmth in his head disintegrated the last of the migraine's haze. "Let's go."

She pulled on a purple puffer coat, locked the door, and turned. Noticing the missing security team, she gave him a wide-open-sky smile. "They left?"

"People do what I say."

"I'm sensing that." She stepped closer to him than anyone ever dared and placed a hand on his upper arm. "I'm glad you're better. It hurts me when I see the Alphas suffer so harshly. I have a Water friend who gets terrible nausea, and I haven't figured out how to help her with that yet. Why do the Betas not experience pain?"

"In the Natura class, Betas are less powerful than Alphas, so my guess is they're less subject to these types of maladies. Since the power levels are less with each step down in the coven class, I've never heard of Gamma- or Delta-level people suffering from mild ills. It's not a big deal. We don't have human disease issues to worry about, so I'll take a headache over diabetes or cancer."

A satisfied smile brightened her expression. "It's nice you mention the coven class. We're all Naturas, but try telling that to my grandfather. I've never understood this whole everyone-stays-in-their-lane thing or utilizing the witches and warlocks as housekeepers or in some kind of servant role."

He agreed and felt her reply. Kind of. Warmth spread up his arm, the sensation tingly, soft. His Fire element responded, pushing and nudging against his skin like a pet wanting to nuzzle its owner. He pulled back at the familiarity, noting the way his energy reacted like it knew her.

"We'd better get going. I'm hungry." His mouth watered, and not just for Southern cooking.

"You're going to love this place, I promise."

Something stirred inside him. Something he hadn't felt in a long time. He'd made her happy, if only for a little while. Her life was about to be nothing but shit, and he didn't care, really, but he had a sense of *what the hell?* It wouldn't cost him anything, and in the end, his greatest wish would be fulfilled. If he made her smile? Maybe the Goddess would make his blaze-of-glory death painless.

She pushed the button for the elevator. They stepped inside, and in the silent ride down, he memorized her scent, her voice, and the way she moved and baked everything about her into his element's memory, setting her up in his senses like a passcode on an alarm.

They crossed the lobby, and two Air bellmen opened the double doors leading to the street. He reminded himself to keep his power in check. Other than Elspeth and Lach, the entire building housed humans. He stood beside her at the curb while the doorman hailed a cab.

She looked up and gave him another blinding smile. "I'm warning you now, I'm not hiding in this apartment anymore. Today, we'll do lunch, and I need to stop by my office in Hell's Kitchen." She put a hand on his arm, touching him again like they were old friends. "You have no idea how much I appreciate it just being you and me. My other guards never spoke to me, and I...well, you're different. I'm sorry about yesterday. I misjudged you, right down to your element." Her smile shifted from sunny to sly. "What'd you call Earths? Dirt diggers? I've heard Fires called hot plates, mug warmers, camp lanterns, Bic flicks. I can't remember them all."

"Bic flicks?" That insult was new. Of course, no one disrespected *him*. Ever. Still, her pretty pink mouth stirred up some fluttery, flickery shit in his dick. When a taxi arrived, he let her slide over before joining her.

The cab pulled away. She scanned the street like she was memorizing it, and her reduced attention made him aware his energy levels were still lower than he liked, despite the magic of her froufrou oils.

Maybe tonight while she was asleep, he'd coat the apartment walls in a Fire cage and arrange a recharge somewhere in the building. The lobby bathrooms would work. A janitor's closet. A stairwell. Wherever.

Ten minutes and multiple blocks later, the cab stopped at a red light. Aleron did another scan, got elemental crickets, and found himself grateful for the silence. The more she talked, the more he saw her as someone different. A non-Lennox. Which was purely delusional.

Sure, she'd relieved a headache, a bad one even, but seeing her as anything but a pawn was dangerous. He hadn't counted on the collateral damage being a kind, beautiful unicorn, but she had Seanair to thank for her fate.

Best thing he could do was eat, run her errand, and get her back home. Where he could stop all this she's-different bullshit and shore up his plan to kill her grandfather at her wedding.

CHAPTER
SIX

The cab pulled up in front of a West Village building that needed a facelift twenty years ago. Aleron reached inside his jacket for his wallet, but Elspeth was already handing two twenties through the partition. He wondered why he had attempted to pay. He was responsible for paying for…well, nothing. Seanair was the money man, so what was with him acting like he should pay, let alone do *anything* other than play bodyguard?

He did a quick scan before she got out, and he followed her onto the curb.

"You tipped ten bucks on a thirty-dollar fare?" he questioned, noting how the sea of people on the sidewalk parted, the usual steer-clear effect of his six-five height. He motioned her beneath the awning and grabbed the door handle before she could.

She walked into the dive called Down Home and looked over her shoulder. "I like to recognize people who work hard and let them know I see and appreciate their efforts. I know how it feels when you're not."

Lennoxes didn't pay anything forward. They paid themselves.

His stomach growled as he stood behind her at the wait stand. The place was packed already, likely due to the deep-fried aroma. With his Elite One role taking him all over the world, he hadn't smelled home-cooking this mouthwatering since high school. An older woman showed them to a table in the corner, and he took the seat facing the door.

She fanned her face and pulled off her coat, hanging it on the back of her chair. "I'm surprised I'm so warm. It's below freezing today, and normally goose down's not enough to keep out the chill. Must be this place." Taking a deep, appreciative inhale, she sat down, her expression melancholy. "I'll probably miss this restaurant most. By the way, this is only the first stop on my Goodbye, Manhattan Tour. Prepare to eat out a lot."

If every place on her bucket list was like this one, maybe he wouldn't mind a few weeks' delay in his revenge.

He cut a glance at her, and his curiosity got the better of him.

"So why the Russians? I can't see Yuri Burkov taking you out for grits and greens. He prefers champagne and superyachts to fried food and checkered tablecloths." He gestured toward their small table.

"That's easy. They have a treatment that stops the progression of the tripowered disease. When I get married, Lach gets the treatment, which gives him time until I can find a cure."

"Hate to tell you, but there's nothing easy with the Russians. Any so-called treatment might be poison more than cure." He leaned toward her as she shook her head in disagreement. "I'm not kidding."

"You aren't the first person to warn me, but it's the only option left, and I'm taking it."

A waitress breezed by and left two iced teas on the table.

"You've seen evidence of this treatment?" He picked two sugar packets from the container between the salt and pepper.

"You sound just like my best friend." She held out a hand. "Try the tea first. It's already sweet." She took a sip from her glass, and a pleased smile tugged at her pretty mouth. "I've seen the data. All their patients are still alive years after their first protocol."

Yeah, but data was only as good as the inputs, and the Russians were master manipulators.

"Be careful. Even if you think you're doing the right thing to try to save your family, it can go sideways." Goddess, did he know that.

Her hand slid across the table, settling over his like an old friend's. "Are you speaking from experience?" Her gaze cut to his jaw. "Is that how you got that scar, trying to save someone in your family?"

"I don't like to talk about it." Especially not with her. "Besides, the scars you see aren't always the worst. I don't want this thing to blow up in your face. You're…too kind to have something bad happen to you."

She was *too* a lot of things.

He wanted to ask more but didn't want to risk souring her growing trust with his nagging doubt. The Russians were hand grenades with the pins half out. Seanair understood the regime better than anyone, so Aleron's question was, what was Seanair getting in trade for his granddaughter?

"Listen…" He had to take control of this convo. "No more trips to Freddy's. I pulled the info about the other night off of Seanair's daily report. I'm guessing he doesn't know, since the violation's not in the Elite One database, and it doesn't seem that Lach will say anything."

"Thank you, but…why would you help me like that?"

He could give her some truth. "Freddy's a straight shooter. No BS happens on his watch. Plus, rosewater lightning's damn good."

Card played. He probably ought to tell her that swill would fuck her straight up if she drank more than two. But there'd be no more secret outings to Freddy's.

A different waitress pulled up beside their table with a notepad and pen ready. "What'll you have?"

"You're the expert." He deferred to Elspeth on the ordering.

She started in with a few questions about the specials. His attention snagged on another waitress, this one carrying a massive tray loaded with steaming food. His mouth watered as his senses went on full alert to bacon, bread, and…wait. Was that a lemony something?

"We won't go hungry." She gave a nod of thanks to the waitress, who finished scribbling down their order as she walked away.

"So, this place reminds you of Savannah? The Deep South's a far cry from New York."

"Especially the cold. I've been here since after boarding school, and I never get used to it." She took a saltine and swiped it with butter. "My best friend, Kazumi, hates the cold worse than I do."

"Water element and daughter of the Water Magnus?"

She took a drink of tea and tipped the glass at him. "Very good."

"I wasn't going to mention it, but your file is pretty light on friends and confidants."

She gave him a sardonic look. "You're surprised? Besides the obvious with the breeding of powerful children, a Passive's of little use to most Alphas, so the majority of Naturas don't acknowledge I exist."

"You're a Lennox."

"Right. My name and superbabies are my only redeeming qualities."

"I didn't mean it that way."

"What did you mean?"

"Well, you're nice, and you seem fun, and you're attractive, so I'm sure you date."

And you cured my goddamned headache like a nurse boss.

Laughter poured from her. She sat forward, and her hair fell in a long, brown curtain, shielding her face.

"What's so funny?" Unease crawled up his neck at the light, airy feeling inside him.

"Your intel is terrible. Sure, I can get laid if I want to, but I want someone who'll actually see me not as a means to an end, but as a person with feelings and needs and dreams." Her smile faded. "Well, I *did* want that, once upon a time." She pulled a small menu from beside the napkin holder. "You should check out the desserts. I always get lemon meringue pie, but I hear their pecan is great."

"You like lemon?" He recalled the last dessert his mother had made him. Lemon cake with lemon glaze.

"Lemons are Mother Nature's finest creation, best served, well… any way. I love lemons. In fact, after Lach's visit, I'm out of lemon candy." She flagged down a waitress. "Can I borrow your pen?"

The woman put a ballpoint on the table and kept going.

Elspeth picked it up and wrote *lemon drops* on the inside of her wrist.

"You know, most people text themselves. Or use a notes app."

"Habit. I started this in grade school and can't quit. Seanair gave me a task one time, and I didn't have a notepad with me. I forgot, and he was so disappointed in me. His censure nearly killed me."

His hand shook with the urge to punch Seanair right in his damn mouth. Aleron reveled in the anger and welcomed the sensation overtaking the calm he'd learned—the hard way—to cultivate. He'd long ago shoved down his feelings and focused on facts and goals and the plans to achieve them.

"I love lemon too." He ignored the strange balm soothing his irritation.

Her long hair spilled over her shoulders, two beautiful brown swaths framing the deep V of her sweater. Fine. She had great tits. Round, ripe, just-right globes he wasn't going to get to handle. Had to be the only reasons he spent half a second considering her no-friends sob story and her lemon love. He'd expected a cheekbones-contoured, collagen-filled, dressed-to-the-nines diva. So, she was different. BFD.

Unfortunately, the curl of satisfaction inside him at her no-boyfriend situation wouldn't flatten. She didn't date. Or if she did, it was the rare, lucky punk who didn't act like a rich douche. He didn't think she was a virgin, but the idea of her underneath some pompous, undeserving asshat ignited something in him he couldn't ignore.

Why did he even entertain anything about her other than how she figured into his goal? He certainly didn't care about anyone anymore. His mother had disowned him. His brothers had likely forgotten him. He sure as fuck didn't give half a shit about a Lennox.

For today, he had to bank his primal fury and pretend to be at ease. He couldn't risk tipping Elspeth off. Not when he was so close.

A waiter put a huge tray on a stand in the aisle, steam curling from every bowl of butter-bathed or grease-coated vegetables.

"I catch a hint of a Southern accent sometimes," Elspeth said. "Where are you from?" She eyed the fried chicken, green beans with bacon, fried okra, creamed corn, and biscuits bigger than her fist.

"Louisiana. Small town." His stomach growled, aching for the feast to begin.

Conscripted into service at eighteen, he hadn't been on a date since high school. He chanced a glance at her while the waiter placed the bowls on their table and decided he liked how it felt to have a conversation. An odd thought, for sure. He didn't talk to people. He executed orders, picked up payments, laid down Seanair's law, and didn't get chatty doing it.

She smiled like she was happy with the food and the place.

And him.

It was hard to admit he had a spark of respect for a Lennox, but with her, it was hard not to.

"I'm still surprised I don't know you. I know all the Alpha-level families." She picked up a spoon and scooped a little of everything onto her plate, handing him the utensil so he could help himself.

"Alpha-level powers don't always translate into Alpha money. My family's working class."

She huffed a laugh. "My grandfather isn't known for altruism, so if you're in his elite group, it's because you're powerful and he asked for your help."

Fire energy crackled beneath his skin.

"He didn't ask. I volunteered." He picked up his fork. The metal heated, and he tamped down his temper before the tines could glow hot.

"How generous and loyal of you. I'm glad Seanair sent you and not another one of his stone-faced pillars who answer me with clipped replies. I know it's not their job to be friendly, but you act normal around me." She leaned across the table toward him. "It's nice."

She sat back and smiled, the move so easy and right, like they were old friends.

"It'll probably be the quietest job you've ever had. I don't have a chef or a butler like the rest of my family. I don't want a Beta Natura serving me or a poor witch or warlock making my coffee or cleaning my toilet."

"You have something against the coven classes?" He rested the spoon in the green beans and started in on a biscuit.

"No. I think the way they're treated is shitty. They don't have innate power, but they're still Naturas. I don't have innate power either, but I get a hall pass and am considered Natura because I can amplify an Alpha's power at conception and birth superbabies." She dug into the creamed corn on her plate. "If I could change anything about who we are, I'd give the coven classes equal seats at the governing table and eliminate all the class crap between the Alphas and Betas. I'd get rid of the arranged-marriage part of Kindred, too, and focus on archiving births, deaths, and marriages."

"I'm not sure your grandfather would support your grand plans. His position's clear on the witches and warlocks."

"He calls me his little idealist and dismisses me. None of those things will ever happen, but I let the ideas guide how I treat people."

Fine. He'd gotten her completely wrong. The Lennox Passive was an anomaly in more than just power.

He stabbed his fork into a small hill of green beans just as it hit him. Power. Buzzing by like an angry bee. His Fire flared across the table like a camera flash.

"Is something wrong?" She set down her tea glass.

Upon their arrival, he'd scanned a ten-block radius and left traces of Fire marking the perimeter to trip any trespassers. He checked again, verifying someone crossed his Great Wall of Fire line but retreated.

"We're good." He forked the beans into his mouth and held them on his tongue, savoring the salt and bacon flavoring.

He went in for another bite and the sensation hit. Pressure. Subtle and slow. Like the walls were creeping in. He whipped out a swath of power, scanning the room, searching for the source. Nothing. No Naturas for blocks. *What the hell?*

"What's with the scowl?" Her brow furrowed, a smile curling her mouth. "It's okay to admit you're enjoying yourself. I won't tell."

He scanned the immediate area. Sending out his Fire energy with a force that would clock a Natura good if they were in range.

"No. Everything's fine." Or he was losing his mind at the normalcy of it all. How having lunch with her seemed so natural and…right. He'd forgotten the beauty of simple pleasures, of enjoying a meal with someone he liked.

The waiter returned. "Can I get you any dessert?"

"Lemon meringue," they both said, followed by Elspeth launching another of her distracting smiles.

She glanced at her watch, turning her attention to him. "We'd better get it to go. I need to get to the office and back home. I've got to start transition planning on Kindred."

A few minutes later, a waitress left a to-go bag and a check on the table.

He moved to get the bill, and she snatched it up.

"No, I'll—" He stopped, reminding himself that he worked for her. He wasn't out on a date. A normal social life didn't apply to him.

"Let me," she said. "This is the first time I've been out with only one other person in a year." Her hand slid across the table and over his, and he swore he felt the heated curve of her fingers down to his bones. "Well, outside of Freddy's." A twinkle of mischief in her eyes threatened to short out his heart. "This was the perfect last visit to this place. Thank you."

He looked at her face and fell into her deep, green gaze. Her sincerity stung as much as her gratitude. Seanair never thanked him. No one did. He was feared, shunned, his life a murderous haze of assignments. He was on his last one. The final hurrah, and he would not let her kindness kill his plans.

She handed a passing waitress cash and the bill and told the woman to keep the change.

"Let's walk to the office. It's only ten minutes." She stood and strung her purse across her body, shrugged on her coat, and grabbed the bag with their pie. "I'll sure miss this place." She made her way through the packed restaurant toward the door and called over her shoulder, "You should come back here after I'm gone. You obviously appreciate their food, and that makes me happy."

He followed her through the crowd. Something warm and right stirred deep inside him, then curdled. She might be happy now, but she'd hate him soon enough. At the exit, he gave a last look around and snatched a business card off the reception podium.

Maybe he'd come back. If the pie turned out to be good.

Out on the sidewalk, he cast out his energy and confirmed the area was Natura-free.

"We're good to go." He drew up beside her on the sidewalk and got snared in the aura of her perfume.

The sky had gone winter gray, and a blast of wind sliced straight through his jacket.

"It's not far." Her brisk steps clipped up the sidewalk. "We'll go up Ninth Avenue."

They continued on Hudson and veered onto Ninth. He liked Chelsea, with all the trees, ironwork on the building fronts, and its stunning array of architectural styles.

As they walked side by side amid a sea of pedestrians, Elspeth didn't seem to notice how others stepped wide to avoid him. He noted the cars parked against the curb had mere inches between their bumpers.

"How do you live here?" he asked. "It's so crowded with…humans."

"Everyone minds their own business. Humans don't know anything about me, and Manhattan has close to two million of them. I'm more at home here than in some area full of our people. It's funny. Even though I have no innate power, I'm counted as Natura because of the baby thing, but since I don't have that interior vessel like the witches and warlocks to call and hold power, I'm not one of them either. I swear this whole innate-versus-called-power BS has reached its peak. I might as well be human."

"You aren't human." How could she compare herself to those self-indulgent twits? All they did was buy, buy, buy and fill the earth and sea and even outer space with their trash.

"From what I've seen, power's not all it's cracked up to be."

It was pointless to argue with a null. If she'd ever felt power, especially Fire, she'd laugh to hear herself say something so cavalier. The notion of her having Fire consumed him, but he killed the idea of her regenning with him, as the last thing he needed in the middle of a crowded sidewalk was a boner.

They crossed 21st Street, and he walked slap into a full-on wall of Earth energy. Not rotting. Not pure.

But way the hell off.

She grabbed at her throat, her mouth wide open, face red like she was choking. He knew instantly. That energy was pouring down her throat. He grabbed her hand. Yanked her into an alley. Encased them in a vault of Fire. Tugged her tight against him.

"Hang on. I got you." He summoned what little Air power he could, put his mouth over hers and kissed her, gently pushing the energy down, directing it toward her lungs, becoming her personal oxygen mask. He shored up his first Fire wall protecting them, circled his second mantle around the attacking Earth, capturing it between his two walls, and compressed the Fire barriers.

The Earth energy struggled, flailing and smashing against his invisible Fire compactor.

Her arms slid around him, and she upped the kiss. He didn't think as he swept his hands under her ass and lifted her. Turned and pressed her against the side of the brick building. Focusing on the thread of his Air energy, he gave her all he had, giving her back her breath.

That damned Earth energy was trying to kill her. He sensed its intent, the heaviness of its plans to fill her lungs and burst them. No fucking way. Not on his watch.

The warped presence stroked and suckled at his energy field, searching for a fissure to slurp its way inside. A shriek cut through the alley, the wail shrill and sick, the otherworldly Earth's call piercing his senses. Vined tendrils slithered up his protective barrier, writhing to get to her. He perceived the power as male, then female, then a genderless but sensual slide of other.

He tapped into that rare place where the last of his control met the lawless wild of his free Fire. He unleashed his restraint and launched an obliterating strike. Red, turbulent energy flew toward the invisible mass. He sensed a wall rising, and...*oh, shit.* His power ball was going to bounce off that Earth wall and strike him and Elspeth like they were bowling pins.

He didn't give her a warning, didn't give her time, just absorbed her into his innermost aura, the sacred space of orgasm, where he could twine his energy with hers and push power into her. She arched against him, gasping at the fusion of whatever Passives held with his Fire. He tucked her life-force beside his and held the fuck on, shoring up his shields against his own energy.

If she died, he'd go with her.

A richness filled him, the purest Fire and her Passive essence interweaving in a braid of breath-stealing pleasure. A strangled sigh left her, her hips flexed against him, and he breathed her in, tightening his embrace for the impending blow.

The blast hit him hard. His body smashed into hers, pinning her against the brick, and he grunted through the pain of waiting for his shields to absorb the Fire reverb.

The air rippled, and he sensed the Earth floundering.

Pressing her tight against the wall, he flung out a hand and slung a last-ditch, murderous swath of Fire energy, a full-out incendiary shimmer that would cling-wrap itself around the Earth mass. The blast tore from him, a torrent of powerful Fire at levels he'd never used.

A screech ripped through the narrow space, bits of brick pelting his shields. A crackling sounded, like the ground splitting, the Earth energy breaking apart. A clap of thunder split the air. Spits of sleet littered the ground. Human screams came down the alley. Footsteps clattered. Horns honked, and tires screeched. He pulled her to him and ran, ducking beneath a delivery door awning. The freak storm continued, the sleet now hail, gunfire pellets pounding the metal roof overhead as he covered her with his body.

The energy's foulness tore away. Gone, no trace but for the white marbles of ice covering the ground.

"Aleron?"

"One minute, baby." He scanned the alley, held her, made sure the thing was gone, and did the weirdest damn thing. He pressed his mouth to the top of her head, closed his eyes, breathed in something that smelled so Goddess good. "Are you hurt?" He didn't think so but assumed nothing—not after that fuckery.

"No."

Leaning back and looking her over, he felt his whole world

shrink to her wide eyes and hair tousled by his hands. He threaded his shaking fingers into her hair, pressed her back against a metal garage door, and kissed her. Sweet Goddess, she tasted of smoke and rain, air and life. He lost himself in the soft press of her breasts against him, the rush of her breath, and the sweet grip where she clawed the front of his shirt.

A tiny, faraway voice cried, *What the hell are you doing?*

He broke the kiss. "Elspeth, look at me."

Her head lolled, her expression slack, looking drunk from the Air energy. "Kiss me some more," she whispered.

"We have to go." He rested his forehead against hers, seeking to slow his breaths and sharpen his mind.

For one outrageous moment, he imagined he didn't have to stop, imagined they didn't have to leave. He dug his fingers into her hips and envisioned the tearing of their clothes as they both rushed to get the barriers gone between them. He pictured driving in, filling her, saw the flush on her cheeks and her half-lidded eyes as thrust into her. He wanted her right there, in the alley, against the wall, the salt from her sweat-drenched skin rich in his mouth.

Sirens wailed in the distance. A human had obviously called 911. Goddess, he'd screwed up. He hadn't remembered to hide the extent of his power and probably left some nice, black scorch marks on the brick. Shit, he might have torched a car or, Goddess forbid, a building.

He'd earned his towering-inferno reputation.

A mass of energy pushed against him, and he knew.

The restaurant. The walls closing in. He'd sensed something and written off the sensation. That Earth abomination had sized him up, right there in the restaurant, and judged him beatable.

And he'd dismissed the whole thing being distracted by…her.

Her hands slipped into his hair. "More." She kissed him, her lips gentle and soft and searching.

He should push her away. She was energy-high and—

The truth clocked him. Air was a truth serum and melted away falsities. She was kissing him because she wanted to. With her logic dulled and the truth unhindered by reason, she'd continue to pursue anything she wanted until the high wore off.

"Hey. Elspeth. Baby." He pulled back slightly. "You have to stop kissing me."

"I don't want to." Her bottom lip teased over his mouth. "I've wanted to kiss you since you mouthed off to me. You talk to me like I'm a normal person. Take me home. Have sex with me," she whispered into his mouth.

Great human Jesus.

"Elspeth, listen to me. You're telling me these things because your brain's filters are down."

"I know. I like it. I can do what *I* want." Her head met the metal of the garage door, her expression soft. "You're not attracted to me. I'm sorry I misread—"

"I am attracted to you." Shit. Where were *his* fucking filters?

As if called, the first of his mantles returned to him, the energy seeping into his skin. The second one that had been his father's gave them a wide berth, surrounding them and guarding against the Earth energy's return.

A lazy smile pulled at her mouth. "I knew you felt it too. You're a good person, and we could be good together, for a little while. I'd like something good to remember if things go bad after I'm—" She blinked and sucked in a deep breath. "Everything hurts."

"Yep. That's the Air hangover."

"Put me down. Put me—" She scrambled away several steps and retched.

Shit. Maybe he'd given her too much Air, but he hadn't known how to control it. His Air was latent. He'd never pulled that much, let alone knew how to use it help someone.

"I've got you." He gathered her hair in his fist.

His second mantle did a weird thing, ballooning into a bubble, encasing them both. He tried to call it to him, but the energy wouldn't budge. Instead, faint orange flames licked over every inch of her, the light pulsing and dancing around her.

"Can you see the Fire?"

She'd stopped vomiting but still had her hands on her knees. "That's you?"

"Yes." He scanned the alley as she straightened, distrusting the thing had truly departed. It dawned on him then. "You've never seen this side of what we are, have you?"

Her stare went miles long.

"I've seen flowers preen and bloom for my cousin. I've watched Fire dance between Lach's fingertips. My cousin Kerr burned me once when I was a teenager. He tampered with my mug of chai tea and hid the heat until I picked it up. Lach found out, and it never happened again." She slowly raised her gaze to his, her chin quivering. "I know about enriching soil and managing temperatures, filtering the air of pollutants and cleaning up seawater. I know how our elements drive industry and why many of us come from old money. The few high school classes I got to attend outside the regular ones didn't cover filling lungs with dirt."

There could be only one man behind her ignorance—Seanair. One part of him agreed with keeping her far away from their ugliness. The other wished Naturas could reincarnate, because after he killed Seanair, he'd raise him up like a zombie and kill him over and over again for not letting her take advanced-level classes. Marrying into Russian royalty, she needed full understanding of their capabilities.

In that moment, he realized he wasn't Seanair's only victim. It made sense, in a messed-up way, that their brutal leader kept the tightest reins on his own family.

He held out a hand, the desire for her to feel safe with him more important than finding and obliterating whatever had attacked her. "If you have questions, ask. I promise to always give you the truth, no matter how hard the answers."

He understood the danger of lies, and the one he'd keep from her was his plan for her grandfather.

She took his hand, and he pulled her to him, wrapping his arms around her. "Don't be afraid. I won't let anything happen to you. I give you my word."

"What was that thing?" The heat of her words seeped into his shoulder.

"An Astrux, I think. I've never felt one that strong."

"Do I want to know what an Astrux is?"

Her arms tightened around him. He noticed the anomaly. The small spot squatting beside his burning need to torch something. A strange corner. A tired place. That longed to steal her away and hibernate somewhere, nothing but the perfume of her shampoo and her body's softness in the space.

"It's improperly released energy." He'd share what he knew of the phenomenon. "If a Natura dies, and their energy isn't properly released back to its source, it roams the earth, stuck in a human-like purgatory, like an invisible, sentient cloud of power. Normally, they're frightening and can cause some turmoil, but I've never heard of a mass this large and powerful."

"But if it's Natura energy, why couldn't you sense it before it struck?"

Good fucking question.

"I'm not sure. It's gone now." He didn't think, just kissed the top of her head and narrowed his gaze on the tiny balls of ice in her hair and melted them.

He cast out his energy, out of the alley, down the streets, clocking every Natura in the vicinity with a stay-back warning. How many humans had experienced the storm? What was the damage? Man, Elite One was going to have to scramble to cover up this shit. He'd call in and check the cleanup status as soon as he got them home. Wait. *Home? Them?* He shook his head at the slip.

What are you doing?

Another great question, which begged a central one. What was more important? His mission? Or some woman he'd never see again once she was married?

Stay. Focused.

Stress made everyone do weird shit, so this cuddly, kissy, huggy version of himself was as messed up as that Astrux.

"Let's get you back to the apartment. I'll seal us in and figure out what's going on. Okay?" He put her at arm's length and lowered his head even with hers.

Her hand came up, cradling the scarred side of his face.

She nodded and leaned to look behind him. "That terrible thing ruined our pie." Her words slurred.

He looked over his shoulder at the smashed white bag on the ground.

"I'll get you some more. Here, walk beside me." He tucked her under his arm, because he…well, he was just being nice. That was all.

They walked up the alley. His senses on full alert, he scanned every brick and car and person as they waited for a cab, certain of only one thing.

That Earth energy wouldn't give up.

CHAPTER
SEVEN

Her heart would not slow. Not in the cab, not in the elevator, not at her doorstep.

Everything hurt. Like she'd been a car, and that thing had been a wall. What hurt most was the lies. Or, rather, the omissions. All the things her loved ones hadn't told her, Seanair, Lach, and Kazumi included.

Lach, she understood, at least from a protective-big-brother perspective. But Kazumi? Ever since seventh grade, her best friend had known her big nonnegotiable—she never again wanted to feel less than. Right now, she felt like a clueless, privileged twit.

The poor, brainless, sheltered rich girl.

Ms. Passive girl living in her protected Passive world.

"Keys are in my front pocket. You'll have to get them." She put a hand on the doorframe and tugged her purse over her head, her leg muscles signaling they were about to go on strike. "It's taking everything I have to breathe."

And dry-swallow the bitter pill of her ignorance.

Her purse thumped on the carpet.

"Turn around and look at me." Aleron's hands rested on her shoulders, and he put her back to the door. "What's going on? You're having trouble breathing?"

She looked up at his face. The deep furrow of his dark brows. The tightness of his hard jawline. The angry pink of his scar. He looked ready to kill the first thing that moved, right down to the dust motes.

"My lungs ache, and my pride's taken a significant hit too." She shook her head. "They felt better when you gave me your Air, but now they feel like deflated tires."

His concern morphed into a deep frown. "I need to put a hand over your ribs."

"Why?"

"Because if I injured you, I'll be able to tell. If I caused it, I can fix it faster than if the Astrux did it. You said you were better."

How could she tell him that in his arms was the best place she'd ever been?

"Let me check." He started at her side, his wide palm gliding toward her stomach.

Delicious warmth baked into her skin, and though she couldn't sense the immense strength of his Fire, she marveled at the obvious physical power beneath his gentle touch. A twinge of pain came from nowhere, and she winced.

"You just hit a tender spot." She put a hand over the area, wishing she could stem the ache settling into her muscles.

His fist pounded the wall.

"Shit. *Shit.* I'm sorry. Let's get you inside."

"Why are you mad?"

"Because I seriously screwed up." He scooped her purse from the carpet and strung it around his neck, the thing hanging down the front of him like a name badge.

"You saved me. It's the one thing I'm certain of."

"I fucked that up too. I'm not in the business of saving people." He looked down and reached toward her jeans pocket.

Her stomach tensed at the swipe of his finger through the thin pocket material. He had her apartment door open in seconds.

"I need to lie—"

Her knees gave out.

His arm wrapped around her waist. "I got you."

In a blink, his arms locked tight and firm beneath her knees and around her back, and her cheek was resting against his collarbone. The door slammed like he'd kicked it closed.

"Let's get you into bed."

Yes. Yes. Her eyelids grew heavy. Everything came back. His power. His rage. His brutality. She had no idea how power release worked, but if there were some kind of internal doors involved, he'd thrown his wide. Everything open. Fire on blast.

His warmth crept into her, down her side tucked against him, in the bend of her knee, the side of her breast where the tips of his fingers rested. He'd taken a great risk to save her. That thing that had poured itself down her throat, thick as bread dough in her lungs, had sought to destroy her. Her heart gave an extra hard *thunk*.

She remembered the vines, the snakes of power he'd ripped away from her, enduring the brutal bites himself.

"It tried to kill you. It wanted me dead, but whatever that thing was, I felt its hatred for you."

"You shouldn't have felt a thing." He placed her gently on the bed. "How's your breathing?" He sat beside her, his gaze taking in every inch of her like he was a frantic nursemaid.

Thank Goddess, she'd felt something.

"Passives should at least be able to recognize when someone's about to fill their lungs with sludge." She tried to take a deep breath. "I need to sit up and get out of this bra."

"No, you don't. Be still."

"Have you ever worn a bra?"

He gave her a look that made her smile, despite the pain, the confusion.

The aching, unmet need.

"Imagine jamming yourself into a too-small jockstrap. My ribs ache, and I don't need a band digging into them. Would you like a rubber band around your balls?"

She didn't think it possible, but he blanched. "I can't believe you said—"

"I have brothers. Stop giving me the what's-a-proper-girl-like-you look—ooh." She rubbed at a zing of pain under her boob.

"Roll onto your side."

"I can unhook a bra."

"So can I." He cocked an I've-done-it-plenty brow.

"Fine." She moved to turn.

His warm hand rested on her waist, guiding her. She braced a hand on the other pillow. The mattress moved, shifting as he climbed onto the bed behind her. Cool air kissed the skin right above the waistband of her low-slung jeans. She sensed the thin strip of fabric tucked between her cheeks and remembered—

His touch grazed over the edge of her thong. She heard his rough rush of breath and felt the slight tug of fabric as he lifted the band of her sweatshirt. Time turned into the sweetest of gifts. The moment drew out. His knuckles brushed warm and tentative over her skin, the band of the bra pressing into her and slowly releasing.

"Fuck."

Yes. Please.

She didn't have the strength to pleasure herself, let alone him. No way was she going to lie there and not savor every inch of him. It'd been a long time. So long since she'd been with a man. There'd been Eamon, her first boyfriend. Then a human in college. A few Naturas on rare wild nights out. One in a limo. One in a bathroom stall at a club. Naturas who'd gone on to marry the women she'd introduced them to.

"I need to call a doctor. You're...bruised."

She jostled as he got off the bed. If he called for one of their physicians, Seanair would know, and then she'd have ten guards, maybe more. She'd be confined to her apartment. Trapped inside the white walls. No park walks. No bakeries. Her Goodbye, Manhattan Tour would be canceled.

"No. Please don't." She struggled to sit up, pressure building in her temples. She was giving up everything, and she wanted a month. A month to say goodbye to her life. "If I really felt like something was wrong with me, I'd tell you. My lungs ache, and I have zero energy. That's all."

She didn't feel gravely injured, more like she'd gone from couch to marathon.

In a day.

"I'm out of my depth here, and I'm not going to play doctor when we have a team at Lenox Hill who makes house calls."

"Give me your Air. One more time." She remembered the alley, his mouth, and his glorious power filling her. Great breath of winter, she'd inhaled his magnificent, life-giving Air. "Please." She closed her eyes, trying to re-create the sensation. "It felt so good when you were inside me."

Her eyes flew open at her choice of words. She met his gaze. A flicker of orange heat flashed deep in his brown eyes. Had he lost control of his power, or had he let her see it? Naturas concealed their energy around her, their gazes either soft with pity or sharp with triumph.

"If a doctor comes here, I won't be able to leave this apartment again, and if that thing wants to get to me, it will." She suffered no illusions about her predicament, the situation not new. "I think you surprised it, but you're stronger than it is with your two Fire mantles or…well, you're a Dual with the Air you gave me." The phantom scent of clean, crisp air teased her nose. "Do what you did one more time. Today was the best day. Before it went to shit, I felt…free." She met his hard gaze. "The other night at Freddy's and today, I felt *normal*. I'm about to give up everything. *Please.*"

He folded his arms behind him and assumed the stone stillness and dead-eyed stare of her usual guards. She sensed her freedom slip, her last hurrah unlatched and drifting, floating to join her uncertain future.

A grave sense of loss crept over her.

"Where's my phone?" she asked. "I'll call the doctor myself." Goddess, when Seanair heard about this…

She turned her head toward the windows soon to be her only link to the outside world.

"I'll do it." He came to the left side of her bed into her sight line.

"I don't want your pity."

"Do you remember how I gave you my Air?"

She shifted her gaze up to his. "That's not something I'll ever forget."

"If I do this, you can't tell anyone about my Air energy. No one else knows I have it. It's saved my life more than a few times."

"You know the full story about my brother." Her muscles grew heavy, her body seeming to sink farther into the mattress. "I'll keep your secret."

"Lie on your back."

She did, never taking her eyes from his, her heartbeat accelerating as he climbed onto the bed and straddled her hips. His arms crossed, and he pulled his sweater over his head. The black T-shirt underneath pulled tight across his chest and biceps. Muscles. Hard. Flexing. His body a solid mass of them.

"It's hot in here." He eyed her with cool indifference.

Her gaze cut to the hollow of his neck. His heartbeat punched against his skin.

You'll never tire of a night with a Fire.

The memory cemented as he placed a hand on either side of the pillow and leaned toward her. Her hair rustled. A light breeze tickled over her face.

"I have to go slow this time. Those bruises may be from me."

"If they are, I know you didn't do it on purpose."

"I should have been more careful."

"You didn't have time to be careful. You saved me. That's all I know." She cupped the side of his face with the scar.

"Whenever you're ready." Her need to know the mark's history faded as his mouth drew closer and closer to hers.

He kissed her. Her mouth opened on its own. The strangest press of power pushed its way inside her. A gentle strength. A coolness filled her mouth and streamed down her throat, much like that rosewater lightning, the temperature warming like he realized the air had been too cold.

Her breasts swelled, and a longing ache bloomed low. Goose bumps broke over her skin. An immediate warmth blanketed her. She recognized the sensation and realized he was the reason she hadn't been too hot or too cold since he'd arrived. She arched up, wanting to feel his warmth, his heavy body pressing against hers.

She wrapped her arms around his neck, toying with the chain that hung there, and pulled him closer. Closing her eyes, she remembered the smile he'd given her at their shared love of lemon. The image shifted, back to the alley, where his expression had been murderous and his hold on her steel. He would have scorched the earth for her, would have been a one-man wrecking ball of destruction to save her.

He would have died. To save her, he would have sacrificed himself.

The soreness in her lungs dulled. A sense of rightness like she'd never experienced washed over her. She should break the kiss and let him rest, but she didn't. She laced her fingers into his hair. A faint groan rumbled from him.

She wanted him. Inside her. Driving and grunting and sweating above her. His gruff exterior hid a selfless man. One who, in the face of sheer wrongness, did the right thing. The noble thing. She wanted to feel the stretch of him, the scrape of his stubble, his harsh huffs of breath all the while never taking her eyes from his.

He broke the kiss. She immediately felt the loss of his warmth. She had felt him. Not his body, but his power. She'd felt the caress and lick of his Fire. A call wanting to be answered.

"Take off your sweatshirt so I can heal the bruises."

The rush from the alley returned, when he'd filled her with his energy, and something so incredibly right snapped into place. Exhaustion seeped into her arms and legs, her body a leaden lump.

"Let me help you." His gaze softened like he could sense her lethargy.

She tried to arch, her muscles useless, but he managed to shift the shirt up her body and gingerly guided it over her head.

His eyes glowed orange. Red. A tiny ring of blue edged his irises. His hand covered the right side of her lower ribs.

"Oww." She winced at the tender spot.

"I'm sorry." The light in his eyes died. His gaze rounded, his mouth firming, his expression grim with shame. "I've never harmed anyone before that I didn't want to hurt."

He'd said he didn't save people.

"Do you kill people for my grandfather?" Her gut gave a knowing nod.

"Not all Naturas use their powers the way they were intended." He gently palpated her sides.

"But you kill them, and my brother does too." She aired the suspicion she'd long held but hadn't wanted to verify.

Seanair kept her out of the way, but she'd overheard things when she was younger, when her grandfather had been less careful.

"Yes. Close your eyes. The light will be bright."

She did, and her other senses opened. A glorious smoke hovered under her nose. A rapturous heat caressed her skin. Pure, raw pleasure sizzled inside her.

A rush of breath escaped her. "Stop."

"Does it hurt?"

"No," she managed, not about to tell him if he kept up his healing, she was going to have the orgasm of her life.

"The bruises are fading. Let me do something less intense." He shifted down and hovered his mouth over one side of her ribs.

He took a deep, long inhale, then blew like he was extinguishing birthday candles in slow motion. A faint orange stream colored the air and bubbled like peroxide over the tender area. Damp heat sank into her skin and covered her in an electric-blanket warmth. Her eyelids fluttered.

"Rest now." He started to move.

"Stay." She slid her hand over the covers toward him. "Stay until I'm deep asleep. I'm scared." The memory of the thing's hold came alive as her vision grew hazy.

"You have nothing to fear as long as I'm around." He lay on his side, too much space between their bodies. "I've got you."

He did have her. With him near, she felt untouchable, his power infinite and immense and numbing her in the most exquisite sense. Goddess, the heat of him kindled deep inside her. Deeper still was the feel of him. His arms around her. His mouth on hers. The thing she sought to cling to wasn't his Fire, but his touch. It'd been so long since she'd been held. The shelter of his body had rocked her way more than his power, and she longed to snuggle into him, bury her nose in the bend of his neck, and wait for those Goddess-blessed arms of his to pull her close.

She found his hand and curled her fingers through his warm ones, her mind fuzzy, trying to re-create the feel of him. "Do you know how long it's been since I've been touched?" She struggled to lift her eyes to his, knowing she should shut her mouth, but she needed him to know. "No one hugs me. Family sometimes, but not like you. In your arms, I feel like everything's going to be okay."

She tried to hold his gaze, but her eyes wouldn't stay open.

Her last thoughts were of him and an impossible dream.

He pressed his hand into the mattress and slipped it from beneath hers. A small sigh sounded, but she didn't wake. He'd almost decided to sleep beside her in case she had a nightmare. The urge to comfort, protect, and soothe her prodded at him like a hot poker.

He couldn't stop thinking about what she'd said, how she'd looked at him. His last hug had come from his father, right before they'd split up on the trail heading for the chapel. About half an hour before his dad had been murdered by Seanair.

Twelve years since, he'd had more than a handshake. He didn't hug his regens. He gave, she received, and they went on about their business. He'd had a girlfriend in high school. Caitlin. Young love. First love. Though they'd never gotten a chance to have sex. He'd lost his virginity at twenty-four, the night he came into his full power, his Fire settling in with the assistance of a tender assigned by Seanair to service him.

He didn't understand why it'd felt so right to protect Elspeth, shield her. This primal protective streak for her buzzed and spit inside him like a broken power line. He liked her in his arms, her breath warm against his mouth and her soft body tight against his.

Of all the people he could be attracted to, why her? The granddaughter of the man he hated with every single cinder of his Fire.

He shouldn't do it, but he couldn't stop his hand from moving gently toward her, his knuckles skimming the soft curve of her jaw.

She was beautiful and kind and all of the things he'd once envisioned he'd have.

He longed to hold her one more time. Let her rest easy against him. Fall asleep with his nose buried in her hair.

He climbed from the bed and crept across the carpet, chastising himself for letting things get so out of control. He had a goal, one shot to achieve it, and he kept…dreaming. Dreaming shit that wouldn't come to pass. His life was set, and any dreams he'd had died with his father.

Leaving her bedroom door cracked in case she needed him, he vowed to set fire to any further distractions. He cast a second swath of Fire, sending it across the floor and up the walls, making sure to reinforce the windows and the vents.

A spark of holy-shit realness shot down his spine. He had a problem. A big, powerful, invisible problem. How did he battle an unseen enemy? Within sight distance, Naturas could see each other's auras. Waters were blue, Earths green, and Fires red. Airs were white and kinda glittery, like walking party sparklers, making them easy prey. Even if Naturas couldn't see each other, their energy emitted a signal similar to cell phones, so they essentially announced their presence like pings on a radar.

That Earth energy had come out of nowhere.

He dug his cell from his pocket and checked the screen. *Shit.* Twenty-seven texts. Four phone calls from Elite One HQ.

He pulled up the last one and fired off a response.

Inferno: Unicorn in lockdown. Sensed problem. Initiated total isolation. Unicorn fine.

Elite One never used real names, but he wished he'd given Elspeth a different one, as he wanted to think of her as *his* unicorn, not anyone else's.

EOHQ: Zeus wants full report. Hold for check-in.

Inferno: Assignment was to protect unicorn at all costs.

EOHQ: Zeus ordered sole access to your cell. Lockdown, but for him.

What? The point of total lockdown was so a location couldn't be determined. Kinda important to hide when dodging a covert ball of festering energy.

Inferno: Affirmative on access. Zeus only.

EOHQ: What was that thing? A squadron's investigating. Two non-responds.

Inferno: Which two?

EOHQ: Flicker And Kindling.

Shit. The two newbies.

Inferno: No idea on the cluster. Keep me posted.

EOHQ: Will do. Zeus wants unicorn on display.

Of course, he wanted to trot his show pony all over town.

Inferno: Affirmative.

He shoved the phone into his back pocket. Something about today didn't sit right. Astruxes attacking humans was usually a petty annoyance. Drenching them in freak storms. Blowing papers off desks. Messing with heat so hot pots seemed cool enough to touch. Commanding birds to take craps from trees on the people passing below them.

The free-range spirits were angry at being separated from their energy source, but they didn't congregate en masse, and they harangued humans, not Naturas. Even more, Seanair had strict rules about dispensing energy upon death. A prayer was spoken, and the freed element energy returned to its figurative mother ship. Period.

Disobeying Seanair's rules earned Naturas a visit from Elite One, and those visits ended only one way.

He gave a last look through the small gap in the door and studied his pretty unicorn.

Yeah, it'd been a lifetime ago since someone had held him like he meant something.

That was the problem with Elspeth. She made him soft. As a rule, he didn't hesitate. Ever. He didn't feel anymore either. For years, he'd bathed in ferocious anger, replaying his father's death over and over until hatred charred his emotions.

Her chest rose and fell in a soft, easy rhythm, her hand still extended toward where he'd been.

The soft hum from the car-filled streets blanketed the room as he looked at her, and he allowed himself to admit the small truth. He'd never kissed a woman he wanted. Sure, he needed women to recharge his element. He wasn't into men, but they'd work too. Sex was a servicing, a function.

He'd burned away all traces of that foul Earth energy and tasted Elspeth's true essence. Odd that he'd gotten spice and not sweet. Since he'd inhaled her freely, he'd discerned her every thought. She'd judged him honorable. Secretly kind. Desirable.

His unicorn had a dirty little mind.

If she hadn't been completely wrecked, she'd wanted them skin to skin, with him deep inside her. He shut his eyes, needing to kill this strange sensation dogging his every move. A waffling. A weakness. A want.

He wanted her with a desire bordering on wild fury.

How could he want someone he hated? She was a Lennox. He loathed her like the rest of the arrogant lot.

He studied the swaths of brown hair draped over the white sheets. The pale skin of her shoulder peeked from beneath where he'd tucked the comforter around her. In the hour he'd lain beside her watching her sleep, he'd decided she was naturally pretty. Thick, long lashes. Her nose turned up slightly, and he'd had to stop himself from toying with the tip.

Even in sleep, there was a steadiness about her. An ease. An honesty he didn't know what to do with. Try as he might, he hadn't found anything to hate or even frown upon. Well, her brother's situation and her asinine engagement, but he shut that shit down.

He returned his focus to Seanair, self-anointed Zeus, and waited for his anger to froth and rise. He called up the worst day of his life and conjured up the smell.

Burned flesh had a distinct odor, one that baked into his senses, that he wouldn't dislodge. If he'd seen his father die, his brain probably would have dulled the memory, lessened it over time so he could return to some new normal. Scent was different. Scent took him right back, hiding like a scared gopher between the pews, that strange crinkle, and then...charred skin.

He set his Fire free, flames coating his palm. He could create a fireball, set her bed aflame, let her burn in his power-induced sleep.

One Lennox down, too many to go.

The idea of anyone harming her unleashed a vicious fury. Smoke wafted from him, the fumes of his anger seeping from his skin. He realized he couldn't do it. He would never allow harm to come to her. He was as certain as he'd been in that alley.

He would die for her.

He scrubbed a hand up his face. He'd hurt her by accident. He'd been trained to take life, not to save it, and he'd gone into overkill with his energy. Shame filled him. He owed his dad, owed him to finish what he'd started and get that Fire cuff off that motherfucker Seanair and start the search for the true Fire Magnus. As an emissary, the cuff would make him unkillable, but the moment he found the rightful wearer and removed it, he'd be dust in the wind.

Yet, here he was, lusting after a lemon-loving unicorn.

His dick pushed against his fly. Damn thing demanded sustenance, especially once he'd absorbed his father's Alpha mantle. Naturas liked their sex, but trying to keep two mantles charged was proving to be daunting.

Turned out his little brain wasn't so smart, as it wanted to sink into someone who could do nothing for him.

He had to get his act together. Solve the Astrux mystery. Figure out what was going on with this asinine gala.

The strangest sensation washed over him, an odd taste inside him he didn't recognize. Guilt. A feeling he'd long squashed. He didn't have a remorseful bone in his body. He couldn't, and do what he did. His admittance to her of his role stung. He eliminated horrible people. Not the petty-crime types, but assholes who took out cities with hurricanes. Folks who had no problem burning thousands of acres to damage another Natura's position. Two weeks ago, he hadn't blinked at torching a bunch of Airs who'd attempted to get away with popping a few tornados to rip up downtown Atlanta to teach another Air family a lesson.

She moaned in her sleep, and he breathed in her exhalations.

His dick firmed to the point of pain.

He couldn't escape the flavor of her emotions swirling in his senses, her desire potent, alluring. Why was his body reacting like she was a refueling power station? She couldn't recharge him. Elementwise, sex with her would be like tapping a busted electrical outlet.

He shook his head. He couldn't leave her now. He'd Fire-sealed the apartment, but bringing someone in to regen later tonight wasn't a risk he'd abide.

He'd have to take matters in hand. He turned and headed for his room. Goddess, could he sink any lower? There was nothing wrong with masturbation for pleasure, but pumpin' the chump for regeneration purposes was like filling the energy tank with the cheap gas. Alpha Fires didn't top themselves off, not on the regular anyway, and his two mantles required steady servicing.

One of the last conversations he'd had with his father snuck into his thoughts, a man-to-man convo right before everything changed.

One of these days, his dad had said, *you'll meet someone who'll check every box. I'll never forget the day I met your mother. Tried to deny it every which way, but I was done, son. Cooked clean through to my soul. Anyone can have sex. When you're with your true other half, in that moment where you give energy freely to each other, you'll know the purest, greatest love.* His dad had socked him square in the arm. *Then you'll know exactly why I chase your mother all day, every day.*

The words bounced around the hollow space inside him, a crevice left by death. A take-care-of-business twinge shot through his balls. There'd be no one for him. No wife. No family. He'd sign his own death warrant the moment he ended Seanair.

He walked through the guest room and into the bath. If he didn't take the edge off, his resolve to keep it all business with Elspeth wouldn't last. He went to take off his lace-up boots, and fuck it—

Yanking open the holes of his button fly, he made it to the sink and turned the hot water on full blast. Jerking up the drain stop, he watched the basin fill and hoped the water would be hot enough. He should have taken care of business before he'd made his bargain and dismissed her other guards.

He shook his head at his mistake and shoved his jeans and boxers to his knees. Dick hot and hard in his one hand, he plunged his other one into the scalding water.

A grunt caught in his throat as he siphoned the heat from the liquid. Warmth. Life. *Goddess, I need more.*

He stared at himself in the mirror. A vein popped in his forehead as he strained to channel the flow of thermic energy from the water. Yellow light crept up his arm and disappeared beneath the T-shirt's sleeve. Inhaling deep, he started to pump, tightening his fist until his cock turned a strangled red. He stared until his reflection glazed over, his shaft thickening and growing harder, his breath coming quicker.

It wasn't enough. Flying solo was never enough. The skin on his hand pinked in the scalding water. He bent more at the waist and leaned his weight onto the sink.

He closed his eyes, felt her phantom lips on his, took things further and imagined slipping inside her, what he'd do to her. Her dark hair spilled across the white sheets. Her sexy, smoky rose scent clogged his senses. He cast aside his excuses and let the truth of her desire fill his lungs anew. She wanted him. Him.

No one wanted him. Not even his own family.

His mouth watered as her desire spread through him.

He grew impossibly hard. Exhaling roughly, he took a harsh breath and upped the jerk of his hand. The pithy heat from the steam did nothing. He needed to come. Come while doing a massive energy grab. He sought another heat source and looked to the wall. Thank fuck. Heated floors. He tore his hand from the water to hit the switch for the radiant coils beneath his feet. He scrambled out of his boots, ripped off his socks, and curled his toes against the warming tiles.

He caught sight of his desperation in the mirror. What a

disgrace, allowing his Fire energy to get gutter low. He didn't deserve his father's mantle. He flipped the scalding water back on, plunged his hand into the stream, and resumed pumping his cock with his right hand.

What would Elspeth would say if she could see him now? Weak as a newly powered, jerking himself off, about to pop a blood vessel under the strain of yanking power through his feet and hand and wringing out an orgasm to open the place inside him where his power resided.

He closed his eyes, opened his first aura, tried to get his element to absorb the heat in his heels. He worked himself sore, teetering on the edge of orgasm so he could open his second shield.

Sweat trailed into his hair. He raised his head, focused on the sheen of sweat on his face, and tried to picture her. What would she look like when she lost control? Would the V at the top of her mouth pull flat? Would she cry out loud or breathy? Even though she was a Passive, would the green in her eyes glow? Would his eyes turn the shade of hers if she could conceive?

A smile pulled his mouth tight as he imagined himself behind her. Driving into her. Imagined his name coming from her mouth. Breathy. She'd be breathy, and that pale skin would flush pink. His mind played a game of musical positions. His breathing grew faster, his heart beating furiously. The picture formed right in front of him of her green eyes, unfocused, his name a ragged breath from her full mouth, the smile on her face when his eyes turned the green of hers, telling her she could have his baby if she wanted.

A wife. A family. His dream.

With her.

A shudder ripped through him. Red smoke filled the room. His vision went crimson.

"Els-*peth*." Her name came out in a strangled grunt.

Jets of heat shot from him, down his hand, across his thighs. A hunger like no other tore through him. A night. One. With her. That's all he wanted. No mission. No revenge. No death. No Lennoxes.

Just her. And him. Taking their fill of each other until they were breathless.

He pinched his eyes shut. Why'd she have to be beautiful? And smart? And kind? She was supposed to be a bitch. Self-righteous. Judgmental. A typical Lennox.

Fire energy crackled over his skin and sizzled away the sweat. The red smoke retracted and reabsorbed into him. He assessed his energy levels and ground his jaw. Not enough. Not nearly enough if he had to battle an enemy he couldn't see. That strange Earth Astrux would have killed her, its energy salivating and starving to devour her life-force.

Over his damned dead body would it have her.

He looked himself over in the mirror, all stubble, scowl, and scar.

He'd fallen so far, so far there was no way up. No glimpse of the boy who'd wanted to follow in his father's footsteps.

Something flickered in his mind, an idea killed, probably the last dying cinder of hope he had another option besides death. That something good waited for him at the end of this long road.

Who was he kidding? At the end of his journey was a cliff and only one way to go—over. Since he'd gotten his father killed, he didn't deserve a future or anything more.

Not even the fantasy of Elspeth Lennox.

CHAPTER
EIGHT

Elspeth awoke to easy breaths and streams of morning light spearing through the windows like someone had turned up the intensity of the sun. She looked to her left, where she hoped to find Aleron still asleep so she could secretly study the man who'd kissed her back to rights.

She rolled onto her side and tucked her arm under her head, unable to stop looking at the indentation of his head in the pillow. The sense of loss, of sadness, that he wasn't there was almost a physical blow. She tested her ribs, finding the soreness gone. Which sent her now fully awake brain chasing the memories of the horror in the alley, of the attacking thing she couldn't see and down a rabbit hole of a thousand questions.

On top of those endless brain loops, she'd received a crash course in the dark side of her people. She should be frozen in fear. If this could happen in New York, where she was protected by family, what could happen thousands of miles away, in a massive country, with no one who knew her?

And how did she explain that a pair of intense brown eyes, a scowl, and a scar hushed her worries?

Why had she met him now? At a time she couldn't pursue him? She tried to chalk up her attraction to the flood of emotion from yesterday's events, yet it was the diner that had done it for her.

His non-frown at the chicken. His semi-smile at the pie. His attention on her. He'd *heard* her. Hadn't dismissed her questions. Hadn't kowtowed to her because of who she was. He'd treated her... as an equal. Sure, he'd brought up the status thing, but he'd responded to her as if she were normal. After a lifetime of being treated like a freak, that was pretty heady.

And then he'd kissed her.

Even as hidden a romantic as she was, she'd laughed at books and movies where a heroine was supposedly this big, tough, badass woman who slept her way through armies but would be taken out by one kiss from the sexy, enigmatic hero. So not believable.

But now she understood. Understood in a way that shook everything she knew.

She hadn't slept her way through armies, but she was no wallflower. What she and Aleron had shared, and survived, no one would understand. Between the diner and near disaster in the alley, she'd seen the man beneath the stoic guard exterior.

That Goddess-awful Earth energy had done one good thing. Surviving the attack had put her and Aleron on an island of shared experience. Enduring power of that magnitude and coming out alive connected them in a way that turned days to years.

And now?

His touch, his taste were seared into her, his smoky aroma baked into her very essence.

If a kiss could do that to her, what—

The doorbell rang.

Kazumi and the dress. Right.

Crap. She had so much to do before the gala, and all she could think about was gazing into Aleron's brown, brown eyes and feeling his mouth, so firm and soft but insistent on hers.

She launched herself out of the bed and across the room, and a sense of lightness bloomed. Zum made everything better. She raced into the hall, focused on the door and the second ringing of the bell, and collided with a mass of warmth and muscle and skin. Her hands pressed against his bare middle, and she swore heat shot from her palms and settled between her legs.

His arms captured her like she belonged in them. The woody, smoky scent of him, still heated from blankets and sleep, hit her, and everything stopped.

His long, strong fingers closed around her wrists. "Have you forgotten the door-answering rule?"

No, and she hadn't forgotten what that deep voice did to her either.

She caught the flare in his eyes. A quick hit of orange. Arousal. She'd seen it last night in her bedroom. He cut his gaze away and tried to hide it, but those abs of his were tense, his shoulders rigid.

She didn't want to consider the electricity between them, but it was there—and not one-sided.

"It's Kazumi." She held on to his gaze. "You're not dressed. I can get it."

He took her hand and pulled her into his room. "Come here." He grabbed a shirt from an open duffel bag. The longer she stood there, the more his scent filled her senses. Sweet Goddess of Man Cologne, the whole room smelled of him. Of Fire. And man. And...*yes.*

"Not a word about yesterday." He yanked the shirt over his tousled hair, the play and flex of his muscles the brightest of shiny objects. All tanned skin and brute strength. He turned, pulling the black T-shirt down, but not before she saw the thin trail of hair disappearing beneath the waistband of his jeans.

"She's my best friend. She's a vault of secrets."

"I know who she is to you, but if you tell her, don't think she won't tell her mother. She will. She'll think you're not safe." His gaze warred with hers.

Zum never hovered, but when they'd been at Freddy's, she hadn't strayed from Elspeth's side. She'd always had the sense Zum shielded her in some way. Telling her BFF a ball of invisible Earth energy had tried to fill her lungs with dirt...

Aleron was right.

Zum, never the soul of patience, pounded the ornamental knocker. "Get that big-ass Fire to answer the door."

"Any Water BS, and she's outta here." He gave her an I-mean-it glare, then opened the locks.

Zum stormed in with her outstretched arm holding a long, black bag. "Great Mother N, girl, what the hell's going on here?"

Elspeth shouldn't have smiled, but she couldn't help it. Zum was just over five feet of indignant huffery in her black jumpsuit and platform sneakers, and Aleron was all six-five of stoic badassery. Still, it would be a toss-up as to who was more pissed off at the moment. He might be looming over her best friend, but Zum wasn't giving an inch, even if her neck was craned all the way back to look up at him.

"Kazumi, this is Aleron Foussé, my guard until the wedding. Aleron, my best friend, Kazumi Fukada."

The two all but circled each other like cats with arched backs trying to decide who was going to strike first.

"Both of you, back off." Goddess save her from elemental arm wrestling.

"Foussé? The Fire family?" Zum draped the dress over the back of the sofa and folded her arms, her classic battle pose.

Wait a second. "You know them? Him?"

Zum's smile was all teeth, no eyes. "Not him personally, but yeah, Mom's mentioned the Foussés. He's the one you texted me about? The Elite One ass—"

"Yes!" She widened her eyes to try to tell Zum to zip it. They'd talk all things Aleron when they were alone. "We've worked things out. Everything's great."

"'Great' and 'guard' aren't two words you usually put together." Zum fussed over the garment bag, her tone taking a guards-with-benefits direction. She turned and did a thorough visual assessment of Aleron like he was a car she was considering purchasing. "Did you hear about the attack last night?"

Hmm. Maybe he'd passed Zum's initial inspection, since it seemed she'd backed off of her impending hurricane attack on Aleron and was as smooth as deep water.

"I haven't heard a thing. What happened?" Shitshow averted, she moved toward Zum, her stomach knotting at her best friend's stark expression.

"I can't believe it. A Natura couple was killed. Murdered in their brownstone." Kazumi scrubbed her hands up her face. "The deaths were strange, and there were Earth signatures everywhere, like the energy had no control. Mom says there's some weird-ass shit happening, something about a disturbance with released energy. Whatever it is, it's not good."

"That's horrible." Her pulse kicked up, the truth a clog in her throat. After what had happened the night they'd gone to Freddy's, she almost brought up the witches, but she didn't want to breach the confidentiality about Zum's mom and the meeting.

"How were the bodies discovered?" Aleron moved to the other end of the couch, standing like a lava-filled Hulk, all heat and menace.

Zum arched one of her perfectly plucked brows. "The human cops and Con Ed showed up, since whatever did it decided to burst the water and gas lines for an entire block. It's headlining every news channel. What have you been doing that you haven't heard?"

Aleron pulled his phone from his back pocket and thumbed across the screen. "Fuck."

"Hard fuck, chief," Zum agreed. "Elite One better get their shit together, or humans won't be buying the 'natural disaster' BS much longer. Con Ed can only get blamed so many times." She blinked, then rubbed her eyes. "Holy… No wonder I feel like I stepped inside a campfire. You have two Fire mantles?"

Aleron's nostrils flared. He drew up straight and folded his arms behind his back. Irritation buzzed inside Elspeth like flies on fruit. He didn't have to stand at freakin' attention in front of them.

"My father gave me his mantle a long time ago." His gaze shifted to one of Lach's paintings.

Zum's expression smoothed. "I'm sorry for your loss."

Aleron's jaw worked, but other than the almost infinitesimal movement, he didn't so much as blink.

Kazumi didn't seem insulted by the lack of response. Instead, she took the dress and walked toward Elspeth's bedroom. "I'd better shake this out, or it'll be wrinkle city. Join me in the bathroom in two minutes."

Elspeth was used to her best friend's mercurial shifts but felt the need to explain when Kazumi was out of earshot. "Don't mind Kazumi. She can go from floodgates open to Zen water garden in a heartbeat."

Aleron met her eyes but stayed stonily silent.

She cleared her throat and tried again. "I'm sorry you lost your dad and that I didn't say something before." The weight of grief was one she was used to carrying. "My parents died when I was a baby. I know what it's like to miss someone. It's a wound that won't heal."

His dark expression deepened, and she was more grateful than ever that he was assigned to *protect* her, because for a moment, he looked like he wanted to burn both her and Kazumi into the rug.

"Don't say anything about the Astrux." He glared down his misaligned nose.

She didn't know what she'd done wrong, but she was glad for the excuse to get out of range of Aleron's rage-filled eyes.

"Zum's waiting. You can stand down, okay? Everything's all right."

He pinned her again, without so much as shifting his weight. "Everything is far from all right. Don't drop your guard, and don't get chatty."

Her hackles rose, dispelling any momentary weakness she'd been caught in. "Don't you forget that you're my guard, not my boss. I'll let you know what my plans are after I've visited with my friend. You're free to go back to your room, or patrol, or whatever else it is you do."

She didn't wait for a response and instead donned the mask she'd worn for years to conceal her thoughts and feelings. Moving through her room and into the bathroom, she stopped short, awed at what came naturally to most Naturas.

Goddess love Waters. Zum was using one hand to direct the steam coming from the hot water running in the sink onto the dress she'd hung from the robe hook. The fabric smoothed from neck to hem, the material releasing every crinkle in a cascade like special effects in a movie.

"Let's see Rowenta come up with a steamer like that." Elspeth couldn't contain a smile at her tiny friend's concentration.

Zum's expression transformed from intense to amused in a blink. "Not in a thousand lifetimes." She gestured to the dress. "I trust no one but myself with Burmese lotus flower silk."

"I don't either," Elspeth agreed, as if she had a clue about silk from Myanmar versus any other place on the planet.

"Do you like it?" Apprehension notched a line between her bestie's brows.

How did her badass friend have one speck of doubt about herself? Every creation Kazumi made was something beyond magical.

She took Zum's hand and gave it a squeeze. "It looks like you took a million emeralds and melted them to make this. It's stunning, and I love it. You're amazing. And you gave me no hints at all the other night that you'd outdone yourself again."

"Girl, I had to get up and sew the next morning and put my needle into overdrive to finish. You have to look like ten million bucks tomorrow night."

A wave of nausea hit her at the thought of the upcoming gala. Seanair's events were spectacles, with the Lennox family on full parade.

"What's wrong?" Zum clutched her hand tighter. "Did I mess something up?" She was scanning the dress like she'd dared to miss snipping a thread.

"I'm…not used to color. I wear black to everything. I like to blend in at these events."

Zum wagged a scolding finger. "No, no, no. No more haute funeral looks for you. You're almost twenty-four, not ninety-four. You've got curves, and it's time the world sees them."

"I don't know…" She stood and noted the deep plunge of the neckline and the slit up the leg. "I'm no prude, but I normally don't show so much skin at family events."

Who was she kidding? She'd never shown that much skin anywhere.

"Normal is boring and no longer part of your verbiage." She gave the dress a game-show-host wave. "I call this the Manslayer. All those chickenshits too scared to ask you out because of Granddaddy's death stare will be crying in their cocktails. My goal, though, is to see how the Russian responds once he sees the photos of you online in this dress."

"You're baiting my fiancé?" She jerked her head toward Zum and about choked on the word.

Surely she could be forgiven for forgetting. She'd signed the contract only three days ago, and for the love of the Goddess, she hadn't even met Yuri yet. She'd been too busy dealing with Tall And Broody, who was somewhere out in the living room, and getting attacked and then having the Fire kissed into her.

"I'm dangling you like a gorgeous, tasty carrot to see if he bites. It's the racy-text test. Tabloid photos will be online before you even make it inside the hotel." Zum stood and folded her arms, a super-pleased smile on her face. "Actually, this gown is my middle-finger salute to your fiancé. Has he bothered to text, call, Snap, anything?"

"We've had no communication other than the contract."

"No communication? Do you hear yourself?" Zum took the dress in hand and unlatched the straps from the hanger. "I may be glamming you up, but I'm still not down with this whole thing. My mother says the only reasons anyone deals with the Russians are oil and gas." She looked over her shoulder as if she could scan the bedroom through the walls. "I want to hear all about the Elite One man in your living room. Come to think of it, where's the rest of your security detail?"

"Aleron's like ten guards in one, so the others were reassigned. I'm enjoying the privacy."

And him pushing Air into my lungs with his mouth.

"Good thing he's not your gala escort, or the paparazzi would have a field day. It's still us, right? The chick power posse?"

"New York's Powerpuff Girls." Elspeth laughed at the memory of going back to their college dorm wasted and watching the silly show.

"I'm still Buttercup, and you're still Blossom."

"Not sure I'm the leader of anything, but I wouldn't mind having Bubbles's supersonic wave-blasting power."

"You're going to have plenty of power at Seanair's soirée. You'll be a siren no one can resist."

She felt her expression fall. "That's not power. That's being on display like a prize pig. I'm a guest like everyone else. It's not about me."

"Oh, it's so about you." Zum's tone was shrill. "Your grandfather does nothing without a plan. The event may ostensibly be about honoring Jon Costa's promotion, but now that the engagement's official, Seanair's making a statement."

"It would have been nice if the statement had included an 'I love you,' or even 'congratulations.'"

Zum ran a thumb over Elspeth's cheek. "I'm sorry, E. Your family sucks in the emotion department. You should've been a Water like me."

A lighthearted laugh escaped as she pulled herself together.

Zum unzipped the back of the dress. "It might surprise you, but I actually approve of Seanair's heavy-handed gesture. A two-mantled Fire is like toting around a turbo Easy-Bake Oven of protection, which is called for after what happened last night." She gave Elspeth's sweatpants the stink eye. "Now strip, and let's get this fitted."

Elspeth didn't hesitate. She and Kazumi had been dressing and undressing in front of each other since boarding school, so she pulled off her nightwear and held out her arms for the dream of molten green in Kazumi's arms.

The silk flowed over her in one smooth kiss and fit as though the fabric couldn't stand to be away from her skin. A zip and a button and she faced the mirror, her mouth agape.

She looked…amazing.

Even with no Spanx. Even with no makeup. Even with her hair a mess.

"Holy adjective attack," Zum breathed, her eyes shining with pride. "Stunning. Dazzling. Spectacular. You're going to be a one-woman boner fest."

Normally, she and Zum cracked themselves up with their banter about men. All this talk about guards and boners sent her thoughts to places she couldn't go.

They moved into the bedroom, and Elspeth stood before the triplet of mirrors in the corner. She wasn't vain, but she had to be scrupulously conscious of her appearance when she met clients and had installed the trio years ago so she could be sure she was tucked and put together without any help. Now, the vision reflecting at her from three angles was anything but neat, buttoned down, and business-like.

The neckline plunged. The halter snaked around her neck as though her throat was being caressed by a lover's hands. Her shoulders were bare, and from nape to waist, her back was exposed. Her personal bits were fully covered, but the allure was how much Kazumi had left to the imagination.

A sharp knock was followed by the door opening before she could respond.

"I need to—"

Aleron's words died in his throat as he looked at her, devouring her bared skin with his eyes and then taking in the plunging front in the mirror.

She wasn't sure how much of her he'd seen last night, but it'd been enough to make his breath catch and his hands jittery while unhooking her bra. Now, he stood transfixed, and her heart pounded as she imagined his eyes on all of her, taking her in. She anticipated what his kiss would feel like on places besides her mouth.

Kazumi's laughter was a rippling brook of amusement. "Down, boy, or you'll scorch yourself."

The moment of unbridled lust in his gaze sharply turned to disapproval.

"Need I remind you you're engaged?" Aleron ground out.

For a split second, she'd felt beautiful. No, gorgeous. The light, the fire, the heat in his eyes had nearly melted her in the best of ways. She'd felt like she was honey, and he'd needed to devour every sweet drop of her.

Now, she prayed some rogue Earth would cause a freak earthquake, and the floor would split open and swallow her.

She caught herself and called on the vow she'd made on her twelfth birthday that she would never cower in front of anyone ever again.

She straightened and summoned the haughty coolness she used with most Naturas.

"Did you need something?" She refused to address his remark.

He gave a sharp nod. "I'm going outside to do a perimeter sweep. I'll lock the apartment. Don't try to leave."

"I know how to unlock my own doors."

"Not that kind of lock." Zum folded her arms. "He's trying to put me in my place too. FYI, Waters can't be contained."

"I won't be long." He glowered at Elspeth.

If she hadn't known better, she'd say his feelings had gotten hurt, but given the way he was acting, she wasn't so sure he had any.

The front door closed.

Zum's eyebrows shot up in a what's-that-all-about arch. "He's a li'l crabby Fire. Maybe he needs a colon cleanse? I've got the will and the Water."

A laugh burst from her. Goddess love her filterless bestie. If the thought formed, Zum spoke it. "You are incorrigible."

"It's why you love me."

"One of a million reasons," she whispered, her mood since the attack a roller coaster of twists and turns.

She'd shoved aside yesterday, the event so terrifying it seemed unreal, but her best friend was the realest thing in her life. Soon, there'd be no more Kazumi pop-ins at the office or her apartment, no more *it's time for a mochi run* texts. No more impromptu drinks at places like Freddy's. She'd long considered Kazumi a sister, a sister who hugged the breath from her, a sister she laughed and cried and commiserated with.

How would a FaceTime friendship last?

There were no hugs on FaceTime.

"Help me out of this." Elspeth reached for the buttons at the back of her neck.

Kazumi stepped in, and in seconds, the silk slid down her body, leaving her naked except for her undies. Her best friend stopped abruptly. Stared.

Her fingertips grazed over Elspeth's lower back. "What the hell are those?"

CHAPTER
NINE

"What are what?" Elspeth twisted to look in the mirror.

"These." Zum pointed at the faint yellow marks, her fierce frown full of *don't give me any bullshit*. "I'll forgive myself for missing them in the bathroom because that mirror sucks. But this looks like you've taken up bronc riding."

She couldn't lie. Not to Zum. But she wasn't going to spend her last weeks in New York under house arrest. And after the way Aleron had just made her feel, he could shove his orders about what she could and couldn't do up his ass with the stick that was already there.

"Give me a sec to get dressed and make coffee, and I'll tell you. If you promise not to tell anyone, including your mother and especially Seanair."

"Let me put this back on the hanger, and then you can tell me something I know I'm going to hate." Zum took the dress into the bathroom.

When they were together again in the living room, Elspeth sighed in relief at being back in jeans and an NYU sweatshirt, her hair tamed into a ponytail.

"So, spill." Zum accepted a mug with both hands. "You know the rule, chicks over dicks. Or in this instance…" She cast a glance at the front door. "Best friends over assassins."

"What?" Elspeth followed Zum's gaze.

Zum sputtered the sip of coffee she'd taken. "You don't know? I thought you knew every Natura alive."

"Hardly. I can't know that many people."

Or anyone advertising themselves as a hit man.

"In this case, I have to give your Godfather Granddaddy some props." Zum took a careful drink, her glare coy. "In light of recent events, sending his top killer was a smart move."

Elspeth was still trying to process the last twenty-four hours, and her brain refused. She understood security. Understood situations sometimes got rough. Understood sometimes force was necessary.

"His top…killer." The alley came back. His rage. His ferocity. His burn-the-world-down power.

"You think Elite One hosts garden brunches?" Kazumi fired a get-with-it-girl glare. "Listen, the guy's got a serious rep and probably tons of baggage. I know he's protecting you, but be careful. Fires like that flare up, and you don't want to be caught in the flames. You can't have a job like that for long without losing your soul or your mind, but as I always say, Seanair don't care. He's probably using the guy up like he's somehow using you for this marriage gig."

Goddess bless, she was done arguing about the wedding, but Zum's assertion couldn't be right. Seanair's businesses weren't all aboveboard, but assassins? Who was he killing?

Funny, though, this thing she shared with Aleron. She sure understood being used up.

"Honestly." She took a seat on the sofa, exhausted by the whole idea. "I didn't know Elite One existed until he showed up."

"Whoa, girl. Back up." Zum sat a couch cushion over. "You have got to be kidding me. We don't talk about security and all that shit all the time because it's a regular part of our lives. You're a Lennox. I'm a Fukada. We've been raised in this BS."

"You have been anyway."

Zum clapped her free hand over her face. "I honestly never think about it with you. And I can't believe Seanair never told you, but suffice to say, if you've got an Elite One assassin at your back, I'm as reassured as I can be."

Her body tensed like her subconscious refused to consider Zum's words.

"Seanair and I aren't exactly chatty with each other." The word *assassin* silenced a whole lot of whispers in her instincts but flooded her mind with questions.

"Yeah, but some things shouldn't be skipped." Zum sighed and put her mug on the coffee table. "Let's get to the nitty-gritty. What the hell is up with those bruises, because by the Goddess, if that Fire fucker hurt you, I'll—"

"He saved my life."

With as few words and as little emotion as possible, she gave Zum the details of what had happened in the alley. Her mangled pride made her leave out the specifics of what went down after they'd returned to the apartment.

"K. Need to move." Kazumi paced a path across the living room and back. "You say it's an Earth, but hail's a favorite Air tantrum, and Hell's Kitchen became in ice machine yesterday."

The door opened, snaring their attention. Aleron shut the door behind him and stopped short.

"Why would you tell her to keep what happened from me?" Zum ground out.

Even without power, Elspeth sensed the rage coming from her friend and felt an equal assault from Aleron.

"Because I haven't figured this out yet, and I want to keep her alive." He came toward them, his tone ripe with challenge.

"Well, if that whatever-it-was surprised you, we have a problem."

"That's an understatement, even from a Water."

"Stop with the elemental pissing contest." Elspeth shifted her glare between them. "I need both of you."

Even as the words slipped out, she knew how true they were. His earlier mention of her engagement still stung, but after what they'd shared yesterday, she knew he would do anything to protect her.

She captured her friend's gaze. "You just admitted there's nothing more powerful than an Elite One guard. He may a supreme jerk, but he's going to keep me alive. There's no doubt he saved me yesterday, and I owe him."

Kazumi stopped short, a veritable war raging on her face as she stayed lost in thought. In the span of a moment, she moved to stand in front of Aleron and bent to one knee.

She bowed her head and held out her right hand, palm up. "I owe you a debt. Whatever you need, name it. I can feel your protection swirling around her, and it's the strongest I've ever felt. You saved the best friend I'll ever have, and I'm indebted to you for the rest of my days."

Aleron blanched, his eyes wide.

Elspeth's throat jammed, stinging and clogging with the certainty that leaving Zum was going to be brutal, harder than almost anything she'd ever done.

"I did my job." His gaze sliced to the floor and back to the wall. It seemed to take divine intervention from the Goddess herself, but he took Zum's hand and pulled her to her feet.

Some semblance of understanding passed between them. They gave each other a nod. Hopefully, a truce of sorts.

"Can we all sit down now?" Elspeth gestured toward the couch and chairs.

To her surprise, neither her stubborn friend nor her even more stubborn protector hesitated.

"I wasn't the only one hurt in this process, Aleron. You need to tell Kazumi everything. She may be able to help you. I know that thing will be back."

"If it does, I will destroy it." Aleron sank into the side chair.

Zum gave a decisive nod. "I'm all for Astrux annihilation. I've regenned with numerous Earths, and that skunk vibe settled over the city right now isn't anything like the walk-on-the-wild-side-of-nature hangover I know."

He bristled at the mention of rejuvenating elements. She sensed a constant tension in him, but that strain no longer read like anger. He'd been with her for three days, and he hadn't left her alone. She knew single Naturas and Duals refueled themselves regularly, and

Aleron had two mantles. Though she had no idea of his regeneration requirements, she imagined keeping a double shot of Fire fueled and firing at his levels took twice the sex.

I wish I were a Fire.

Her first instinct was to kill the urge. Avoid the pain. Stay away from the hot truth.

Instead, she simmered in it, recalling his burning intensity and the sear of his kiss. Her lips tingled with the phantom feel of the hot crush of his mouth, and the skin of her back was aflame where he'd unhooked her bra. She remembered the flex and tension in his biceps as he'd balanced himself above her.

"Let's form a pact." Zum stood. "A Water and a Fire combining forces is like a blizzard in human hell, but stranger things have happened. Mostly, I don't like the halo hanging over the city. With the gala tomorrow night, I don't want you cremating me if things get dicey and I need to drown something."

"What halo?" Goddess, she hated being in the dark all the time.

"Nothing you should worry about. Elite One's handling it." Aleron's jaw firmed like he wanted the subject closed.

"What he meant to say," Zum's tone scolded like a teacher correcting a student, "is that there's a weird elemental vibe hanging around, like someone's using the elements in a way they shouldn't. There are also these little fissures, like something's poking holes through the veils of elemental energy that circle the planet. Think of it like driving and the car occasionally makes a weird noise. Nothing catastrophic, but enough to know something's wrong under the hood."

"You are fountain of information." Aleron stared Kazumi down.

"I prefer river of knowledge." Zum batted her eyes. "Her grandfather treats her like a child, and that's not how I roll. There are no secrets between me and E. Now are we making a pact or not?"

Aleron looked warily at Zum's offered hand. "If the thing comes back, it'll read my signature and see you're aligned with me. I don't want a reprimand for putting the Water Magnus's daughter in danger."

"I'd like to see someone try to reprimand you," Zum scoffed. "Don't judge me because I'm pint-sized. I'm going to rock that thing like a hurricane if it comes anywhere near Elspeth when I'm around."

"All right, Half Gallon. Let's do this." He placed his hand above hers, palm down.

"Game on, Easy-Bake."

A glow lit the space between their hands. A sleeve of blue light climbed to Aleron's elbow and sank into his skin. The same process occurred with Kazumi but in dark orange.

They both winced, as if the actions had hurt.

"What does that exchange get you?" She'd never seen anything like it between her brothers or cousins.

"Think of it as a Natura friendship bracelet so we can't kill each other." Zum's cheeks puffed, then deflated as she blew out a breath. "I can see why people don't do that on the regular."

A phone rang, the theme from *Jaws* coming from the bedroom.

"Hold up. That's my mom. And I need to get the shoes. One sec." Zum dashed from the room.

Elspeth turned, wanting him to tell her more about pact.

Aleron had propped himself against the back of the sofa and was busy raking his gaze, long and slow, down her. "I'm sorry about what I said. The dress was amazing. You looked—"

The tips of his ears reddened, and his gaze cut to his boots. This big blaze of a man was shy?

"I looked what?" She needed him to finish the sentence and confirm the cause of the flush creeping up his neck.

"Beautiful." His eyes locked with hers. "So damn beautiful."

Why did she have to meet him *now*? How was she going to forget how he'd saved her, how he'd kissed her with such care, how his hushed breath on the bruises had tingled and tortured the skin below her breasts?

"Did I look like a Lennox? Is that what you saw? And now that I'm back to jeans and a sweatshirt, everything's fine?" She had to know if he saw her as the woman in the file Seanair had sent him.

"No." A red haze seeped from his gaze and hung in the air between them. "You're Elspeth to me now. Just Elspeth."

Not a Lennox.

Not a means to an end.

Not a connection with access to Seanair.

"Thank you." She didn't swipe the tear speeding toward her jaw. "No one ever sees me but Zum and Lach."

She bit her bottom lip, a bad habit that kept her emotions banked. In a little less than month, he'd be gone from her life. The shredding was slow, the ripping in her chest feeling like punishing little tears. There wasn't anything between them but a small something. A shared, horrific experience. A sense of shell-shocked relief. A bond, so tiny and fragile, a thread she wanted to strengthen.

"I promised you the truth." He hunched his shoulders and pushed off the sofa back, resuming that Goddess-awful military stance.

"If things were different—"

"Your life is decided, and I am not of your station." He stared ahead, dead-eyed and straight, like a Buckingham Palace guard.

The protocol crap again.

She slipped off the sofa and went to him, stopping within arm's length.

This close to him, her body was nothing but heartbeat and breath. Her fears crept in, crawling from those deep places where she'd stuffed them, and she jammed the idea of him killing people back inside and slammed the door.

Her heart thumped hard, like it was trying to break through her ribs to get to him. What if she didn't feel this way with Yuri? What if Yuri didn't want her, or worse, what if she didn't want him? What if there was no chemistry between them, and sex was rote and only conception-focused?

Her feelings for Aleron had flared deep and in an instant, rooting in complicated ground. Crisis revealed character, and yesterday, he'd been nothing but honor and determination and selflessness. In the moment when he'd saved her and she'd taken that first free breath, he'd claimed a part of her heart. What he'd done… There were no words, no thanks that would do. Inside her was a mark, deeply buried and sharply carved with his initials.

"Don't speak of yourself as beneath me again. A man who would lay down his life for someone else is the very best of people. I will never forget you, and if circumstances were different, I'd want to explore this thing between us. Don't deny you felt something yesterday when I know you did."

"I learned a long time ago that what I want and what I get are two different things. I will protect you at all costs." His gaze fixed on something over her shoulder. "Let me do my job, Elspeth."

Dread spread through her like a noxious cloud. "That thing knows your signature. It wants to hurt you."

"I'm unkillable." His stance widened, and his gaze steeled.

"Stop doing that."

He bristled. "Doing what?"

"Standing there like you're something for me to command. I'd never do that, and I don't want you to have that expectation of me." She moved closer and put a hand on his sweater, the pec beneath warm and firm. "Nothing's unkillable. We're not immortal. I don't know what benefits an extra mantle bestows, but Naturas do die."

"Are you worried for me?" His gaze shifted to her hand.

"Yes." She stepped into him and rested her forehead on his chest. "Now that I know what you can do, I'll worry about you forever."

His body went taut beneath her, but she didn't move back. No, she tortured herself further by breathing him in and holding that blessed smoky goodness in her lungs. She didn't know why she could smell his element, and she didn't care. She merely prayed the scent would bake into her senses and never leave.

"Mom. *Mom.* I'm leaving in ten minutes." Kazumi's voice drifted in. "Yes, I'll take a different route home. Yes, I'll be careful. Yes, Elspeth's fine."

A pang of guilt echoed inside her. Kazumi and her mom were tight, and now a lie rested between them.

Warm hands rested on her shoulders, and he gently slipped

from beneath her touch. He moved back beside the fireplace, his all-business expression back.

Kazumi flounced in with a pair of strappy sandals hanging from her fingers. "No one says no to Prada, especially not at sixty percent off at the Barneys closeout. We'll play Cinderella, and I'll slip on the shoes." She waved a come-here hand at Aleron. "A little help, please, new best friend. Can I call you my hot friend? Get it?"

"We've formed a temporary alliance." He came over and held out a hand, staring down at Kazumi like she was butter and he was a frying pan.

"Easy-Bake's too much work. I'll shorten it to EB. It'll be our secret." Kazumi earned a long sigh from Aleron.

Elspeth took Aleron's hand and lifted one foot to let Kazumi do her thing, then the other. His hold tightened, not like yesterday, but a grip strong and warm and soft.

Kazumi's mouth opened in a joyous O. "I am a genius. If you look this sexy as hell in jeans, when you put that dress back on, you're gonna set eyeballs on fire."

She gave Zum a cut-it-out scowl.

Aleron let go of her hand and returned to the sofa. A fire lit in the fireplace, his gaze on the flames, which suddenly burned higher and brighter.

The *Jaws* theme blared again.

"I've got to go. Mom's going cyclonic. I'll call you tomorrow, and we'll make gala plans." Zum shot her a stink eye. "I'm officially repeating I'm not happy with this Russia disaster, but I'll always have your back."

"Nothing's going to jeopardize what I'm doing for Lach." Anger rose at the idea of that Astrux interfering with her plan. Buying her brother time was her only trump card, and no one—even an invisible power—was going to ruin it.

"And they say Fires are stubborn." Kazumi rolled her eyes. "Be safe, chickie."

Walking down the hallway, she waved a hand at Elspeth's, "I will."

"I'll protect her," Aleron interjected.

"You'd better."

The front door clicked shut.

Aleron closed his eyes and held up his hands. Orange light baked into the walls, drawing up the windows, across the ceiling, and sealing every crack.

"I'll order pizza, and you can do whatever it is you do until tomorrow night. I'm overriding my orders, and we're not leaving this apartment until then." Aleron headed hastily into his room.

Elspeth turned to the fireplace, her gaze going long, her instincts aflame that things were about to get worse.

CHAPTER
TEN

Tension had filled the last day and a half as she and Aleron had engaged in a fierce battle of *let's ignore each other*. Of course, not talking to someone whom she was dying to talk to only made her want to talk to him more as her thoughts fixated on what they'd done two days ago when they *hadn't* been talking. She could close her eyes and conjure the feel of his mouth on hers and imagine his kiss moving lower...

Elspeth stopped a few feet from the open double doors and took in the palatial candlelit ballroom. As usual, Ross and his sidekick Egan, had done a mind-blowing job with the details for the gala. No expense had been spared in the decadent space at the St. Regis hotel.

Filled with round tables, the room glittered with centerpieces of opulent greenery surrounding gold and bronze taper candles. Hundreds of yards of sheer tulle hung from the ceiling, tied back with cording, giving the effect of the room being surrounded by sparks. The chair covers had been perfectly pleated so each seat mimicked a miniature throne. Every piece of silverware and stemware had been precisely positioned, and every one of the room's fifty guest tables had a perfect view of the dais in the room's center.

She glanced at the platform draped in cascading swaths of gold fabric and resisted the urge to roll her eyes. The evening was meant to honor Jon Costa and his promotion to Northeast lieutenant, with the ceremony more like a coronation than recognition of the man's loyalty and service. The Costas held the patents to several fuel-injection processes. If it involved heat or combustion, a Natura family probably owned the business. Rich beyond belief, those attending tonight had garages full of fancy cars and lived at even fancier addresses.

In addition to New Yorkers, the New England crowd had garnered invites, all old-money Naturas who loved their galas.

Still, everyone in attendance knew who the real guest of honor was. The person turning heads from conversations in the lobby and drawing attention from the open bars. A woman about whom they wouldn't dare whisper or publicly complain was upstaging the Costas' evening.

Her.

The woman marrying into the Russian syndicate.

"Ready?" Aleron stood off to her right.

"I'm never ready for these Goddess-damned things." She met his brown eyes.

"You look incredible." He kept his gaze on her face, his expression uniform. Anyone looking would have seen a guard doing his duty. "Someone pisses you off, let me know."

"Thanks. I will." A pang resonated in her chest at the admiration in his eyes and the resolve to protect her in his voice. What had she done to insult the Goddess that she met a man like Aleron literally a day after she agreed to marry a total stranger? "You don't look so bad yourself." She smoothed her dress, hoping he wouldn't see the interest in her eyes.

Aleron in a tux defied words, and several cougar types had nearly broken a claw to get a look at him when they'd walked into the lobby.

"Here goes nothing," she muttered, her legs leaden. There was so much on the line tonight, and she reminded her ridiculous heart to get over any silly dreams of fairy-tale endings. There was one route to save Lach and no fairy godmother to swoop in and save her.

She held her head high and drew her shoulders back. The emerald dress fit like a lace glove. A last glance in the mirror before they'd left her apartment had her loving her body. Goddess bless Zum for providing Elspeth with the ultimate middle finger to all the jerks who'd stare at her. She wouldn't have another chance to flaunt her curves so blatantly, and she was going to floor the engine tonight.

She stepped into the archway, but before she'd moved hardly a foot, Zum barreled toward her like the tide rolling in, dressed in a clingy red silk jersey gown, her slicked-back, jet-black hair striking.

She slipped an arm around Elspeth's waist, her other hand holding a drink, and shot her an all-teeth smile. "Where in the hell have you been?" Zum asked. "I'm sweating up my Spanx, and Seanair's cutting a sharp eye in my direction."

Even with the princess-cut diamonds sparkling in her ears, Zum's eyes stole the show, their blue-tinged, icy hue reminding Elspeth of a glacier.

"He knows I'm never the first guest and that I usually sneak in. If he wanted me here early, he should have contacted me." She steadied her breath to calm the forest's worth of butterflies in her stomach.

"True." Zum looked over her shoulder at Aleron. "Looking sharp, EB. So far, I've detected no elemental funny business."

"I feel safer already, HG."

Easy-Bake and Half Gallon. At least they were getting along.

Zum held up a finger as she knocked back the rest of the clear liquid in her highball glass, the pine scent of gin distinctive. "Saw Seanair 2.0. I have to say, I kinda dig your middle bro's surfer-scientist vibe, even though he has the personality of a starched tablecloth."

"Graham is nothing like my grandfather." Elspeth had seen her brother rarely once he'd left for college, the lab and academia his preferred family. The middle sibling and an odd duck, Graham had never gotten along with Lach, or, really, anyone. He'd taken off for Cal Poly right after high school. Now he was almost thirty, and beneath his windswept light brown hair and smarter-than-thou smirk hid a wickedly brilliant mind.

"Give him time. We all know who's next in line." Zum put a hand to her mouth and winced. "Sorry. I'm two gins in. Don't listen to me."

Elspeth smiled at her tall, deeply tanned brother's approach and supposed he was somewhat misunderstood too. Lach was a doer, an artist, a dreamer. Graham was a thinker, a planner, and painfully blunt.

"Has Seanair seen those yet?" She nodded toward Graham's low-top trainers, thankful he'd had the sense to go monochromatic, black, and leather.

"Not sure. Don't care."

No surprise there.

She stepped over and hugged him. "What drew you away from the lab?"

Graham ran a hand through his rough-cut hair. "Who else? When Gangsta Grandpa calls, it's in my best interest to answer. He says he wants to talk to me." Obviously wishing he were anywhere else but there, he folded his arms and looked around, shifting from side to side, the movement subtle but there. Fire and Air Duals could *not* be still.

"Are you sticking around for a few days?" She hoped to get some time with the brother she rarely saw.

"Hell no. He'll talk, I'll listen, then I'm back on a plane." He stopped fidgeting, and his expression turned awkward, like he didn't know what to say. "Since I can't refuse a family command performance, I'm getting a beer. If I have to be here, I will be buzzed."

A chime sounded. Graham gave her a sardonic smile and headed into the crowd. In seconds, three hundred or so people moved slowly toward their seats.

"I suppose we should head to our table," she said to Kazumi as they watched her brother make a beeline for the bar, the crowd parting, making way for an almighty Lennox.

They walked toward the center of the room with Aleron close behind.

"I've never had dinner on a throne before," Kazumi said. "I'll bet the food tastes better up on Mount Look At Me." A rosy blush crept into her cheeks. "Oh, and I saw Ross. He's freakin' awesome and switched my assigned seat with Graham's so I can hang with you."

"Are you ever going to ask him out?" She looped her arm through Zum's.

"There's no point. I like him too much to just fuck him, and my parents expect me to marry a Japanese Water before I become Magnus."

"I'm sorry." She'd seen one too many sets of meddling parents. There weren't many families with the Fukadas' strength, but a pairing with a powerhouse Earth like Ross might gain them more than they'd ever dreamed.

"Don't be sorry. It's the bane of children of traditionally minded parents everywhere." They stopped a few feet from the dais steps, and Kazumi pulled her aside, shooting Aleron a give-us-some-space look. "Here's the scoop. The Costa family, Seanair, and the three of us are up top, so it should be nice and boring. And I asked Mom about the Foussés, and she said to check the archives for the Winter's Hail Coup."

"Okay." She couldn't recall seeing anything about a coup anywhere in the database. "Do me a favor and ask Ross to look in the archives for me?"

"Sure thing." Zum wagged her brows and one-eyed the bottom of her cocktail glass. "I need a last gin before I ascend to my seat. You want anything?"

"No, thanks." She looked to Aleron, cupped her hand, and tipped a pretend cocktail.

He stepped back into hearing range and glared at Zum. "No drinks. I'm on duty. You are too."

Zum waved a dismissive hand. "Liquor's mostly water. This is like taking communion. I'm fine. Mom says the weird Earth vibe over the city has diminished to almost nothing, thank the Goddess."

Surely the night would go without incident. With this much power in the room, the Astrux wouldn't dare show up. Every element was represented, the room awash with bespoke tuxedos, diamonds, and Alpha-level power. Plus, the staff was made up of mostly Beta-level Natura, so only a blatant fool would dare show up uninvited.

"I'm sorry your mother didn't get the Northeast lieutenant position. She deserved it." Elspeth spied Masako Fukada holding court in a group of Waters.

"All's fair in love and organized crime." Zum raised her glass in a mock toast. "One last thing. Don't think I've forgotten about your birthday. I've got big plans for you, girl. We'll get through this snoozer gala, and then we're getting our party on after Yuri's visit. Maybe we'll do a repeat trip to Freddy's and bring Easy-Bake with us. A gallon of rosewater lightning might get a smile out of him."

So what if she didn't have power? She should cut loose this year anyway. Twenty-four was supposed to be a major birthday for Naturas, and she could still have a damned party. "I could stand to live a little before I go."

"Good, because it's already planned for two days after Yuri leaves. Back in a flash." Kazumi dashed for the bar as another take-your-seats chime rang.

Aleron followed close behind her up the steps to their table and pulled out Elspeth's chair, then took the seat to Elspeth's right. Elspeth read the name on the place card to the left, and her heart nearly stopped. She hadn't considered Rob Costa, Jon's son, would be there, much less seated next to her. Not with his illness, or rumored "poor health." Once diagnosed, Naturas with the tripowered disease did a slow disappearance, fading from public events and work, until their existence was forgotten.

But tonight was all about Jon Costa, appearances, and saving face.

She glanced again at the card as Jon came toward her, his hair now a distinguished gray. When was the last time she'd seen him? She couldn't recall, but his warm smile hadn't changed. He reached into his pocket as he came around the table.

"You look lovely, so like your father. It's been too long." Jon held out his hand. A small, iridescent white bead lay in his palm. "I found it a few days ago at our beach house. We don't see them much anymore, with what's going on in our oceans, but I hoped you might like it."

"You're always so kind to think of me. Thank you." She took the pearl and leaned up so he could kiss her cheek. Jon Costa had been a midlevel lieutenant for years and as devoted a father. "Congratulations. Your promotion's much deserved."

"Thank you. It's always good to see you, Elspeth. Your parents would be so proud of you." He went to his seat as a gorgeous redhead who had to be his daughter took a seat beside him.

"I'm Liz." The redhead nodded, her eyes full of concern for Rob.

She latched on to the usual pleasantries to get her head back in the game. Seanair christened the top of the stairs, and with her grandfather mere feet away, she had to pour on the poise and grace.

She finished her how-are-you, I'm-fine, isn't-this-a-beautiful-night nonsense with Liz, then leaned forward to take a drink of ice water. There was no reason to feel hurt that Seanair had made his way through the tables below, shaking hands and slapping backs, but hadn't even glanced her way.

Two hands grabbed the seatback beside her. Jon's and Liz's expressions tightened, and she didn't have to look to know Aleron had tensed up like a lion sensing a threat as he watched a man so obviously sedated he shouldn't be standing. One look, and the rumors proved a sad truth. Rob Costa, Jon's tripowered son, pulled out the chair and took his seat.

All she could think was she was witnessing Lach's fate. He'd spend his last days as a shell, a medicated shell, barely able to function and wanting to die.

She took a harsh breath. No. No, that wasn't going to happen. As the Goddess was her witness, her brother was not going to die a slow, dishonorable death. Not while she had one breath left in her body.

Or one uterus to sacrifice to the Russians.

Whatever it took…

CHAPTER
ELEVEN

No, no, no.

Aleron caught the problem, the Fire stench like burnt hair. He'd assumed the place card a courtesy thing. He hadn't imagined the guy would dare show up. Elite One had been tracking Rob Costa for weeks. Rob sitting next to Elspeth was a nonstarter.

Kazumi came to the table, and he used the opportunity to pull out her chair as an excuse to whisper to Elspeth, "Switch places with me."

"Elspeth dear, you look positively gorgeous," Seanair drawled, stopping him in his tracks.

Their leader practically glowed, his eerily magnetic charm like a beautifully poisonous snake drawing the gazes of the room's guests.

Elspeth rose and put a hand on Aleron's arm, her expression *don't make a scene, it's fine.*

Right. 'Cause a Passive could tell exactly what was going on.

She moved toward the gloating bastard.

"Hello, Grandfather." Elspeth leaned in and kissed his cheek. "It's been a while since you've seen Kazumi. I asked her to join us."

The sugary scent of her white lie caught in Aleron's throat. She was covering for her event-planning cousin, Ross, of course. Seanair had likely dictated the seating arrangements and wouldn't appreciate a last-minute switch.

Seanair nodded at Kazumi, and his eyes sparkled, no doubt because he was trying to figure out how he could use the change to his advantage.

"Miss Fukada, what a pleasure to have you join our table. I think so highly of your mother."

Seanair's sour lie grabbed at Aleron's senses like a swallow of skunked wine.

"Thank you, sir." Kazumi gave a slight nod, her eyes a little too gin-glassy. "I'm honored."

Aleron's power coiled, ready to strike. Jon Costa was all smiles except for several quick glances at his obviously ill and high-as-a-satellite son. Why would Seanair want Rob at the table? Rob had maybe a month before he met his maker. No one knew. Why bring that danger into the room? Why—*shit*. Just when he thought Seanair couldn't be a bigger asshole. Rob was obviously the night's special shiny object, something Seanair could dangle in front of Elspeth, a live example of where Lach was headed.

So she would go through with the wedding.

"Let's all take our seats, shall we," Seanair ordered, the words clearly not an invitation.

Everyone obeyed, and Aleron shifted his chair toward Elspeth, throwing up a third layer of Fire energy around her.

"That's not nec—" Liz stopped at the grip of her father's hand.

Aleron raised his brows, a simple move that shut smart people's mouths.

The drugs would likely prevent any sudden outbursts, but tripowereds were unpredictable, and he would take zero chances with Elspeth's safety.

Then, of course, she did the thing he needed her not to do. Invited damn disaster.

"I'm Elspeth Lennox." She put her hand on Rob's. "I'm sorry I didn't introduce myself when you sat down. It's such a pleasure to meet you, Rob."

Rob stared at his plate, his gaze moving to the three wineglasses at the corner of his gold-trimmed place setting. His head turned slowly, like the move pained him, and he rested his gaze on their joined hands.

Goddess don't let him suffer too long.

Aleron fired off the prayer to the Goddess he wouldn't call benevolent, but the poor guy. To be caged like that, a sound mind inside a rebelling body, feeling your self-control slip.

Goddess kill him. Kill him if he ever got like that. Kill him before his poor family had to do the job. He'd seen the tripowered disease as a nuisance, something unlucky Naturas got that he then had to handle—and fast—before the afflicted took out, say, a bridge on a major freeway. Like the woman a few years ago in Atlanta.

Rob's bloodshot eyes evidenced the fight he waged. The gravely ill man wanted *out*. In that moment, Aleron lost what little respect he had for Jon Costa.

Rob was alive only because his father didn't have the balls to end his terminally ill son's pain.

"Th-thank. Y-you." Rob looked up at Elspeth and struggled to form a smile.

Several servers arrived, refilling water glasses and setting down fresh bread and butter. No one else at the table gave Rob even a cursory glance, as if ignoring the illness would make it go away, except Jon and Liz, who stared at Elspeth like she was the second coming of the humans' Christ.

Elspeth rubbed the back of Rob's hand. "I've known your father for years, yet you and I've never met. I'm happy you could come tonight. Your dad deserves this honor. He's such a good man."

"He is." Rob managed a short nod.

Aleron picked up his water glass, his gaze roving the tables below like a good little bodyguard. Seanair chatted up Kazumi for several minutes, moved on to Jon and Liz, then spent several minutes giving specific instructions about champagne to a poor Beta-level server.

Aleron listened to Elspeth's un-Lennox-like small talk and genuine interest in Rob, who seemed to perk up like a wilting plant that'd been given water. He caught the stares coming from the people at the tables below, those lingering glances from guests captivated by Elspeth's permeating charm, their eyes wide that she'd treat an obvious outcast like he was the same as anyone else.

Seanair stood. Silence swept through the ballroom.

He lifted a crystal goblet, and the other guests followed, turning the large space into a twinkling field of raised glasses. "Before we begin the celebration of Jon Costa's much-deserved promotion, I'd like to propose a toast to my beloved granddaughter."

Seanair turned a hawk's gaze on Elspeth. She smiled, though the color drained from her face. Beneath the table, Aleron fisted a hand in his napkin, the need consuming him to grab her, shield her, take her away. He cleared his mind, killed his anger, and schooled his expression to avoid Seanair's detection.

One day. Sooner rather than later. That callous son of a bitch would enjoy every painful tool in Aleron's element bag of tricks.

"To Elspeth's happiness with her betrothed, Yuri Burkov, who'll join her soon here in New York," Seanair proclaimed, hoisting his glass higher. "I welcome the alliance between our families. May Elspeth and Yuri's upcoming union be prosperous and blessed."

Aleron cut his gaze past her smile of pure grace to her lap and the wad of silk in her hand. She slipped her other hand from Rob's, raised her own glass, her smile faltering when she noticed Rob's slump back into catatonia. She nodded, turned her head to acknowledge the room, and took a sip from the tall flute.

Aleron's gut twisted at the actuality of her leaving.

Something still didn't sit right with this arranged marriage. He wanted to hear more about this treatment for Lach. Better yet, see how the Russians managed to halt a disease that had no mercy. Elspeth finished the champagne in her glass in three swift sips.

"Please excuse me." She rose from the table and looked to her grandfather, who gave her a curt nod.

Aleron stood, shot a quick I'm-on-it-sir glance to Seanair, and trailed her down the steps. A short train of rich emerald silk billowed out behind her. She moved quickly through the ballroom, across the lobby, and into the ladies' room. Rapidly scanning, Aleron sensed no other element energy inside. He'd give her two minutes. No, one. He leaned back against the wall, checked his watch.

Seanair's voice snuck into the lobby through the closed ballroom doors. Speech time. Maybe tonight he'd be more long-winded and give Elspeth a chance to breathe.

He cast out his power to check on her, and a wave of sorrow pummeled him. He punched open the first and second doors and heard the gasps and sobs and retches.

"Elspeth, it's me." He wasn't sure she heard him.

She'd barely made it into the stall, the door not closed, her hands braced on the toilet seat.

"Leave me. Alone." Her breath hitched, and she raked her hand over the toilet paper roll, ripping off a long swath.

He raced to the sink, grabbed a stack of fancy hand towels, and dampened them.

"Let's get you cleaned up." He came up behind her.

She took several deep breaths, then straightened. "I'll do it. Cleaning up vomit and hot messes isn't in your job description. Give me some space."

He moved back, eyeing how small she looked with her shoulders slumped and her hair in a sad swath cutting across her face.

"Do you see? Do you see now why I'm giving up everything to save him? Do you see what Lach's going to become if I don't do something?"

Streaks of black trickled down her cheeks, her irises a brilliant green against the red rims of her eyes. He should honor her request to stay back, but he couldn't. He couldn't leave her standing there in tears. He couldn't leave her alone. He looked over his shoulder toward the door. No one had followed to check on her, but it wouldn't be long before someone did.

"I got you." He dabbed at the trails of mascara with a cloth.

"I can't let Lach get like that." Her folded arms tightened at her midsection. "I can't...that can't happen to my brother, and I can't fail. This treatment is the *one thing* I can do to help not only him, but our race. I've grabbed the only straw there is."

His heart faltered, and he remembered all the things he'd assumed her to be. She was supposed to be a penthouse rich bitch, draped in diamonds and makeup and attitude, with standing appointments and a staff. Like he was a straight-up killer with no heart, no emotion, no humanity.

He'd judged her, expected her to be Seanair's protégé, a typical Lennox who cared about power, not people. Yet, here she was, wanting to save not only her brother, but their race from a dreadful, debilitating disease.

"Come over to the sink." He took her arm and walked to the wide basin.

A chime sounded. Elspeth reached beneath her arm into the dress and pulled out a phone. Questions pelted him about how she'd stashed a phone there, but her exhausted sigh had him bending to get into her sight line.

Her head fell forward, and her phone hand dropped to her side. He grabbed the cell to see what had upset her.

You look gorgeous. I'm excited to finally meet you next week and finalize our plans. Yuri

"Looks like he passed Zum's text test. It's not racy, though." Elspeth turned on the water, leaning over the sink and rinsing out her mouth. She checked her face in the mirror and shook her head like she was a hopeless cause

He frowned at her Lennox-like tone and the stiff-upper-lip posture he didn't like on her.

"Why didn't Seanair buy the treatment?" He placed the phone next to the sink and swept her hair over her shoulders. The strands were thick and soft, and he remembered how his Air energy had stuttered when he'd braced himself above her, all of him, in awe of her.

"The Russians refused money. They want powerful heirs, and that requires me." Her chin quivered, and her nose had reddened. "I know the treatment only buys time, but it's better than the alternative." She picked up her phone. "What if I don't feel anything for Yuri? What if there's no chemistry at all? I want my brother to live until we find another option or a cure." Her expression crumpled, her eyes pinching shut. "But a part of me doesn't want this. At all. How can I be so selfish? This is life-or-death for Lach, and I'm worried I won't fall in love."

She put her back to him, grabbed the edge of the sink, and started to sob. Her shoulders rounded, and her head hung in misery.

The weight of her sadness tore at him, his Air ability to sense others' emotions suddenly cranked up. He put his hands on her shoulders, turned her, and pulled her against him. She stiffened, and he tightened his grip.

"Breathe. I've got you." Frustration boiled inside him. All he could do was hold her, and Goddess, why couldn't he do more?

Her hands rubbed up his chest, a guarantee she'd push him away. When her fingers closed around the lapels of his jacket instead, something loosened inside him.

"I've got to find a way to accept this. Yuri's going to be here next week. My poker face only holds for so long."

He cringed at her flat, hopeless tone.

The idea of her faking anything with the guy she was going to marry ripped off the internal duct tape he'd slapped over the memories of his sappy-in-love parents. There was something comforting to a kid to see his mom's coy smile and his dad's cocky grin. To watch his dad sneak up and wrap his arms around his mother's waist while she was making dinner.

He pressed his lips to the top of her head. Kissed her hair. Didn't move. He slid his hand up the dress to her exposed upper back and traced easy twirls beneath her hair. Rocking her slowly, he swayed, a dance to the world's slowest music.

She stiffened and pushed away. "I can't be near you like this. You make me want things I can't have."

"I won't pretend I don't understand, but we both know you and me, we...can't."

"I can't what? Want you?" She stuttered a harsh laugh and returned to the sink. "Too late, I'm afraid." An eon, an eternity, passed as their eyes met in the mirror. "I want a chance with you."

He shut down his instincts, hard and fast. There was no chance. There was no want.

"What we want isn't in the cards, Elspeth. I'm sorry."

She grabbed a guest towel, dampened it, and swiped beneath her eyes and around her mouth. She tossed the used towel into the bin.

"This is why I hate makeup." She studied her reflection, taking another towel and leaning forward to touch up beneath her eyes. "Let me put myself back together. I have to get back, and I'm sorry. I'm sorry you had to see me like this."

Her scent wove into him, a complex, strange aroma laced with hints of fresh air and flowers. If he hadn't known different, he'd have thought her powered.

"Don't be embarrassed. You're beautiful. And kind. Lach is lucky to have you." He wanted to go on, but words weren't enough.

She held up a hand. "No more compliments. Please. You've done more for me than I deserve, and I can't keep hoping for something that won't happen."

The need to reassure her, something completely foreign to him, ran over his common sense. "No, it can't happen, but I'll always be here for you. Even after this is all over."

She leaned back against the counter, her Lennox game face back on. "You can't promise that."

"I can. You can call me whenever, from now until the end of time, and I'll come to you. Help you."

"Help me. How noble," she scoffed softly. "Would it shock you to know what I want with you is far baser and more primal?"

How little she knew him if she used *noble* to describe him. But he was deadly serious. Absurd as the truth was, he'd protect her if she asked for him, but he couldn't give her what she wanted, no matter that his body was hard and straining toward her, willing to agree to whatever she proposed.

She couldn't understand how the ordeal in the alley had fused them, joined them in a way that could never be severed. He wouldn't lie to her or give her false hope. Nor would he admit that, every minute, she peeled him like an onion, ripping away years of self-preservation and focus. He had to get her to that altar. He had to answer the Goddess's call. He had to avenge his father.

But for as long as he could, he'd be her watchman.

"At the end of the day, how do you think this would work?" He wondered how she could ignore the obvious. "I'm working class, and you're the granddaughter of the most powerful Natura in the world. If your grandfather discovered I'd laid a finger on you, what do you think would happen?"

He gave zero fucks about what Seanair would do, but he had to distract her and get her focused on something besides him. And he needed to get his own body and wild-ass thoughts in line before he fucked up not only her world, but the plans that had ruled his life for the last twelve years.

"I find I don't care what my grandfather thinks anymore. All my life, I've tried to gain his approval. I finally like myself, and I'm proud of who I am. I'm enough, even without power. I am enough."

No, she was *everything*. Everything he'd once hoped for and dreamed about. She was the future he'd once foreseen for himself, the embodiment of what he'd wanted from life. He'd longed to do a Fire job, siphon off the world's rising heat, return the swamps' temperature to normal levels, come home every day, steal up behind his wife while she was doing whatever, wrap her in his arms, and make love to her on the closest flat surface.

"You are enough, and you're also right." He pulled out his phone and checked the time. "We've got to get you back to the table. But tell me, before we head out, how this treatment you're trading your life for works. I'd like to run it by some friends."

She gave herself a final glance in the mirror. "I'm no scientist, but my understanding is they push the element into the patients to complement the third one that shouldn't be there, effectively neutralizing the third power by giving them a fourth."

One, there were no quad-powered people. A Nexus was a myth, the biggest pie-in-the-sky dream in the world, the Natura version of every Marvel and DC superhero rolled into one. Two, there was no way to artificially augment a power. As a Natura, you were born with power, or you weren't. If you were a witch or warlock, you either had an inner vessel to fill with called power, or not. Period.

"How do they push an element into someone?" Thank the Goddess, his attempt to get her to change gears worked.

"It's closest to a human bone marrow transplant. They have to take a Natura's inherent powers down to nothing, like lowering a human's immune system, then they take the marrow from the bones and add the fourth element via some process they haven't told us about yet, then slowly reintroduce the reconstituted marrow back into the patient." She smoothed her hair, tucking a strand behind her ear. "I've seen data on thirty people. The time to equalization's different for each person, but they're all stable." She met his gaze. "Best of all, since they started the treatment, no one's died."

He didn't know what to say. If it were one of his brothers, he'd do whatever it took to help Emeric, Laz, or Zeph, estranged or not.

Still, this "science" sounded more like a sham. "We can't just add energy to our bone marrow like syrup on pancakes."

His second mantle wouldn't have taken hold and bonded with his primary one if his father hadn't died.

"There's more to the process, but they won't reveal more than the basics until Yuri and I are married. Believe me, our scientists were skeptical too. This treatment is the one thing I can do for Lach, and maybe others. If sacrifice is my superpower, then I'll be a lamb."

His brain stalled. A full-on time-out. How could he could have been so wrong about her? He'd gotten glimpses she was different, and he'd assumed her lack of power would have made her helpless.

But then she'd turned the tables on him and made him want. Need. Desire.

Damn it all to human hell. He had to shut down all the thinking and get back to doing. Get her back to that table. Get his priorities back in order.

Get her to the chapel.

Kill Seanair.

Die in a firestorm of revenge by the North American powers that be.

Simple, really.

A knock sounded.

"Elspeth? Are you in there?"

A little zing zapped him right in the invisible friendship bracelet. Of course, Half Gallon would show up now.

Elspeth caressed his cheek, the heat from her palm stilling him. "Thank you for this." She gestured vaguely around the bathroom. "You're a good man, Aleron."

There was only one good thing in that room, and it sure as hell wasn't him.

More damned knocking.

"Just a second," she answered, her tone pitched high.

She flipped the lock and opened the door.

"Holy wilted prom date. *Girl.*" Kazumi dug frantically in her purse and pulled out a long black tube. "Praise be for Chanel. Hold still."

Kazumi turned on the tap and got to work restoring Elspeth's mascara, then pulled out small black cases of makeup, muttering under her breath as she touched up Elspeth's face.

Steam finally poured from the sink, and little HG shot him a glare. "Behold the power of water, Easy-Bake."

She did a voilà-wave thing and channeled the cloud of heated vapor toward the dress. The wrinkles vanished.

"I've got soooo many skills." Kazumi linked arms with Elspeth and headed out the door.

He walked the required step behind, repelling the curious looks of passing guests with his trademark I-will-fry-you glare. The clamor of ballroom conversations rose higher, Seanair's speech evidently over. Utensils clinked against plates. Waitstaff poured in and out of the room.

You're a good man, Aleron.

No, he wasn't. He was a machine. Paid to hurt others and eliminate complications. The one who was going to kill her grandfather without an ounce of remorse.

Why had he held her, comforted her, wiped away her tears? She was inside him now. Her scent. Her emotions. Her laughter. Her kindness.

Her heartache.

He'd kissed her for much longer than he'd healed her, which made her a problem now on par with Seanair. The idea of killing the spark in her eyes when she looked at him...

Goddess, how had he aced becoming his own worst enemy?

They climbed the steps with Kazumi pulling him aside at the top long enough to whisper, "We need to chat later." She proceeded to the table, going on about champagne and tequila and celebrating with the Costas.

"So glad you could rejoin us, Elspeth." Something dark cut through Seanair's light blue eyes. "You missed my speech by two minutes."

"I'm sorry, Grandfather." She sat after Aleron pulled out her chair. "I wasn't feeling well, but I'm better now."

He took his seat, keeping his gaze on their leader, sensing the coming strike with no way to counter the cruelty.

"Don't worry, dear." Seanair picked up his champagne and tilted the glass toward her. "I'm used to you missing the mark."

Elspeth didn't respond but picked up her dessert spoon and tapped through the hardened sugar top of her crème brûlée.

Everything in Aleron revved to incinerate Seanair right there. He met his boss's gaze and cut his glance to Rob Costa, having to use a poor, dying man as a sickly scapegoat to explain his power surge.

Seanair fired off a control-yourself frown, then resumed drinking and eating and charming the table's guests.

He schooled his expression and focused on his plate, adding one more thing to his list of problems. Something wasn't right about the arranged marriage or the treatment, and the little spout of Water he'd made a pact with didn't like it either. Then there was that cocked-up Astrux still out there.

He'd kill Seanair, but first, he decided, taking a nice long drink of his water, he was going to make sure Elspeth Lennox wasn't making the biggest mistake of her life.

CHAPTER
TWELVE

Elspeth glanced at her computer calendar, which showed the week blocked off in solid purple. She hadn't planned on working forty hours in three days at the office. But after a weekend of being only feet away from Aleron but a million miles apart, she'd take hellacious hours at Kindred over the torture of his silence.

Aleron had canceled her Goodbye, Manhattan Tour, and the snowball of things she had to complete had started its final roll, and she felt like…stopping. Pushing a pause button on the world with only her and Aleron in it.

Humans considered Mother Nature a cruel bitch, but Father Time was the remorseless thief.

She closed her eyes, focused on the beat of the thing that kept her alive, and realized the one power she'd wish for over all others.

Time.

She'd stop time. Right now. Freeze it. Lach's disease wouldn't progress. Her marriage contract would remain locked in the Kindred database. And she'd have Aleron all to herself. They could explore each other's bodies, confide their secrets, fall asleep and awaken in the shelter of each other.

"Want to order salad Niçoises from the new French bistro down the street?"

She looked up, realizing Ross had walked in, and Goddess

knew how long he'd been standing there. "How about cheeseburgers, fries, and lemon bars from the deli on the corner?"

His mouth rumpled, his expression going full sour professor. "You had that yesterday."

"Comfort food." She straightened the files on her desk, not about to mention she'd had a tough time buttoning her black, skinny jeans today—the ones with generous stretch.

"You still planning on the lace mermaid gown? The one you selected prior to your French fry bender? It's not boding well for the final fitting." He held up his hands at her scowl. "No judgment. I do the same thing with chocolate, but we need to call the seamstress at Bridal Reflections to see about changing out the zipper for a medieval lace-up with an expansion placket."

Elspeth took a seat in her desk chair and put her hands firmly on the armrests. "You're absolutely right. I'll take a cappuccino and an order of lemon bars instead. Caffeine and sugar should get me to quitting time."

Ross winced. "I'm not sure that's a better solution, but to keep you from turning into bridezilla, I'll go place the order and check on Egan. He's been digging in the basement files since the morning after the gala. Why did Kazumi ask me for—"

She bounced a frantic finger against her mouth, cutting her eyes toward the lobby. "I don't want him to know I'm looking into it," she mouthed, *him* being Aleron and the issue being the Winter's Hail Coup.

Maybe there was nothing to the event, but the facts weren't adding up. Aleron wasn't listed in the database with the Foussés or anywhere. Guillaume Lucien Foussé was nowhere to be found either. In fact, she'd had to get his father's name from Kazumi, and Bill, as the man had been called, didn't exist in the Natura birth or death registries.

Realizing Ross hadn't left, she looked up.

"You okay?" A sharpness speared his usually kind eyes.

No, and she wasn't going to be ever again.

"I'm fine, Professor Lennox." She straightened a pretend bow tie at her neck. "But I'm busy putting together a list of everything I do so when you and poor Egan inherit this job, you won't want to put a hit out on me."

His expression softened. "You can't help it, can you."

"Is that a question?"

"It's a statement. You can't help thinking about everyone but yourself."

She tried to exude a no-big-deal vibe she was far from feeling. "Some people in our family make that damn near impossible. If staying focused on not leaving you in a giant sinkhole keeps me from worrying about Lach and wanting to kill him, consider it a lucky break. I haven't heard from him, and he won't answer my texts."

Ross snorted. "He thinks he can hide from me, but I always find him."

"You know where he is?" She sat forward.

"He's at the southernmost point of Argentina. He stayed at the gala for five minutes, then headed straight for JFK."

Her brain stalled. Lach hadn't replied, yet he was okay enough to take a long-ass trip? "What's he doing there?"

"My guess is he's meeting with Isidora and they're about to leave for Antarctica. They see each other three times a year. The person who pays the bills knows all the secrets. That's how I know where he is."

"Do I want to know why he's meeting with the Antarctica leader? Isn't she in her early fifties?"

"I hear she's quite the hellcat. Looks like a tall Halle Berry with ice-white dreads and a voracious appetite for sex. What's not to like?"

She wanted…*needed* to believe Lach had taken his playboy ways on a global tour despite her every instinct screaming the truth was much bigger.

"Isidora has what elements?"

"She's an Earth and Water Dual and scary powerful. Trust me, my Earth energy's glad she lives far away. Isi's got a sense of…let's call it swamp justice."

"Swamp justice?"

"If you piss her off, she's not gonna wait for a council or judgment to fix things. She's gonna put you somewhere you'll never be seen again, and all without a trace."

Ooh-kay. She'd had zero experience with the woman, but it couldn't be a sex thing with her and Lach, as her elements could do absolutely nothing to boost his Dual Fire and Air. So, if it wasn't sex—

Why couldn't it be?

A rush of heat bloomed in her breasts and between her legs. She'd never thought to ask, and why would she since she had no elements to recharge? Once Naturas came into their power, did they have ever sex without an energy exchange being involved?

"You're right. I don't want to know." She conceded if Lach had been seeing the woman on the regular and returning home, apparently unharmed or turned into an ice sculpture, he was being his most charming self.

Ross headed for the reception area. "Be back in a—"

"Wait." Her nerves got the best of her about the quest for info about the mysterious coup. "Shouldn't you be the one doing the searching in the hard-copy archives, and not Egan? I know he's tasked with more than his on-paper responsibilities so Seanair's spies won't report that he's serving more than coffee and answering phones, but this information's not in the system for a reason."

Disappointment cut across his expression. "I would never do anything to jeopardize this family."

"Of course you wouldn't. It's…you know how Seanair is about the coven classes."

"I thoroughly vetted his family before I gave Egan the internship. It takes miracles to pull off what Seanair expects of me, and our warlock is a miracle worker."

Something told her that unearthing buried information about the Winter's Hail Coup could be devastating.

"If you trust Egan, then I trust Egan." She wished her instincts would take a lunch break. The sense of something looming even worse than the Astrux wouldn't go away.

"I trust him with you, and you're not someone I'd ever risk. Be back in a few." Ross disappeared into the reception area.

She looked down at the next line item on her transition list. Birth plan.

She had no human prudishness about the contractual conception timeline. It was simply logistics and legalities. But, Goddess, she had a few days until she met Yuri. The man who was going to be screwing her from the moment they said, "As the Goddess wills" to each other until she popped out the required superbaby.

Why couldn't the Naturas have some advanced in-vitro thing that made this all as cold and clinical as the contract?

Egan stepped into her doorway and cleared his throat.

"What'd you find?"

He set a large accordion binder on her desk. "Five days and eight hours later, I found a box stashed in the back of the file room. We're talking the dusty, musty, moldy part in a dark corner with cobwebs, which this warlock doesn't dig. But, Ms. L, there is some serious stuff in this file."

"You're supposed to call me Elspeth."

"Baby steps."

She eyed the caution creeping into his expression. "Whatever you read, you can't tell anyone. This information was deliberately removed from the database long before I took over Kindred."

Egan made a zipping motion across his lips. "I'm not particularly happy that you know I've read what's in there." He nodded toward the file. "I'm off to the back office to print some other things I found but wanted to get this to you first."

He left without another word.

She opened the binder, pulling out a picture of three handsome young men, their shirt collars unbuttoned, beers in hand, the guy on the end with a fat cigar in his mouth.

She turned over the photo.

Jacques Foussé. Seanair Lennox. Gregor Kralj. 1972.

The pose was so...schoolboy. So...dudes having a good time. Jacques...wait. She'd seen Aleron's grandfather's name in the database. How long had the Foussés known her family?

Her eyes stopped on the image of Gregor Kralj as she thought about their forty-five-minute video call yesterday, negotiating the time-line for his granddaughter's eligibility in Kindred. The Texas farmer's request had been simple enough. He didn't want Jette to have to quit her job as a nurse. Work wasn't a valid reason for deferring an eligibility listing, but Elspeth hadn't hesitated in agreeing to postpone the woman's listing for an additional five years.

Somebody needed to be able to chase their dream. Might as well be Jette Kralj. And she'd gotten an incredibly grateful farmer pledging to help her whenever she needed.

She couldn't quit studying the picture, her gaze moving to Jacques Foussé. The height. The build. The eyes. He towered over the other men. The Foussés obviously had a long history with Seanair. Jacques had died a long time ago, but why weren't his son and grandson listed in her supposedly accurate database?

"What happened?" She pulled out some papers, all of them Bill Foussé's. Birth certificate. Report cards. Natura Academy exam scores. Solid hundreds across the board for one, two… She thumbed through page after page of test results. Perfect scores for eight straight years on all his Fire exams.

"What happened to you, Bill Foussé?"

She took out a small manila envelope, turning it over and bending open the brad. Reaching inside, she pulled out several uniform service patches. Five years. Ten. Twenty. She stared at the last one. The one for thirty years read Guillaume Lucien Foussé, Elite One commander-in-chief. Aleron's father, who was also deleted from all mention in the records…

Had there always been a Foussé protecting the Lennox line?

Panic clogged her throat and churned into a coil of dread. Why did Seanair have so many of Aleron's father's personal effects? She flipped through the remaining pages to a stack of pictures at the back. Two boys, about thirteen, the big brute's arm draped over the shoulders of the scrawny kid with the smartass expression. She turned over the photo.

Jacques Foussé. Seanair Lennox. Fire punisher crew.

Looking through the rest, she watched two lives unfold and a friendship grow, from boys to teens to young men. How could a friendship between two families just fall off the map? By all appearances, Seanair and Aleron's grandfather had been best friends.

On her desk, she noticed the corner of a page with an embossed seal. She pulled the paper from the stack. A death certificate. Two handwritten notes were taped to the back, the edges frayed like they'd been ripped from a book. She recognized the beautiful cursive as Seanair's.

Fire Magnus Log. Year of our Goddess 2010. January.

I write this entry late, for I still know not what to make of the death of my best friend's son. Jacques Foussé was family to me, his son, Bill, becoming one of my own after Jacques passed. Bill violated the sanctity of my worship during Winter's Hail communion to beg me to appoint him emissary for the Fire cuff. He beseeched me to fix the Fire element and search for the true bearer. I always took his counsel, just as I took Jacques's. I was startled, and then my vision burned red with suspicion. For the first time ever, I lost control of my power. I recall talking to Bill through the haze of my anger, but what followed is a blank. All I do know is that I killed Bill in front of his own son, Aleron. Bill died at my own hand, but I cannot offer amends. The other Magnuses are weak, and war is coming. I will not step down when there's so much to lose.

Aleron is mine now, in service to me for the rest of his life, because the Oracle forbade me to kill him. I marked the boy's face. I have beaten him to within inches of his life in the name of strengthening him. I do not recognize this dark side of myself since my wife passed.

Dear Goddess, since Mathair left this earth, it seems I know only death. My heart is numb, my chest a void, a black, graceless space into which I've fallen. I fear the dark side of my elements are overtaking me, for I do not understand this new, constant craving to hurt Aleron and mold him into my harbinger of death.

I pray the Goddess forgives my sin of killing in her sacred chapel.

The two guest chairs in front of her desk blurred. Her mouth dropped open. The piped-in music faded until she became only a thing that breathed.

I marked the boy's face.

Her eyes stung, welled. A faint laugh surfaced in her mind. The old Seanair. The one who'd been married to Mathair. Yes, the grief of losing his wife had changed him, but there wasn't so much as a shadow of his former self. Death changed people, but her grandfather had murdered a man.

She couldn't believe Seanair had put such a stark confession in writing, and knew if, in his wildest dreams, that someone would find it, her grandfather would have rendered the pages into the finest ash.

A great weight hung heavy in her chest, the mass a tombstone, the truth a grave, the facts unspeakable and plain. Seanair had irreparably harmed the man who'd barreled into her world and stripped away the illusion that her duty-bound life would be enough.

If she could blame only Aleron's kiss, this growing cloud of agony would eventually pass. He was getting paid to protect her, but his quiet kindnesses were choices. She understood the conflict in his eyes now, those red flashes of anger. Yet, he still kept her coffee the perfect temperature, chased the drafts away in her apartment, made her stretch in comfort instead of shivering in misery. She looked to her empty coat hook on the wall, and the knot in her throat grew. The high temperature today would be in the twenties. The wind made it seem colder, but from the moment they'd stepped from her apartment building, the fifteen-minute walk to her office had felt like it was seventy-five and sunny.

Her warrior guard had a discreet stillness to him, an innate goodness for which he didn't want credit and he'd never admit. Beneath the blazing shields of his Fire lay a good-hearted man. A man who cared for her and didn't expect anything in return.

A man she desperately wanted to know.

She covered her face with her hands, wishing she could make sense of the horror. What did she do now? Seanair's malicious crime was unfixable.

"Food's here." Ross walked in with a small tray, his gaze wandering for a place to set it.

She jerked, swiping at her face, and stuffing pictures and papers back inside the binder.

"What happened?" Ross nearly dropped the tray on the chair. "Elspeth?"

"Wedding jitters." Her thoughts jumbled and blurred like a shaken snow globe. "Is Aleron still in the lobby?"

"Yes. Do you want me to get him?"

"No."

Ross squinted so hard his eyebrows almost met. "You look like you just witnessed either a miracle or a massacre."

She yearned to tell him what she'd found out, but she needed to talk to Aleron first. This was about him, about his life. He must have gone through absolute hell after losing his father so violently—right in front of him—and then being forced to serve the very murderer who'd taken his dad from him. She swore her body weighed a thousand pounds, the weight of the information too much to bear. How the hell was she going to figure everything out before the wedding?

Egan came in at a jog and stopped behind one of her guest chairs, close to a ream of paper clutched in his hands. "I've got something else to show you."

Ross looked between the two of them. "Do I need to know about this, or can I go back to the piles of work threatening to crush me? I have the final couple's shower details to approve and a wedding I still need decisions on, like location, flowers, food."

Irritation rose at his demands, but she could remove the wedding bullshit from the list.

"The Carlyle Hotel. Irises. Heavy hors d'oeuvres, no dinner," she rattled off. "Full open bar and a custom dessert selection for every table."

"Lemon everything?"

"No." Her thoughts drifted to a scarred man. Change that—a scarred *boy* who'd become a good man. Yuri wouldn't get lemon. "All chocolate. White, dark, whatever's most expensive to feed our fake friends."

"I can work with that." Ross waved and strode from the room. "Later, kids."

Her gaze locked on Egan. "Did you show this binder to anyone?"

"No."

"Where did you find it? Specifically." No way would Seanair let this reign-ending information out of his personal files. How did everything get from the Savannah house to here?

"In a box with Lach's things."

Oh, shit. Her brother's favorite saying exploded in her mind.

Knowledge is power.

Lach had stolen the file and put it in a place most people wouldn't think to look. Brilliant move, but now that she'd had a second to think, it was pretty easy to see that what Lach wanted was leverage.

To stop Seanair from killing him before the disease did.

She looked at Egan's stricken face. "It's all right. I know this is a lot, and I appreciate you bringing it all to me. I'll protect you, Egan. I promise." She took a deep breath, but no way were her nerves anywhere close to settling. "What bomb do you have there to drop?" She nodded at the papers he held.

Egan handed them over. "In the witch and warlock world, this information's worse."

She flipped through the pages, all of them copies of receipts dating back over ten years. "Who is Magdalena Wiedzma?" She checked again. Every dollar amount was the same. "And what does my grandfather pay her to do for twenty-five hundred dollars a pop?"

She did the math, noting the stack represented over a million dollars.

Egan walked over and closed the door, then took a seat in one of the empty chairs, bracing his forearms on his knees. "She's a witch you don't want to cross. She's a witch no one admits to knowing. Most of all, she's a witch you don't want knowing you."

"Why not?" She hid her embarrassment that she knew next to nothing about the covens. She tried to excuse herself because her world consisted entirely of Alpha- and Beta-level Naturas, but that was the bullshit every privileged class told themselves about those they deemed beneath them.

"Magda only deals in darkness. The white witches won't even speak her name because of the shit she does, the experiments. Many have tried to take her out and failed."

"Tried to kill her?"

"Without hesitation. Some would settle for binding her, no matter how grotesque that is to even think, much less do. But if we could bind her? Yes, we'd do it."

"Why would my grandfather associate with her?"

"The only reason anyone goes to her. They need something brought back to life, or they've got a massive problem and aren't squeamish about how they fix it."

Seanair's diary entry had been filled with regret. Her conclusion clocked her between the eyes. Surely Seanair wouldn't try to resurrect Bill or Mathair, or both.

She stood and went to the windows behind her desk and looked down at all the oblivious humans scurrying on the sidewalks below. For a moment, she longed to be like them again, to go back to before an invisible mass had filled her lungs and tried to destroy her.

"How does she bring something back to life?" Her cheeks heated at her ignorance.

"It's not physical. That's TV. But there are some who believe the spirits of the dead can be called back to this dimension."

Goddess on the rag, could this day get any worse?

A knock sounded, and the door snicked open.

"Excuse me," Aleron said. "You have visitors coming up the elevator."

"Tell them I'm out of the office."

Aleron's gaze was a cold, empty beam over her left shoulder, his arms stiff and pulled back, hands clasped behind him. Like a soldier. Just doing his job. "It's Yuri. With three others. The Russian delegation, I suspect."

Her eyes cut straight to his scar, her heart thudding so erratically, she feared it might up and quit.

"That's my cue to go." Egan stood and picked up the tray. "I'll put the food in the kitchen for later."

She gave him a smile and a nod of thanks. They had more to discuss, a lot more, but there'd be no more revelations about the witch world today.

Which was fine. She couldn't take any more.

Egan made it into the lobby right as the elevator chime rang. Aleron about-faced and filled her doorway, his back to her.

"I'll notify Ms. Lennox you're here," Egan announced, his voice louder than usual.

"I'll see myself in," came a cool, Russian-accented voice. "You may remain in the lobby," he said, likely to his guard detail.

She couldn't make out the exact movement outside the door, but the frigid current coming from Aleron contradicted his brash Fire nature. A figure moved in front of him, but she couldn't see much around the mountain that was her protector.

"Out of my way," the same voice said.

"Ms. Lennox receives announced visitors only. You'll have to make an appointment."

"Let him in, Aleron." She recognized Yuri's power play and didn't have the energy for a big showdown.

"As you wish." He backed into the room and reassumed his militaristic stance in front of the credenza opposite her desk. Sparks scattered up her arms and down her body, the sensation powerful, but tempered.

She made a show of looking at her watch, hoping she could see the energy she faintly felt. No light or color covered her arms, but the same smoke scent smoldered in her senses, a reminder that, even now, he still protected her.

She shoved the terrible truth of his father's death into the darkest corners of her mind and donned her well-used, don't-fuck-with-me armor.

The man who walked in glided with smooth purpose toward her. His blond hair was swept back like it'd been styled by the wind on the bow of his yacht. She'd seen a dozen photos of his megawatt smile and figured them staged and the perfect use of tabloid space. He did know how to dress, though. His slacks, shirt, and cashmere coat in gray tones fit him like the finest of gloves. The leather of his black shoes appeared butter soft. Underneath all the finery, intelligence flourished in the depths of his forest-green eyes. The man was nothing short of gorgeous.

His gaze ran over her, and his smile pulled tight. "That's a beautiful sweater. It matches your eyes."

"Thank you." She forced herself not to check, but she was pretty sure she'd worn a fuzzy acrylic sweater with her black jeans and knee-high boots.

"I opted to dispense with the formalities and meet you first privately." Yuri came around the desk like he had a right to crash her personal space.

"If your lead-in is to buck tradition and show my grandfather who's boss, I'll warn you it's not wise to poke the tiger."

"Agreed, but that depends on who you think the tiger is." He extended a hand. "Yuri Burkov."

"Elspeth Lennox." She returned his firm grip with one of her own.

"I like that my future wife speaks her mind." He brought her hand to his mouth. "It's a pleasure to meet you, Elspeth Lennox. You're even lovelier than your photographs. If all our children look like you, my people will want as many heirs as we can give them."

Really? Serving arrogance and sex as appetizers was not going to get him the entrée.

"Let's get married before we start talking about consummation."

Yuri blinked, caught off-guard. "Of course, though you can forgive me for being eager to be with my future wife when she is as beautiful and intelligent as you."

She took her hand back and gave him a tight smile. "You should know I'm not one for flattery. While I'm being honest, it would have been best if you'd given me notice you were coming."

His keen eyes pinned her, trying to read her. "But then I wouldn't have had the chance for a candid conversation with you. Our every move is scripted, and I was determined to have one moment not on a spreadsheet. Just between us."

"Then you shouldn't have been born a prince."

She couldn't stop a quick glance at Aleron. *Just us?* Was Aleron invisible to this man?

Her stomach soured with realization. To Yuri, a guard wasn't a person. Wasn't worthy of notice.

She started to speak but saw Aleron quickly shake his head, so she switched her attention back to Yuri.

"Would you like to sit?" she managed, waving toward her office chairs.

"No. I have something for you." He pulled a box from the interior of his jacket. "I'm sorry I did not get here sooner to give you this."

He opened the lid to reveal a diamond the size of the damn moon.

Her hands shook, her eyes glued to the ring so she wouldn't look at Aleron.

She couldn't do this.

She had to do this.

Her stomach knotted, and her heart squeezed.

Yuri took the ring from the box and reached for her left hand, gingerly sliding the wide platinum band down her finger.

Breathe. Breathe.

She gave a quick glance to Aleron and saw the blue rings around his irises. Wishing telepathy was real, she bit her lip, wanting to tell him she didn't want Yuri. She wanted him, only him. The moment stretched, all the brief, incredible moments she'd had with Aleron crashing together in a crushing wave.

She forced out her next words. "It's beautiful."

And horrible. And devastating. And soul-breaking.

"I'm delighted you like it."

I hate it.

"The stone's been in my family a long time," Yuri continued. "If you like precious stones, you're marrying the right Earth." He held her hand gently and brushed his thumb over her knuckles. "Now that we've made it official, I do need to rush off and go poke a tiger."

He gave her a smile she assumed was supposed to be playful, inviting.

Keep breathing.

"Until this weekend, then," she managed, her body numb.

"May I kiss you?" His gaze searched her face, a knowing tilt at the corners of his mouth.

"Not yet." She held up a hand. "I'm not ready. I wasn't prepared for this."

It was clear he wasn't pleased, but he hid it behind a polite nod. "Until the festivities tomorrow, then."

He turned and strode into the lobby, Aleron following.

She dropped into her chair, wondering if her brain and soul were still in her body.

Her new life would start soon. Sooner than she'd planned.

As the ache in her chest diminished, leaving a black hole of nothingness in its wake, a chill came over her, and she wasn't sure how she'd survive the bitter cold of Saint Petersburg.

CHAPTER
THIRTEEN

Aleron stood beside the stone column in the Plaza's Palm Court atrium, the violins' high, vibrant notes carrying over the hundred or so guests. The music should be soothing, and yet it made him itch.

Memories of his dad coming home after an especially hard day at "work" assailed him. His body would be tense, his eyes haunted. The boy hadn't known his father's true job or what his duty had cost him, but he'd watched his mother hold his dad. Talk to him. Take him to their room. When they'd come out, his dad would be less torn and battered. Not healed exactly, but able to hold it together.

He understood now.

He'd had that moment of haunting in the alley, worse than any dark assignment he'd ever completed. And he'd had an instant of being held and feeling stitched back together in Elspeth's apartment.

Watching her with Yuri was like he'd been split open from neck to gut with a dull sword. And his beautiful, emerald-eyed Florence Nightingale couldn't make things better this time.

She'd cured him. Healed him. And he knew now she'd relieved more than a mere migraine.

When the Russian slipped that ring on Elspeth's finger, it had been a slow slice on his soul. A stinging, burning, brutal assault. A broiling agony rekindled every time he glanced at her, the fantasy of her with him aflame.

He tugged at his collar and lowered his body temperature so he wouldn't sweat up his expensive assassin-wear. The fine fabric of his sweater scratched, the Italian loafers' leather rubbed, and his worsted-wool slacks chafed. He kept his bodyguard-on-duty expression extra bland, but he wasn't sure how long he could look at her standing beside that Russian douche.

Shooting a punk-playboy smile at one of the guests, Yuri placed a hand on the small of Elspeth's back, and Aleron's Fire reared up. He'd never lost control and didn't know what to make of his element seemingly flipping him off and firing up shit that couldn't happen.

He looked away and raked his gaze over the guests. Most of the well-wishers were older, the women decked out in sophisticated suits, expensive jewelry, a few in hats. The men appeared bored, at a couple's shower because they had to be, all stuffed shirts and stoic and getting their late afternoon scotch on.

Elspeth was nothing like them. Her hair was down, draping in easy waves over her shoulders. She'd worn green again, the green that lit up her eyes like jewels, and little makeup. She was classically beautiful, stunning when she smiled, but incredibly adept at camouflaging her lovely soul.

I'm used to you missing the mark.

Seanair's cutting comment at the gala crisped inside him like burnt toast.

His pulse thumped, fueling fury at her grandfather's cruelty. He had no idea how Seanair could view her as anything but smart, resourceful, and resilient. She'd taken her lack of power and brushed it aside, like energy meant nothing, and focused on her family. Loved them. Was sacrificing everything for Lach.

Missed the mark?

Yeah, when Aleron got that bastard into the chapel where he would let his defenses down, he'd be missing zero marks. Seanair had a bull's-eye on him that Aleron would nail with a firebolt.

He scanned the room, but his eyes kept going back to her. He zeroed in on the Earth d-bag trying to loop a finger through hers and forced his expression to remain bland when she deftly avoided his touch and sipped her champagne. A monster more ferocious than revenge reared up, ready to rip that Russian to shreds and barbecue the pieces.

Standing in the quiet front corner beside one of the massive potted palms, he could admit he wanted her. He couldn't have her, but that didn't mean he'd ever stop hungering for her. He'd like to say his thoughts were gentlemanly, but why lie? A part of him did ease when he was with her. Other parts wanted to claim her. Pick her up, take her away, and keep her for himself. He looked down at the nine-hundred-dollar loafers Seanair insisted on for some weird-ass dress code he called *smart*. Smart bodyguard? Smart assassin? Another reason the man had to die.

His gaze came around to her again as she served up the same combo to another congratulatory guest—the halfhearted laugh, the pseudosmile, and the slow blink.

And there went another slice of his willpower. More than a sliver this time. And a truth so potent and fiery he put a hand on the massive marble column to steady himself.

She could be the one, the great love his father had told him to strive for.

His forever.

His Fire blazed inside him, pushing against him, wanting out. Elspeth couldn't do jack for his element, but the fool energy gave zero fucks. Best to admit he'd hopelessly, brilliantly, forever burn for her and dream of what could have been between them.

But he'd play the game today. The one where he tried to look everywhere but at her.

And fail.

"Easy-B." Kazumi popped out from behind the plant.

Half Gallon. Exactly the person he did not want to see.

"Did you hear ol' Astruxy's back? The ground split open fifteen minutes ago in the middle of Harlem." She tipped up her champagne glass.

He'd known that thing wasn't done.

His Elite One associates had better get on that shit and fast. "Is anyone hurt?"

"Not as far as we know. Lucky for us, everyone knows about the 125th Street Fault, so our people at the US Geological Survey are calling the incident an earthquake."

Aleron scrubbed a hand up his forehead. "The energy's sloppy and desperate. Let's hope we don't run out of believable explanations."

"Let's hope Elite One destroys the thing soon."

"Yeah." A raucous laugh in the corner interrupted his thoughts.

Seanair. Entertaining a small group of Russian VIPs near the fountain. The old tyrant wouldn't be laughing for much longer. His gaze hopped to another contingent of Russians walking up to congratulate Elspeth and Yuri.

"Are you going to roast him like a chicken or blacken him like a fish? I can't decide if those eyes of yours are set on slight sear or extra crispy."

"Not too bright of you to talk about killing a future king within earshot of other loyal subjects."

"If you don't have the firepower, I could drown him in his bodily fluids, but that whole Water submersion tactic is so…unoriginal. I'm thinking death by invisible undertow. Harnessing the energy of tide pulls is a fine Water art." She glanced sideways at him. "Deep down, I'm an artist."

He glared at the saucy little Water who downed the rest of her champagne. No way was he engaging in this conversation. There were too many Airs in the room who might sense his ass-kicking vibes.

"The bar's right there." He nodded toward the trellised stand anchoring the center of the open area.

The last thing he needed was for Seanair to catch him chatting up the *incorrigible Water*.

She pointed at her wrist. "You can act like you don't like me, but the little bracelets we share say you're my pal."

"We have a pact we will soon sever."

"We have BFF potential."

"We have a mutual enemy."

"Enemies plural, Easy-Bake. I'm no fan of Seanair, and I can feel your extreme dissatisfaction with two men in this room. I share your sentiment."

"Seanair was right about you."

"That list should be short."

"You are incorrigible."

"That's his nicest word for me. That old fogy hates me because he can't touch me. Elementwise, my mother's as powerful as he is, and that's a total ball-scraper for him."

He funneled his Air energy toward her to check her sincerity. The bitter stench of her exhale clocked him right below the ribs. Holy shit, his little smartass Water ally hated Seanair. Hated Yuri. Hated everything about the whole couple's shindig and didn't even try to hide her disdain. He got a whiff of all kinds of Water-borne catastrophes she longed to inflict on the Plaza's Palm Court.

He glanced down at his surprisingly destructive ally. "I don't want to think about that man's balls, but if you're into that kind of thing, go for it. I would tone down the hate, though. There's a lot of windbags in here, and you never know who's sniffing around."

Laughter and the clamor of conversation filled the area. Clinks of champagne flutes. Servers carrying silver trays filled with hors d'oeuvres circulated around the open atrium. His gaze went back to Elspeth. The guests wouldn't see it, but he knew her now, knew her smiles and expressions. She had one hand folded across her stomach while the other held on to a flute like it would fly away.

Kazumi nudged him. "Advice taken, but, dude, you keep looking at her like that, and people will suspect you've done more than guard her body."

He wasn't sure what happened. If a vein popped in his head. If the connection between his mouth and brain severed. Or if something mowed down his self-preservation.

"I have to figure out how to get to Russia. She'll need me over there."

Kazumi whipped around and faced him. "Holy shit. That's what I've been sensing but couldn't place the emotion. That's not protection. You care. For *her*."

He should deny it and back waaaay up from that assertion. But he'd underestimated Kazumi's observational skills, and Goddess help him, he was tired of his two-faced life.

"She's a great person. She's kind and loyal and beautiful." He stopped there, afraid he wouldn't be able to if another word slipped out of his mouth.

Kazumi's eyes narrowed. "She doesn't put up with your bullshit either, does she?"

No, she didn't. But he wasn't going to stand there and wax on about something that couldn't happen.

"It doesn't really matter what I want, or what any Natura wants. Our lives are set, yours included, but I can protect her. I'll do everything in my power to see that she's safe."

And how's that gonna work? You're gonna kill her grandfather at her wedding, survive the hell storm of power that'll rain down on your ass, and then jet to Russia to play bodyguard?

Yep. He'd fried his last brain cell.

"You're perfect for her." Kazumi nudged him again.

"Maybe you should slow down on the alcohol. You've clearly already had too much."

He checked his watch. Five minutes to go, and he'd scan the entry and exit points again. Other than human pickpockets, this part of Manhattan didn't see too much trouble, but he didn't want the Central Park pond ending up in the lobby if that Astrux decided to cruise to the Upper East Side.

The *Jaws* theme blasted from Kazumi's purse, and she shoved the champagne flute into Aleron's hand, scrambling to answer the call.

"Hey, Mom. Wait. What? Slow down." Kazumi put her back to him, plugged a finger in her ear, and hunched to better hear the call. "You're sure? Yep. I'm on my way."

She turned and fumbled to get her phone put away. "Where are they going next?" She looked to Elspeth and back to him.

He didn't give details to anyone, but the stark expression on Kazumi's face had him offering up the truth.

"They have a private dinner with Seanair. I'll know the location soon and send the reservation information."

When Seanair dined out, he made reservations at several restaurants, deciding at the last minute which one to keep so that his location remained unknown.

Kazumi's hand clamped around his wrist. "Once you know, text me, and I'll meet you."

"What's going on?" He discreetly pulled from her grasp as Seanair's cool gaze hit him. "Is there some kind of problem?" He gave his boss a nod before resuming his slow perusal of the room.

"I'll know soon." She started to leave but stopped, her back to Seanair. "I know he's watching us." She took back her glass and turned her face up to his. "I can't say anything yet, but if my mother's right, some serious shit might be going down."

CHAPTER
FOURTEEN

Elspeth climbed from the taxi, Aleron following behind her, and made her way to the private entrance for Le Bernardin. Seanair reserved the salon often, preferring its privacy and dedicated waitstaff over that of the main restaurant's dining room. She stopped several feet from the entrance, flexing her hand and staring at the magnificent diamond weighting her finger.

Goddess, it was happening. Really and truly happening. Beneath the awning, the stone caught the glow of the heated torches, a slash of light hitting her eyes. She made it into the elevator, not looking at Aleron, not thinking about what and who awaited her. The landslide had started, pulling her with it, down a terrible, steep hill to her wedding day. No more delays. No more wishing it wouldn't happen.

She stepped from the elevator and stopped outside the glass door.

"Is something wrong?" Aleron's low voice vibrated inside her, the short distance he'd maintained between them miles wide.

How did she explain the emptiness? How could she describe that when she tried to predict her future, the answer was a desolate landscape of nothing and no one meaningful? Her life would be devoid of sparks. And it would be a life she'd chosen because there was no other choice. Her dream had truly died. She'd hoped to grow to love Yuri, but first she had to get to like.

A photo album starring the man at her back flipped its pages in her mind. The surprising softness of his hair. His smile at lemon me-ringue. His wrath in the alley. His brown eyes staring down at her. His mouth on hers. His arms around her at the gala.

All of that was destined for nothing but memory now.

"In a different time, place, and life, I wouldn't choose this. I would be exploring things with you and hoping they'd lead where I want them to go." Her body hollowed, like the words had drained her dry.

A labored breath cut the silence.

"Elspeth—"

"It's true." She faced him, not willing to make excuses anymore. "I've accepted my fate, but I won't lie and say it's what I want. We have something, and it could be good. Amazing. I'm thankful to at least know chemistry is an actual, tangible thing and that I've experienced it once. With you."

He looked to the floor and back to her. His brown eyes burned a rose red, and his gaze softened, holding hers so gingerly, his stoic mask falling away. "You are my one good surprise." His jaw firmed. "I'll give you my private cell. If you ever need me, for anything, call, text, whatever, and I will come to you. No matter where I am or what I'm doing, I'll stop the world to get to you."

She nodded, unable to look at him any longer. As the foolish wish of having him faded away, she couldn't dream of him any longer or stare.

"I have to go in." If she didn't step away now, she'd do something she shouldn't.

Aleron's phone buzzed. "Seanair's pulled up, and Yuri's already inside." He toyed with the ends of her hair. "You look beautiful."

"I'm dressed for a funeral."

He smiled, a sinister one that would scare the fire out of even the most powerful Natura. "Maybe you'll send the subliminal mes-sage that if he ever does anything to make you unhappy, it'll be *his* funeral."

After growing up with two hotheaded brothers and an over-bearing grandfather, she hadn't thought she'd be attracted to someone heavy-handed, but she loved Aleron's ferocity. His loyalty. His dependability.

If he pledged to have someone's back, he'd have it in spades.

She had no doubt he would scorch the earth—for *her*, and not because she was a Lennox.

Her gaze shifted to his scar and the files she'd read but didn't want to wholly believe. She could sense it now, Aleron's hatred on constant simmer, the truth a harsh line he saw every day and one she now couldn't deny.

She didn't know her grandfather. She'd bought into the facade he'd carefully constructed. She'd believed him on those few instances when she'd asked about the rumors about her family. Perhaps she'd been naïve, so determined to prove herself that she hadn't questioned further when things didn't sound right. She'd been so focused on people-pleasing, she'd been used, manipulated, and—Goddess, what a horrific lie she'd swallowed.

Now wasn't the time, but she would tell Aleron she knew the truth and ask him how she could help. Nothing would bring his father back, but maybe… She needed time to sort through the situation.

She took his hand in hers, squeezing it like she'd never let go. "Thank you. For everything. You're a good man, Aleron. The best."

He stiffened and cut his gaze away from her. "Kazumi wants to know where you're eating. I'm texting her the location. Will you cover for me if it comes up?"

"Of course." She tightened her grip, not knowing why Zum would crash the dinner since she despised Seanair.

A chime sounded.

Aleron stepped back and folded his hands behind him as the elevator doors opened.

Seanair strode into the small lobby with three guards in tow. "Station yourselves at the downstairs entrance," he ordered over his shoulder. "No one comes up without my permission."

"Yes, sir," one of the men answered, the others following him back into the elevator.

"Good evening, Elspeth." Seanair gave her a perfunctory nod like she was an acquaintance. "You're dressed rather harshly this evening. I much preferred your dress at the Plaza." He took in her black, long-sleeved shift and classic pumps.

"I'm dressed for business." *And the demise of my dream.* "This is a transaction, and I want no doubts that I'll honor the terms."

"Of course you will." Seanair turned to Aleron. "You'll remain out here."

"I want him in the room," she countered, wanting him in sight. "Yuri's guard will be in there."

And she couldn't let him go. Not yet.

Goddess, not yet.

Seanair's gaze cut to Aleron. "Very well. I love a good reminder of who's more powerful. Keeps things civil."

Aleron's expression remained perfectly plain. "Are you ready, sir?"

"Yes." Seanair turned to Elspeth. "I'll do the talking tonight."

Didn't he always?

"As you wish." She longed for the Grandie she'd loved with all her heart before Mathair's passing.

Aleron opened the glass door. Seanair went in first, and she followed, feeling the barest touch on the back of her shoulder, a you-got-this graze she hadn't realized she needed.

"Elspeth. Seanair." Yuri stood at the circular table set in the room's center, his guard stationed at the far end of the long room.

Etched-glass windows spanned one of the walls, the wood-coffered ceiling elegant, the room's soft lighting perfect for a sophisticated experience. Three simple place settings with black chargers, silverware, two wineglasses, and a champagne flute sat atop the white tablecloth. A blown-crystal vase graced the center, filled with red and orange mixed flowers with ribbons of greenery.

She took the spot to Yuri's right, leaning in to give a hurried kiss to his cheek. He turned his face at the last minute, his mouth brushing hers, and it took everything she had to keep from slapping him.

Goddess, he'd better be glad she had no power.

He stepped around her and shook Seanair's hand. "I'm glad the three of us can spend time together. I'm returning home tomorrow to handle a situation. My father has died."

"I'm so sorry." *Argh. Foot in mouth.* She hadn't known King Mikhail had been ill, yet Yuri's tone had sounded as if an ivy hadn't been watered and been relegated to the compost pile.

Or maybe he'd been counting the days until he could take the throne.

"I believe he's been ill for some time. My condolences." Seanair's reply came off as if an old car had finally conked out. "I believe congratulations are also in order, Your Highness."

They all settled at the table.

"Thank you." Yuri brushed his hand down her arm. "I must return for the state funeral and other events, but I will not allow for a delay of our wedding." He took a drink of water. "I hope a quick announcement of an heir will ease my…our subjects' mourning."

"I'd like nothing more than to be a great-grandfather. I'd have much to teach the little one." Seanair's blue eyes glittered with warning.

A waiter walked in carrying an uncorked bottle of red wine.

"I went ahead and asked him to let it breathe," Yuri proclaimed, like he'd cured the humans' cancer. "Shall we toast?"

"Of course." Seanair leaned forward, his tone as if the idea had been his.

A man in a superbly cut suit circled the table, adding a small serving to Yuri's glass. He swirled, sniffed, and tasted, finally nodding his approval. The sommelier filled her glass first and made the rounds, then backed away in perfect subservience.

She forced her mouth to maintain what she hoped was a semblance of a smile, noticing the strain between Yuri and Seanair, wondering if she'd unconsciously winced at everything they'd both said or if her expression screamed *hell no* to having Yuri's baby.

She had to join the conversation, add something here and there. Regardless of Seanair's directive to keep quiet, she wasn't about to give Yuri the belief that she wouldn't have a voice as his wife.

Aleron stood directly across from her seat, to the right of the door, his stare focused over her shoulder. Her throat tightened with a ball of building regret. How selfish she'd been to demand he stay in the room. He didn't deserve to hear this bullshit, and here she'd made sure his face would be rubbed in it.

"To my bride, a great beauty who'll make a beloved queen." Yuri raised his glass.

"And to Russia's new king. Long may he reign for the good of our people." She nodded in acknowledgment, certain she wouldn't get a drop of wine down.

"Cheers." Seanair clinked his glass against hers and took a sip. "Now that we've attended to social niceties, I'd like to know how the treatment is coming and when we'll receive the remainder of the protocol."

"According to my mother, her people have prepared the remaining documentation and updated our records."

"Your mother runs the program?" She didn't remember that information being in the original correspondence.

"Yes. She's a scientist. My parents met in London at university many years ago. She's the brains behind the technology utilizing much of the same procedures as the human bone marrow transplant. It's believed the marrow's where the third power is housed, so it's removed and replaced with that of a healthy Natura. She's quite optimistic, as everyone who's received the procedure has survived. The fact we've stopped the deaths is quite a feat, given what's occurred in other countries."

She'd earn Seanair's death stare, but she'd ask anyway. "If it's that promising, why haven't you shared it with other nations? Every Natura wants the disease eliminated."

Yuri gave her a warm smile. "They're going to love you, you know. My mother wasn't embraced by our people, as she valued science over her royal duties. But that turned out for the best, I believe. I'd love nothing more than for my country to claim this victory. We're maligned because we keep to ourselves, but our first duty is to our own people."

Goddess, not the nationalistic crap the humans practiced. One planet. One people. Maybe she'd be able to effect change by raising little global citizens and being a face for the Russians in Natura circles.

Seanair and Yuri engaged in small talk as the waitstaff wheeled in a tray, placing napkins in their laps and plates of mixed greens on the chargers.

Her stomach turned. She reached for her water, half listening to them talk, and took in her future husband. His tousled, blond hair swept back from his forehead as though he'd combed his fingers through it. His forest-green eyes seemed somehow lighter, brighter maybe. Yuri Burkov was handsome. From what she could tell, he was all toned muscle beneath his open-necked dress shirt and cashmere jacket. She wasn't sure how she'd ever have sex with him. Well, the how, yes. But there was zero sexual attraction on her end.

Seanair's phone rang. He pulled it from his Lennox-plaid jacket and frowned.

"Excuse me a moment." He stood and walked to the end of the long room.

"Notice anything different about me?" A knowing grin lit Yuri's face.

No. Crap. She had to say something.

"You look nice tonight, but you looked nice the day we met." She held out her hand, hoping he'd focus on the ring and the coat of polish she'd slapped on her fingernails.

"It's my eyes." He gaped at her with an intensity that sent a shiver through her. "They changed after the couple's shower. I noticed in the car. They're the shade of yours."

"Oh." She blamed her lack of interest in him for forgetting Natura biology. "I'm fertile." Quick mental calendar math estimated her at a week past her ovulation cycle, which meant she'd be in the exact same condition when they married about three weeks from now. She shot up a quick prayer to the Goddess, thanking her for giving Natura women control over their reproductive choices.

"I notified my physician after we met yesterday, and he charted you'd likely be able to conceive during our honeymoon."

Her heart pitched straight for her stomach.

"And we're quite compatible. The blood sample you had to submit as part of the physical—it was shipped to me, and I drank it."

She picked up her water glass and cut a glance at Aleron.

She caught the flash in his gaze, his two mantles ablaze. Blue fire. Hotter even than white. Shit. Lach had told her early on that blue fire was bad news.

"I had no idea you could—"

"Blood sampling's something royals do, to test compatibility before they marry. If I'd taken ill, we'd not have been a match. Our children will be incredibly powerful."

She'd lost the will to respond or care. Goddess, she just wanted this night to be over.

Seanair came toward the table. "We have visitors coming up, Masako Fukada and her daughter. I'm hoping they're only going to extend their best wishes, but I'm curious how they knew we were here."

Her grandfather looked straight at her, his eyes alight with censure.

"I texted Kazumi where we were. We're going to get together when we're done here," she lied, hoping her grandfather wouldn't inquire any further.

"You know how I feel about her."

"She's my best friend."

"I believe you mean troublemaker." Seanair frowned. "You seem upset. Anything else you need to tell me?"

My fiancé told me he could knock me up right now.

"Not upset, a little nervous. Yuri and I were speaking about... children, and I know nothing about being a mother." She turned to Yuri. "I lost mine when I was young, and my grandmother raised me."

"Your Mathair loved you dearly," Seanair crooned, a glimpse of the Grandie she remembered shining through. "Of all the grandchildren, you were her favorite. I'm sure you'll remember the things she taught you when the time is right." He looked to Yuri, then her, knowledge alight in his ice-blue eyes. "I'll be most pleased when this good news comes to pass."

Great. Now everyone was on the same page that she could get pregnant. Goddess, she wanted to dive out the window, but opted for picking up her wineglass and taking a big ol' swig.

Aleron turned and opened the door.

Masako Fukada walked in, the undertow of presence rippling from her belied by her conservative navy suit. Kazumi came up beside her, dressed for a night on the town, her hair mussed like she'd been running, her glare a riptide of anger for Yuri.

Ms. Fukada bent at the waist, bowing in traditional Japanese custom. "Good evening, Seanair. My apologies for interrupting your evening. Unfortunately, I bring disturbing news of which I don't believe you're aware."

Elspeth looked to the table as a ripple disturbed the water in her glass, the liquid spinning, a small funnel teasing the center.

"Do go on." Seanair sat back in his chair and crossed his legs.

"My connections within my element extend all over the world, even to your country." The Water Magnus looked to Yuri and then Seanair.

Kazumi's gaze cut to hers.

"The Russians' treatment," Masako continued, her tone smooth, "while promising, contains a flaw. While it's true none of the treatment's recipients have died, they also haven't awakened. They're all in comas, Seanair. I'm sorry."

Elspeth jerked her gaze to her grandfather. "Did you know this?"

Fear sliced though Seanair's blue eyes. He *did* care for Lach. Goddess, he really, truly still cared for the grandson he used to play tennis with for hours.

"I did not." His narrowed gaze swerved to Yuri. "Is this true?"

Her grandfather knew everything. Everything. This whole thing had to be a trick, just as Lach and Aleron and Kazumi had insisted.

"I don't know." Yuri toyed with his silverware. "But my father's last words to me make sense now. He said, 'Better to go an earthquake than a ripple.'"

The room seemed to shrink, the air heavy and thick.

Those were King Mikhail's wise last words? His last official photo was probably of him shirtless and bareback on a horse.

Everything around her muted. There was no treatment. Not one Lach would take or she could imagine. Her brother, lifeless, hooked up to machines?

Never.

Her brother had nothing now. Nothing. Her plans, her goal, the one thing she could do was…gone. She had no power, no way to help him, no alternative but to watch him die. As long as she'd had an option, she'd had hope—which had gone up in a twist of smoke.

"That's not acceptable for Lach." Her fingers found the ring and slid it from her finger. "He's either full of life and tearing through it, or he'll return to Mother Nature as motes of Fire and Air. He can't be sedated or contained." She looked to Seanair. "He's balls to the wall, pedal to the floor, or he isn't my brother."

Seanair's gaze shifted from her to Yuri and locked on him, his glare set to deep-fry.

She looked to Kazumi, the turbulence in her blue eyes contradicting her stoic expression.

"There must be some mistake." Seanair's tone was knife-sharp. "Why did you not come to me sooner, Masako?"

Ms. Fukada stood as still as a placid lake. "I'm telling you only because my daughter refuses to allow the friend she considers a sister to make the biggest mistake of her life. I'm doing this for her, not for you."

The petite Water Magnus and Kazumi turned and walked from the room, a tidal wave of power flowing behind them.

Elspeth pushed the ring toward Yuri.

"The wedding is off." She got up from the table and headed straight toward the exit.

"Not off. Delayed." Seanair's words stopped her short. "The next-highest bidder begging for my favor will be pleased."

She knew it now, had no more doubt about who her grandfather had become.

"Life isn't all about power." She kept her back to him and kissed the memories of her Grandie goodbye.

"In our world, my dear," Seanair's voice lowered, "it most definitely is."

CHAPTER
FIFTEEN

S tanding in front of the living room windows, Aleron took
another sip of coffee and stared through the leaves to
the tree-lined street. Elspeth's apartment faced Central Park,
and while small, her unit had to be worth at least two mil, maybe
three. He sent a wave of power through the apartment, vanquishing
the persistent chill of February. Outside of the bus stops, this part
of town didn't feel like it was in one of the world's largest cities. As
he watched the clueless humans going about their day, a few of them
scowling up into the scattering snow, he felt...small, for the first time
he could remember.

Insignificant. One Natura of many who'd lived through the centuries and who'd meet the same end.

His plot to avenge his father's death had been stolen from him,
and the fleeting, sweet taste of revenge had turned sour and foul.
The same question rose, the one he'd asked himself for twelve years.
What had he done as a child? What grave sin had he committed for
Mother Nature to keep his goals ever out of reach?

He took another drink and decided he'd try the ritual his father
had taught him. When it came to the Goddess, his dad's approach
had been uncomplicated.

Check in, son. All She wants is your trust.

Maybe that's what was wrong with him. He never checked in.
He was more of a drive-by guy throwing up a quick, two-finger

"hey" and going about his day. Sure, he observed Winter's Hail and Summer's Epiphany, but maybe She wasn't as impressed by his rogu-ish charm as he'd hoped.

Might as well try that thing Elspeth had done with the oils that had made him feel something. Ease. Quiet. Peace. Maybe her candle had opened some mystical, unknown connection.

He likely was spiritually dead. Since the dinner and Masako Fukada's revelation a few days ago, he'd felt...nothing. He'd tried to call up his anger, which wasn't too hard given it was his go-to fuel for everything he did. Time had rusted his rage, a slow oxidation of ev-erything that mattered, until he'd become a robot. His brutal plans, his fiery dreams, the one task She'd chosen him to complete, and he couldn't.

Maybe if he talked to Her, he'd get some kind of direction. A memory came from the past, so far back, so faint he barely heard it, but he recognized his mother's laughter, teasing him that he needed to do less talking and more listening. The echo of her voice nearly sent him to his knees, another sign he'd let his barriers down, and that weakened him. He'd shoved every drop of memory of his mom and brothers into the furthest reaches of his brain. He'd had to purge them from his soul the day he'd destroyed everything connecting him to the Foussé line.

With a volcanic force of will, he rammed it all back again, snarl-ing at himself to get his brain back on the business at hand, even if he didn't want to do the very thing he could no longer avoid. Maybe, if he did listen, he'd hear the woman's voice that had been in the chapel the day his father had died. If he tried hard enough, prayed hard enough, maybe she'd come back and give him an order, since following orders was the one thing he was good at.

He tipped back the last of his coffee and set the cup on the table. It had to be close to noon. His delivery would be here soon. It'd better be. And Elspeth had to wake up and come out of her room at some point. He couldn't be sure, though. After yester-day's fourteen-hour work-athon, she had to be exhausted.

He picked up the candle she'd left on the table, snagged two from the mantel, and went to his room, leaving the door cracked in case she got up. He'd go a full fifteen minutes with the Goddess, ask Her to show him the way, and see what happened.

If not, he'd come up with plan B. Seanair was killable. Naturas weren't immune to knives or bullets. Sure, using human weapons was the ultimate disgrace, but after all he'd done, it wasn't like he had some stellar reputation to uphold.

Although he wasn't exactly overflowing with character, with the wedding off and the chapel out, he was currently at a loss on the best way to get rid of the blasphemous tyrant, so time to kiss up to ol' Mother N.

Looking to the bed, he opted instead to stretch out on the carpet, placing one candle to his right, the other to his left, and holding the third one over his heart. All three came to life with a half thought.

He closed his eyes. The heat kicked on, and the carpet fibers itched through his long-sleeved T-shirt. A few minutes dragged by, his breathing loud in the quiet room, and doubt crept in. He imagined a different world for Elspeth, one where she got to live out her dreams.

For now, she was heartbroken over the loss of the treatment for Lach. He'd watched her order Ross and Egan around, but he'd seen beneath the armor of the dark gray power suit she'd worn yesterday. Any other time, she'd have been confident, sexy as hell. But she'd looked broken, and if he could do anything, have anything, he'd want to put her back together again.

"Help her. Ease her pain," he whispered, feeling foolish raising up his discount prayers. Wait. He'd better be more specific, so She'd know. "Help Elspeth Lennox. Help Lach Lennox. Don't let him die. It will destroy Elspeth, and she's been crushed enough by life."

Anger crept in that something so bad could happen to someone so good. Elspeth wasn't perfect, but she tried so hard to please her grandfather, her cousins, hell—everyone. She was kind and beautiful and... Why did she suffer when ugly-souled sleazebags like her grandfather got away with literal murder?

"Shit, prayer is not my forte." His eyes popped open. "Sorry. *Sorry*." He held up his hands, and the candle on his chest wobbled. It was probably good he didn't go to chapel, as he'd get chased out or knock over the altar and burn the place down. "Give me a sign. I'm not sure how I can do what You want now."

The candle's heat pushed deep and wide, and the flames of both his Fire mantles flickered gently inside him.

"I'm the worst of Your children," he admitted, whispering the truth without a shred of manipulation. It wasn't like he could fool Her, but the confession hurt more than he'd expected. "I did nothing to help my powerless father in that chapel. I disgraced my family. I serve a man who knows nothing but tyranny. I want to do one thing worthy. Just one. Show me. Whatever it is. I'll do it, and I won't fail this time. Please."

The squeal of a hinge on Elspeth's bedroom door sounded.

He sat straight up, snuffed the candles with a blink, and scrambled to his feet amidst the tails of smoke.

Yeah, that had gone great…

He jogged into the kitchen. "Hey."

Should he wish her *happy birthday* now or wait? Goddess, he sucked at this being nice thing.

"Hey. You made coffee."

She turned around, and he nearly died.

Her long johns clung to her every curve, the gray waffle weave clinging to her breasts and hips. Wisps of hair stuck out like she'd been attacked by a band of Airs. A sleep wrinkle spliced her cheek. He caught a hint of mint, so she must have brushed her teeth, and that rosy perfume of hers weaved its way inside him.

She was the most beautiful, mussed-up thing he'd ever seen, and he knew—for sure—he would protect her until his last breath. Maybe he shouldn't have prayed for divine anything. He didn't need a mission from the Goddess, because he wasn't leaving Elspeth. Hell, he had to come up with a brilliant reason to stay on as her guard, because the first thing Seanair would do, once the wedding-drama dust settled, was reassign him.

The man never let his hammer stay in the toolbox for long.

"Aleron?" Her hand cupped his arm, her expression confused. "Looks like we both need coffee."

"I'll get it. You sit." He nodded toward the chair. He should grab his mug from the living room, but he didn't want to chance her fixing her own cup. At some point yesterday, he'd been shot by the sentimental fairy, determined to do something nice for her on her birthday, and it all started with her favorite drink.

"I'm not going into the office today." She took a seat at the tiny, two-person table in a chair he'd likely compact like an aluminum can. "Ross and Egan don't need a repeat of yesterday. I may have been a little…much."

She'd been a hurricane of accomplishment.

"I was impressed with your supervision skills." He kept his back to her to hide his smile. Goddess, she'd been so like him. Burying herself in work. Running Ross to death canceling wedding plans with the precision of an Elite One mission. He'd even felt for Egan. Digitizing a basement full of paper files and getting them uploaded to Kindred would take the young warlock a year. He hadn't complained, though. In fact, he'd seemed a little too eager and ass-kissy, but he apparently liked his job. Judging from the guy's pricey threads, the Lennox gig must pay well. He took two mugs from the cabinet. "Black, right?"

A phone chimed.

"Right. Zum can't come over today. She says something's up with the Waters. Have you heard anything?"

"No." He'd checked in with Command earlier. The thing in Harlem had been handled, and there'd been no sign of the Astrux, which was weird. Energy released improperly at death didn't move around a lot. It collected and festered and sat, growing like an elemental mold, so there should be a decaying cloud of Earth energy sewage parked somewhere in Manhattan.

A second chime sounded.

"Zum says, 'Tell EB I will call him later.'" She looked up as he set her morning elixir in front of her and gave him a half smile. "She likes you, you know, and she doesn't like anyone."

"She tolerates me. To her, I'm an ugly piece of furniture she can't move." He took the seat opposite hers and hoped the chair was stronger than it looked.

"Nope. She gave you a nickname, and that's Kazumi love. Most of the time, when it's just us, she calls me E, and well, you know I call her Zum. It's hilarious she calls you EB, like you're my sidekick."

He shoved down the urge to volunteer to be her wingman, obliterated the desire of being her anything.

"She'd better keep the term of endearment between us. I have a reputation to uphold." He'd roast the first chump at Elite One who likened his power to a toy oven.

He pulled his phone from the front pocket of his jeans so he wouldn't have to look at her and gave a quick check of the screen. Radio silence. Seanair hadn't issued one directive since the dinner. He chanced a glance at Elspeth and caught her dead-eyed gaze. Half of him wanted to pull her out of that chair and kiss her breathless, while the other wanted to hold her and promise to make it all better. He didn't like seeing her so sad, and he didn't like this weight on his mind that he couldn't fix the Lach problem for her.

Fuck. This whole Elspeth thing made him weak. At the core of his power, maybe he did have a child-sized oven.

Half Gallon had the strength of an ocean, though. He'd seen the look on Kazumi's face when she'd left the restaurant, the conflict swirling in her ocean-blue eyes. She'd saved Elspeth from ruining her life at the same time she'd destroyed her dream of a healthy Lach. Little HG had grit. He'd underestimated her, too, and he could admit, in his head, that she was all right for a Water.

"I need a favor." Elspeth put down her mug.

"Sure." Finally. Something he could do.

"Well, a question first. Can you sense how far along my brother's illness is? Like if he's close to—you know, the end." Her gaze dropped to the napkin she was shredding to bits.

Her exhaled thoughts clogged his throat, the air thick with her sorrow and desperation. She still wanted to save Lach, didn't want to give up, but there was this steely, weight-of-the-world truth inside her, a terrible burden of acceptance she couldn't ignore.

"I can sense the health of his energy. There's been no report of contamination of his base-level elements."

Her green eyes went wide. "There are reports?"

He didn't want to tell her most of what her grandfather's enforcement group did, but he'd tell her this part. "Elite One keeps tabs on all tripowered people."

"How many are there?"

"The number's growing. The more polluted the world becomes, the sicker some of us grow."

She bit her lips and tried for that non-expression she'd worn at the office yesterday.

"I figured Seanair was having Lach watched. It's difficult to actually hear it." She brushed away the mess she'd made and wrapped her hands around the mug, leaning toward him like a starved plant drawn to sunshine. "I need you to promise that, when it gets bad, when it's Lach's time," she whispered, her eyes glistening, "you'll tell me first."

"What are you going to do?" His heart fired like a cannon. She had no idea what an unhinged tripowered could do. No goddamn clue. Many times, there was no heads-up. Buildings burned. Rivers overflowed. Tornados ripped towns apart. Avalanches mowed down ski villages.

"I don't want Lach's legacy to be one of destruction. I don't know much more than the basics about power, but after what I witnessed with you in the alley, I realized he's strong enough to level this city and out our secret. As much as I love him, the earth can't exist without us, and I can't let him risk not only our people, but the entire human race. With two mantles, you'd be strong enough to help me handle the situation and not get hurt, right?"

His heart fired another round at her worry for him. That's what the Goddess was going to do. Kill him with Elspeth's kindness.

"If something happens, I'll take care of it." He kept his tone light, but she wasn't going anywhere near an unleashed Lach.

"I'm not asking you to do it." She sat back and clenched her hands. "I understand now how dangerous my brother, unchecked, would be. But if he doesn't have the capacity to make sound decisions, I'm going to be the one who ends his life, not some Elite One SWAT team who doesn't know him. No one really understands Lach but me. Most of the time, he's a sarcastic asshole, but he's got the best heart. I'm the one person he lets see it, and I won't let him die with anything but dignity." She let go of a long-suffering sigh. "I trust you completely to do the right thing, and I can't say that about many people in my life anymore."

He didn't know what she meant, but he wasn't asking. Not today. But he wondered what the hell she believed she could do against an out-of-control Natura about to go supernova.

This wasn't how he'd pictured this day at all. Sure, it wasn't going to be the happiest of birthdays, but he'd wanted to try to lighten things up a little. Give her a bit of space and levity to take a breath.

"Right now, he's supposedly left Argentina for Antarctica with Isidora," she said, her tone *I don't know what the hell that's about.* "Do you know her?"

"I know of her, and I've seen her at the continent president council meetings I've attended with your grandfather. She's…quiet."

Ice-queen quiet and a tad on the freaky side.

"Ross implied Lach has something going on with her. My brother's an adult, and I know more than I care to about his escapades, but I'm…I'm afraid." Her voice went deathly low. "One of these days, he'll go off on one of his jaunts and not come back."

Definitely not how Aleron had planned her birthday to go.

He leaned across the table and offered his hand. "I'm sorry."

Goddess, was he sorry. He understood powerlessness. Deep sadness. The utter misery of not being able to prevent the death of someone you loved. There wasn't anything else to say. No words would ease the pain of loss. No thoughts. No prayers. Nothing.

He needed to turn this convo around. Throwing her a pit-of-despair party and building her a diving board wasn't the soirée he'd wanted.

"Have you investigated human treatments?" He had to offer her something.

Where was that delivery dolt with his gift?

"I'll find something else. If there's one thing you should know about me, it's that I never give up. I can't." She took his hand and squeezed, her glassy eyes meeting his. "I need to talk to Graham again. His work involves infectious diseases, and he's been overseeing Natura research on the tripowered disease. Maybe they've made some progress on how to develop a cure. He's not the best at keeping me updated on that stuff."

Nope. If he could help it, she wasn't working on her birthday.

"You said you were taking the day off," he reminded her.

"That was silly to even say. I can't waste time."

"You need…what do humans call it? A mental health day?" Goddess, give him something to get her to stop working.

He was going to make her smile if he had to sing Goddess-damned Harry Styles songs and show her he had the dance moves of a malfunctioning robot.

The doorbell rang.

Fucking finally.

"I got it." He put out a hand when she started to get up.

"I'm not sure who it'd be. Deliveries are left downstairs."

"It's something for me." *For you.*

He moved down the short hallway and opened the door.

"Receipt's in the envelope." The guy handed him a white box and walked off like he'd delivered a bomb.

Ah, New Yorkers.

"Thanks." He closed the door, wondering how he'd surprise her now. Or maybe she'd hate a surprise, so he should hand her the box and hope for the best.

Ah, hell. He and *best* were definitely not friends.

The most delicious scent he'd ever smelled cut across his nose.

"I'm going to get dressed, and then I have a few calls to make," she called from the kitchen, then came into the hall, looking from his hands to his face. "What's that?"

"A surprise. Well, not a surprise. A thing. A tiny thing. For your birthday." Okay, he was eight again and had gotten busted stealing warm cookies from his mom's kitchen.

"You got me a surprise?"

Her timid smile stabbed him right in the heart, and the blade twisted.

"I did. Go back in the kitchen, and we can open it." He nodded in that direction, wishing he'd had a chance to look at it first.

"What is it?" Her tone turned a bit bubbly.

"Don't laugh." He came up behind her and put the small package on the table. "I got you a cake. It's kind of a do-over since we didn't get to replace the pie we lost in the alley."

Her hand brushed over the name engraved on the lid. "This isn't any ol' cake. This is from Brooklyn's best bakery. They don't whip up cakes to sit around for purchase." She met his eyes. "You planned this."

Kind of. Most folks made things fast if the price was right.

She bent at the waist, her nose an inch from the top of the box. She took a long inhale and straightened, her smile wavering. "It's lemon. You remembered," she whispered, her chin quivering.

"Happy birthday, Elspeth. I'm thankful for this day and that I met you. I meant what I said. You truly are my one good surprise." A warm, fuzzy feeling spread inside him at the sincerity anchored deep in her eyes. "Go on. Open it."

Her hands shook as she lifted the lid.

Sweat formed on his brow as she took in the pale yellow, round cake. The baker had done a kickass job with the elegant cream swirls dotted with little lemons and green vines covering the edges of the top and down the sides. He'd asked the baker to mimic the bushy Meyer lemon tree he remembered from back home, the one that had provided the fruit his mother had used to flavor his favorite desserts.

He watched her face, riveted by the smile creasing her perfect mouth.

"I'll get plates and forks. You get it out of the box." She turned toward the cabinets.

He caught the catch in her voice as he unfastened the tabs at the sides so he could lift out the six-inch cake, thinking it'd been worth every penny to see her happy. He took in her exhales and absorbed the bittersweet cocktail of emotions.

As he pulled the cake from the box, relief burned steadily within him that he'd chosen the reusable porcelain plate option from a local artist the bakery used. Little lemons and green leaves had been hand-painted on the white rim, the design on the girly side, but he hoped she'd use it and think of him after he got reassigned. And he would be put back on his regular rotation eventually. Knowing Seanair, he'd be lucky to still be around next week.

His gaze drew to the elegant script of her name written beneath the words *Happy Birthday*.

"Elspeth." He loved the taste of her name across his senses.

A gentle hand landed on his back. He turned, his power flaring that she stood only inches from him.

"I've never received a nicer gift." Her gaze slowly searched his face.

"I'm glad you like it." He stepped to her and swept her hair behind her ear.

"I do, but that's not the best part of the gift." She closed the space between them and rose on her tiptoes, her mouth hovering off his. "I like the way I feel when I'm with you. I'm happy." Her lips softly and sweetly brushed his.

CHAPTER
SIXTEEN

er eyes closed as a feeling of rightness flooded her. She wrapped her arms around his neck and strained to maintain contact because he was so tall. He didn't return the kiss, and she almost stepped away. Then his tongue brushed her upper lip, his mouth moving over hers, the intensity building, rising, until he was kissing her like she was life's first breath.

So much had happened that she couldn't remember all the things they'd experienced together, but it felt like everything. He felt like everything. She could be with him now. He was the shiny thing in the broken pieces of her life, the bright spot in her dark heart.

She was free.

Free to pursue him like she wanted.

And oh, how she wanted.

He broke away sharply, leaning down and pressing his forehead to hers, his large, warm hands cupped around her face. "We can't. I'm going to get reassigned." Tension rippled from him, the room's temperature rising. "I want you so much, you have no idea, but you're not a fling. I can't tell myself this won't mean anything. I can't treat you like a regen when you're so much more."

She closed her eyes, overwhelmed by the care in his voice. There was so much between them. So much electricity. The need for connection.

"Look at what's happened since you got here. We have no idea what'll happen tomorrow, but we have now. We have this day." Goddess, she wanted longer. "I don't know how, but no one's taking you away from me. The only way I'll let you leave is if you want to go."

His forehead tensed against hers, his eyes pinched shut. "You deserve better, Elspeth, better than me. You deserve someone who can be in your life. We're not the same status. There's no public future for us, and I don't want a secret life for you. You're not from a family where you can do whatever you want without consequences."

Goddess, why did he think he was such an awful person? All he'd done was protect her. He'd never hesitated to put her first in that alley, even though he could have been hurt. He'd held her while she'd cried in the bathroom at the gala. And now he worried for her reputation. Her. The null. The nothing.

She leaned back, looked to the cake and back to him. She wanted one thing. One thing she could call hers.

"Why would I want to let go of the best thing that's ever happened to me?" She dropped her watery gaze to his mouth, lingered, and longed to feel the press of it against her own again. "Your concern for me makes me want you even more. You respect me. You *see* me." She trailed her finger down the scar. He was so brave, so brave and so...good. "Be with me."

The knot in her throat held, inching larger as the seconds burned between them.

"I'm not a good man. I've done horrible things." His hand raked through her hair and settled on her jaw.

"You're a good man to me."

"Do you know how I got this scar?" He turned his head so the mark was a blaze right before her eyes.

"Yes, I do. I read a diary entry of my grandfather's. I know everything, and I don't blame you for hating him. I'd rather focus on what I want, rather than what Seanair's done. His list of sins is longer than I ever imagined, but I won't add losing you to that list. I won't let him take this from us." She looked at the cake and back to him, her tone laden with intent. "Have you ever had cake sex?"

He did a double take, and his gaze darkened. "No."

"It's a birthday party game. I paint my favorite parts of you with icing and cake." She shot him a sly smile. "And lick it off."

Two blue rings lit around his reddened irises. "You shouldn't tease me like that. I'm struggling to do the right thing."

"You're struggling to do what you think you should do, not what you want to do." Desire pooled inside her. "I want you so bad I ache."

His finger teased below her bottom lip. She closed her eyes at the sensation, the heat spooling like wildfire, her pulse alive beneath his touch.

"I am lost when it comes to you." He cupped her jaw, his face coming toward hers, nothing but desire in his gaze. His tongue drew across her upper lip, little licks and nips building to teeth and breath and a hot-as-lava kiss. "I'm done fighting this," he said into her mouth, his hands sliding up her face and slipping into her hair. "And I get to go first on this game."

A delicious heat sizzled in her breasts, between her legs, her body alight for him. His arms went around her, his hands gripping her ass as his searing kiss sent a shower of sparks over her skin. With her hands clasped around his neck, she realized the feeling was him. All him. No Fire. No power. Like they were two humans who wanted nothing more than each other.

He wanted her. Just her.

And she wanted him.

Her fingers found the edge of his shirt. She pushed it up, groaning at the muscles beneath. Her gaze went to the rings hanging on a chain around his neck.

"What are these?" In all the chaos, she'd forgotten to ask about them..

The desire in his eyes dulled. "They're the only things I have left of my dad. His wedding band and a relic that didn't destroy itself. I don't like to talk about it."

She was sorry she'd brought it up, sorrier still as she realized she'd assumed something about sex with an Alpha.

She teased a finger along the corner of his mouth and leaned up and gave him a quick kiss. "I won't mention it again. I wondered…" Goddess, this was embarrassing. "Since I have no power and can't refuel you, can you enjoy sex without a power exchange?"

"If it's with you, I'm gonna enjoy it." His arms crossed in front of him, and he tugged the shirt over his head, tossing it to the floor. "You're nothing but good for me. Feel what you do to me." His eyes dipped slowly south and back to hers.

She drew her hand down his warm chest, tracing her fingers over his firm pecs and into the dips of his abs. Reaching the waist-band of his jeans, she didn't let go of his stare, watching his eyes go molten as she cupped the firm heat of him.

"You have no idea how hard it's been to stay away from you." His breath came faster.

She drew back, tugged her shirt over her head, and let it fall, her breasts swaying free. Cool air hit her skin and instantly warmed. He was taking care of her again, tending to the smallest of her needs. The little things were how she'd known. The coffee. Her food. How she never had to zip her coat anymore, even in February. Things he wasn't paid to do but did anyway.

"Then don't stay away anymore." She took his hands and guided them to her breasts.

"Goddess." His eyes flared red as he cupped her and teased his thumbs over her nipples, his wicked smile lighting something wan-ton deep inside her. "You're so damn beautiful." His hands went to her hips, and he backed her to the wall. "Tell me again how this cake-sex game works." The flames in his irises burned bright against the whites of his eyes.

"We have to be completely naked." She pushed him away enough so she could hook her thumbs in the waistband of her long johns, pushing them down slowly and toeing them off.

"Mother N." His wide eyes narrowed to a wicked gaze, promis-ing the best possible burn.

His jaw tensed, and his throat bobbed as he swallowed. She'd never considered herself provocative, but seeing his reaction made the last of the old voices go away. For the first time, she was gloriously in charge. It was heady to feel sexy. Flirtatious. Desired.

No, *desire* was too tame. This was craving. Deep. Raw. Insatiable.

She reveled in the clink of his belt buckle against the tile, the swash of his jeans, the slaps of his boot laces, the gentle whoosh of his socks.

He straightened to his full height and palmed himself, his cock long and hard and ready. "Turn around. I want to see all of you before we start."

Her heartbeat surged into her throat, her nerves alive, her thoughts firing like bottle rockets. Two things weren't small or even medium-sized on her: her boobs and her ass. But the old voices telling her to be embarrassed were silenced by his hum of pleasure as she obeyed.

His hands grazed her shoulders as he split her hair and pushed it forward onto her breasts. His finger teased slowly down her spine, tracing a circle in a sensitive spot where the bones ended and the want began.

"I have dreamed of this." He kissed his way down the trail his fingers had taken, her need growing with the brush of his breath against her skin. He went to his knees behind her, his hands spanning her ass as though he'd found perfection and had to be sure she was real.

He gripped her hips and turned her, his head drawing back so he could look up at her, stark, raw need carving his features into harsh lines. "I want to take this slow, but I'm not sure I can. Not the first time."

Desire raged and consumed her, her body a breathless, needy thing.

"What? You think I'd only want you once? You are a fire I can't extinguish."

He pressed a kiss below her belly button, and a hard shiver went down her body.

"I think I know how to play this game. I'll paint frosting here." His finger trailed across her lower belly. He eased back, standing enough to lean toward the cake and scoop a glob of icing with his finger. "Now, where was I?" He returned to his knees and swiped a long, sugary stripe in the spot he'd kissed. "If I'm going to win, I'll need a baseline. Widen your stance for me."

Her heart went into overdrive. *You'll never tire of a night with a Fire.* She somehow managed to move.

"The goal here is to decide which I like better, the taste of lemon or you, right?" He cocked a brow.

She nodded, the word *yes* stuck in her fist-tight throat.

With his other hand, he dragged a finger through her slickness and sucked it clean, his eyes closing. "Definitely sweet, but I need to play a few rounds before I know for sure."

Honestly, she hadn't been sure where her wild-ass cake-sex comment had come from, but hell yes, she was going to play.

His tongue did a slow drag along the path of icing. Her stomach tensed, the nerves there electric, live wires of want and need and lust splintering through her veins.

"First birthday present of the day, and round one." A dark smile pulled across his face, and he pushed toward her, lifting one of her legs and placing it over his shoulder.

His hot breath washed over her sensitive skin. With one of his hands braced against the wall, he grasped her ass cheek with the other, his fingers digging in the more he licked and sucked and teased her. Her head fell back, her body stringing tight, tight, tight at the feel of his greedy mouth.

There he was, giving himself to her again, seeing to her satisfaction, putting her needs first. The tension built, her body on fire. So close, so close, so—

The orgasm struck, her eyes slamming shut, her breath a harsh moan. Her hands smacked the wall, one landing on his, her nails scoring his skin. She pitched over, falling into sensation, nothing but a black sun of bliss eclipsing behind her eyelids as he wrung wave after wave of pleasure from her.

"Aleron," she cried, his strong arms holding her up, his grip tight as he kissed her inner thighs.

His rested his forehead where he'd licked off the icing, his body taut. "*That.*" His breath was ragged. "Was better than cake."

She focused on the heat of him as he rose, the dusting of hair on his chest tickling her along the way. "You like me better than lemon?"

His hands cupped her bottom again, and he lifted her like she weighed nothing. "I like you better than everything, no contest."

He kissed her, his body pressed against hers, the tease of his teeth sending shivers down her. Goddess, he was intense, the urgency in his grip, the heat in his eyes, his voice dark. A glorious smoke mingled with his breath and the leather-scented soap she'd put in his bathroom.

She breathed him in, all in, the essence of him the sweetest high.

Her eyes locked with his, and her breath caught at the need blazing bright in his hot gaze. "You're the first thing I've ever gotten that I wanted."

Something had broken free inside her. She wasn't following the rules anymore. She would make her own.

Rule one? Aleron was in her bed, and inside her, as often as possible.

"I'd forgotten how to want. Until you." His words, quiet as they were, drowned out the refrigerator's whirr. Everything slowed, the room around her receding until she was surrounded by nothing but the sight and sound and scent of him.

Hers. All hers. This man she couldn't get enough of.

"Come here." He helped her get steady on her feet and guided her to the small rug on the floor. His gaze predatory, he followed her down, bracing his hands so she didn't absorb the full weight of his naked, hard body.

"Guide me in. I'm dying here." He ground against her.

She slipped a hand between them and found his hot, hard length. He wasn't a small man by any stretch, and a curl of worry sprang that she wouldn't be able to take all of him.

"Stop thinking." He breathed near her ear. "I'll go slow until you're ready." He leaned back, his head lowered, watching her position him. His eyes met hers as he slowly pushed inside. "Tell me if it's too much."

The stretch burned enough to let her know she'd be oh-so-yummy sore tomorrow, but she couldn't look away from his hot gaze, her body a riot of sensation. No one had ever looked at her like that. No one had ever wanted her so openly. No one had ever made her feel so desired.

You'll never tire of a night with a Fire.

No. No, she wouldn't. Not with him.

He inched his way inside, a sheen of sweat across his forehead, his muscles straining as he patiently pushed all the way in. "Mother N, you will be the death of me, and I'll go with a smile on my face. Are you okay? I don't want to hurt you."

She kissed him, teasing his lips, tasting a sweet blend of herself and him. "Trust me to tell you if it's too much." She smiled against his mouth. "You won't break me." She squeezed her muscles around him, ready to see him let go.

He groaned, breathy and low, and thrust. Found his rhythm, his abs tense as he grunted. Goddess, he was strong, his hips moving faster.

Her foot kicked the table. Something fell. The saltshaker, maybe. She didn't care. He took her orderly, pristine world and messed it up, mussed her up, made what she'd missed in life oh so clear. He managed to hit a sweet spot inside her, over and over. Her body tightened, the low coil twisting and tensing, and—

Her eyes rolled back. His hands fisted in her hair, and she came apart, straining and gasping and calling his name.

He jerked hard, her name a hoarse, harsh shout. He fell against her, pinning her to the floor, their world nothing but breath and sweat and heat.

She opened her eyes, staring blankly at the stove, her senses focused on the lock of her ankles at his back. She sensed a strange line had been crossed, one that would forever change their futures. For the first time since that disastrous night when she and those closest to her had discovered she would have no power in her lifetime, she felt…seen. Whole. Wanted.

"I…you're…incredible," he huffed into the hollow of her neck as her fingers toyed with the damp waves of his hair along the back of his neck.

A wave of exhaustion swept over her. After that, he no doubt—

"Stop thinking, baby. My Air can't sense your exact thoughts, but I get the gist of what's going through that pretty head." He gently pulled out of her and helped her up, tugging her against him. "You've only unwrapped the first present. You're going to receive many, *many* gifts at this private birthday party." He took her hands and pulled her toward the hallway. "Let's grab a shower, and then I'll feed you cake properly."

She loved this teasing side of him, this lightness between them they'd not experienced before.

"What if I want more cake improperly? It's my birthday." She poked at his chest, and he caught her finger in his fist.

"This day'll be filled with improper things." He pulled her toward her bedroom and into the bath. "I aim to keep a sated smile on your pretty face."

No, he'd aimed for her heart and had stolen it.

She turned on the shower.

"You aim to please, do you? Then I'm giving you *all* the party favors."

His playful smile was one she hadn't seen but made him look younger and even more handsome. Ten minutes passed, maybe ten hours, as he gently washed her from head to toe, taking the time to point out and pay attention to his current favorite spots. Before they threatened to exhaust the city's water supply, he turned off the taps and reached outside for a fluffy towel.

He wrapped her in the oversized sheet and tugged her toward him, nipping at the spot right below her ear.

A laugh escaped her. Goddess, when was the last time she'd laughed? "I don't need this anymore." She tugged at the edge of the terrycloth, letting it fall to the floor, and raced for the bed.

He was on her in seconds, scooping her up and turning to absorb their fall onto the mattress.

"I'm getting the cake. Be right back."

She watched his mighty fine ass as he strode from her bedroom, the man a masterpiece of muscular art, and realized the problem. He'd ruined her for anyone else. What they'd experienced, what he'd done for her, to her… She'd seen the man beneath the armor, the one she'd bet he'd never shown anyone else.

And she wanted that man. More than anything.

He came back in, holding the box and a fork. The bed jostled as he climbed in and settled beside her. He sliced a perfect bite with a little lemon on the frosting and held it near her mouth. "Happy birthday, Elspeth."

She slid the cake from the tines with her lips.

"Good Goddess of fruit, that's delicious." She reached for his hand and the fork. "Your turn." The game started, and they took turns feeding each other bite after bite of
perfect lemon.

He finally put the box aside, lying down beside her, his nose near hers on the pillow.

"I'm hungry again for something better than citrus." He teased a finger down her cheek, his expression serious but serene.

"Then let's make sure you're fed until you're full. It would break my heart for you to go hungry on my birthday." Or on any day, she didn't add, wanting to take this, take him, one glorious day at a time.

He smiled, part angel, part devil, and rolled on top of her, kissing her and making love to her for hours.

When night finally fell, and she lay wrapped in his arms, his body pressed against her back, his soft snore rustling her hair, she closed her eyes, her last thought that she wanted this man with a fury she didn't recognize.

And she vowed to find a way to keep him.

CHAPTER
SEVENTEEN

Aleron opened his eyes and stared straight into a mass of long brown hair. Elspeth's rose scent invaded his senses, the perfume pushing through him, the aroma strong in the heated space they shared. He carefully extracted his legs intertwined with hers, his body heavy with a strange, sated energy, and rolled to his back. She couldn't refuel him, but as he stared at the ceiling, he chalked up the boost to just being with her.

She stirred, turning toward him as if searching for him in her sleep. Her chest rose in a long, slow swell, releasing more easily, eyes turned up ever so slightly as if she were laughing in her dreams.

The tops of her breasts peeked from the comforter lying loose across her body, toying with him, calling to his hands, his fingertips, his tongue. He studied her smooth forehead, the straight line of her nose ending in a cute button, the curve of her mouth that had damn near destroyed him last night. Her expression was so relaxed, so coy, he almost thought she was awake and playing with him.

He'd never woken beside a woman. Never spent the night or more than an hour, tops, with one to regen. He couldn't call last night sex. Sure, in the textbook sense, maybe, but even a hint, a whiff of the physicality of what they'd done sent a bolt of lust through him. What they'd shared, what she'd given him... Goddess, his pulse accelerated at the memory of the blissful strain on her face as she came undone around him and the look of unbridled sin in her green eyes as she described, in great detail, what she was going to do to him.

He eased back the covers, his morning wood now log-straight, and slipped out of bed. He'd better get away from her, or he was going to kiss her awake and start her day with him worshipping her with his mouth between her legs.

He looked at the clock on her side table. Ten a.m.? What the hell? Sleeping so late was a first since his teen years.

He studied the sweep of her dark eyelashes against her pale skin and the sliver of white through the tiny parting of her full mouth. Her hand pushed into the space where he'd been, and a deep exhale rushed from her, the peace of her expression returning at finding his lingering warmth.

She looked like she'd found forever. With him.

And he'd seen it with her in the horizon of her eyes.

She felt like a home, a place he wanted to live, a place he didn't want to leave. She was so…lovely. Not pretty or smart or funny, but all three. *Lovely* encompassed all three. *Lovely* was something he'd never tasted before, and he didn't know what to do with the feelings flickering inside him. She wasn't marrying the Russian, so how could he find a way to stay with her?

He headed for the kitchen, his brain empty of ideas, but his heart full. He imagined the moment he told Seanair.

I quit, you disgraceful cockbag. I'm taking Elspeth far away so you can't ruin her. She's mine. I love her. And you can bend over and take it straight to your throat if you—

Yeah, he'd be ash right after the word *quit*.

He walked to the counter, found the coffee, and got a pot started without really thinking about it. It was a good thing the ritual was hardwired, because all his brainpower was focused on her. He couldn't give her up. He *wouldn't*. It didn't matter that she couldn't refuel him. Goddess, his power might go to shit, because he didn't want to regen, ever again, by sleeping with someone else. She was all he wanted, all he needed, damn his elements to the far corners of the polluted earth.

He recognized the slow squeeze of his heart. The pang he still felt for his mother and his brothers ever since they'd all stopped speaking to him.

His father had been right. His gut had given him the heads-up the moment Elspeth had opened her front door. That poke in the instinct had signaled a hard left for his life.

He loved her. Was in flaming, burning, pure-as-Fire and Air love with her.

The coffeemaker sputtered and steamed. He toyed with the rings hanging around his neck, something other than bitterness stirring inside him. His Fire energy stretched from a flicker to a steady flame. He felt...*good*. Damn great, actually. His insides tingled, all smoldery and warm, like he'd tossed back a couple fingers of whisky.

He stood at the window over the sink, not giving a damn he was buck-ass naked. He'd check in with Command in a bit, but he wasn't about to cover up. In fact, he planned to play human today, go biblical, and Adam-and-Eve it in the garden of her apartment all day long. Maybe she'd be up for a test of which was better, cake sex or bacon sex?

Hell, why choose? Both...with long, long showers in between where he'd use up bottles of that froufrou bodywash, playing bubbles with every single inch of her. He could see doing that for the rest of his days.

A breath of worry whispered over the back of his neck.

How could he think of abandoning his plan? How had the idea even formed? Twelve years. Twelve years of dreams, every detail specific and gory. How he'd do it. What he'd say. How he'd feel at the wide-eyed, oh-shit rounding of Seanair's eyes when the tyrannical leader realized it was game over.

Revenge had saved him, fed him, fueled him through every Elite One assignment.

He owed his brothers and his sweet mother. His parents had been so in love.

But he'd fallen for a smart, sexy, sweatpants-and-hoodie woman trapped in a ballgown life. Even though Seanair was a cruel, flaming asshole, Elspeth still cared about him. No matter how much her grandfather cut her with his words and put her down, she still held some smoldering candle of affection for the old ball bag.

A terrible, traitorous tug at his heart unearthed a truth he couldn't deny.

He could not kill Seanair and also have Elspeth.

No analysis needed. It was either love Elspeth or kill her grandfather. Standing there, her scent baked into his skin, the decision... Well, there wasn't one. His instincts flared anew, the flame steady and sure.

It had to be her.

He grabbed a glass from the cabinet, turned on the faucet, and availed himself of Manhattan's surprisingly tasty tap water. He waited for the rebuttal, for his brain to go *hell no* and for his heart to harden and recommit to revenge.

It didn't come. No argument. No guilt. Nothing.

Nothing but sweet warmth washed over him, and a fragrant peace laced the air.

He swallowed the last gulp, put the glass in the sink, and felt it. A disturbance in the Fire seal. Power teased through his hair and over his face. He jerked at the flood of sensation, looking around the kitchen.

Power struck him in a full-body press, pushing him into the counter. A strange new zing twirled with the Fire inside him, a burst of... Air? Not hair-dryer level, but a hurricane.

He searched deep inside himself, going still at the element count.

Two. Not just Fire, but a fully formed Air. No more halfsies— the gift from his mother was no longer latent, but a tornado fueling the flames.

How had his Air gone from faint to a roar, and why now?

He went still. Energy lashed his insides, the Air stirring and whipping and chasing his Fire. He marveled at the sharp increase in power, how his inferno of power now had afterburners. Static crackled over his hands, the normally orange light now tipped with white.

How on the Goddess's great earth had this happened? How—

A breeze shot through the room, ruffling the roll of paper towels, sliding the spoon rest into a stove burner, knocking over the saltshaker.

Not buying what he was feeling, he closed his eyes and ripped open the figurative door to where his energy resided. There was Fire, shacked up next to...

Impossible.

Naturas didn't just gain extra power. As if insulted, the Air energy inside him seemed to stand and fist-bump his Fire. His hand slapped the counter at the kick to his lungs. A cyclonic whirl of wind surrounded him then calmed, like his Fire had shepherded the Air.

He was a Dual, a Goddess-blessed Dual, and a damned strong one too.

How in the blazing fuck had that happened?

Power brushed him. Just a stroke. A tease. A test? He glanced behind him. That energy was different. Unease yanked his instincts. He checked the apartment's shields again. No fractures. The sensation increased, its force building, like he was being sandwiched between two large, invisible masses. He shoved back against the power. Earth. Where was it coming from? A breeze smacked his face. Air that didn't belong to him.

Confusion still ruled the moment, but a heightened awareness jerked his head toward the bedroom.

Power glided over his bare feet. Up his legs. To his middle and over his arms and neck and face.

Not one energy. Not two.

Four.

And not *his.*

He checked his shields again. Walls, windows, vents, wires. Covered in Fire energy and holding. Had that nasty-ass Earth Astrux come back and brought friends?

A scream came from the bedroom.

He stepped into the hallway, and a tidal wave of elements pinned him to the wall like he was a bug on a board, the energy a blitz of assassin-level strength. He clenched his fists.

Her name clawed up his throat in a roar. He called upon his Fire, pulling, sucking, wrenching every molecule of heat within reach. Like an engine revved, his element flooded him, and he leaned into the tornado of Air and flames and fury.

He broke free and lunged into the bedroom, razor-sharp control and temper ablaze in brutal fury, primed for total annihilation. If anything happened to her. If anyone dared to touch her...

He stopped dead.

He jerked and doubled over, the violent retreat of his Fire and sloppy retraction of his Air smashing inside him like two crashed cars. He fell against the bed, slid to a knee, and grunted against the sword slice of pain.

Bands of colored light circled Elspeth. Green. Blue. White. Red. Like some miniature aurora borealis having a festival over her skin.

Eyes wide, her chin trembling, she was on her knees on the bed, her fingers fanned over the sheets as she braced, her naked body shaking and seemingly pinned by magnificent power. Her scent, the one that had invaded his every pore, permeated the room, the provocative blend smoldering with Fire essence and stroking his element.

"What's happening to me?" she cried, her voice shaky and high.

Red and white threads circled her hips, bathing her in a radiant fountain of color, the bright ribbons changing to green and blue.

Not trusting his eyes, he scanned the room.

Elspeth and him. Alone. No one else. No *thing* else.

He counted the colors. Fire's red vapor clung to her skin. Air's white outlined her body. Earth's green and Water's blue chased each other from top to toe.

It couldn't be. That hadn't happened in—no.

The phenomenon transpiring before him supposedly existed only in legend. Every family longed for such luck, the winning ticket in the Natura genetic lottery.

That wasn't real.

But the evidence didn't lie.

He inhaled the plethora of aromas from the elements dancing

around her, ripe and thick in the room. Smoke. Dirt. A spring breeze. The salt of the sea. Mother Nature's finest and purest gifts.

The arrival of one's element was a private moment, the recollection of that fateful day an intimate agony of pleasure and pain.

"Aleron," she gasped. "Help me."

He raced to the bed, realizing the champagne-like bubbles of power fizzing over her were now seeping into her.

"What's happening?" She tried to straighten but fell forward onto her hands, gasping. "I woke up, and they were there. It's too much." She shoved a fist over her mouth, leaped off the bed, and rushed into the bathroom.

He followed and took her hair in his hands as she dry-heaved. He sensed power, not danger, but he barely had a finger on her, and his hand trembled.

"You're a Nexus."

A swath of Fire cut through the room, and the towel beside the sink went up in flames. Shit. He yanked the cloth off the wall, rack and all, and threw it into the tub. Twisted open the tap. Good Goddess, she had no idea what she was doing. For a split second, he thought he'd set the damned thing aflame, then knew instantly how wrong he was.

He'd had six years of training to learn how to control one element.

She'd had no training at all on all four of them.

Holy elemental wrecking ball.

"It's okay, baby. I've got you." He went to the floor beside her, pulled her into his arms, and circled his Fire and Air around her.

"What's wrong with me?" she moaned, curling into him. "And why do I feel like I drank a bottle of vodka and then went toe-to-toe with a steamroller?"

In the bedroom, his cellphone went off, song blasting and phone vibrating on the bedside table. Led Zeppelin's "When the Levee Breaks." Kazumi.

Not now, damn it. Not now.

"What's a Nexus?" Elspeth gasped out.

"Short story is, you got power-jacked by all four elements and are hemorrhaging energy. Goddess, you're buzzing like a kid hopped up on Mountain Dew and Pop Rocks. Come here." He guided her toward the rug and pulled her onto his lap.

"My head hurts so bad." She winced. "What...how..."

She slammed the heels of her hands against her temples so hard it scared him. He took her wrists and pulled them down so she wouldn't hurt herself.

"Look at me," he ordered, repeating the command louder when she didn't obey. "Elspeth. Look. At. Me."

She finally met his eyes, and he drilled his gaze into hers like his captain had done to him during training.

"You can do this. You have to trust me."

She shook her head, and he pulled one hand up to kiss her knuckles, gently biting the ridge and startling her.

"Do you trust me?" He feared her answer.

Finally, she nodded.

"Okay, take a breath—not too deep!" He had to be precise with his instructions so she wouldn't accidentally level, drown, or torch something. "Tell me what you're feeling. Exactly. Break it down like you're making a list."

Her frantic gasps slowed, and she maintained eye contact as he saw a hint of her panic ease.

"I...I can tell the energies apart. Earth and Water hurt. It feels like surf crashing onto a beach in my temples."

The phone rang again. The same song abruptly cut off. A what-the-fuck punch came through his "friendship bracelet" and clocked him between the eyes.

"Aleron, I'm scared," she whispered, burrowing into his neck, her fingers curling around the chain and clutching the relic and his dad's ring like they were life rafts and she'd been tossed off the *Titanic*.

Her whole body tensed against his, and right as he thought she was better, she arched as if she'd been shot. Her shriek of agony filled the room and nearly destroyed him.

He pulled her closer, wrapping his arms and legs around her as if his strength could shield her from the maelstrom inside her. Her nails dug into his back, hard.

Goddess. He didn't know what to do. He'd never—

The moment of his father's death returned, the memory blinding and instant of how he'd been shielded from the blistering heat. Could he give her his father's mantle? Let her borrow it for a little while? Help stabilize her with his Dual elements like a remote control?

"Sit up, baby. We're going to try something." He smoothed her sweat-stained hair away from her face and gently pushed her back, shifting her in his lap so he could reach between them. He frantically searched his fear-scrambled brain to recall how his father had divorced his mantle and put it into the relic.

"Hurry." Her arms clutched her middle.

"I got you." He kissed her temple and hoped to hell it worked.

He put the vessel between his lips and spoke the Latin words inscribed on the inside of the ring.

"Et ego dabo vobis omnia mea."

He closed his eyes as he realized his father had truly given *all I have to you*. Seconds passed, and a tearing sensation burned deep inside him, spreading over his skin like a full-body Band-Aid being ripped off.

The ring vibrated against his mouth. He tugged the necklace over his head and freed the relic.

"Give me your hand." He took her right one and slid the jeweled band down her ring finger.

A violent tremor went through her.

"What is that?" She sank against him, her breathing taking on a reediness he didn't like.

"My father's mantle. It'll be strong enough to contain the other elements until we get help. Imagine you're a stove and pretend you're adjusting the gas to an easy burn. My primary mantle knows yours, and I'll help it behave. Pretend we're best friends and our Fires are holding hands."

As he'd hoped, his bad joke made the tiniest smile play on her mouth.

Holy shit, this was a long shot…

"The Fire and Air are calming down." Sweat dotted her brow. "The Earth and Water are pissed, but it's like they're locked away."

"You'll have to forgive the mantle for being a bully. Think of your powers as first-graders, and you just gave them a timeout. They're not hurt. We just have to get them to chill out in the corner for a sec and behave."

His phone rang again. Pounding drums and a wailing harmonica and driving guitar.

"That's Kazumi." He looked closely at her face. Goddess, she was pale. "We need her help with the Water. Who do you trust to give us a hand with Earth?"

"I trust both my cousins, but Flora's stronger than Ross." Her head lolled, her eyes half-lidded as she almost dozed off.

"Let's get you back in bed." He helped her to her feet, then picked her up. Even with his mantle, she was leaking energy like a hot air balloon with holes in it. If he felt battered by the ripples thrashing him, he couldn't imagine what it was doing to her.

He placed her gently on the mattress, covered her naked body with the quilt, and went around to the other side of the bed. He picked up his phone off the nightstand and hit Kazumi's number in the call history.

He didn't even hear the call connect.

"What the shit is happening over there?" Kazumi yelled as he held the phone away from his ear. "Is the Astrux back? There's a bullhorn bat signal coming through this bracelet."

"Slow down, damn it! Not over the phone." He balanced the cell between his shoulder and ear and looked at Elspeth, who'd fallen into a restless sleep. "Just get here."

His heart thumped at the dark circles beneath her eyes and the sweat-dampened hair matted against the sides of her face.

"Is Elspeth okay?"

A terrible knot grew in his throat.

"Call Flora, don't say a word to anyone, and get both your asses over here." He ended the call.

He climbed into bed beside her, pulling her naked body against his, her back to his front. Her fitful, jerky sleep made sense, as she was literally in power overload, and her body was trying to shut down. He dialed up his Fire, slowly so he wouldn't startle "the kids" and slowly upped the strength of his new Air. With more care than he'd taken in a decade, he finessed his power into a healing circle around her, containing her elements within an invisible fence. He remembered his twenty-fourth birthday and the moment his power had arrived. He'd been sitting on the hearth next to a massive fireplace in the Fire quarters at the Elite One compound.

He'd sat there, feeling like he'd been dipped in lava, his skin burning like it was on fire. For a moment, he'd been terrified, incapable of sorting all the sensations taking him over bit by torturous bit. It had been overwhelming and horrific, his entire being consumed by pain and power.

Dear Goddess, what the holy hell was it like to have all four arrive at once?

"Help's on the way." He pulled her closer when she didn't respond. "I've got you."

Her full weight pressed against him, seeking contact with him at every possible point. Her breathing didn't slow, staying more labored than he wanted.

"Don't you dare take her away from me," he swore softly to Mother Nature, adding another layer to the Fire wall surrounding the apartment and wishing the Water and Earth cavalry would hurry the hell up.

CHAPTER
EIGHTEEN

"I can't get this." Elspeth looked down at their joined hands, the shakes not subsiding. Her cousin Flora was known for being oblivious to the term *personal space*, but for the first time, Elspeth felt the opposite of uncomfortable. Something inside her strained to move closer, and the powerful Earth leaned in just as much.

The hour she'd spent with her cousin, holding handfuls of leaves and dirt and breathing in the scent of the soil Flora had brought in an urn of pure gold, somewhat steadied the sensation inside her that she could only describe as a massive wall. A wall she felt certain had the capability to crush things like taxis or split things wide…like streets.

"I know this is a lot and you feel unsteady, but I can tell you're good for now. Earth's a little more forgiving than the other elements. Once you can leave the apartment, I'll show you our ways outdoors." Flora broke away and slipped her feet back into her Birkenstocks. "We'll leave the city and find a secluded place in a park where we can lie in the leaves, our nude bodies flush with the ground, with nothing between us and our elements. You'll feel disconnected until we get you truly grounded, but you'll be all right for a while."

Naked in Central Park. That'd take, oh…fifteen seconds to get arrested.

She looked up at her six-foot-tall cousin and saw her in a different light. She had the nature goddess thing going on, her body lithe, her long, stick-straight hair falling almost to her butt. Flora never wore makeup or perfume, didn't paint her nails or color her hair, and dressed only in natural-fiber garments, if she decided to put on clothes.

Elspeth's Earth energy pushed at her skin, her element wanting to attach to Flora, like meeting like.

"You can't stay a little longer?" Her body felt heavy, as if her muscles had turned to cement. "I got no heads-up on this, not one thing, and it feels better to have you here."

Flora's green eyes glimmered with exhaustion. Goddess, Seanair worked her cousin into the ground. She spent most of her time traveling and optimizing soil on large farms, the owners paying Seanair millions to max out their crop yields. In her downtime, Flora either worked to clean up polluted soil or tended her physical element and spiritual practice religiously, her life in clear devotion to their creator.

All in all, Flora was the best of them. The Lennox who lived a simple, devout life.

And had ridiculously strong Earth energy.

"I have to go." She gave Elspeth's hand a gentle squeeze. "I missed my flight to Mexico, so I have to get to the airport to catch the next one. If I get there too late, the client will contact Seanair." Flora whipped the golden sheet of her silky hair to one side. "Don't worry. You're going to be okay. Mother Nature protects Her most important treasures."

"I'm not feeling like a treasure at the moment."

"It seems unfair, but She hid you all this time to keep you out of danger. If you thought families wanted you when you were Passive, that's nothing compared to what they'd have done to get you if they'd had even the tiniest hint you were a Nexus. There are families among us who don't care how they get what they want, as long as they get it."

Selfishly, she'd been too exhausted to think much beyond how the secret world she'd wanted with Aleron couldn't exist any longer. She hated that he'd stationed himself outside her front door, insisting her Earth and Water elements would settle quicker if he wasn't in the apartment.

"Won't I be out of balance without more guidance? This Earth feels like I'm toting around a mountain."

Flora's arms wrapped around her and pulled her tight. "After you work on Water with Zum, handle the dirt, rocks, and leaves I left you. Smell them. Taste them. Take their essence into you. They're sourced from the world's few remaining unspoiled places and will settle your energy. When I get back, I'll introduce you to Freddy."

"Rosewater lightning Freddy?"

Flora's smile turned sultry. "That man can make a tonic. He's a sweet regen, too, when you're in need of a silver-fox Earth daddy."

Given she felt like she'd been hit by a truck that then backed up and plowed over her a second time, sex was the furthest freakin' thing from her mind.

Flora stepped back and hoisted her backpack higher on her shoulder. "When you need to regen your Earth, let me know. Freddy's not for the uninitiated. Someone female or genderless may be best. Feminine or neutral energy's more measured in its approach. No matter who you choose, don't let your elements weaken too much. You'll know, as the energy will feel lethargic. Regens are different for everyone. Some need every few days. Some can go a week or more. You'll have to listen to your energy and stay charged and ready." She pressed a kiss to Elspeth's forehead. "You're going to be magnificent. I just know it. Let Aleron take care of your Fire and Air."

Goddess, she could not consider that now with everything such a mess.

She tried for a reassuring smile. "He's…it's complicated."

Flora's expression turned serene. "No, it's not. He cares for you. I can feel it. I'll give you one piece of advice: Play by your own rules. Not Seanair's. Not our society's. We owe nothing to anyone but Mother Nature, and She has blessed you beyond measure."

Thanks, cuz. No pressure there.

She followed Flora out of the kitchen. A red halo sputtered and flared around her cousin's body as she passed through the Fire shield. Aleron had protected her with this invisible elemental armor, which appeared to be quite complex and strong. How long would it take her to learn how to protect herself? How to shield those she cared about?

Goddess, why hadn't her powers come with a thick instruction manual? Hell, they had a dating app. Why couldn't there be a here's-how-you-work-your-powers app?

Her breathing slowed, and she waved to her cousin one last time as the elevator doors closed. How had she forgotten about regeneration? She'd have to refuel. Would she need four times the sex to keep all her elements charged? What was she going to do about Earth and Water? Tension inched up her throat at the thought of being with anyone besides Aleron.

She heard Aleron say something through the clamor of her what-if scenarios.

"Elspeth?" He pushed off the wall where he'd been standing with Zum and leaned into her sight line. "Is something wrong?"

"No." *Yes.* "I'm tired." She blinked herself to rights. "What did you say?"

The line of concern between his brows deepened. "I said I'm glad you have Flora to help you. Her brother's a real piece of work, though."

She remembered when she and her cousin, who was two years older, had been in elementary school. Lach had had a reputation he followed through on with his fists, so no one had bothered Elspeth. But Flora's twin brother, Kerr, hadn't defended his sister from the kids who'd made fun of the towheaded, pigtailed, pudgy girl who talked to the trees on the playground and apologized to her broccoli at lunch.

The scrap of memory left a fresh cut. Flora had been a kind kid, too kind, and the others had bullied her for her imagination. And Kerr had let them.

"There's not an honest atom in that asshole Kerr's body," Aleron said. Tension flowed from him in hot waves.

Which was why she was glad she rarely saw Kerr.

She looked up at Aleron. "It's weird that they're twins but so different. Kerr could learn a lot from his sister. She's a kind, free spirit who doesn't get her validation from others. She knows her talents, stays true to them, and prefers to leave a soft wake in her path. She'll be here every time I need her. She's always had my back."

His hand cupped her jaw, his thumb grazing her cheek. "Are you sure you don't want her to be in the meeting when you tell Seanair?"

She took his hand in hers.

"When we meet tomorrow, I'm going in alone. It's time I make a stand with my grandfather. He's not going to tell me how to use my power."

Zum nudged her arm. "E, we need to get moving."

"Go commune with Water." His smile was strained. "As soon as I drop my shields for any length of time, your Nexus secret will be out. I want you as strong as you can be when that happens."

She leaned up, kissing his cheek, and willed herself to be strong. She didn't want to tell Seanair, didn't want to leave her apartment, didn't want to do anything to disturb the new, beautiful, fragile bond budding between her and this man.

"It won't take long." She didn't like him staying in the hall. He'd insisted, though, and Zum had agreed.

She closed the door, putting her forehead against it and breathing for a second. A whirling sensation continued to stir inside her, like Air was chasing Fire. Earth tugged at her like it was playing Jenga with her bones. Her Water rolled and shifted with storm-tossed waves battering her insides.

"Come with me. You're hurting." Zum's hand landed gently on her shoulder.

Elspeth turned. Her best friend's expression had turned serious and she'd changed her clothes and was wearing a robe. They went into the bathroom, the room dark, the only light coming from the small, high windows.

Zum closed the door and went to the tub, turning the taps on full blast. Her irises lit and bathed the room in a soft glow. "Humans live for their holidays and weddings, celebrating days involving their divinities, traditions, or other people. Naturas honor a few days, but one's truly special: the day of their birth. The day Mother Nature delivered us here and blessed us with a part of Herself, giving us all we need to do good." She came to Elspeth and took her hands.

"I think a lot of Naturas, of…us, have forgotten that."

"Which is why we have to stay committed to the rituals. We must connect with those like us, to nurture the power inside us so we become our best, most powerful selves." She cradled the sides of Elspeth's face. "I'm honored to still your Water. Take off your clothes, and I'll show you what only Waters know."

The robe dropped to the ground. She'd seen her best friend in the buff a gazillion times, the two of them used to undressing in front of each other since boarding school. The soft light kissed Zum's short frame, her small breasts pert, the thatch of hair at her sex dark and thick. Where Elspeth was all curves, Zum was an ode to feminine sculpture, a study of soft angles, her body a gorgeous work of art.

Her heart thumped as she pulled off her pajama top and slid down the bottoms. She unhooked her bra, her breasts too heavy to go long without one.

She studied her friend, Zum doing the same, and she wondered why humans often despised their bodies. The lines and curves and the blend of bone and muscle and fat created a unique beauty unlike any other.

Zum offered her hands, palms up, and curled her fingers with Elspeth's.

"The twelve-year gap between our twelfth and twenty-fourth birthdays is a critical time." Zum's eyes glowed a faint blue. "We train every day so that when our power arrives, it's not crippling. Water's often dismissed as the weakest element because we seek equilibrium. Each body of water on this planet strives to connect, whether via rivers and streams or underground. Our element requires we seek each other's comfort more than the others. The heavy pollution demands more energy to properly clean the liquid we all need to survive."

"It's amazing." She sensed a part of her reaching out, almost desperate for the embrace of the largest element on the planet.

Zum's gaze cut to the bath. "I'm going to take you into the water and curl around you like we're twins in the womb. There's nothing sexual in this ritual, but we often need bodily contact with nothing between us."

"Is this true for all elements?" Her mind raced in a frenzied quest to learn everything she could.

"Yes, although I don't know the others' private rituals. The connection's way more intimate than sex. Each element has a way to connect, like children who sleep all tangled up like puppies, but we've stopped doing that. We don't even shake hands for fear of revealing our power. Which is why sex has taken on a bigger role, though it has nothing to do with our spiritual side."

"What'll we do?" She noted the water had neared the top, the room warm and humid.

"I'll be behind you, my body curled around yours, as the Gemini. The water twins at birth."

Zum climbed in, not letting go of her hand, and positioned them so Elspeth was closest to the wall. Her pulse accelerated.

"I don't touch people." She had last night, and she suddenly wanted Aleron with an urgency she found hard to fight.

Or rather, people didn't touch her. She now understood the inability to deny an element's need for contact with one of its own kind, the yearning of Water inside her turning desperate.

"We'll take deep breaths and submerge in the water. Let your breath out slowly, then reach for me with your mind. Seek my energy, and my element will seek to still yours. We'll stay under as long as we can. If you start to panic, squeeze my hand, and I'll help you."

Her breath came fast, her nerves flaring. "I'm nervous."

"Elspeth." Zum took her shoulders, turned her, and placed a hand over her heart. "Be still. In here. Seek calm." She sank into the water.

Elspeth followed and propped up on an elbow, her back to her best friend.

"Take a deep breath and go under. Blow the air out slowly and don't inhale."

She took a deep, openmouthed breath, closing her eyes as she sank under. Water plugged her ears, muting the glug of bubbles that sputtered from her as she started to exhale. The space in front of her brightened, and a warm blue colored her eyelids. It didn't take long to empty her lungs, and a thread of panic coiled.

Zum's hold tightened, her best friend's hands cradling her breast and stomach, the hold motherly and reassuring. The water churned, the whooshing sound soothing her mind to blank. Her muscles seemed to relax, one by one, her pain sinking, its grasp loosening. Her mind and body floated, peaceful and stagnant, like a leaf in a puddle.

Something brushed over her, a gentle lapping at her skin, the water washing her, cleansing her, preparing her for some strange birth. She couldn't feel her friend anymore. Water energy flowed away from her, Zum's going into her, the two of them intertwined in this sacred elemental womb. Her temple pressed against something soft, and she sank into a bottomless void, floating down, down, down, toward a dark freedom.

A force yanked her up, her body breaking the surface of the water. Her breath went in, out, water flowing from her mouth. Zum eased up behind her, drawing her back against her chest, her hands wrapped around Elspeth's ribs.

"Half an hour. That's good. It's what you needed." Zum's grip tightened as Elspeth's body wrenched and fought for air.

"I can't breathe." She jerked and gasped, a spray of water projecting from her mouth like vomit. "Let me go. Let me—"

"Don't fight me. Your Water will obey mine." Zum shifted, her grip lifting Elspeth's breasts, her hold ungodly strong. "The first time sucks, but your Water's coming to heel, and I didn't want to tell you the ending when the middle part's so good."

"Let me turn," she sputtered, water draining out of her ears, her eyes, her mouth.

Zum loosened her hold ever so slightly. "I'm not sure what's better, having full knowledge of what happens or going in unaware."

"Did I take on water like a sinking ship?" Her ears finally popped, and her hearing cleared.

"It's a good analogy, but I don't fear drowning, because I know how to give myself up to my element. That's what you did. You welcomed the water inside you, and you won't encounter this resistance again. Be glad you'll only have to go through this initial process once."

Thank the Goddess.

She hugged Zum tighter, burrowing against her, so grateful for the friend she considered a sister.

"The Naturas survive by seeking succor from each other. You have never known the need, the urgency, whereas we normally have years to acclimate. I'm sorry this was frightening." Zum's words vibrated against Elspeth's cheek. "I've shown your Water where to live inside you, and a switch has been flipped that you can't undo. You will have to tend it now, and when it needs communion, if I'm not around, find any source you can submerge in, but there must not be anything between your element and you."

Rivulets of water ran down her face, the trickle from her mouth slowing. "So I breathed in the water?"

Why hadn't she choked or drowned?

"In a sense. Think of your body as a cup that was filled and then drained. Water enters everywhere it can until we're full. Fires surround themselves in flames and don't burn. Airs can walk straight into a funnel cloud. Earths bury themselves in dirt. You'll have to honor all of your elements to keep them spiritually sound, and you'll have to have sex with an element or its complement to fuel its strength."

"I don't want to be with anyone but Aleron." She let her head loll and her eyes close, uncertain she could take hearing anymore truths. She glanced up at Zum. "You know I'm not completely ignorant of our ways, right? Like knowing there are lesser ways to regen without full-on sex?"

"I never thought you were ignorant. 'Intentionally uninformed' is a better term, and I'm sure you can thank Seanair for that. I shouldn't have assumed anything and told you more."

"Maybe. I should have demanded more for myself and asked." She shrugged a shoulder. "A few years ago, I put a contract together for incompatible elements. She was a Fire, he was an Earth."

"No shit?"

"No shit. Their families were prominent enough to be on the registry without being really powerful. Both families agreed because the two really loved each other. It was cool. One of the few true marriages for love I did. The contract, though, specified the details of the regen, that the other had to be in the room, watching. I glossed over some of the specifics because it felt like I turned into a peeping Elspeth, but I admired how they talked through everything and made sure they were comfortable. The love between them was incredible, but it was the total trust that they'd work through things that blew me away."

"You mean if either one couldn't handle the sex outside the marriage?"

"Yes. Who knows what happened in the years since, but yeah, that part of the contract was a big deal. All this is to say I'm not completely ill-informed. Even though I've been treated like I was a human for most of my life, as if I was a mutant thing that had slipped between the bars of the gates, I'm still a Natura. I've always been a Natura."

"Of course you are." Zum's smile went from warm and understanding to wicked. "I can't wait to watch you rub these assholes' faces in it."

Strangely, nothing inside her agreed with that idea. She'd expected the desire for payback to be a slow, calculated simmer, a gnawing need to punish those who'd sneered at her or, worse, simply ignored her existence. She felt nothing, or rather, it was more of a fog, a mist she'd have to wade through to figure out how she'd live as a Nexus. She needed time to process, but her elements seemed to recoil at the thought of revenge, as if they wanted her to do more, to do...better.

"I'm sorry. My brain's all over the place."

"Girlfriend, it's called exhaustion. I don't know if it's different for a Nexus, but I can sense the lethargy of your Water and Earth. Once Seanair knows, I'm sure he'll give you immediate access to a tender." Zum's cheek rested against her head, the two of them slouched like toy dolls. "Aleron knows what's required. I'm sure he's already thinking about the issue, but it's a transaction, and you don't have to be with the same person twice. It's your choice. You do realize why they're used?"

Since she'd never had to consider regenning, she hadn't given any thought to why so many Alpha-level Naturas often recharged with Betas.

"Passives are element seed-passers who level-up power. I never spent time worrying about the kind of refuel sex I didn't need to have."

Zum sat up, the water swirling as she turned. "Betas only until you marry. Alphas don't regen together unless they have absolute trust in the other. Power grabs are real. An Alpha seeking to multiply their energy can steal another's with a one-way pull. The take without the give is the Natura equivalent of rape."

The truth about Kindred's full purpose settled over her, stealing her breath.

"That's the reason for the contracts, for the guaranteed levels of power—the equalization clause—between the couples. I've basically been brokering agreements so one person's not more powerful than the other. That they can refuel each other and enhance their power without the risk of theft."

"Like sex, Kindred's a necessity. There are also Alphas who engage in full, cyclic, honorable sex with their Betas." Zum's mouth pressed into a sad smile. "Because of who my mother is, because of who I'll become, I have to be careful. You do too."

She didn't want to think about adding one more item to her list of things she'd have to beware of. "That's terrible."

"It is," Zum agreed, resettling against her. "But with humans degrading the planet faster than we can fix it, many Naturas have tossed aside their morals to do whatever's necessary to stay as strong as possible to fix the planet. That means mergers for power and pairing with partners you can trust." Zum's finger teased along the edge of the tub. "I get why you feel the way you do. Sex has become a vitamin we swallow, a necessary thing to keep us going when the true food's finding our...perfect half. The person we want to come home to, the one we can be vulnerable with and truly let down our guard with." She threaded her fingers through Elspeth's. "Be careful if you're physically with someone you don't completely trust."

"I will." Frustration clawed at her insides. "Right now, it makes me ill to think of being with anyone but Aleron."

Zum's hand stroked over her hair, slow and steady. "We need two things to function: physical connection and prayer. Naturas don't clutch their pearls at sex like prudish humans do."

"I'm not being a prude. I'm...good Goddess, I don't even date. I was about to get shipped off to some eager-to-procreate Russian, but I've found a man I want. Now you're telling me I can't have *just* him."

"I'm not telling you anything, because you shouldn't even exist, yet here you are, so we'll figure it out as we go. But a couple pieces of advice." Zum released her hold. "If you don't want anyone to know who you're sleeping with, check yourself after you recharge. Signatures linger, so you'll want to conceal the energy you've taken in. I usually picture throwing a blanket over it, so it's like a ghost only I can see."

Goddess, she had so much to learn, and now there were sex ghosts?

"If I feel any more clueless, I'm going to lose it." She closed her eyes, sinking into the comfort of their bodies being skin-to-skin, the contentment of being cared for lulling her into a near stupor. Exhaustion weighted her entire being, and her Fire and Air had resumed their crazed game of chase inside her. "How do I give someone power?"

Zum's chin rested on top of her head. "I really do hate your grandfather. He should have at least educated you on more than the basics for your family's elements."

She had to acknowledge, after a lifetime of trying to hold a place for her grandfather, that she didn't really know Seanair and wondered if she'd ever gotten any true affection from him or if he'd faked his way through her childhood. Her whole life suddenly seemed like a lie.

"I fear he's done terrible things, but I can't worry about that now. Do I have to do anything special during sex to refuel, or does it happen naturally?"

Images from last night with Aleron filled her mind. She wanted to go back to being an ordinary woman, back to being a nothing.

"When you're almost there and you're wound so tight you're seeing stars, you'll feel a push, like your energy wants out to go to your partner." Zum's serene tone was hypnotic, like gentle waves washing ashore. "Then you'll sense a pull, like your body wants to take what it's about to give. You know that moment right when you pitch over and it feels like something's flown free inside you?"

"Yeah," she answered, her mind replaying yesterday's many moments with a man she couldn't see living without.

"That's when the energy cycling happens. And it's...everything. No matter who you're with, in that moment, you're nothing but your element. It's transcendent."

She wondered what that would be like with Aleron but remembered the new rules.

"Even with someone you don't really know?" Her heart fluttered, like it wanted to stop.

"Sweet friend, when you're in that moment, you know everything about the one you're with, which makes it beautiful and vulnerable."

"Right now, I'm trying to keep Fire and Air from ripping up my insides." And trying to keep the remnants of the small meal she'd had earlier in her stomach.

"Aleron can fix that problem." Zum sat up, the water rocking and swirling, her expression solemn. "Your energy's the most soothing I've ever felt. It's even better than my mother's. We may have to have regular Water sleepovers. My element's at peace for the first time in a while."

An idea occurred to her, though she wasn't sure how it'd work.

"Maybe I can help Lach." She recalled touching Rob Costa's hand at the gala. He'd seemed to become more alert at the contact, though she hadn't had any power then.

"E, I think it's time you start accepting what's coming." Zum stood, water dripping down her body. "I've looked high and low for alternatives.

It's a long shot, and it'd be a stretch to find something that would actually help Lach. Have you consulted any witches or warlocks?"

"Seanair says all they can do is call elements. I'm not sure what good that would do. Although I don't know him that well, I could ask Egan." The young warlock had proven eager to help before.

"Seanair excels at telling others they're not worthy. It's time we think out of the box, and that's the only one that came to mind." Zum stepped from the tub and grabbed a towel off the bar.

Her gaze drew to her best friend's thin legs, and her hand shot to her mouth. "Look at your thighs." She got out, Zum handing her a towel, and went to her knees, tracing a finger from her friend's ankle up to her inner thigh, the vein thick and blue. Several branches shot from the main one. The streaks reminded her of rivers. The ones on her breasts splayed like snowflakes.

"I need to go." Zum dried off, a hint of irritation in her tone. "This happened after the last person I had sex with. I was a veined mess."

"Did I do that?" She stood, fearing her power had a mind of its own.

"I have no control over the timing of when Water will decide I should take over from my mother. All true keepers of an element bear physical signs. Legend has it that's how Mother Nature marked her chosen ones. I'm close to becoming the Water Magnus, but apparently the marks have to settle in permanently. It looks like my body's going to be a roadmap of the rivers of my vascular system. Come here." Zum pulled her into a tight embrace. "When Flora comes back, commune with her in a location of her choosing. Your Earth is better, but it needs someone of her power level to tame it."

The ache in her lungs began to subside, but she hoped an Earth-communing ritual would entail rolling around in the leaves and nothing more.

She stopped Zum's search for her clothes. "Hey, I need to thank you. That was…amazing."

"That's what the rite is for. I'm honored I'm the one who got to perform it with you."

"I'll never forget it." She breathed into the calm, new bond with her best friend.

"I won't either. Now that you've been through the best and the worst of it, we'll have plenty more to talk about. Make sure you partake of every element. If you don't, that's when trouble starts."

She followed Zum into the bedroom, wrapped in a towel as the petite Water got dressed.

"There's a piece of good news you're overlooking." She sat on the carpet to put on her high-tops.

"What's that?" Her mind drifted to lemon cake and last night.

"If you do for the Fire boy out there what you just did for me?" Zum smiled, nodding toward the living room. "You could be everything for him. You could calm his Air and answer the call of his Fire."

She could…Goddess, after everything he'd done for her, she could finally be there for him.

"I want more than a regen with him." She wanted her bestie to know exactly how she felt.

"Good, 'cause I'm pretty sure he feels the same." She held up her hand and pointed to the bracelet on her wrist. "Either I'm getting pings of stress because this is taking so long and he wants in here, or he's firing off a hurry-up code. EB's set on broil. Best let him back in even though it's fun as hell to mess with him."

She followed Zum to the door, feeling like a toddler hounding a babysitter. "When will you be back? I have so much to learn."

"You know I wouldn't leave you if I thought you weren't ready." Zum pulled her in for another hug. "Water emergencies are easy to fix. Find water and get in it."

"I don't know what I'd do without you." She cherished the new closeness between them, the connection beyond anything she'd ever experienced with her cousins or brothers.

"You won't ever have to know since we'll be BFFs forevah." Zum hooked her hair behind her ears and opened the door. "It's your turn, EB." She punched him lightly in the arm. "Get her Fire and Air where they need to be. It's time to show Seanair who's the true elemental boss."

CHAPTER
NINETEEN

Elspeth grabbed the oh-shit handle as Aleron pushed the Mini Cooper to its limits.

Taming four powers was like being on a never-ending roller coaster and trying to not puke while enjoying every thrilling second of the loops, the stomach-wrenching drops, and the halting jerk at the end of the ride.

She turned off the satellite radio, unable to take any more Megadeth while racing up I-87 for Tarrytown. She understood Aleron's anxiety about the meeting, his simmering rage at Seanair, but she patted the door handle of her poor little car in apology for having to endure a Fire's wrath.

Her phone buzzed in her pocket, and she pulled it out to check the screen.

Lach: Knew you were a legend. Had a feeling Mother N was playing tricks.

Aleron had been right. Once they'd left the building and he'd dropped his shields, the Natura rumor mill had blown up.

Where are you? Call me!

Can't. You got this. Will teach you how to kick Fire and Air ass soon.

When will you be back in the States?

After a minute or so with no response, she sighed, wishing she could see him. With her new powers, she would be able to sense Lach's elements and would know exactly what was going on.

"Is something wrong?" Aleron's gaze cut from the road and back.

He'd been unusually quiet this morning, bringing her coffee and toast to the bathroom while she got ready. He'd wanted one more day to work with her, but it cost him too much energy to maintain the shields on her apartment. She had to admit that she might need Seanair's help, and Aleron had, too, which nearly sent his temper into orbit.

"Lach texted to tell me he knows. If my Nexus news made it to Antarctica, then Seanair surely knows."

And she could only imagine what her grandfather would say.

"Seanair misses nothing." His gaze stayed steady on the road. "Try not to worry about Lach. If he's with Isidora, he's in good hands. She's rumored to have a soft spot for rebels." His words were meant to comfort her, but the thought of Lach so far away upped her worry.

Frustration rode her, as she needed to get up to speed with her elements quicker. She'd made progress, but not fast enough. Aleron had wanted to work with her for another twenty-four hours before she saw Seanair, but that wouldn't have been enough time to make a major difference.

Today was the day.

"I understand why it bothers you, but I need to see Seanair alone. He won't harm me, and it's important to me to say what I need to say. My history with my grandfather is complicated and strained. I'm done with his half-truths."

She needed to learn *everything* about the Lennox family businesses, not just the Kindred part. A foreboding came over her at what she'd discover.

The steering wheel's leather creaked under his grip. "He's no doubt already cooked up a plan to maximize your value to him. You're now his most valuable asset."

"He can't order me around anymore. I'm strong, and I think he'll find me much less agreeable." Not yet as strong as Aleron, but she'd get there. "Trust me to address the situation, okay? No matter how I feel about my grandfather, I'd rather have him with me than against me."

He downshifted and took a corner hard, the engine's high-pitched whirr and the squeal of the tires filling the car as they raced past the statuesque, leafiness of überwealthy suburbia. Tarrytown. Thirteen miles outside Manhattan, but an hour by car in traffic, with the feel of a small town but with gated driveways, stone walls, and megamansions.

"It's not you I have a trust problem with." He made the turn onto her grandfather's street.

She couldn't have this conversation now, but they needed to talk about his father and his family. There was still so much she didn't know about the situation, but there had to be something she could do to hold Seanair accountable.

"I'll get in and get out." She let go of the handle as they whipped into the drive. "My goal's to leave the matchmaking business to do something more important. I have all the elements in me, which means I should do something for the good of *all* Natura."

She eyed the two solid-steel posts standing in front of a gate flanked by two massive, stacked-stone columns, repeating her vow to herself silently. She could do this. She could do this.

She *would* do this.

She didn't come to the Tarrytown house often, preferring to meet Seanair in the city. There was no call box or guardhouse, but the whole area reeked of money and mistrust with fences and security staff and cameras everywhere.

"You should know he's had Elite One watching your brothers and cousins." His gaze cut toward her. "There's so much for you to learn about the true nature of his businesses. Yes, he looks after North American Naturas, but protection comes at a price. He's had someone in California keeping tabs on Graham in the lab. He knows every move your cousins make. He's got a team ready to deploy should Lach lose it."

Her stomach turned at his confirmation of her suspicions. She did have a lot to learn, but her grandfather couldn't deny her access any longer. She was counting on him wanting to keep his Nexus close, and she wouldn't settle for anything less than being in her grandfather's inner circle.

And keeping Aleron. Her bodyguard would not be reassigned, unless he wanted to be.

Large, obvious, stay-away cameras mounted in the surrounding majestic trees swiveled toward them. The posts lowered into the ground, and the massive, wrought-iron gate slid back slowly in its track.

"Promise me you'll give me the time and the chance to change things." She rested a hand on his leg, the power coursing through them both thick inside the car.

To hold my grandfather fully accountable. To get justice for your family.

"I promise." He put the car in gear and pulled through the gate.

He stopped the car and shifted toward her, stroking a hand down her face.

"Trust me to handle my grandfather." She slid her hand over his on the gearshift. "And trust us. I don't care about class bullshit or Natura expectations. I'm choosing my future, and if you want to be with me, I want you in it."

She shifted in her seat, knowing she'd fallen for him, a massive face-plant into the best man she'd ever met.

"I fully intend to take on real responsibility, and I'm counting on you to educate me." She wagged her brows, hoping to lessen the tension she sensed whipping a firestorm inside him.

"Call me Professor anytime." He took her hand, giving it a gentle squeeze. "We can't ignore the Earth and Water situation forever."

"Later," she whispered, not about to entertain the idea of sleeping with someone else. "Let's get this over with." She trained her gaze on the long, straight driveway striped by two wide swaths of green grass.

He put the car in gear, and they went straight up the drive, faster than she would have, and he eased the car into the circular turnaround with practiced ease.

"He definitely knows," Aleron bit out, his frustration palpable in the tiny car. "The power dampeners are off."

"What are those?"

"Relics fueled by blood to dampen the powers of those who haven't been given clearance. Seanair likely took a blood sample from you and your siblings and cousins as babies so your energies wouldn't be affected."

Looked like her grandfather's many homes were actually elemental fortresses.

Aleron surveyed every pebble, flower, and blade of grass as he walked beside her up the wide stone steps to the front door. As they moved beneath the portico, the knowledge settled deep inside her. The love of her life stood beside her. Aleron was…home. A home all of Seanair's money couldn't buy. A security she'd never had.

Looking at the doormat, she concentrated and tried to create the same safety cone around him that she sensed he'd placed around her.

Protect him, she ordered her elements, facing him and staring up into his face. *Guard him like you guard me.*

Light shimmered around him, a quick rainbow of red, white, green, blue that hovered, caressing him, then disappeared into his skin. She could sense the barrier, an invisible force field she didn't think he could detect.

Thank you. He's important. She recalled how it'd felt to commune with Water, how the honor went both ways. A zing went through her, a we-got-him elemental salute, and a surety resonated inside her.

She could do this. She could have him. She could help her people and figure out how to save Lach.

She went up on her tiptoes, clasped his waist, and kissed him.

"Might as well start this meeting on my terms." She gave him a last quick peck, his wide eyes awash with red and white, his new Air cozying up beside his Fire. "Wait in the foyer. I'll be fifteen minutes."

She went to turn the handle, and the door opened.

Seanair's longtime butler, Miller, extended his hand. "Miss Lennox. What a pleasure. What—Goddess *bless* me. You're real." He bowed like he'd walked up on a deity, his tone filled with awe.

She walked into the rotunda with its soaring, twenty-foot

ceilings and its polished walnut floors. Everything had a recently cleaned sparkle, and the scent of pine perfumed the air. As Miller closed the door, she sensed his Beta power.

"I'm the same person, Miller." Would every Natura act this way around her?

"No. *No.* I—he wants to see you right away." Miller rushed down a long hallway.

"Brace yourself. He'll be angry." Aleron assumed his guard position by the front door.

Anger frothed inside her. Seanair wasn't going to treat him like a second-class Natura anymore—or anyone, for that matter.

"Can you not stand like that?" she whispered harshly, keeping an eye out for Miller. "It's not like that between us. It will never be like that between us again."

"I won't make things harder for you." A don't-test-me look darkened his expression. "When it's just us, I'll be myself. In public, I'll be what others expect me to be."

His gaze shifted to the grandfather clock.

"He will see you now." Miller turned back, and his gaze swung between her and Aleron.

She followed the butler down the long corridor, sensing Aleron close behind.

Miller opened the door to the grand library overlooking the gardens, bowing again as if she were a queen.

She gave an I'll-be-okay nod to Aleron, who stood at attention off the entry, and walked in.

The door shut with a sharp click, almost like a gun cocking.

Her grandfather sat at his desk, *The Wall Street Journal* open and shielding his face. Light streamed through the wall of windows behind him, but he didn't lower the newspaper.

Fine. She'd play his power game.

And win.

She took a seat in one of the two chairs facing his desk. Fire crackled in the fireplace to her right, flanked by floor-to-ceiling shelves filled with books, their mustiness teasing her nose. What she wouldn't give to shut herself in this room alone and dig through his library of ancient tomes. Surely someone must have penned *The Complete Guide to Being a Nexus.*

"How long?" Her grandfather neatly folded the paper.

"How long have I known?"

"Yes."

"Since yesterday morning. I got a birthday visit from the power fairy." She sensed the brewing storm fogging up the room but couldn't stem her irritation at his cool treatment. "Flora and Kazumi know. They had to help with Earth and Water. I was a mess."

His elbows on the armrests, Seanair tapped his fingertips together. No smile. No warmth.

"Who tended Fire and Air? Wait, let me guess. The man I watched you kiss outside my front door on my camera feed?"

"Yes. Aleron's been a lifesaver." She met his glare, not about to hide who Aleron was to her.

"I'm sure he was." He crossed a leg and eyed her like she'd tracked mud across the carpet. "It was a mistake to not trust me first. You could have spawned a tornado as easily as a light breeze. Ages ago, Nero started the Great Fire of Rome because he thought he could shirk his training."

"Aleron handled the situation perfectly." Her hackles erupted. "If you'd allowed me to take upper-level training after boarding school, I wouldn't have been so clueless."

"It would have been cruel of me to rub your nose in your deficiencies." He waved a hand, as if bored.

She caught the curl of Air energy teasing her nose. "If you want to know my capabilities, ask."

She cast off his attempt to measure her strength and mentally high-fived herself at the catch. Maybe she wouldn't be a complete failure at this Nexus thing.

Seanair pushed back in his chair, his hands still joined.

"Aleron's crossed a line I didn't think needed drawing. He seems to have forgotten our agreement. I'll have to deliver a reminder."

She gripped the arms of her chair. "He's a good man. He's

protected me. If you try to harm him or anyone in his family—again—you will be sorry. I know exactly what happened to his father, and you will pay for what you did. You killed that man in cold blood."

"Is that what he told you? I suppose you know everything now that you're a legend come to life. A know-it-all Nexus isn't what I need."

She'd wanted to talk to Aleron before confronting Seanair, but she couldn't keep quiet.

"Do you think I'm going to support your assassination-fits-all policy? You *ruined* the Foussé family. You took everything from a young boy and then condemned him to a life as a hit man because you chose power over your supposed best friend. Bill Foussé was an honest man dedicated to doing the right thing, and you *murdered* him."

Red flashed in the blue of his eyes.

"I regret the event."

She'd come with the tiniest hope she could salvage something with him, get a glimpse of the Grandie she'd once known. When was she going to stop thinking the best of people? He'd changed for the worse, and the only good thing left were memories.

"I don't know you anymore. Mathair died, and you became a monster." Her Fire ignited again, and her hand shook as she tried to keep from lighting up the curtains.

"You have no idea what I deal with on an hourly basis. You are, however, full of surprises." His gaze drew down her as if seeing her for the first time. "Some of my goals may no longer be out of reach."

Oh, please. Did he really believe his own bullshit?

"*Your* goals? Naturas aren't people to you, they're…disposable."

His eyes turned a stormy blue. A cunning smile pulled slowly across his face, and a breeze rustled her hair.

"Do you really believe your Mathair died of heart failure?"

Her elements stilled to an eerie calm, her pulse a drum in her ears.

"That's what you told us. That her heart stopped."

"Guess who stopped it?" The lines at the corners of his eyes deepened. "Nothing smart to say?" His eyes narrowed, his pupils pit viper sharp. "I did it. The day she tried to puncture the lungs of your brothers and squeeze them flat like spent balloons."

He'd loved Mathair. More than life. More than them. More than anything.

"I don't believe you. Lach was, what? Eighteen. Graham was sixteen. They'd remember that."

"Not after ingesting a memory tonic." He rolled his eyes at her evidently non-poker face. "Witches are occasionally useful."

"Mathair had the tripowered disease?" She couldn't remember any signs or symptoms and grasped for the only thing that made sense.

"Yes, and she turned in a blink. Manageable to murderous is usually how it goes, so forgive me if I don't lament openly about your brother," he spat. "Every time I look at him, I relive killing my wife."

"Grandie." His old name slipped out, and she slapped a hand to her mouth.

"Don't you dare pity me. That's what leadership *is*. You sit here and insult me when you haven't a clue what's at stake. Her death was an agreement we made together should the situation turn fatally south. You should make the same deal with Lach now that you can pull it off."

A cocktail of resignation and dread stirred and burned sour in her stomach. She got up and went to the fireplace, uneasy at the ripe, raw Fire and Air energy circling the room. Seanair came up beside her, approaching her as if she were a chessboard.

"I'm not wasting my time on matchmaking," she told him. "I don't know enough yet, but I can feel something's odd with all the elements." She'd noticed an occasional speed bump in her energies, or maybe that was her not knowing what the hell she was doing. "I'm not kissing Natura ass anymore either."

"No, but they'll be kissing yours. There is a better role for you. I need to bring back the Natura High Court. You can be the sole Judex." He looked from the flames to her.

"People will not accept another Lennox acting as a dictator."

A low laugh rumbled. "You have so much to learn about our people. Most of them are not the do-gooders you believe. They act like children trying to steal each other's elemental toys."

"Let me guess. Your version of justice equates to punishment." She met his gaze and held it. "Our people sound broken. I'll work to heal them."

"Are you taking the role as Judex or not?"

A sense of *this is it* ripped through her.

"Yes." She wasn't about to ignore her gut.

"You cannot marry him."

Her breath caught at the abrupt change in subject.

"My relationship with Aleron is none of your business," she managed, her tone daring him to continue.

"I smell his energy signatures all over you."

Shit. She'd forgotten Kazumi's warning.

"I'm not breaking things off with him."

"Then he's as good as dead."

She turned, folding her arms and priming her elements. "You will not harm him."

"Relax," he chuffed, like she was showboating. "I won't have to kill him. There are numerous powerful families around the world who will do whatever it takes to get a Nexus, and who knows to what end? The possibilities are limitless, but I've not considered them, as there hasn't been a recorded Nexus in over three hundred years. Taking out a problematic bodyguard is easy. Aleron can hold off ten, probably fifteen Duals, but he wouldn't survive a gang of twenty or more, and you're not strong enough yet to fight them off yourself. But keep him around if you want a bull's-eye on his back." The swirls of blue in his eyes turned tornadic. "You need me, Elspeth, whether you want to admit it or not."

"I'll get more guards." Accepting his help would be stepping a toe on the dark side.

The rumors she'd heard off and on were true. The ones he'd outright denied.

"You're a ticking nuclear bomb to which no one knows the codes. Until you rein in and hone that hemorrhaging energy, you're a liability to Aleron and our family. When word gets out your powers are real, the war that's been brewing will start." Seanair went over to the bar and poured his usual whisky. "Graham will handle the politics. I had no idea when I called him home for the gala that this was in our immediate future, but now he'll not delay ascending to my position. I can no longer wait until my death is imminent to pass the Fire and continent president torches. No," he said, as if talking to himself, "he'll need me to walk in tandem with him as he learns dangerous ropes."

Shit. No wonder her usually teetotalling brother had drunk a bar's worth of liquor that night. But why start training Graham now? Naturas lived to be well over a hundred. Seanair probably had another thirty years left to rule.

"Have you told Kerr about Graham?" she asked. "He thinks he's getting both jobs."

Her asshole Fire cousin might be the one to burn down Manhattan, especially since Graham wanted nothing to do with Natura politics.

"Kerr's working on something for me and doesn't need the distraction of disappointment."

"He's considered the job his since boarding school."

"Kerr thinks the world was created for him. His talents lie elsewhere." He tossed back a solid hit of his drink. "You have your first issue to handle tomorrow as Judex."

"That's fine." A finger of worry scratched at her. "But I won't give up Aleron. We'll keep the relationship discreet for now."

"There are no secrets in our world."

Her elements stirred at the veiled threat in his tone. "Then I'd better work on gaining strength. I'll kill anyone who tries to harm him."

She struggled to stay on task, but the cyclone of her grandfather's revelations and the idea of danger to Aleron wouldn't settle.

"Since I'll be Judex, you need to appoint an emissary for the Fire cuff. You need to make the move soon. Kazumi is the rightful bearer for Water. If you want to hold on to your continent leadership position, doing the right thing now may save you later."

Zum had never liked her grandfather, and yet Elspeth still yearned for a man who was nothing of his former self. Her Grandie was dead, along with the last ember of hope she could somehow resurrect him. Seanair had better watch out, or someday Zum might challenge his continent rule—with Elspeth as her wingwoman.

"I'm the sole reason North America enjoys peace." Seanair eyed her with disdain.

He wasn't used to his grandchildren talking back to him, most especially her.

Well, too damned bad.

"All I've ever done is try to please you, to show you that although I was powerless, I was still worth something." Her eyes welled. Screw it. He could deal with her angry tears.

A crush of Air and a blast of Fire cut through the room. Her energy rose, deflected, shoved it away like he was nothing more than a human.

"You think I'm such a terrible grandfather?" he seethed. "I raised you like you were mine when those vile witches killed your parents, and now I know why they were so determined. Somehow, they knew a Nexus was coming, and they didn't want whoever it was to live. You were lucky your Mathair kept you, Graham, and Lach home that day, or you'd have been in that car."

"Did witches really kill my parents?" She hadn't believed his assertion long ago.

"I can't prove it, but I've questioned several I believed to be involved, and they eventually caved."

He'd killed them. Tortured them. Her hands shook as the brutal truth of her grandfather's role became perfectly, viciously clear.

"You're not the same. When Mathair died, you and every shred of love you had for me died too." The froth of her anger whipped power, heavy and thick, inside her, drying the last tear she'd ever shed in front of him.

"I won't give up the cuff."

"Then I predict someone will take it from you." She stared at the flames in the fireplace, pleading with her Fire to calm.

They faced each other. He seemed older, tired, yet his power pushed against hers like it was thrilled to meet someone worthy.

"The cuff is all I have left of her. Several months after her death, she spoke to me for the first time as the cuff's Oracle and told me I had to keep it. That the rightful owner would reveal themselves, but that she wasn't allowed to tell me who it was." Her grandfather looked at the floor, his gaze long. "I don't expect you to understand. You've never been in love. The cuff's the only way I can hear her, and I'll go to my grave listening to her lovely voice. Graham will begin training for the continent presidency, but he'll not get the Fire cuff until my death."

"Graham's not the rightful bearer. There's supposed to be a mark, a sign." She thought of the pronounced blue of Kazumi's veins.

"Lennoxes are born to lead. We've ruled for two hundred years, and with you and Graham in power, that won't change." His expression shifted to one she'd seen the night of her twelfth birthday, when she'd become a nothing to him and all the power-reveal party guests. "There's nothing more to discuss but your first job as Judex. You're going out to Montauk tomorrow. Elite One has informed me Rob Costa's at the end. Take Aleron and monitor the death. Rob's last wish is to die on the beach. Build a bonfire so you have something to point to if a human calls the police to report smoke or flames."

"I'm not going to watch a man die." Her gut twisted into knots.

The deep blue of his eyes lightened, and she realized he was actually Air dominant.

"You're likely going to assist the process when he resists. The will to live fights the rising elements. Elite One monitors all tripowereds and often handles the deaths. As Judex, you will likely have to order a Natura's death before the disease gets out of hand. If you can't accept that responsibility now, then you'd better find somewhere to hide. Maybe Isidora would let you join her on an ice floe in Antarctica." Seanair scoffed like he was dealing with a petulant toddler. "Otherwise, man up and do your duty. Aleron knows what to do, and you need to see the end so you'll know what you're dealing with. Lach doesn't have much time."

"How long before…" She couldn't get out the rest of the words.

"Unless he takes a sudden turn, I estimate six months. He thinks cryogenic therapy along with Goddess knows what else Isidora's doing down there is going to delay the inevitable, but it won't. She says his Water's rising."

No. *No.* There had to be something her power could do. How could she gain four elements and still not be able to save him?

"One last thing." His expression went ice cold, obliterating any last trace of her grandfather. "You're not going to break centuries of tradition by marrying beneath you. Power breeds power, which is what we need if we're to undo the humans' environmental mess. If you want war among the families, choose Aleron Foussé. My best advice?" He went to his desk, opened a drawer, and returned with a black business card, shoving it into her hand. "Text that number and get a Beta tender to service that Earth and Water."

CHAPTER
TWENTY

Aleron peered out the guest room doorway, listening to make sure Elspeth was still in the shower. The whoosh from the water pipes in the wall had stopped. No clanging or other kitchen noises. Certain she must still be in her bedroom, he grabbed the candles he'd used to commune from the bureau and gathered up others he found, hurrying into the living room and lining them up along the coffee table's edge and across the mantel. Checking the seals on her apartment for the millionth time, he closed the blinds on the sliding glass door and turned off the lamp on the side table.

Irritation zinged along his nerves as he surveyed the room. He'd wanted to do that ambience thing. Her first regen should be special. She deserved so much more, but instead of fancy, he'd managed dollar-store cheap.

"What are you doing?"

He jerked at her voice.

Elspeth stood in the archway, a short dress accentuating her luscious curves. Super short. Black on top. Green on the bottom. She came toward him, her nipples peeking through the lace, the skirt skimming the tops of her thighs and teasing him with what hid just out of sight. Something revved inside him, already turned on. Heart, lungs, dick. Pumping, breathing, hardening. She chewed her lip and fidgeted like she thought she'd chosen the wrong thing.

"That dress is amazing," came out of his mouth. Wait. *Gown* would have been better. Tiny gown? Sexy gown?

"It's a chemise."

She turned around slowly, letting him see, his eyes catching something white hanging beneath her arm.

A tag.

He forced down a smile at her sweet naiveté. "Is it new?"

"I've had it for years. I've never worn it, or…" She looked to her feet, back to him. "I've never had anyone I wanted to wear it for." She tugged the bust. "Zum made me buy it. It's a little tight."

He made a mental note to let Half Gallon know he owed her a big-ass favor.

"No, it's not." Noooo. In fact, a size smaller would be perfect so those amazing breasts would stretch the lace even more.

"We need to commune and regen. Can those happen at the same time?" She took in the candles, the combined light from the dozen wicks dancing in her eyes.

"They're typically separate. I normally commune alone." Well, if twice a year could be normal.

She was so innocent of their ways. They'd had sex, which easily scored as first place in the best-ever category. His pulse raced, because this wasn't about being her lover. He could do sex with Betas. That was an easy exchange of power, but his spiritual check-ins with the Goddess happened rarely, and he wasn't sure how to respectfully introduce someone into the sacred side of their element. And then there'd been his first regen, consisting of fifteen minutes in an Elite One dorm.

Damn it, she deserved so much more.

He'd never understand how the most powerful Natura in the world, an elemental virgin, had ended up with a man like him.

"I've got to be straight with you. I don't know what I'm doing." He took in the lovely fall of her hair, the vibrant green of her eyes.

"I think you've done just fine." Her eyebrow lifted in a saucy arch.

He stepped in and kissed that perfect brow, then shook his head. "No, sweets. I'm serious."

"Is it because I've never regenned before?" A red flush climbed her neck.

"Yes, but not for the reasons you think." He kissed her other brow, berating himself for embarrassing her.

Goddess, he should tell her the truth. She could decide if she'd lower herself to refuel in his shoddy version of a sacred place.

"In a proper regen, you're surrounded by your element. There are private apartments in the city we could rent that are designed to help us experience the best of each element. In our case, my case, we'd breathe smoke. We'd bathe in flames. Every atom surrounding us would be in service to Air and Fire. This is the cheap version." He gestured toward the candles and the fire in the fireplace.

"There's nothing cheap about this." She turned, taking in the room. "This is—this is priceless."

She didn't understand, and he should have taken the money out of his savings. Found a way to get her to a safe room. It wasn't like he couldn't spare the cash. He didn't like spending blood money, so he'd shoved nearly every dime he'd made into a mutual fund, vowing it would go to a good cause upon his demise.

She perused her apartment again, her expression brightening. "I don't need fancy. This is private and perfect."

"It's not about fancy. It's about letting our elements have free rein. Regens charge our power. Communing strengthens our faith so we don't lose our way. If I could, I'd take you to a cave for both." He recalled the one he and his brothers had played in as kids at home, its true purpose revealed in his advanced Fire classes. "The best ones are underground. Primitive, but it's the closest we've got to First Fire, the moment of creation when the original spark ignited inside us."

"Come here." She tugged him close and stepped into him, her arms wrapping tight around him, her body pressed against his as if he was the only thing she wanted in her world. "I just need you. That's all."

He knew how to fuck, understood how to submit to the primal part of himself and take a woman the way he'd had her the first time. He'd taken her several times, the break inside him widening a little more with every release. It wasn't the mechanics of ejaculation. It was the hole she'd made in him, a gap in the fortress around his heart, the fissure she'd used to sneak inside. He didn't want this to be a regular regen, a basic function, some furious, empty action that would be over in minutes.

He pulled her to the hearth, his instincts begging him to do more for her. "I don't know how to do sweet or fancy or romantic. I don't have the right words, but I swear I want this to be special for you. Your first regen should be…everything."

Like she was.

To him.

"The fact you care enough to want more for me is enough." She leaned in and traced his collarbone with the tip of her nose, and the tender touch nearly undid him. "We'll have our cave someday." Her gaze shifted, taking a quick zip around the room, her green eyes locking with his. "You see me and accept all of me. The good. The not so good. Like I see all of you and want more."

He looked in the mirror above the mantel. Checked his eyes. Still brown. For the space of a second, part of him admitted he'd love to see his eyes go green, the signal she was fertile. A breath later, he cursed a silent streak. The thought of his child in her belly was a dream, but it would be a nightmare to her if she knew the things he'd done.

His old friend anger rose. Tomorrow, she'd walk into the most dangerous situation he'd ever experienced, her power nowhere near strong enough to withstand the wrath of a tripowered meltdown. Time to get his head in the game and take care of her, not daydream like a man with a secure future.

"I need you ready for tomorrow." He could give her a shot of massive strength. A spill of words idled inside him, promises he longed to make but couldn't keep, but he had to give her a truth she needed. "Here's something important you have to heed. If you're with an Alpha to regen, always use your Air to detect their intent. There are those who wouldn't hesitate to steal your power."

"Is this the Alpha version of 'the talk'?"

He gave her the scowl that garnered Natura attention. "I'm serious. I know someone who's been power-raped, and they've never fully recouped their energy."

"I hear you. Kazumi's warned me too. There's only one Alpha I'm regenning with, and I trust him." She gently poked him. "Have a little faith in me, okay? I'll be fine tomorrow because you'll be there. I never worry about my safety when I'm with you. I don't worry about anything, actually."

His worst fears tumbled up and out of him.

"I worry about losing you. All the time. My nightmare is something happening, and either I'm not there, or there's too many of them, and I can't fight them off."

Her soft expression sobered. "What can I do to make you not worry so much?"

"Kick my ass." Power was the one thing he did exceedingly well. "When you can level me, and I can't get up, I'll feel somewhat better."

Only when she was strong enough, when his Fire submitted to hers, would he attempt to relax. He scoffed at himself. Who was he kidding? He'd never not worry about her.

A laugh bubbled up, the sound vibrating through their clasped fingers. "Sounds like a Natura smackdown. I'll need a cool stage name."

Great. "I'm not joking."

She had to understand so she wouldn't learn the hard way.

"Hey." She pulled away and tapped his chin. "When it comes to regenning, I have no idea what I'm doing. You're set to give me a feast of energy, and I might give you a cornflake in return."

"I like cornflakes." *Oh, yeah. Cereal sexy talk.* One more sex foul, and she'd toss his ass out of the game.

She toyed with the chain that held his father's rings.

"The only worrying I want is your skin sliding slick against me, your mouth learning mine, and you straining and driving inside me so I can give you something I don't want to give anyone else."

The words wouldn't come, not sweet ones, but he could give her his dream of a true regeneration, a new ultimate fantasy he'd had to craft with candles and an apartment-sized fireplace.

"There's a slab of stone in a cave I know." He slipped his arms around her, his hands low on her back, his chin resting softly in her hair. "The surface is smooth, buffed to a gentle curve by centuries of use. Branches and sticks and leaves litter the floor, with a narrow path to the altar. I would lead you there." He leaned away, bending so their eyes met. "I'd lay you down and light the kindling around us. We'd breathe smoke and stir the flames to rise and lick over us, burn and whip the world around us, and join our elemental bodies until you needed no more. I would feed you all that I have and give you all that I am."

Her eyes glistened in the fire's glow. He blinked away a rush of moisture, his body tight with apprehension, his soul a wide-open space she could destroy.

She tugged at the towel around his waist. Goddess, he'd forgotten he'd come from the bath to pull together his genius idea of doing something special.

"Undress me," she whispered, her expression open and raw and innocent.

Damning his nerves, he slipped his fingers beneath the thin straps of her chemise and teased them down her arms. Slid the stretchy fabric over her breasts and hips, the wisp of material a soft crush against the carpet.

Words from his inner vault returned to him, his father's words, about how he'd know when he found the right one. He'd not only found her, he longed to claim and keep her, build her a pyre only they'd light.

He took her to the floor, putting his back against the rug and easing her gently over his body, her mouth inches from his.

"I feel it." Her eyes closed, her nose flaring with a deep breath.

His finger traced the lovely angles of her cheekbones, crested the soft rise of her nose, and glided over the V of her mouth. "Feel what?"

"The call of your Fire." Her eyes opened, their green a straight pin piercing his heart. She grinned, and something teased at his elements, her energies beckoning him. "The allure of your Air."

Heat simmered beneath his skin. His heart struck his ribs. The last of his doubts descended back into the memory tomb he kept tucked far away, the place buried deep beneath his elements, where he hid his last good keepsakes of recollection.

He kissed her. Not the assassin. Not the elements. Him. Curling his fingers through the silky strands of her hair. Sucking her bottom lip into his mouth, the plump flesh tenderly caught between his teeth.

Closing his eyes, he focused on the flame in his mind, the gentle stirring of his hair, awakening his smoldering Fire and nudging the newborn breeze of Air to life.

Her irises shifted to a faint orange, the little threads of lightning splintering bright white. Her scent filled him. Rose and the newness of spring in the air. The errant thought came he had no clue how his new power would react or if he could control the exchange. She smiled down at him like he was her whole world, and his worry disappeared.

"Take me inside you." He didn't recognize the need in his voice, something so much more than desire, something he'd never known existed, much less could have. "Your Fire's dominant."

"Is that good?" She sat up, her breasts beckoning him, full and ripe, in a gentle sway.

His breath rushed in at the glide of her fingertips over him, at the point of him against her softest skin, the push inside, and the beautiful, final breach, his eyes rolling back as she took him in fully.

"I'm still Fire dominant." His mouth opened at the slow rise and soft sheath of her tightness. "It means…we're the best match."

He reined in his element's need for fuel, willing himself to build her up to a slow, breathless burn. The desire in her gaze shot through his veins, and his skin colored a medley of sunset hues.

"So good." Her eyes glazed over, the drunken pleasure of energy a heady rush of sensation. She moaned, going all the way up and slowly down, her hips rolling, her hair spilling all around her.

He sent a wisp of cool air across her breasts, and her nipples hardened to tight, pink buds. Desire swarmed him, a need to claim all of her. Body, mind, and element. He yearned for all of her, every scrap she'd feed him, wishing for more than a few hours to tend her. He grabbed her waist, stilling her.

"Wait, baby, or it'll be over." She was going to kill him, especially if the untold levels of power he sensed swirling around them went any higher. His death would be a slice of erotic heaven.

"Too excited, Mr. Foussé?" She tensed her muscles around him.

"Don't do that. Yes," he wheezed, his beautiful death certain.

He slid his hand near where they joined, his fingers teasing the spot urging her forward on a broken breath.

"Yes. Right there." Her rasped confession surrounded him.

"Tell me when you're close. Together is best." He prayed he could hold out long enough.

His body and brain were reduced to primitive function at her slick, wet heat. He circled two fingers, feeling her tighten, her soft moans hardening him to painful fullness.

A breeze tossed her hair, feeding the flames in the fireplace, the whoosh growing.

"I feel it." She resumed her slide, up and down, increasing the speed, waves of crimson rippling from her skin, the air around them blustery. "I need it."

"Take my hands." He threaded his fingers through hers, his arms straining as her head fell back.

"Almost there. Almost." Her mouth dropped open, and she rode him hard, losing herself in the rapid build of elemental power.

A tight twist coiled inside him, building, burning. A blowtorch of flame shot up the chimney. Candlewicks flared, wax spilling over the table. Her hair lashed her face. Air shoved into his ears, his nose, his mouth.

"Aleron." She came down on him, hard and frenzied, a long, soft groan filling his ears. Her back arched, and she froze, all sensation reduced to a rapturous lock-and-release around him.

Glass shattered. The air swelled and retracted with a slap. A wall of power wrapped tight around them.

Fire and Air pummeled him. A breath punched from his lungs. Bursts of bright light blinded him. His hips jerked, and he came so hard, tears leached through the tight pinch of his eyes.

As if they were in the very cave he'd craved, they were engulfed, surrounded, encased in a cage of flame. As wave upon wave of orgasm shook them both, Fire consumed them, taking the offering of their union and giving back an inferno of power.

A brutal squall of Air funneled a vicious vortex around them, the power terrifying and terrific and beautiful. Flames licked over their skin in a frenzy of fiery tongues. An orange fog stirred thick in the room. He sensed his back leaving the floor, her body hovering just above his, the tornado of energy cocooning them in light, in air, in the perfect state of grace.

It took moments, eons, but the heat slowly receded, and his body met the rug again. A grave sense of loss plagued him at the departure of their elements, but he looked around wildly, sure the apartment would be a three-alarm blaze.

No.

It was just her. And him. His Fire sank deep and warm in his skin, his breath filling his lungs with the purest Air. An unfathomable satisfaction fanned out inside him, an indescribable satiety seeping into his muscles, his bones, his blood.

He blinked, his nose near hers, the full weight of her body a balm. The mist blanketed them, arcs of static forking through the orange fog, the air laden with the scents of smoke and ash.

She tried to sit up.

"Stay." He tightened his arms around her. "It's a halo."

"Halo?" She slumped against him, her nose stroking along the side of his neck.

"Elemental fallout. It's a blessing."

"I understand now. You must crave this."

He shook his head. "I've never transcended. I never believed in the mystical enlightenment stuff they teach in Natura sex ed."

"I understand why they call it a blessing."

"I don't count myself in the blessed category." He kissed her forehead and breathed in the rightness of their mingled scents. "At least I didn't used to."

He wished for a do-over, a taking back of all his sins, a return to when hope and a single dream filled his heart. He'd wanted a family. Wanted to find a wife, to make a home, fill it with kids, and take care of them. Love them.

Damn it, why did his mother and brothers keep reappearing

in his mind? He'd banished their memories, committing them to ghosts, who kept returning to haunt him.

"Let me sit up, and I'll show you a Fire communion while the elemental afterglow's still here." He quick-kissed her hair and helped her rise, getting them situated so they faced each other, their knees touching. "You're definitely Fire dominant." The fading pink in her gaze thrilled him. "We wouldn't have had a halo if you weren't. Most Duals will tell you that while their powers are balanced, one of them takes the lead."

He tried to blink back the disorienting hangover that followed what they'd done, but he had no way to process that nuclear-level regen. In all the locker room talk at Elite One, nobody had ever bragged about the whole universe spreading out before them after sex.

"Is it always like this?" She looked up at him.

He pushed the sweat-matted hair from her face and took her chin, dragging his thumb along her jaw. "I don't know. It's never been that way for me."

A smile tore across her face, her laughter low and sultry. "Can we do it again?"

He leaned down, cradling her face and kissing her mouth like she'd break. "We can absolutely do it—"

He sensed the ribbon curling toward them from the fireplace. Their heads jerked toward the hiss of flames, surprised gasps coming from both of them.

"Hold out your hand and watch." He stretched out the arm closest to her.

She followed his lead, and he shortened his reach, hooking his pinkie with hers.

The light spooled a solid orange with little flickers of yellow along the edges. The bright band tapped her thumb, bouncing to the next finger, leaving an arced orange trail as it kissed each tip. The thin band flattened, widened, the ribbon a bracelet racing around their wrists. He stared at the circle of light, watching it whip and dance and spin, as if Fire was performing for them. Gently, the light slowed and fizzled, disappearing into their skin. The budding essence of Air whirled inside him, stroking his Fire, an invigorating effervescence traveling the length and width of him, his skin showered in sparks.

A long, slow breath left her. Her head rested on his shoulder as their joined hands lowered to his leg. They stared at the now calm embers, his temple leaned against hers, watching the soothing flicker of light.

He wasn't sure how long they knelt there, not saying a word, sitting still in the presence of an otherworldly form. He couldn't explain how he knew, but he obeyed the unspoken order and pulled her to her feet.

"Come to bed with me." He kissed her knuckles. "Let my Fire and Air feed yours again."

He didn't know what to do with the adoration sparking in her green eyes. He followed her into the bedroom and spent the next hour upon hour losing count of how many times he entered her and how long it took for her cries of his name to turn hoarse. They slept and they woke, and he brought her to bliss, again and again, until his muscles begged for rest. He curled his body around hers, bringing his arm over her, her full breast filling his hand.

And fell into the deepest sleep.

CHAPTER
TWENTY-ONE

E lspeth stared up at the gorgeous beach house, wishing she could stay inside the Mini Cooper. She'd driven this time, to have something else to focus on besides impending death, and had peppered Aleron with a barrage of questions so she wouldn't have to face a cold, hard fact.

Even coming into all four energies, it'd taken the ritual with Kazumi and the halo in the sexual afterglow with Aleron for her to accept what they were—living, breathing elements—at their core, that they were *other*.

Seeds of element power planted and matured to ripeness in the confines of a human body. An "other" meant to return to its original form.

They climbed from the car, heading up the stairs and taking the wraparound deck to the boardwalk.

As they crossed over the dunes and reeds stretching down the beach, the line a sandy sentry between the sea and several jaw-dropping homes, the wind whipped at her navy maxi dress and long cardigan. She focused on the horizon at the ocean's edge and considered their final destination, the infinite bounds of the universe where all Naturas once floated freely, shuddering at the idea of leaving her human body now that she knew what wonders her people felt every day.

She stepped onto the beach, her Fire energy keeping her nice and toasty, the sand pushing between her toes. She needed a diversion from what awaited her. "Why do you think Seanair's tapped Graham as his replacement so soon?"

"I'm sure it's not a good reason." He toyed with the chain around his neck, his polo shirt and dark slacks plastered against a muscular body she now knew so well. "Seanair's great at the shiny-object trick. The transition of power will draw attention from whatever his real goal may be." He moved toward the firmer sand at the water's edge. "When I'm in the situation like you're about to be in, the one thing I'm sure of is I'm saving others, even the humans who don't deserve what we do for them. The reason we tolerate their disrespect of the planet while we try to teach them to do better is we're responsible for their evolution. Once we get them to a place where they know how to heal the environment, we can return to our original element form. Essentially, the earth will return to a human Eden, but for us, it will be Natura paradise again."

"That'll be a while. They have a lot to learn."

"True." He stopped and put his hand on hers. "Listen, I know it's hard to believe, but what you're seeing today isn't a sin to our people. I respect the hell out of Rob for handling a situation that only ends one way. Once he immolates, all three elements will return to the source, and he'll be healed. Our afterlife is one of elemental unity and spiritual joy, which is why we commune, to feel and pay respect to pursuing purity. It takes guts for him to go out on his own terms."

"I wish there was a way to save him."

"If Rob doesn't do this, his elements will overtake his mind, and he'll lose his memory of anything earthly. Whole families have been killed by an out-of-control tripowered." He shook his head. "Damn, I wish you didn't have to do this."

She wouldn't stress him further by admitting she wished the same thing or conceding that she actually saw Seanair's point. If Lach decided on a similar end, she had to know what she was dealing with, because no way would she let her brother die alone. The thought of gaining experience with essentially putting someone in a Natura Faraday cage until their elements broke free of their body nearly crippled her. Aleron would help her today if she needed it, but he couldn't bear all the responsibility, and *Goddess*, she could not screw this up.

If becoming Judex meant she'd order death, then she needed to see the result of her actions. She hoped to change the job's responsibilities and allow families more control rather than ordering Elite One to handle the problem like Seanair had done for years. But she couldn't worry about her new role right now. Nor could she think about Lach. Her only concern had to be honoring the wishes of a dying man and helping him, if need be, leave this world with dignity and grace.

"I don't want to be sheltered from what we are." The ocean's saltiness pushed into her, the sweet tang of turbulent waters riding the wind. Aleron's Fire and Air vibrated at a higher frequency, the timbre of being fully charged, but beneath the smoke of his steady rumble of power were the fumes of an emotionally exhausted man. "Life's not always beautiful, and we can't ignore the parts that aren't pretty. Rob needs us, so we're here."

He pulled his cell from his pocket, frowning at the screen as they crossed onto dry sand, heading toward a dense thicket of trees.

"Elite One's reporting an odd energy in the city, elemental in nature but off. I don't like this Astrux thing. It's been quiet for too long, so I'll teach you about shields when we get back to your apartment. Yours combined with mine is the level we need. That thing wants you, and I sure as hell don't like you being exposed out here."

"We have to accept the risks." She couldn't think on it now, and great Goddess, they didn't need one more thing to worry about. So much had happened, the attack in the alley seemed like ages ago. Her biggest concern now, though, was the fear Seanair had set her up to fail with Rob.

But she wouldn't. Not with Aleron there to help if she needed him.

Rob's sister emerged from the trees. With every step toward Liz, Elspeth's anger rose. She wondered again what point her grandfather wanted to prove with this assignment. That Lach had no hope? She wasn't giving up. She would find another option. The choice hadn't made itself known yet.

"Ms. Lennox." Liz's long black dress rippled seaward.

"Elspeth, please. Or whatever you'd prefer."

"I'd prefer not to see my brother die. I'd also prefer no witnesses, but Seanair demands his proof, so here you are." Liz pushed back the fall of her red hair, her fair skin highlighting the dark circles underneath her eyes, her lacy dress not hiding the extreme thinness of her body. "I hope there's a flare of decency in all that power. He's to feel no pain. Understood?"

Aleron stepped forward. "I'll ensure it's instant."

"I'm sure you will." Liz cut a piss-off glare at Aleron.

"You have no need to fear me today or at any other time." Elspeth didn't try to ease the moment with a smile or trite sentiments.

"You're a Lennox. Forgive me if I don't take you at your word." Liz's glance went from her back to Aleron. "My father may pledge his allegiance to Seanair, but I don't."

"That's fair," Elspeth conceded. "I hope, one day, you'll have a different opinion of me." She reached for Aleron's hand, but he stiffened and stepped toward the path leading to the jetty.

Her heart blamed Aleron's distance on the stress of the assignment, but her gut shook its head. She wanted to believe he'd withdrawn because they weren't alone and he was keeping their relationship quiet as they'd both agreed. But she'd caught him watching her along with his intense stares at nothing, as if he searched to solve the world's problems, or maybe just hers. He thought he knew what was best for her, and if it meant them being apart, he was wrong.

Another problem to add to her growing list.

Liz led them into the thicket of shrubby trees. "Rob's last good day was the one after the gala, after he sat next to you." She stopped at the clearing. "Did you do something to him? For those few hours and the rest of the night, he was better."

Aleron's hand landed low and warm on her back.

"Nothing other than talk to him." Her stomach knotted at the note of hope in Liz's question. She understood desperation. "If I could spare Rob, I would. I'm unsure how much you know, but my brother's dealing with the same thing. That's why I initially agreed to marry into the Russian dynasty. Unfortunately, their treatment isn't what we thought it was. My brother'd never allow himself to be placed in a coma."

"Rob wouldn't either." A resigned smile pulled at Liz's mouth, an angry red line below her bottom lip as if she'd been biting it. "The brightest stars won't be dimmed. They're either white fire or nothing."

White fire. That's Lach. And he'd always burned bright in support of her.

Liz's gaze switched to the two men standing at the point's rocky edge. "I can't believe you've been blessed with all this power and can't do anything to help Rob. I know what I saw. He was better. You somehow made him better."

She clung to the strength heavy in Aleron's focused gaze. She'd had no power at the gala, or had she? Had Rob's brief improvement been her doing?

Liz's fingertips swept over her cheeks, her chin quivering. "Let's go. He had a moment a few minutes ago where he didn't know me."

They headed for the two men saying their last words to each other. Aleron tapped her arm, letting Liz walk ahead.

"Erratic behavior and dementia are normal at this point." He kept his voice low. "His energy's splintering. Contain him the best you can. Think of it like surrounding him in bumpers his power can bounce between. This won't take long, but even if it's risky, let's give them a few minutes. Prime your powers. Once you preload, you can extend your reach. Give him about a six-foot diameter so his energies won't sense a challenge."

On the drive up, he'd briefed her on Fire and Air, giving her the terminology required to command the energies until her power synced with her mind and the two worked in tandem.

Fire sprang to life. Air swirled around her, teasing over her skin and toying with her hair. She readied Water, looking out at the distant waves and focusing on an undertow.

Wield.

A wall of energy came from her left. She threw out a hand, and the invisible force held, undulating and rippling.

"It's the word and the speed," he whispered.

Return. Slowly.

The energy crawled toward the sea, piercing the water and leaving no wake. Her arms tingled, her nerves electric. Too much.

"You're doing great. I would have doused myself."

She smiled at the compliment. Juggling three elements was hard enough. Time for the fourth.

Wield.

Nothing happened. She gave the command again. Waited. Earth reminded her of Lach's bulldog sitting down and refusing to budge the moment someone put on her leash. She considered a rest, then slipped off her sandals. The second her toes dug into the sand, the barest tremor vibrated beneath her feet.

"If you feel his Water collapse, you can bolster it with Earth or more Water, whichever you feel steadier with." Aleron returned Jon Costa's nod. "They're ready. You'll be fine. Surround Rob, and I'll be your backup fence."

They headed for the end of the jetty.

"Are you sure we can't—"

"There's nothing you can do to make this better." He slowed as the sand gave way to the rockier terrain of the manmade point. "They've had time to say goodbye, which is more than most people get." He nodded toward the burst of seafoam exploding against the rocks. "The moment he disintegrates, whip his ashes over the sea." His tone deepened. "I don't want them to smell it, as that scent never leaves you."

Her heart squeezed at the pain in his voice, but he wouldn't appreciate comfort. The wound of his father's death wouldn't heal, and there wasn't any benefit to her picking at the scab. They stopped a yard from the Costas, and her elements bobbled around her with two on each side.

While the family bowed their heads and gathered in a group

hug, she stared down the shoreline. On this end of Montauk, houses were large and few. Still, they'd chosen an optimal, secluded spot, as there could be walkers on the beach. A boat in the water. A security camera. Technology, in particular, wasn't a friend to their race. Naturas were now a cell phone recording, long-range lens, or a drone video away from discovery.

Rob lumbered toward them, his gait that of an old man, dressed in navy chinos and a loose, pale yellow sweater. Behind him, the dying sun cast his face in shadow, outlining the softening of a once-toned body.

His energy hit her, the struggle a vicious tug-of-war between Fire and Air and Water.

Goddess bless.

Wrong. So wrong and broken. She willed herself to smile with no hint of her horror. Rob stood in front of her, and her heart nearly stopped.

Trails of red, blue, and white streaked down his cheeks and over his jaw, his elements bleeding from his eyes.

"It's not pretty at the end, but you need to see what you have to fight." Rob put a hand over his heart, like he held himself together. "Feel how my energies are cracking and less distinct so you'll know the signs with your brother."

"I feel them." She eased her energy around the pointed edges of his power, needing to know what Lach faced. "Does it hurt?"

"Yes."

She retracted her power carefully and schooled her expression so he wouldn't sense her distress. Was Lach's energy crackling and shattering the same way? Goddess, they both had the same mismatch, that third wheel of Water so wrong for him, and for Lach.

"Thank you for coming." Jon Costa came up behind his son, his dismal tone matching the slump of his body.

"Of course. We'll help however you need." Elspeth clasped her hands behind her back, not feeling at all qualified, but circling her energies loosely around Rob.

"Give me a little more room. I don't want my power to seek the pureness of yours." Rob's shoulders shook with strain.

She imagined taking her foot off an accelerator, the power less and pulling back. "Is that better?"

"Yes." The word came out pained.

Pressure built behind her eyes at his upturned chin and thinned lips. She tensed her stomach, determined to be strong for the man whose pride was draining his energy. Bruises covered his legs and forearms, as if his elements tried to shove their way through his skin.

She curled her toes tightly over the sandy rock, the abrasion steadying, the ground answering with the faintest quiver.

Rob's expression faded like a board being erased. "Make sure I don't hurt anyone."

Her heart slowed to the point she wasn't sure it still beat. Could she really stand there and watch a man take his own life?

"You've got this." Goddess, he was so brave.

"I'm not afraid." Rob's gaze locked with his father's, man to man. "I'm really tired, Dad. Really tired."

"I know, son. I know." Tears flowed freely down Jon's tanned face.

Aleron cleared his throat. Liz stepped to her brother's side.

There had to be a fix. Some way to transfer energy into him. Or extract the third power out of him. Something. She'd always considered their people so fortunate, their wealth and secret power allowing them to survive through the ages when humans had easily perished.

But here she was, the most powerful woman of their kind, a legend, a fantastically powered freak, but completely and utterly useless at a moment that truly mattered.

She steeled herself, vowing to dive into other options tomorrow. Lach would not die. Not like this.

"Do good and be careful." Rob gave her a weak nod. "Everyone will want you now."

What did she say? What—

"I will find a way to fix this for others. I promise you." The last words came out a whisper. She blinked hard, determined to be as strong as this tortured, courageous man.

She cleared her throat of the rising acid. The small hope she'd held of being able to change something, even a small part, fizzled. There wasn't one damn thing she could do.

Rob turned to Aleron, and his head cocked. "If I find your father, is there anything you want me to tell him?"

Surprise slashed Aleron's stoic expression. "Tell him...tell him I'm sorry."

"Why that?"

"I'm not the man he raised me to be."

"There's no honor left in the bad people you eliminate, brother. A wayward Natura only has one option, and that's to return to the heavens." Rob's gaze glazed over, as if he had difficulty staying focused.

Aleron paled in the dusk's shadows. Her heart about split wanting to go to him, but she had a job. A job she decided she wouldn't wish on anyone.

She erected the first band. Red Fire. Then white, green, blue. Like Saturn's rings. Aleron stood beside her. His power layered between the concentric circles, his Fire and Air to hers. Just there. A formidable plan B, if needed.

"I'm ready." Rob took his father's and sister's hands, and they walked to the jetty's edge. He was a man desperate for release, starving to return to peace and become one again with the rhythm of the universe.

She and Aleron followed, hanging off to one side, close enough to get to Jon and Liz, if necessary. She couldn't picture Lach. Not slumped and swaying like Rob. Not ever.

"I love you, son. I'm proud of you for fighting so hard. I'm proud of the young man you are." Jon pulled both of his children to him, the family huddled in a tight circle.

"You're the best, Dad. I'll save a space for you in the next place." Rob leaned against his father. "Don't let your anger consume you, Lizzie."

"I love you, Robbie." A sob escaped through Liz's wavering smile.

"I love you too, Lizzie Lou."

"Step back." Rob let go of his family and put his feet together, crossing his arms, a mummy standing against a backdrop of dying light. "I'll see you all again in the stars."

Jon and Liz clung to each other, both of them dead-eyed and silent.

Wind whipped through Rob's wavy brown hair and tore at his clothes. Power rose. Immediate and crushing. Fire. Air.

Elspeth dug her fingernails into her palms, g-force pressure driving her a step back. She gritted her teeth, leaning, pushing, shoving against the incredible crush of Rob's primary elements. She struggled to keep the rings evenly spaced and the buffer intact.

The ground beneath her shook. A wave rose behind her.

Holy shit. Holy shit. Holy—

The air swelled and shrank. Thunder cracked, and a boom shook the ground. A deep-red light flashed and spun around Rob. A deafening roar speared her ears.

Everything stilled. Air. Land. Sea. The sunset seemed to hold, the orange ball glimmering in salute.

Tiny lights floated above where Rob had been, black diamonds suspended and shimmering.

Wield. Strong. Heavens.

A blast of wind caught the embers, launching them toward the cloudless sky. Something tugged in her chest, a tiny snippet tearing off and trailing Rob's remains into the twilight.

Her power retracted, and she fell back, Aleron tugging her against him.

Liz's voice tangled with the crash of waves, the traditional version of their prayer blending with the ocean's song.

Her vision wavered, and she sagged against him, trying to make sense of what she'd seen. She blinked, shook her head, a fog of disbelief clogging her mind.

No blood. No guts. No scent. No remains.

Just gone.

A long, low wail carried over the surf's brutal crash. Liz fell to her knees. Jon stood at the rock's edge, his expression blank, an arm extended like he could call Rob back.

"You good?" Aleron tightened his hold.

"I got it." She stepped away and focused inward. The edges of her power felt frayed. Torn. Ragged. She exhaled through her mouth, hoping to blow out the bits of energy she'd ingested.

Aleron wrapped his arms around the shocked shell of Rob's father, pulling him close. He whispered words Elspeth couldn't hear, but she watched the bodies of two grown men tremble with grief.

She snapped out of her daze and knelt in front of Liz, who was rocking back and forth, her body racked with devastating sobs. Putting a hand on Liz's thigh, she opted for silence, not about to offer up a *sorry*. That shit word meant little and did nothing.

Liz raised her head, her cheeks streaked black with mascara. "You have to *do* something. There are others besides the Russians who are working on treatments. If all that power of yours can't fix anything, marry into the fucking syndicate closest to a cure. Our people need help." Her voice broke. "Unless you want to watch your brother scatter to the winds like mine just did."

Liz jerked up and stormed over to her father, putting an arm around his shoulders and guiding him away from Aleron and toward the trees.

Goose bumps scattered over her body at a truth she didn't want to admit. Unlike before, she had no uterus to broker. Sure, she had immense power, but how could she use it to help Lach? If a viable treatment or cure came along in time, she could barter herself in return for the information, but would that be enough?

She had to do something. Lach couldn't feel like that. Fracture like that. Go like that.

Aleron's hand gently grazed her shoulder. "You did—"

"Nothing." She jerked around. "I did absolutely *nothing*."

Not waiting for him, she stormed down the jetty and thrashed through the pine scruff, unable to flee the truth fast enough. As she got into her Mini a few minutes later, Aleron sat down hard in the driver's seat, the car jostling when he slammed his door shut.

"Now you know what we are, what we fight."

"I can't do it." She met his gaze. "I can't do that for Lach."

He looked over at her, his expression unreadable. "Liz was right. Other nations are working toward a cure. If the right one comes along, they'll gladly hand it over…in exchange for you. A powerful alliance is what you need…an alliance I can't give you."

He cranked the car and pulled away, the pea gravel crunching beneath the tires.

She had two options: her brother or her bodyguard. There wasn't a choice. Lach would not share Rob's fate. She'd choose life over death.

And kill the dream of marrying a man she loved.

CHAPTER
TWENTY-TWO

Aleron pulled around the circular drive in front of Seanair's Tarrytown palace. He'd spent the day lining up an Elite One detail to protect Elspeth and had Half Gallon on best-friend duty inside the apartment. He ran through his checklist one more time of the guards he'd handpicked, one of each element, and the rotation schedule he'd created.

He was encouraged her energies had read stronger today, but a report from Command had stripped away the fleeting positive moment. A Montauk Earth family had sensed an unusual presence last night. If he hadn't known better, he'd swear the Astrux was collecting data. Sniffing around. Learning their signatures. Studying its enemy. But Astruxes didn't have the kind of logic and cunning such maneuvers required. He didn't have another explanation, though, and unknowns only increased his paranoia when it came to protecting Elspeth.

Leaving her in the apartment had been excruciating, his Fire and Air and soul erupting in protest. Orange static crackled over his hands, as if his own element flipped him the double bird.

Killing the engine, he eyed the Air guards stationed beside the gas lanterns at Seanair's front door. Jogging up the steps, he shifted his attention to the more powerful Air on the right. He missed the added power of his second Fire mantle, but he wasn't about to take it back from Elspeth.

Besides, his Air had cozied up with his primary Fire and fueled his original mantle way past its former strength.

"Go in. He's expecting you." The woman opened the door.

Inside, two prick Fires he detested stood at the archway of the hall that led to the study. Their power registered as…stale, one guy worse than the other, their energy sooty and sticky, but he didn't stop to question them about why.

Getting this meeting over with and returning to Elspeth took top priority.

Heading down the long hallway, he sent up a prayer.

Goddess, please let this go well.

He stood outside the library, the truth a jagged nail slowly puncturing his soul. Weeks before, he'd planned to kill the man on the other side of the massive door. Now, he was letting go of the one thing that had fueled his entire adulthood. While he knew to the bottom of his rusty soul he'd made the right decision, it'd been far from easy.

He couldn't forgive. He couldn't forget. But he could make a different choice.

And he had.

He'd chosen Elspeth.

Over his father. Over his family.

Dad, I understand now what you meant. I love her. I have to be the one to protect her.

Unfortunately, he'd also accepted that no matter what he felt for Elspeth, he couldn't have her, not like he wanted. He'd been certain his father's death had torn out his heart, but no, there'd been ragged remains. If he could see inside his chest, he'd find a spear, skewering the leftover pieces.

He focused on his Fire and ramped up his Air. Full power. No hesitation. He couldn't afford anything less with Seanair. No matter how this meeting turned out, he wouldn't hurt her by killing her grandfather.

He'd expected to feel guilt, shame, or at least a flicker of failure in the dying flames of his revenge, but a weight lifted. His shoulders, heart, mind, all of him was lighter. He breathed. Deep. For the first time since that horrific day.

His Fire and Air in damn fine form, he sucked in a fortifying breath and walked into the study, straight toward the long desk. A massive tome, its edges yellow and frayed, lay open. Seanair didn't look up as he guided his finger along a line of text that was more symbols than words.

"Come in, Aleron."

He waited for a smartass thought bubble to pop into his head. It didn't, so he stood behind the two chairs in front of the desk, his hands loose at his sides. He glanced around, the décor giving off the country-club feel of the Savannah house, but the bits and baubles were meant to distract, to fool people into thinking the Lennox tartan draped over the oversized chairs by the fireplace was a blanket, not a symbol of power.

The solid wall of books? *Look how learned I am. An educated man could never do such horrible things.* The crossed swords mounted over the mantel on a gold plate? *History, heritage, honor.* Rows of silver, framed pictures marching down the walls? *See what a beloved family man I am?*

All lies. Or, maybe he'd once been a benevolent ruler.

Maybe…not.

Seanair maintained his power play, studying the worn pages as if he were alone. Aleron would let him play his games one last time.

Moving to the wall of family pictures, he bent closer to study the one that caught his eye. Seanair held a little girl in each arm, the dark-haired child with moss-green eyes obviously Elspeth. She looked to be about five, holding a stuffed purple pig in one hand, her head tipped to rest against Seanair's. The sweet grin on her little face exuded utter happiness at being held by her grandpa. Flora had to be the older, towheaded one who had a sunshine smile and the same I-love-Granddaddy posture. Even Seanair's expression was pure proud grandpa, the anger and bitterness missing from his eyes.

Where the hell had that man gone?

Seanair cleared his throat. "It's too bad I can't kill you."

The desk chair creaked.

"Give it a shot." Aleron met the other man's gaze full-on. "You might not find it so easy this time. I don't stand before you as someone who loves and trusts you enough to come in exposed and vulnerable, like my father did."

Might as well start with honesty, since shit was about to get real. Without waiting for permission, he took a seat in one of the visitor chairs.

Seanair sat with his legs crossed, his expression pleasant, like he had all damn day, but a cauldron of fury stirred in his gaze, ripe with the need to call him to heel. "You called the meeting."

"I did." *Out of the frying pan...* "I'm here to resign my position at Elite One so that I can coordinate Elspeth's security detail, effective immediately. I intend to pick and train twelve additional guards, three of each element, to work rotating shifts. Each one must have worked in ultra-Elite units for at least a decade. Twenty-four seven, she'll have a full complement, as it's only a matter of time before that Astrux makes a play for her again. It's been following us around like a hound dog on a blood trail. Reports came in from Montauk this morning about a fog that won't lift."

Seanair stared down his nose, probably pissed Aleron had worn jeans instead of dress slacks with his usual black sweater. "Such dedication. Most others would be impressed, I'm sure, but my question is who's protecting whom?"

There he was. The a-hole in his five-thousand-dollar cashmere.

He bit his cheek and banked his response. Game time was over, but he wouldn't assume anything in the presence of this man.

Normally, Seanair moved on when his victim didn't bite, but now he practically snarled at Aleron's lack of response.

"You're here about protecting her, and yet you sit there coated in her energy, like a pig rolling in shit."

He kept his face neutral. He'd made sure to tuck her energy safely away before he'd gotten out of the car. If Seanair sensed her energy, the only possible reason was she'd sealed him before he left. How? Better still, why couldn't he feel it?

He'd promised himself he'd keep his wits and his mouth in check. He checked his watch.

Five minutes. Not exactly a record.

Time to play a card from Seanair's deck and deflect. "Why did you really agree to send her to Russia?"

"Careful now, son. She's none of your business, and you're not a Lennox."

Nope. No posturing today.

"She's my only business. There's no Fire stronger to protect her, and now I have an Air sidekick." He let his fuck-you smile fly. "Which means I get read in on need-to-know matters from now on. Which families have already been in contact about her? I didn't ask Command, as I know you're keeping the details close on this one." He primed his power, letting his Air out enough so Seanair would sense the equality of their energies. "I won't allow you to trade her like a baseball card."

Fury simmered, low and tight, in his gut. The need to take Elspeth far away from this tyrant fogged his better judgment. He almost missed the sensation. Peroxide bubbles on skin. He chanced a look around, noting Seanair either hadn't noticed or acknowledged the energy.

"That fetid Earth has been gone for days now. It wasn't strong enough to stick around." Seanair dismissed the situation as if a fleck of dirt had caused the citywide rift in elemental energy. "Isidora says the problems aren't caused by an Astrux, and she'd know."

Isidora? Since when did Seanair consult with the Antarctica president? He didn't trust the woman who hunted down improperly released Natura elements and basically ruled an ice island of misfit spirits.

"About your coming in here and ordering me around." Seanair narrowed his ice-blue eyes and steepled his fingers, pointing them like a gun. "You know, my Egyptian's not as good as it used to be, and I have this old tome." He nodded at the thick, weathered book. "I wondered who I could summon to help me with translation. Then it came to me." He tapped his temple. "Did you know your brother Emeric speaks ten ancient languages and seven modern ones?"

Aleron froze, tamping down the brutal rise of energy before he could lash out.

"It would be...unwise to threaten my family." His voice was low, his tone ice, but Fire revved inside him, his Air fueling the flames. Twelve-year-old Emeric's face flashed before him, the last image he had of his brother.

Seanair shook his head. "The problem with young people today is they don't think. They forget their weak spot—or, in your case, spots."

Unease clawed up his neck. He'd written off his heightened awareness as a reaction to entering this viper's den. But he realized now that there was something in the room with him besides the cobra behind the desk.

It watched. Listened. Waited.

He cast out his power, canvassing the walls, hunting for secret doors and hiding places.

"I've spent twelve years in Elite One, training to kill you, and let's be candid. I probably could." He threw out the threat, hoping to elicit a reaction from the invisible spy skittering along the edges of the room, hoping it would reveal itself if it perceived that the danger to Seanair had increased.

"So do it."

Shit.

"No," he countered, disturbed his plan caused little more than a staticky read on the infiltrator.

"So brave."

"In another circumstance, I would, but I don't want to be like you." He stood to his full height. "Striking down your best friend in cold blood. Threatening my family. Those are pages from your playbook." He held the old man's eyes with the ferocity of his new determination. "My father loved you. He always defended you, no matter what you did. Told my brothers and me we were to respect you and do what you asked." He bent far enough to brace his hands on the desk so he could lean in. "I've given you twelve years. You're not getting any more."

"Or you'll what? Kill me? Yes, yes, you already said that."

Goddess, could he be more out of touch?

"Do you think people like having you as their continent president? I can assure you, all Fires hate you as Magnus. That cuff never belonged to you, but you've continued to wear it and degrade the element. They're not showing you respect, Seanair. They're biding time until you can be toppled."

"I don't concern myself with people's opinions of me. They want stability, a safe place to live to do their jobs and commune with their elements, and I provide that. They may not like my methods, but they adore the peace I keep. No leader is appreciated in their own time. History will be my vindication."

Elspeth's cloak of protection warmed around him, reminding him to keep his eye on the ball. None of this was about Seanair. It was about Elspeth, whose first act as a powered Natura had been to envelop Rob Costa in the mightiest mother of all powers, cocooning him in grace and peace. With her first display of her gifts, she'd proven herself worthier than the man before him had ever been in his entire lifetime.

"Once she's fully up to speed, Elspeth will overthrow you, which for you will be a fate worse than death. She cares for people. I've already seen it. You thought to teach her a lesson by sending her to Costa's immolation, but all she came away with was empathy and determination. She'll find a way to cure Lach, return honor to this family, and she'll heal our people." He leaned in a few inches more. "Why would I want to kill you? Then you would miss the torture of watching our people turn their backs on you."

Seanair folded his arms and settled back in his chair. "Until such time as your pathetic threat comes to pass, I'm still in charge, which means I control this continent and all the families on it. A French Air dynasty has a more promising treatment than the Russians, so it was a good thing those plans fell apart, leaving me able to give Elspeth to their eldest son in exchange for the data."

"You disgusting son of a bitch."

"Not bitch, my boy. My bloodline is unrivaled, which means Elspeth's is, too, and it's precisely why she'll never be yours. Another thing you've forgotten is how to count, so I'll remind you she has four elements and has to recharge all of them. She'll need an Earth or a Water tender." He tilted his head and held up one, two, three fingers as if counting off. "I guess that'll shift you to second string. Have fun on the bench."

His hand shook. Fire blew through him in full torching fury.

"Apologize. Right now. You will not speak of her that way."

Ignore him. She's his favorite, and he can't admit he's wrong.

He jerked around at the sound of the woman's voice. Shit. He searched the room. Nothing good ever followed that Goddess-forsaken voice.

"Did you hear that?" He scanned, flung a swath of Fire, cycled a funnel of Air.

"Hear what?"

"The woman from the chapel." Memories of that dreadful day erupted and nearly brought him to his knees.

"You can hear Mathair?"

Wait. Seanair could hear her too?

"I heard the same voice the day my father died."

"Interesting." Seanair shifted in his chair and put a finger to his chin. "Mathair's the Oracle for the Fire cuff. I heard her the first time right after Elspeth's twelfth birthday. Her voice sustains me, although I have no idea why she'd deem you worthy." He waved a get-out-of-here hand. "Go. Form your security team. She won't need them for long, and you'll be crawling back to me for a job—and to save your brothers. Those twins are the rowdiest Fires." Seanair stood and strode toward the fireplace, throwing out a hand.

A blast of flame flew up the chimney. Satisfaction oozed thick and warm inside Aleron. He had gotten to the old bastard.

It's time. Take care of my granddaughter.

He wrenched around.

Four sharp hisses pierced the air.

His side stung. Burned. He looked down at the dark spot growing on his sweater. The hell? Fuck, it hurt.

A grunt sounded. Seanair arched, his eyes wide as he fell forward.

Training kicked in.

Pain later.

Observe. Assess. Act.

Deep-orange flames fanned over the floor. His Air fogged the room in a funnel cloud. He jerked around, searched for foreign elements, the Astrux, any explanation. Nothing. No energy but his own. His mind sharpened. His body numbed.

Seanair slid to the floor. A red stain spread across his dove-gray sweater, the spot blooming and shiny. Blood ran down the side of his neck.

"Hey! Get in here!" Where the hell was the front-door cavalry?

He threw up a fence. Blazing Fire. Cyclonic Air. He fell to his knees beside Seanair and saw that his skin was sallow, horror bright in his eyes.

"It stopped working. The potion." He sucked in a ragged breath. "I'm sick, and they know it."

Sick? And who was *they*? Seanair answered to no one except—

Death.

The answer dawned. That's why he'd wanted Elspeth to marry the Russian. Not to help Lach.

No way. No fucking way.

"*You* have the tripowered disease?"

Glassy blue eyes slid to his, and his body coiled with pain. "Yes. My power slipped. Your father…I lost control."

Aleron sat down hard, his energy faltering despite his concentration. "Who knows?"

"A priestess." The lines in Seanair's face deepened with agony. "She did this." His hand flopped toward the fireplace. "Human bullets. Trickery."

"Let's get you on your side, and I'll assess the wounds." He shook off his confusion and helped Seanair turn, grasping the gray sweater at the back and ripping it clean up the middle.

Goddess bless. Two exit holes. Another wound at his neck.

A calm came over him. He pulled at his own sweater, checked his wound. Hole in the fabric. Blood still trickling. Why didn't he hurt more?

He pulled out his cell phone, thumbed the screen. Black. No power.

Something flashed. A loud pop sounded, and the ceiling lights went out.

"They're here," Seanair ground out. "Listen."

He cast out his power. Didn't sense shit.

"I need to call someone." He sat back on his haunches and spotted the landline phone on the desk.

"I'm sorry…about your father." Seanair gasped. "They want the cuff. I appoint…you, Aleron Jacques Foussé, as emissary." He fell to his back, a haze dulling his eyes. "Aleron?" Seanair reached blindly.

"I'm here." He took the old man's hand.

"Watch the witches." His harsh breaths softened and slowed, and his eyes fixed on something over Aleron's shoulder. "My Mathair," came on a long breath.

Two thin circles, red and white, glowed around Seanair's irises, then extinguished.

"Seanair. Seanair!" Aleron collapsed backward, landing hard on his ass.

The red sphere he'd seen many times squeezed through the bullet hole in Seanair's chest. Floating softly like a balloon, the bubble hovered for a moment, the remaining Fire energy rising from the deathly still body. Centered over Seanair's heart, the glowing mass lingered, waiting to be returned to its source.

The sacred words flowed automatically from the recesses of Aleron's mind.

"Goddess, reclaim Your Fire, Your Air from Your child, Seanair Lennox. Freed by death, let the bounty of his energy enrich those who would ripen Your creation. Blessed be, Mother Nature, Creator of Elements."

The freed energy pulsed and shot into the fireplace, a single, roaring flame extinguishing into thick, black smoke. A crisp crackling drew Aleron's gaze to the window, the middle pane now a distorted mass of cracks.

He covered his head with his hands. Air never went easily.

Immense pressure filled the room. The glass panes flexed toward the desk. Reversed. He leaned forward, covering Seanair and ducking his head as the deafening shatter of the panes sprayed shards from wall to wall.

Play dead, Mathair commanded.

He gently closed Seanair's eyes and rested the man's hands beside his body. Air left his lungs like they'd been stepped on. Pain he'd been forcing into the recesses of his mind screamed to the forefront, demanding he look down.

His sweater was soaked. Warm. Sticky. The stain on the fabric growing.

Play. Dead. Now.

A force shoved him flat against the rug. Heavy footfalls sounded in the hallway.

He closed his eyes as the door opened.

"I couldn't have planned this better. I'm gonna finish that asshole. He always considered himself better than the rest of us."

"No, don't. We can't risk your energy being detected on him. It would ruin the whole plan. They'd know we were in on the hit."

Aleron's heart skipped. The two Fires with the sticky, sooty energy signatures.

A pair of feet stopped at his head, but the voice he heard was wrong. Distorted. Or maybe that was the dizziness. He couldn't think. He longed for sleep.

"Where is it?"

The snarl in the second man's voice brought him back to attention.

"It's not on him? Why would the old bastard take it off?"

Beneath Aleron's sleeve, a band tightened midway up his forearm. The Fire cuff.

"Is there a safe in here?"

"How the hell should I know? We got two minutes until the Airs return from sweeping the grounds. We need to go."

"Got an idea. Let's make it appear we took the cuff and send the others back later to search with a location charm. The old man's dead. That was the goal. Cut his hand off at the wrist and put the knife on Foussé. That'll have Elite One suspecting the Nexus is behind the hit. That bitch has to want all four cuffs."

Aleron floated, drifted, heard a whack.

"You got your damn trophy, and it'll bring a mint on the black market. If you're going to get your kick in, get it while I grab the book, and let's go."

A sharp pain pierced his skull, and the world went black.

CHAPTER
TWENTY-THREE

The knock at the door jarred Elspeth more than the text had from the pet-sitting service contacting her about Lach's dog. She opened the door and smiled at the poor young woman struggling to maintain eye contact while nervously ignoring the four guards.

"I'm sorry Lach hasn't responded," Elspeth said. "I haven't been able to reach him either."

"It's so unlike him. We open The Barkleton day or night whenever Lach wants to get Maylene, but it's four days past her pickup, and we're booked solid this weekend. You're listed as the emergency contact." The dog-sitter handed over the leash. "I'm sorry we can't keep her any longer."

"No problem." She stooped down and unleashed the English bulldog. "I appreciate you bringing her over. If Lach has an outstanding balance, call me, and I'll take care of the bill."

"Will do. Bye, Maylene." The woman waved tentatively at the persnickety dog, who turned her head toward the living room like a queen shunning an undesirable subject.

Elspeth closed the door and swallowed the knot of dread. Maylene was the top woman in Lach's life, and he'd never overlook anything about his dog.

"Tell me the diamonds on that collar aren't real." Zum sat in the hallway scratching Maylene's brindled head. Ever the queen, she accepted the homage, her pink tongue lolling out one side of her mouth as she panted her appreciation.

Elspeth went to the kitchen to fetch a bowl of water.

"Like Lach would touch a rhinestone." She turned on the faucet, scolding herself to calm down. "If the collar surprises you, don't ask about the hand-ground raw food he has delivered every seventy-two hours."

Lach's fine. It can't be that easy to get back from Antarctica.

"Order this sweet baby a steak from Gallaghers." Zum rested on her side, rearing back as Maylene tried to lick her mouth.

"I'm about to lose it, Zum." Four texts. Two calls. Aleron hadn't answered any of them. She threw her friend a pleading glance. "Can't you get some kind of 'I'm okay' from Aleron through your friendship bracelet? I lost the warm feel of the protective bubble I tried to wrap him in when we communed."

"I've felt sensations through it before, but none today. Seanair can get a little long-winded when he's on a rant." Zum stood, moving in quickly for a tight hug. "I'm sure Aleron's fine."

"He should have checked in by now."

"And I'm telling you to *chill*. You've got too much on your plate, and you're going to overload your circuits."

"Great. I'm a robot on top of everything else."

"No, you're a Nexus, which is the greatest thing to happen to our people in centuries."

She buried her face in Zum's shoulder. "Nothing like going from zero to hero with no training or even a manual."

Kazumi stepped back, grasping Elspeth's shoulders, her dark brows knit tight. "You're doing great. Seanair should have given you time instead of thrusting the Judex thing on you and forcing you to witness Rob's immolation. Ignore that email he forwarded last night from the French contingent about their 'real' treatment for the trip-owered disease. I swear, your grandfather's machine-gun-leadership style needs a cease-fire."

"Witnessing Rob's return to the source has only made me more determined." She took Zum's hands. "My powers get stronger each day, but the quickest way to get a stopgap for Lach is if I marry into or form an alliance with the family who owns the most promising technology." The weight of what she was loomed large. "Whatever becomes of Lach, I won't be like Seanair and use my power to force compliance or take what I want. I couldn't live with myself if I did."

"You're *nothing* like Seanair." Something dark swirled in Zum's deep-blue eyes. "My mother's working her connections in Asia for information, and her reach is long." She leaned back, her expression heart-attack serious. "Lach's lived a lot longer than the others, and there's got to be a reason for that. He's what, thirty-one?"

"Yes."

"We'll keep at it on Lach." Zum's mouth pulled to the side in a teasing smile. "Try not to worry about Aleron. His strength is more crematorium than Easy-Bake, but don't tell him I said that."

She sized up her best friend. Kazumi's jet-black hair was slicked back into a high ponytail. With gunpowder dark eyeliner, a tight black turtleneck, and leggings, she'd gone Goth cat burglar today. "I love you. You know that, right?"

"I love you too, E. You're my sib from another crib."

"I don't know what I'd do without you. Seriously." She rested her forearms on Zum's shoulders. "This is all too much, and you're keeping me both sane and protecting Manhattan from my monsoon."

"*Girl*, are you listening to yourself? You're trying to learn, in a matter of days, what took me six years. The fact you managed to pool water in the air today is incredible."

Their Water games had been pretty cool, the main issue being how to regulate volume.

"I know. And thank you for trying to distract me from stressing about Aleron not answering my texts." She straightened and spoke the truth baked into her every cell. "I love him, Zum. I know it's fast, but it's real. I can't imagine life without him, but I have to face reality. I can't undo centuries of social protocol because I think the status thing's ridiculous. If I focus on that, my brother dies."

"No worries." She swatted a hand toward Elspeth. "We'll launch

Operation Secret Romance. Aleron can play bodyguard
streets, hot lover in the sheets."

"It won't work."

"It will. EB's broiling over you. You can't let a man like that get
away." Zum's hand covered her heart as she belted out the lyrics of an
old favorite song. "Is this love that I'm feelin'?"

Elspeth covered her ears, unable to endure her best friend's ob-
session for old-school, eighties rock ballads. "Stop. No Whitesnake.
No Scorpions. And for Goddess's sake, no Tesla."

Zum chewed her lip, her singing face morphing to serious.
"Don't give up yet, okay? He gazes at you the same sappy way my
father looks at my mother."

Raised voices came in the hall, followed by a quick knock.

"Ms. Lennox, your cousins Ross and Flora are here, along with a
warlock named Egan. Shall I let them in?"

Goddess on a bike.

"Yes." She came out of the kitchen to meet a crowd of confused
expressions. "What are you guys doing here?"

"Graham called and said to get our asses here, pronto." Streaks
of dirt marred Flora's face, her clothes askew and dotted with leaves
and sticks. "I happened to be in Central Park, as it's easiest to commune in the dark."

Naked. Nope. *No public nudity in the city.*

"We were in Midtown debriefing about the Russians over dinner." Ross stepped toward her. "Do you have any idea what this is
about?"

"No." She motioned toward the living room, her pulse rising.
"Let's wait in here."

They hadn't made it to the sofa when the door smacked the wall.
Maylene tore for the bedroom as Graham pushed inside, Aleron
strung between him and Kerr.

Her heart kicked. Hard. Her instincts flared. The slow slide of
something terrible has happened dredged through her. One look at
Aleron, and the room narrowed.

She barreled through her cousins.

. under the strain, Aleron several inches taller
brother and cousin. "He's still bleeding."

Move the coffee table so they can put him on the
.ered Ross and Egan. She raced to the only person
.. "Baby?" She cradled Aleron's blood-crusted cheeks,
a.. .n screeched to a halt. Cold. Weak. Failing.

He .nergies ripped from her. An explosion of Earth, Air, Water,
and Fire circled him, a twister of Fire and Air whirling a fierce spray
of healing heat and air.

He was dying. The man she loved was—

"No!" The word tore from her in a howl.

Hands gripped her shoulders.

"He's just weak. Elspeth, stop!" Zum's voice broke through, both
her best friend and Flora jerking her back.

"Get him to the couch," Graham ordered, stepping away as Ross
swooped in to help Kerr. Her brother's hands gripped her shoulders,
his face even with hers. "He's lost blood. I've already called the doctor dedicated to Elite One. They're bringing over several pints of a
preparation for a Fire and Air of his strength. Between whatever you
did to protect him and his own energy, he's holding up better than he
should be. He's not dying, Elspeth. I promise. I wouldn't lie to you."

Protest surged inside her, but though Graham wasn't the most
caring brother, she could count on him for honesty. That didn't stop
her from parking herself on her knees beside Aleron's prone body.

"What happened?" She looked up, worry welling in her throat.

"I'll tell you what happened," Kerr snapped, causing her to jerk
her head around. Her cousin jabbed a finger toward Aleron, who
dozed with his eyes half closed. "Seanair's dead. And that shitbag
right there may not have been the one who actually killed him, but
he was in on it and knows what happened to the Goddess-forsaken
cuff."

Graham shot Kerr a back-off glare. "When I need you to answer
for me, I'll let you know."

She turned back to her brother, her mind a muddled mess.

"Seanair's two Air guards found him and called me. They're

guarding his body until I get back. I've sworn them to secrecy on their lives until we can form a plan."

Flames whooshed up the chimney. Her own Fire energy rose and strong-armed Kerr's immense power. While her cousin was a pompous a-hole, oddly enough he was also a devout Natura, honoring and honing his Fire power to incredible levels. She would have thought his fanatical level of devotion to his element would have made him a better person.

"They took his hand!" Fury rolled from Kerr. "Someone hacked off our grandfather's hand and took the cuff." His face morphed into a volcanic mask of rage. "Foussé has a motive. Seanair killed his dad when he tried to take the cuff years ago. Our grandfather told me the whole story. Only family should be trusted. *Ever.*"

An acrid, metallic scent hit her. Blood. Graham's, Kerr's, and Aleron's clothes were soaked with the blood and energy signature she recognized. Her grandfather's.

"It's only a matter of time before this gets out." Kazumi came over and took her hand. "Let me brief my mother. I know she'll want to talk to you and lend her support where she can. She and Seanair didn't see eye to eye on many things, but she did respect his commitment to his elements and to peace, even if she disagreed with how he kept it."

She nodded, her throat clogged with emotion.

Kerr paced at the window, pulling at his hair like he was going to tear it out.

"I'm okay." Aleron grunted as he shifted to a semireclined position. "I won't say no to that transfusion, though. Or an aspirin."

"My bathroom cabinet." She nodded to Flora.

"I've got something better. Give me a minute to whip it up." Her cousin headed for the kitchen.

A strange numbness of disbelief settled in. Too much power. Too much death. Too much sickness. Too much pain.

Goddess above, what do you expect of me?

Kerr stopped pacing, his cold glare hard. "Do you realize what this means? If we don't find that cuff and get it on a Fire, things will burn. Everywhere. You won't be able to stop it. We've got a nuclear-fuel rod walking about Manhattan." He scowled at Aleron. "And you want to kiss our only suspect's boo-boos. How about a five-star dinner and a cocktail?"

"The bullets were charmed," Egan interrupted from the corner. "I sense the disintegrating magic."

Kerr turned his murderous gaze on Egan. "What's a fucking warlock doing in here?"

Ross stepped between them. "Check your prejudice, cousin. He's a fully vetted ally of our family."

"Why don't you grab a bullhorn and squawk it from the balcony? There are families who will gun for us as soon as the word is out. *Literally*, it appears. We have to find that cuff." Kerr gave a harsh nod at Aleron. "And he's going to tell us where it is. If he needs a little incentive, I can help."

Stress poured from Aleron, along with his determination to get off the couch and start working.

"He didn't do it, and he doesn't know who's involved other than two people." Elspeth pushed Aleron back down and eyed Kerr, firing a little breeze around the apartment to remind him that Air gave her the ability to read another person's intent. She faced Graham. "What do you want to do?"

"Why are you asking him?" Kerr came toward them. "The little professor doesn't know shit."

"He's the ascender." Elspeth primed her Water, ready to douse Kerr's hotheaded ass. "Seanair should have told you. I'm sorry."

"He told *you?*" Kerr snipped, clearly indicating he still considered her a step above human trash.

"He told me," Graham interjected. "It's why he ordered me home for the gala. He told Jon Costa, too, as he wanted to train us both on our new responsibilities. He's already spoken the prayer of succession. I was to have communion with him next week for the passing of the cuff."

"I can get you a cuff," Egan said. "Until you find the real one, I can glamour a metal bracelet so no one will know." He pushed off the wall. "You don't need the Natura or coven communities knowing Fire's untended. The longer that stays true, Fires will sense the fissure, and the covens will sense the energy shift."

She stood and placed a hand on Aleron's arm.

Protect.

Power flowed from her like an open elemental spigot, bathing Aleron in a mélange of light.

"Protecting him isn't necessary," Flora said, frowning as she returned from the kitchen. "My brother won't harm him." She handed Aleron a vial. "This oil tincture will work faster than a human pain pill. It'll temporarily make you sleepy, but your Fire will burn off the haze."

Aleron eyed Flora, strain lining his forehead. He tipped back the ampoule and sank against the pillows behind his head. Elspeth raced to her closet and rifled through her jewelry drawer for the cheap bangle she'd worn as part of her genie costume at Kazumi's last Halloween bash.

"Here." She opened the clasp, handed it to Egan, and hoped the thing would fit around Graham's wrist.

"This will work." The warlock turned over the bracelet. "What does the real cuff look like?"

She recalled the few times Seanair had let her inspect it as a kid. "All the cuffs are made from asteroid metal, so the base is iron, but it's about four inches wide, coated in matte gold and etched with hieroglyphics."

Egan nodded. "I'll need to step into the kitchen for some privacy. Be right back."

"You should call your parents at the commune," Graham said to Flora. "Tell them to be on alert. A power vacuum is dangerous until we show some leadership."

"Good idea. Do you want me to head up to Seanair's house afterward? I have a healing ritual I can perform on the grounds that may destroy any residual magic."

"Yes, thanks." Graham turned to Kerr. "You interact with the lieutenants most. We need a plan for a sit-down for tomorrow. Get the word out and set up the meeting on neutral ground. I want a rooftop where all elements can flow freely."

"Seanair holds meetings in the Roxy apartment at Radio City Music Hall," Kerr ground out. "If you'd come home more than once a year for the last decade, you'd know that."

"I hope your assumptions keep you warm, cousin." Graham glanced toward the kitchen. "If the covens are responsible for Seanair's death, we'll need all the help we can get."

"Fine," Kerr said. "I'll head to the Kindred offices and get the meeting notice out to all Northeast lieutenants." He stormed off, nearly trampling Egan as he came out of the kitchen.

"Ignore him." Ross went over to the warlock. "He's assumed since birth that he was next in line."

"Here you go." Egan held the cuff out to Graham, the copycat strikingly similar to what Elspeth remembered of Seanair's. "If anyone tries to sense the magic, it'll feel like Fire but a little off. Blame it on acclimation to your energy. Power looks different to all witches, as the empty vessel inside each of us is unique."

Graham took the cuff but eyed the warlock for a long, assessing moment, finally shifting his gaze back to Ross. "I've got a lot of questions, but for now can you follow Kerr to Kindred and handle the PR plan for the humans and the families? We need to play Seanair's death off as a robbery gone wrong."

"Sure thing." Ross headed for the door with Egan.

"Keep an eye on Kerr in case he boils over."

Egan hesitated long enough to imply he'd rather charm snakes with his hands tied behind his back. "Will do."

The door shut as Graham snapped the glamoured bangle around his wrist, pushing it beneath the sleeve of his Henley shirt. "I'll keep it covered, and hopefully this ruse will hold if no one gets anything but a glimpse of it." He flexed his wrist like the counterfeit cuff already chafed.

"Don't play with it," Elspeth advised. "Don't draw attention to it. We have to appear as if this transition was well in play."

"I'll try, but I need to get going to handle Seanair's body. Oh, shit, I just remembered—"

"I said the prayer," Aleron said, his gaze somber. "His elements retired peacefully."

She went over and clasped his hand in hers, kissing his knuckles. "Thank you. That must have been hard."

"Not really. But even if it was, I wasn't about to let him become an Astrux. Even after everything, I'd never wish that hell on him."

Maylene came out of the bedroom then, hauled her stocky body up onto the couch, and plopped between Aleron's legs, resting her head on his knee with a jingle of her tags.

"Graham, don't leave," Aleron croaked, his voice sounding like his vocal cords had flayed. "I have to tell you something."

Elspeth squeezed his hand. "Stop talking. You're too weak."

"I'm going to be fine," he insisted, pushing himself to a sitting position despite her protests and the fifty pounds of bulldog on his lap. "Now that the others have gone...I have the cuff."

"What?" She looked at him, then at Graham, who'd sat on the other end of the sectional.

"Seanair made me the emissary. After he was hit. Four bullets shot from the fireplace when he lit it. Pull up the sleeve on my right arm. It's midway up."

She gently touched the material, pushing it all the way up to his bicep when she didn't feel or see a thing, and frowned.

"I swear it's there, and apparently I can't be killed until it comes off. I should be dead. Your protection and this cuff are the only reasons I'm not."

And she would protect him for as long as she drew breath.

Aleron continued sharing the details he remembered of what happened, and five minutes later, she and Graham knew everything.

She didn't need her Air to know he hadn't killed her grandfather. He might have done things he wasn't proud of, but he wasn't a cold-blooded murderer. "I already knew you didn't do it."

"I had every reason to want to. Kerr's right." His fingers threaded though hers.

"Why didn't you?" Graham's gaze cut to Aleron's bare arm.

Aleron's gaze shifted to Elspeth, his brown eyes deep and

weighty and only for her. "Because I love you more than I hated him. I would never hurt you, Elspeth. And I would die before I let you be harmed."

"I love you." She brushed his hair off his forehead.

"I love you too." His eyes took a slow trail over her face. "Nothing's changed, though. You have Lach to save, and you can't be with me to do what you need to do."

Her hands shook. Everything within her screamed to tell him he was wrong. Every fiber but one, the truth an anchor.

"We'll discuss that later." She looked to Graham. "Go in the guest room and grab him some clean clothes. Please?"

"I'm glad you're all right." She sensed the Fire struggling to rebound inside him, the wisps of Air seeking to swirl.

Like Dorothy, she wasn't in Kansas anymore, or Oz, or a land close to anything she recognized. She'd landed smack in the middle of acreage for which she had no map, naked and deeply, deeply afraid.

Something cracked inside her. Her heart ached at the loss of the Grandie she'd loved fiercely as a child, but the fracture showed the reality that the man she'd held a secret hope of reconciling with had died long ago. Her Grandie had become a brutal man, a man with enemies she didn't yet know but who seemed far too close.

Her four energies stirred inside her. Pulses of power under her skin revving for a fight. Fear for Aleron had knocked them down, but she grew stronger with every second, and only a fool would count her out.

Graham returned and handed her a small stack of clothing, pulling his cell from his back pocket. "The doc's here. He texted from the lobby. I need to get up to the house."

"All I know about cuffs I learned from my father." Aleron's raspy voice cut through the silence. "I don't know what to look for specifically, but you should have a mark if you're the true Fire Magnus. Anything weird showing up?"

"No." Graham's gaze took a trip around the room. "I'm Air dominant, so it can't be me."

"Kazumi's veins are moving toward the surface of her skin, and they're a deep blue. Her transition to Water Magnus has started. She may be able to help us find the Fire Magnus."

"Be careful, Elspeth. I know she's your best friend, but this is business. Her mother may not be on board with me being the North American president." Graham raked a hand through his hair. "Hell, I'm not on board. I have no idea what to do or where to start. Seanair planned to train me for two years, but that hadn't even started. It'll take more than a village to run this dynasty." He fiddled with his fake cuff. "I'll worry about it later. I need to get to Tarrytown and get the human police involved."

"Graham, one more thing." Aleron pushed up straighter, ignoring Maylene's grunt of dissatisfaction. "There was definitely dark magic in your grandfather's study, and he warned me before he died." He looked to Elspeth. "I know you're fond of Egan, but Seanair's last words to me were 'watch the witches.'"

CHAPTER
TWENTY-FOUR

Elspeth slid across the back seat of Seanair's tricked-out Mercedes. Blacked-out glass. Armored doors. Grade A protection for her now-deceased grandfather, protection she only now understood would be required for her as the most powerful of their kind.

"You're not taking FDR?" she asked Aleron, who was in the driver's seat. She smoothed a hand over her black wool slacks, hoping the double-breasted jacket over the white silk turtleneck shell had been the right choice.

"There's an accident, so we'll go Second Avenue and hit all nine hundred traffic lights."

Great. More time to stew over the sit-down. As the presumptive president, Graham would do most of the talking, while she'd star as the entertainment. Not for her new judicial role, but her status as the four-powered freak.

The fact Graham had advised against riding together to Radio City Music Hall had given her pause. He'd said they should travel separately now, vary their movements. She refused to run scared from whoever'd charmed those bullets that had slipped past Seanair's numerous defenses, but she'd err on the cautious side, especially since her sole interaction with a warlock had been quiet, unassuming Egan.

She moved into the sight line of the rearview mirror. Aleron had been quiet the whole day, having spent the morning on the phone with Graham and working with the interim commander at Elite One. He appeared good as new after the blood transfusion, but he'd been distant and resigned most of the afternoon.

"Any update on Lach?"

Aleron cut a quick gaze to her in the rearview, then returned his focus to the streets, the sidewalk, and the occasional snow flurries. "Isidora confirmed he's there with her, but that's all. I know you're worried, but there's no way she'd let him melt Antarctica."

Lach burning down the world around him wasn't Elspeth's worry.

"If he goes the way Rob Costa did, we won't know."

"You would. If you don't feel the void from Seanair's death yet, it'll come. That trite saying about empty spaces is true for us. The loss of familial strength is real and doesn't rebuild the same way." He cut a glance to the side mirror, changing from the center lane to the right one. "Isidora runs a tight continent, and she's not letting him run amok and chase the penguins. I have zero information on how she manages an island of misfit energies that should already be home, but my guess is she's put him to work wrangling the ones acting out the most."

An image of Lach in a cowboy hat and chaps invaded her brain. If anyone could find a way to lasso wild energies, it'd be her oldest brother. He could wrestle the biggest of them until they slapped the mat and admitted defeat.

She sat back hard against the seat, frustrated, but conceding he was right. She'd tackle the mystery of Isidora later but took comfort thinking the woman had to have more patience with Lach and his disease than Seanair ever had, since her brother evidently hadn't been kicked off glacier island yet. "Do you mind giving me the inside scoop on the families at the meeting?"

"In a minute." He pulled the car to the right to allow a squawking NYPD cruiser to pass. "I forgot to tell you something important yesterday, and I apologize."

He pulled back into traffic, only to stop at an intersection congested with cars and pedestrians.

"You were shot, and Seanair's dead. I can't think of anything worse, other than Lach succumbing to the disease, and you've confirmed he's still alive."

She scrubbed her hands over her eyes. Things couldn't get any more awful.

"Seanair had the tripowered disease."

"What?" The word came out on a breath.

"He said something about a tonic not working any longer, that the witches knew of his illness." He glanced over his shoulder and back to the road. "He also admitted the day he killed my father was the first time his power slipped."

His assertion mirrored the diary entry she'd read, but her anger boiled over. She did the math from Seanair's first slip to now, and the sum of the equation twisted her stomach into truth-soaked knots. Her grandfather hadn't suggested the arrangement with the Russians to help Lach. He'd wanted only to save himself.

"He successfully battled the disease for twelve years and didn't bother to give the treatment to my brother?" She closed her eyes against the hot fury raging swiftly into molten anger.

"I don't know anything about the treatment, but Seanair...he seemed frightened. Of the witches."

Or witch. She recalled the stack of receipts Egan had found. For payments by Seanair to Magdalena Wiedzma.

"I may have something on his source. Seanair was paying big bucks to a bad-news witch."

"If he had any such dealings, he kept it out of Elite One. We had enough to handle with bad-news Naturas." His mouth pulled into an almost smile.

The air shifted and glittered in front of her as if someone had tossed gold dust. Flaky shimmers settled on the seats and dashboard, disappearing into the cream leather.

She leaned forward between the front bucket seats.

He tugged up his sleeve. "Well, well. It's about time. It must feel safe around you."

There it was. On his right arm. Midway to his elbow.

Line after line of hieroglyphics covered the obviously old, dull gold cuff. When she'd been elementary-school age, Seanair occasionally had allowed her to trace a finger over it, letting her inspect the inscriptions and scolding her with a smile when she'd ask to try it on.

Aleron wheeled around a taxi letting out its passengers. "I thought the thing was determined to make a liar out of me."

"When's the last time you saw it?"

"When your grandfather put it on me."

"How does it open?"

"It doesn't. Seanair wished, or willed, it on me." He cut his gaze to her. "It also comes with a ghost bonus."

"There's no such thing as ghosts."

"Sorry. There's no manual, but the cuff comes with a narrator."

"You're losing me." Her stress eased a little at his playful tone. Things had gotten so heavy between them. She longed to go back to her birthday and the lemon cake, before things took a turn for the terrible.

"Mathair's the Oracle for the cuff. She's why Seanair wouldn't relinquish it until now."

"He could hear her…all this time?"

"Apparently from since around your twelfth birthday."

She blew out a calming breath and slipped back into her seat. It made sense now. How often he'd commune. His wistful smile the few times they'd discussed her grandmother.

Tension crept across her shoulders. They'd gone a few more blocks with her counting the Duane Reades to distract herself when she remembered her original question.

"You were going to tell me about the meeting attendees." She shifted her gaze back to the rearview mirror.

"Graham would have invited only those from each family he felt he needed, but you'll see there's disagreement even with those Seanair considered allies. Trust is hard-won and quickly lost in our world. I guarantee we'll have winners for first to lend false support, first to start a territory war, and first to put a hit out on your family. It'll be a twenty-way tie on best ass-kisser."

"At least Jon Costa's with us. He pulls a lot of weight in this region." She'd appreciated his congratulatory call to Graham. Her brother would need a mentor, and Jon would need a distraction after losing Rob.

"He is an important ally, because it's not only the Fires who like him. He's a consensus builder, but don't give him too much credit yet. He may challenge Graham for the continent presidency." His brown eyes met hers in the mirror. "This is far from a slam dunk. Both you and Graham have to uphold the utmost illusion of power tonight, or the infighting will start, and this continent will go down. Naturas were afraid of Seanair's repercussions. When you walk in that room, you'd better reek of power and put everyone on notice, or they'll pounce."

His words lingered in the air like smoke after a fire. All this time, she'd put Lach first. The last six months, she'd focused on him and the Russians and the treatment. Turned out she had a whole other sickness to address. Her people suffered from the plague that was the love of money and power and greed, subverting Mother Nature's mission in their quest for lives that would make Hollywood A-listers look like children playing with board game currency.

"I have to save my people." The statement sat like lead in her instincts.

"It's do or die. Seanair held off the war as long as he could, but there's a power vacuum now, and if you don't fill it, someone else will. You and Graham are the right people. I know it. But the Lennoxes won't pull this off alone. You need a powerful partner, someone with some weight from Europe or Asia. No one messes with the African continent leader, and she has two sons. Kickass Earths. You should call her personally and arrange a face-to-face. She doesn't do online meetings."

The strangest internal heads-up rang bone-deep inside her, and the back of her neck prickled.

"What's that?"

His head turned, security-camera slow. Left. Right. The color drained from his cheeks.

The car slowed at a yellow light.

"Aleron?"

Embers of irritation flared at his silence, but she noted his odd stillness. His head did quick, robotic cuts to the side mirrors, the rearview, the windshield, as he searched for the threat.

A loud pop sounded. The cuff vanished.

Her instincts screamed, *Get out. Get out, get out, get out.*

A musty incense filled the car. An element signature, brutally strong, but ripe with decay.

She tugged at the door handle. Nothing. Punched the button for the window. Dead. The surrounding cars pulled forward, and the Mercedes moved with the rest of the traffic.

"Aleron?" She leaned forward, shaking his shoulder.

He stared straight ahead and turned the knob for the heat to high.

A thick curl of smoke spooled from the vents, pouring into the back, circling into a cylindrical mass on the seat beside her. The swirl slowed, the obscure mass glittering, and black particles like dark shiny diamonds moved, mutated, morphed into—

A man.

She jammed herself against the door.

Pitch-black hair swept back from his forehead. He stared for a moment, as if composing himself. His aristocratic nose, jutted chin, and full mouth formed before her. A dark dress shirt open at the collar revealed a strong neck and hinted at a muscular build. Charcoal slacks. Black shoes. Mid-forties?

A new scent filled her, her eyes watering at its pungency. Trees. He smelled of human Christmas trees. Fraser firs.

"Hello, Elspeth." He turned his head, his indiscernible accent thick, his voice deep and strong.

Coal eyes. Goddess, they were mesmerizing. No, *beautiful*. A velvety, dark gray with filament-like threads of emerald green.

Power shot from her body like fighter-jet countermeasures and walled her inside a tight fortress. Earth, Air, Water, and Fire locked, loaded, and aimed.

He waved a hand, and moss crept across the ceiling, floor, and panels. The aroma of freshly turned soil blanketed the car. "I'm getting so good at being a Natura."

"What are you?" Her Earth energy's impostor siren blared.

"Ah, my first disappointment in you. You don't even recognize one of your own people. I'm Samael." He pegged her with his stony eyes, his smile a wicked white. "A warlock."

Her gaze shot to Aleron, and the car jerked to a stop. His dull gaze and machine-like movements scared her more than watching the smoke that had become Samael coming through the vents. Naturas couldn't take pure element form anymore. Through the millennia, they'd evolved, taking a hybridized human form to blend in. She'd never even heard fantasy stories of someone being able to move as vapor.

She returned her focus to the threat beside her, silent and intense like a black widow spider waiting to pounce. "You attacked us in the alley." She put a hand to her chest, determined to keep her pounding heart from breaking through her ribs.

"I did. I meant to kill you before you came into your power, but I failed, as I didn't know how to disarm a two-mantled Fire." He showed no emotion, no concern, like killing was as normal as taking a shower. "I know now. And it appears he's down to one Fire mantle anyway."

"How could you know what I'd be before anyone else?"

He shook his head like she'd never learn. "Just like your grandfather, discounting the covens."

His power filled the car, the element's signature off-kilter, though one thing was certain—his Earth was stronger than hers.

She didn't dare shift her gaze to Aleron, nor did she...*want* to. Samael had presence, a charisma capable of holding an audience of willing captives. Confident. Regal, commanding, and...nearly pure in Earth form.

That couldn't be right. His energy read as virgin pure, the first turn of terrain. Her Earth pushed against the constraints of her body, seeking the friction of a slow slide with him, element to element. The newness of her Earth craved the power pulsating in his.

"What do you want?" She had to keep him talking, curling her hands to fists in her lap, and demanding they stay put. The Fire mantle Aleron had given her squeezed around her. She'd become so used to the support of his mantle as she trained to control her own Fire, she'd forgotten it was there. Goddess, she'd left Aleron exposed. Why hadn't she given it back to him?

"Stop thinking about how you can best me or save him. You can't." Samael nodded toward Aleron. "I'll pose the same question I asked of your grandfather."

Aleron's breaths came harsh through his nose. She engaged her senses and struck some sort of bubble encapsulating his Fire and Air.

She glared at Samael. "If you harm so much as an eyelash on him, I will cut you down, and it won't be with charmed bullets."

"Convicting me already?" His wide smile wasn't friendly. "I can assure you I'm not working alone, and I'm not a one-trick warlock."

She returned a game-on smirk. "And I'm not a four-powered pushover."

"One chance." He held up a finger. "What have you done with the witches?"

She couldn't stifle her double take. "I don't know what you're talking about."

A tinge of decomposition floated across her senses.

Wrong answer.

"You should beware the fury of a patient man. Killing your grandfather proved to be the simplest of spells. Lach has both feet in the grave, so that's almost done. My Earth's far stronger than yours, and I can best Ross. It'd be a real mudslinger, but I'd win."

Fire shot through her, the skin of her arms glowing red.

"Get out of the car, or I'll get you out." She flexed her Water energy against his Earth, ready to strong-arm him onto the sidewalk.

A warning skittered over her skin, a signal flare from her elements, an assurance that if she threw open the floodgates of her power, she'd lose control.

"Your grandfather treated us like cattle. He wrote off our spells and our glamours and our charms as Natura lite." He hunched a shoulder, and the green threading through his irises deepened. "You push people too long? They eventually push back."

A sensation started at the back of her neck. A crawling. No, a tapping. Like someone sought her attention.

The area warmed, spreading down her body, a heated ooze covering her. A bath of light and heat. Aleron?

Samael uttered low words in a language she'd never heard. Somber. Not pretty, but powerful, and the cadence of the eerie tone flowed through her, filling the car.

"I'll ask a second time since your energy signature is so fresh and new. What have you done with the witches?"

"All I did for my grandfather was arrange unions and maintain a Natura database. Seanair kept me out of everything else." She strengthened her shields at the rumble shaking the car.

"I have no tolerance for liars."

The air shifted. A calm creep of fog spread over the floorboard. Time held, slowed, and the solid surface beneath her moved. Earth energy. Cautious, crawling...crushing.

Nothing at all like Flora or Ross. Or was it? Had she been fooled into buying into the peaceful, tree-hugging reputation of the "quiet, gentle" element?

Anger rose. Primitive and raw. A kill-or-be-killed fury detonated inside her. Her power writhed, twirled, raged at the man who'd threatened something precious. Something new and beautiful. Love for Aleron. Love for the future. Hope for...life.

Her Earth energy rose, a cavernous call from her every cell, an urging to plow Samael down, pulverize him to bits, shove him deep in the dirt.

A choking sound stopped her short. A wretch. A gasp. Aleron slumped over the steering wheel, his body seizing.

"Stop!" She lunged at Samael, trying to break the flow of acid-green light aimed at the front seat.

She hit a solid, invisible wall.

"Stop!"

Horns honked behind them.

"Give me Flora," Samael said.

A landslide of pressure surrounded her. "What? Never." She wouldn't give up her cousin.

Aleron lurched, an unnatural force turning his upper body. Red veins canvased the whites of his eyes. Tendons bulged along his neck.

"Flora will come to me in two days."

"No."

"Flora will be alone."

"No."

"Flora will return when I'm ready to return her."

"Let him go!" She beat at the wall, now a brilliant emerald. Aiming heat, water, everything she had and pushing, shoving, pounding at his shields.

As if sensing Aleron's distress, her Air wasn't having it. The re-inforced glass flexed, bowed, and shattered. Spits of glass ripped her face. Aleron's back arched.

"Yes! Okay! Yes!" The words tore from her throat in a long, shrill scream.

Samael sat back and brushed bits of glass from his slacks as if they were nothing more than a bit of dust. "And so it shall be."

The atmosphere rippled. His body shimmered, disappearing into smoke and glitter, and whisked through a busted window in a vapor-like trail.

Aleron collapsed sideways across the console into the passenger seat.

"Aleron? Aleron! Answer me!" She exited the rear of the car and ripped open the front passenger door, grabbing his shoulders. She strained to push him upright, but her strength was no match for a body of solid muscle.

She pressed her fingertips to his neck, found his pulse, but panicked at his jerky breaths. The blue around his eyes and the bruising circling his mouth faded. She patted her pockets. No phone. Couldn't find Aleron's either.

The rev of a motorcycle cut through the street noise. The grumbling Harley stopped alongside the car, the rider pushing up the helmet's visor.

"What the fuck?" Kazumi shrieked. "My friendship bracelet with your boy is going nuts." Her gaze shifted to Aleron, her eyes wide as she seemed to realize how exposed they all were. "*Ripple.*" She drew out the word in a hush.

An otherworldly blue wave fanned out around them, the power bathing and absorbing into every person on the block and moving to climb the walls of the buildings and flashing at the windows.

"Graham's coming with a battalion of guards. He's called off the meeting." Zum rushed around to the driver's side and took hold of Aleron's body. "Let's get him up in case he comes to. You push. I'll pull. One, two, three."

She grunted, shoving him upright in the driver's seat. Tracing her fingertips over the cuts slicing into his scar, she avoided the bleeding gash over his eyes. A bald fury consumed her. Flashes of blue, green, red, white flared, her power firing like a camera flash.

"Get a grip, E. Now. Don't make me brain-blip those rubber-necking a-holes again."

A black Suburban pulled up. Five men poured out and moved her aside, pulling Aleron out of the car with done-this-before proficiency and putting him in the SUV.

Zum's glare was so like Aleron's, scanning the surrounding area with brutal efficiency. She nailed the obvious leader of the Elite team. "Have someone alert our people in the monitoring center right away. Have them destroy the camera feeds from noon on. If we get word about stand-alone cameras, you'll have to deal with them one on one."

The man's expression sharpened into *don't tell me my job.* "We know this area. We got it."

Elspeth watched her best friend handle the crisis while she could only stand there, staring at the SUV where Aleron was in the back, being checked over by one of the men. Her body, her elements, her soul longed to touch him, make sure he still breathed. His chest had barely seemed to rise and fall, and she couldn't erase the image from her mind.

Kazumi returned and shoved her cell phone into her back pocket.

"These guys are trained in emergency medicine. I called our people at Mount Sinai, and a team will meet us at your apartment. What the hell happened?"

"A warlock happened." Her hands shook, adrenaline still pumping through her. "A warlock who wants a war and can take pure element form."

"That's impossible." Zum motioned her toward the bike and unfastened the extra helmet secured to the back.

"No, it's not."

"What did he want?" Zum threw her leg over the seat and nodded for her to climb on.

"He wanted to know what we've done with a bunch of witches, and he was interested in Flora." She settled on the seat behind Kazumi and put her arms around her friend's waist. She wanted to be with Aleron but realized the motorcycle could get them back to her place quicker than the Suburban. "Let's go. I need to see my cousin and tell her what I've done."

CHAPTER
TWENTY-FIVE

Aleron hadn't believed in the space between life and death where a Natura's consciousness loomed above their human body. His Fire was like looking into a furnace, flames roaring and hot. His Air churned, swirling but stationary, wind waiting to be set free. Then there was his body, the home where his element seeds lived, his human shell, allowing him to blend in and do his job.

It was strange, his awareness floating above his still form in Elspeth's room.

He watched her stroke the backs of her fingers gently down his face, take his hand. An English bulldog rested at the foot of the bed, her body still, her eyes shifting toward the man with *Mount Sinai* embroidered on his scrubs.

"Why won't he wake up?" Elspeth looked from the doc back to the bed.

"His element energy was immobile too long. It's like muscle atrophy in humans when they're inactive for an extended period or bedridden. Neither species is meant to be in stasis." The doctor firmed his mouth. "The primary issue is he nearly drained his Fire down to nothing. May I be candid, Ms. Lennox?"

"Elspeth, and yes."

"I understand you're new to your elements, and while I know little of Nexus abilities outside of old textbooks, I can tell you Naturas have an internal line they mustn't cross. Think of it like the low-fuel light in a car. When the light comes on, you must refill the tank soon." The old doc's gaze softened. "But for us, if we run out of gas, we can't just add more and go. If Naturas completely deplete their energy stores, they die. I've heard anecdotal evidence that some can exist in humanlike form, but I've never seen it. In all my years of practice, I've never seen a patient recover after his levels dropped this low. How did he get to this state?"

Her chin quivered. "A warlock's spell. Even bound, Aleron shielded me. His Fire energy cloaked me the whole time. He...he tried to give me his remaining mantle."

In this half world, he couldn't feel her warmth or her soft skin, couldn't smell the intoxicating combination of shampoo and *her*.

"He had two?" The Fire doc went to the other side of the bed and held a hand over Aleron's midsection. A red glow emanated from his palm, held for several seconds, and retracted. "There's only one now, and it's barely detectable."

"He gave me his second mantle right after I came into my power." She studied the red glow around her hands. "That's why I can wield Fire without thinking. He must've... Goddess, he tried to give me his primary Fire. He was going to sacrifice himself to save *me*."

Damn straight. She still had so much training to do, and her Earth had been nowhere near as strong as that warlock's. When that thing, that aberration, had struck, he'd done what his father had. If he'd had them, he'd sacrifice a hundred mantles. For her.

The dog got up, took several unsteady steps, and plopped her bulky, muscular mass between his arm and his body, her muzzle right in his armpit.

Elspeth waved a hand, her expression animated, both her mouth and the doctor's moving, but the sound had cut off.

What are you going to do?

Something sharp and prickly skittered over his aura.

I'm waiting.

He wondered how he was supposed to speak without the ability to use his mouth.

Mathair?

The voice didn't reply, so he wasn't sure if he'd had a thought, engaged in some sort of telepathy, or hadn't responded at all.

I'm here, Mathair said. *For as long as you wear the cuff, you will hear me. What are you going to do, young man? I can't hold you here forever, and if you're giving up, I must transfer the cuff to someone else.*

I'll keep the cuff. He didn't want to die. He had to protect Elspeth at all costs. *She's the hope for our race. I know it.*

She has many challenges ahead of her. She needs you.

He shifted his attention back to the bed. The doctor had left, and Elspeth sat beside his body, his hand still in hers.

I'll protect her.

That's not what I meant. She can protect herself.

He wasn't about to get into his relationship with Elspeth with her dead grandmother.

"Please, Goddess. *Please.* Bring him back to me." Her voice broke. "I'll do anything you ask. *Anything.* Please, bring him back. I love him."

She stretched out beside him, tucking up against him. "Take back your mantle. You need it. Come back to me, and we'll have lemon pie and lemon cake. Just come back."

She placed her palm on his heart. A blood-orange glow spread down his body.

It was strange what love looked like. Romantic comedies and advertisements portrayed smiles and laughter, sex and sparkly engagement rings. Not a woman begging a man trapped between life and death to come back. No praying, pleading, begging. No smiles and finger brushes over a body badly in need of bathing and care.

"I wanted to kill Samael. I wanted to break his body into pieces, burn them to ash, blow them away. I need you to come back and tell me I'm not a monster. That I'm not like Seanair." Her fingertips traced over his heart. "I have a rage in me now. An appetite for destruction against anyone threatening someone I love."

If he could have felt his body, he knew his breath would be dammed by the clog in his throat, and his heart would burn with a roaring, raging level of love for her that he'd never before understood.

She grasped the lightning inside him ready to strike down those who'd dare to harm what was his. What would always be his.

He got it now, what his father had felt for his mother. What it meant to know you'd found the one you'd fight for until your last breath.

I love her, he said to Mathair.

I know. For now, she's learning her power, but she's a quick study, already ahead of where I thought she'd be. One day, she'll be unstoppable. Mathair's voice held a note of pride. *What do you really want, Aleron? If I could give you one thing for yourself, what would it be?*

Her. He didn't hesitate. *If I could have only one more good thing ever, I'd want her with me for the rest of my life.*

Power isn't our greatest strength.

I never believed it, he replied. *Never understood before now. Love is our strength, and we've screwed it all up.*

There's time to fix. To repair. Not much, but all hope isn't lost.

He thought again of his parents. How they'd touched each other as Elspeth was touching him. Whispered words and shared secrets. His aura weighted, like his soul was a jar and her love was filling it full.

How will I know who is the right bearer? He couldn't sense the cuff, but he could see it midway up his arm.

I'm a ghost, not the Goddess. The true bearer of Water, this Kazumi, her veins have blued, some pushing close to the surface of her skin, like rivers or streams flowing through land. You'll know when you find the rightful keeper of Fire. They'll bear relevant markings and the cuff will sense the call of its faithful ruler.

Great. Hopefully, said *right person* wasn't camped out in a Fire commune on some remote island.

Can I call you if I need you?

I may not answer.

If possible, his spirit might have scowled. He wasn't down with being rude to Elspeth's grandmother, but Oracle-wise, she seemed like a dud.

So surly. What I mean is your call is best placed near a source of

Fire, and my answer will deliver fastest if I'm also near a supply. I travel by Fire, as you will when you die and return to the mother source.

What of our enemies? he asked.

I'm not omniscient. I will pass on what I learn if I observe something concerning. No more questions. This is your elemental last call, Aleron. Will you release your Fire and Air to their source and let your spirit reunite with your father's? Or will you return to her?

Dad? He jerked, looked, frantic to see if he could detect a hint of his father's signature.

Goddess, his father had always known the right thing to say or do. He longed to return to Elspeth, marry her, love her, keep her. But he couldn't.

For the Lennoxes to have a shot at thriving politically, she needed to ally herself with a powerhouse family. A dynasty with clout and connections and unmatched elemental muscle. Aligning with a loner like him would kill her chances of success before she even started and doom her family and the continent to political unrest.

For a second, he ached to fall into one of his dad's lung-squashing bear hugs one last time.

But he had a legend to protect. A legend he loved. A legend he'd have to let go of to see her succeed.

I'm going back to her. There was only one choice for him. *Tell my father I'm sorry for failing him when he needed me most.*

That day in the chapel came back, new life breathed into the nightmare.

The bravest thing you've ever done is weakening yourself so she remained strong enough to fight Samael. I forbade Seanair to kill you that fateful day in the chapel, as there was only one young man strong and worthy enough to tend the Fire cuff in its transition—and that is you.

A sense of peace came over him like a father's comforting hand on a child's shoulder. He'd never fill his father's shoes, but he could share something with his dad.

He could run Elite One and fight a warlock.

Send me back. His Air was prime-time ready to detect deceit. And his Fire? Oh, it was time to *cook.*

He took one last look at Elspeth nuzzling his cheek with her nose, her hand still over his heart, pressing red and white light into his skin. Then she stood, trying to convince Maylene to get out of the bed and eat, but the bulldog let out a snorty sigh and nuzzled the side of his chest.

His two protectors whom he needed to relieve of their guard.

I promise to defend and serve her with everything I have. I'm ready.

And he'd love her from a distance. Close enough to protect her, but far enough away to let her go.

War looms. The covens have spent the last century preparing to take back what they lost. Remember that. Mathair's tone was more kickass grandma than sweet old lady. *Hang on. This is going to hurt.*

CHAPTER
TWENTY-SIX

His eyes flew open. Breath shoved into his mouth, barreling down his throat and overfilling his lungs like they were maxed-out balloons. His Fire and Air crash-landed. He sat up, immediately doubling over. Tears welled and spilled, and the pressure behind his eyeballs threatened to smush them like grapes.

Whatever had put him back together again had smashed his Fire, Air, and human body together like a multicar pileup.

He groaned, and nausea flew up him like fire over dry grass.

"Easy. You're okay." Elspeth's hand pressed on his shoulder. "You're back."

A hot mass of fur and claws stretched and grunted beside him. Maylene rose slowly, snorting and snuffling, eyeing him like he'd had the audacity to disturb a queen. He gave her a scratch between the ears.

"She hasn't left you once. I haven't either."

His hand got a quick slurp. Elspeth got a my-roasted-chicken-better-be-ready glare before Maylene jumped off the bed and jangled her way out of the room.

"Your grandmother isn't a gentle woman." It felt like his not overly helpful Oracle had superglued his Humpty Dumpty ass back together again in mismatched pieces.

"You saw Mathair?" Elspeth sat up, putting some space between them in her king-sized bed.

"Heard, not saw. She made it clear she's a package deal as long as I'm wearing the Fire cuff. Can I get some extra pillows? I want to be propped up." He lifted the sheets, confirming he had on boxers and nothing else. Oddly enough, his gunshot wound had pinked over, the mark depicting months of healing instead of days.

A built-in medic wouldn't be a bad perk for an emissary.

She grabbed pillows off the floor and two more out of a chair, positioning them behind his head. He almost grabbed her, pulled her down on top of him, and held the hell on. But his personal house was on fire, his lungs aching like he'd taken up smoking and puffed his way through an entire carton of cigarettes. He rose, thinking he'd rest sitting up a little more, but things went spinny, and he sagged back.

"I have no strength," He put a hand to his clammy face, certain he must be as pasty and pale as the ceiling, and wished his cuff came with caffeine injections.

"You've been out since last night."

"I lost a day?" Good ol' Grandma left that one out.

The air glittered and sparkled. Heat banded his arm.

"It's still there." Elspeth's head dropped back, and she let out a long sigh. "I'm so glad he didn't get it."

He. Samael.

A soon-to-be-dead warlock.

It all came back. The stench floating through the vents had reeked of rotting dirt. Of invisible rock walls, closing in and compacting him like trash.

"Bring me up to speed." There'd be no relaxing. He needed to get his elements in peak shape, pronto.

"First things first. You have to reclaim your mantle."

"No."

"Yes. You need it."

"Not as much as you do."

Her eyebrow arched, like she was fixing to call him on his crankiness. He knew he was a Goddess-awful patient and wouldn't wish himself on a battle-ax nurse.

"Listen up, my stubborn Fire. With this mantle, it's like my size-eight feet are trying to walk in your size-fourteen shoes." She returned to her seat beside him. "I think it's actually dangerous for me. I blew out level-seven bulletproof windows battling Samael, which Graham insisted shouldn't have been possible since I don't have solid control of my Air yet." She took his hand in hers. "Take it back. I'm not meant to have it, and when we mess with Mother Nature, we always screw up."

"See the bigger ring?" He lifted the gold chain around his neck, the two rings clinking. "Slip it on your finger and then imagine downloading the power into it." He tried to think back to what he'd done when he'd given it to her, but only one thing came to mind. "Try thinking the command *off* and visualize removing a coat. The ring's a relic, and I don't remember my father doing anything special when he transferred his power to me."

"It's beautiful." She took the ring. "I love the square diamonds and sapphires. Is it an Air relic?"

"Has to be. It's from my mother's side of the family. But a relic doesn't discriminate against the energy it's given, regardless of the power of the owner. This ring will hold any element." He shifted to get more comfortable, the move seeming to jar his brain.

Goddess, he hurt. Right down to the hair on his arms.

She slipped the ring onto her pinkie, closed her eyes. Took a deep breath. Froze. Let it out. Pulled off the band and rested it on his chest.

The ring vibrated as it had that fateful day in the chapel.

"It's back." Energy pressed through his skin, his primary Fire flaming hot for the return of its sidekick. "Catch me up on what I missed."

She recounted the attack. The cleanup by Elite One and Kazumi saving the damned day. He'd be wearing their friendship bracelet for a good, long time. Hell, he might hug Half Gallon next time he saw her. That little spout was a keeper, and he'd need her help.

"The only true fear I've ever felt is when Seanair killed my father." He shifted his gaze to Elspeth's, needing proof she wasn't a dream. "Soul-crushing terror filled me when I realized that warlock could have ground me like an ant into the pavement with little effort."

He doubled over at a horrendous cough, his lungs rejecting the elemental sludge he'd breathed.

The doorbell rang.

"I'll get you some water. I'll be right back." He watched her leave and sank into the pillows, debating what hurt worse. Getting shot? Or having his power hurtle back into him like a crater-creating asteroid?

Voices he didn't recognize came from the other room, along with the squawk of a comm device. Guards. Good. He hadn't gotten a solid bead on Graham yet, but he didn't seem like the type to jack around on security. Elspeth had better have an entire regiment camped outside her front door.

"Aleron."

His name was a whisper in a voice he hadn't heard in twelve years. His pulse stuttered.

"Mama?" He brought his gaze up slowly, scared he was seeing some post-concussion mirage.

She stood in the doorway. His throat jammed up, clogged with fear and disbelief. He was uncertain what to say. He'd understood why she'd publicly disowned him, but seeing Ada Foussé made all the despair flood back like it'd been yesterday.

"My first lovebug." Her chin quivered, her eyes filling with tears as she came to the edge of the bed.

She'd aged. Still tall and willowy, but her wiry, shoulder-length hair had more gray streaks than black. She'd never shot fillers and poison into her face, and Goddess knew, he'd been the cause of the lines streaking across her forehead and framing her eyes.

Elspeth came in and handed him a glass of water. "I wasn't sure you were going to make it, so I called her. I showed her an entry from Seanair's journal about what happened that day in the chapel. I hope you're not angry."

Part of him was petrified his mother would tell Elspeth what a monumental screw-up he was and how she should run far and fast, but the agony in her eyes that she'd done something horribly wrong tore at his still-weak heart.

"You did good." He managed a smile, his teeth about the only thing that didn't hurt.

"I'll go heat up some soup, give you two time alone." She gave a small nod to his mother and left.

The door snicked shut softly.

His mom hovered in the space between the wall and the bed, as if she wanted to move forward but wasn't sure yet. He was afraid to urge her over. Afraid her hesitancy was disgust at him for what he'd done. What he'd become.

"You good?" Her voice carried the same gentle tone of concern. One he hadn't believed he'd ever hear again.

"Yes, ma'am." Anxiety took first place in the race of emotions playing smashup in his gut.

"She's a lovely young woman. She told me you gave her your father's mantle and tried to give her your primary one too?"

"Yes, ma'am. I'd have given my life to save hers."

"You love her." Not a question.

"Yes, ma'am." He nodded, blinking hard. "It won't work out, though. I have a duty to her."

"You do, indeed." And there was the I'll-have-more-to-say-on-that-one-later mom voice. "I'm absolutely certain your father's proud of you. Whether he still resides at the source of Fire or he's been born into another body, wherever he is, he loves you and doesn't blame you for what happened. He knew the risks. We both did." His mom came and sat on the bed. "Look at me. I never blamed you for what happened. Not once. Your brothers didn't either."

"I didn't do one thing to help him." He turned his head, unable to meet her eyes.

"Your father and I strategized every outcome. The worst-case scenario came true, and I followed through on the agreement we made together." His mother took his hand. "I disowned you because if I hadn't, Seanair would have doubted your loyalty and killed you. To protect your brothers and you, all ties to your former life had to be cut. So I cut them."

His throat burned as he stared out the window, the sky gray, the afternoon sun missing. "You had every right to disown me. I couldn't give him back his mantle. I'm the reason why Dad was killed. I should have run to him, given him back the ring. I was a sniveling coward, frozen like a weak little weasel, listening to the whole Goddess-forsaken thing. It should have been me."

"No, sir. It shouldn't have and wasn't supposed to be." She put a hand on his arm, gripping tight. "Listen to me, son. Moving on from your father was difficult enough. If I'd lost two of my brave men, I wouldn't have made it. Protecting you was our first priority. We both decided your dad would give you his mantle, as it offered the best protection. Your father didn't fear death, and the last promise I made to him was to do everything I could to keep you alive." Her warm hand squeezed and let go. "And I did."

She was being kind, and so…his mom. But she still didn't know the worst of his weakness.

"If Dad was going to pay, I should have borne witness to his sacrifice. I smelled it. The final smoke. Pain has a scent. Seanair claimed it was instant, but I've killed enough people to know Dad had a moment of agony. And I did nothing but cry."

"No, honey."

"Seanair didn't say the prayer of succession."

"It's okay. I'm certain the Goddess welcomed him home."

"You can't know that." His failure rose, pounding at his temples, cutting off his air. "Mom, I should have been man enough—"

"No!" Air whipped around the room, fluttering the sheets, the magazines on the bedside table, shifting the paintings off-center on the wall. "Your father would have never wanted you to see that. If you take anything I say to heart, remember this: In his final moments, he would have been at peace knowing you didn't watch, knowing you'd remember him as a living person and not his human shell flashed to dust." She gently pushed his hair off his forehead. "Your brothers and I agreed from the moment we learned of your father's death. We didn't want to lose two of you, so we did what we had to do."

His brothers. Goddess, his brothers.

"Are they okay?" He ground his jaw to keep from begging to know if they'd forgiven him.

They might have accepted his mother's edicts to keep him safe, but that didn't mean they'd be willing to ever speak again to the brother who'd caused their father's death. His mother could offer all the lovely words she wanted. It had been his fault, and he'd never outrun the guilt.

"The twins are working security right now at an Air sit-down, but they said to tell you they plan to whip your ass as soon as they can. Emeric will be here later. He's coming to help Graham with continent president protocol and the Fire cuff."

She didn't know he had it, and he couldn't tell her. It'd be safer for her if she didn't know. He erased the thought. She'd used her Air on them as boys, especially on his pain-in-the-butt twin brothers, but he hadn't detected her use of it on him. He needed to keep her from being curious enough to try.

The secret had to remain between him, Elspeth, Graham, Ross.

And *shit*. That other warlock, Egan.

He changed the subject fast. "How long has Em known Elspeth's brother?"

"Apparently, for years. According to Em, nerds unite, and I guess he and Graham share a passion for data. Em was recently promoted to head data scientist and historian at the Global Natura Archives."

Emotion boiled inside him. Anger, joy, agony, love. His brothers were safe and, by the sound of it, thriving and healthy. And his mother had pulled off one of the biggest Natura societal shams ever.

"You fooled Seanair."

"I did what I had to do for my firstborn baby boy." Her hand drew across his cheek. "Now, tell me about this strong, smart, lovely woman."

"Elspeth's still on the hunt for a treatment for the tripowered disease, and the Lennoxes will need all the help they can get to stay in power. I can't give her either of those things." He pulled the chain and found the rings that had fallen to the pillow. "Do you want Dad's wedding ring back?"

His mother's firmed mouth wobbled.

"You kept it," she whispered. "Yes…I…you've had it all these years? Let me help you."

She leaned over him and unhooked the clasp.

"It kept me focused. Well, the rings and the scar."

Her eyes narrowed on the gash that he knew was hidden a little by his scruff.

"How could you—oh my goodness. You've carried this mark all these years? Aleron Jacques Foussé, you heal that right this second."

"Sure, Mom." Anything to focus her on something besides Elspeth.

He watched his mom slide his father's scuffed gold band onto her left ring finger. He blinked several times to make sure she was real. His mom. The woman who'd taught him to love.

He placed his palm on the scar and called up his Fire. Heat tingled and zinged over the spot he'd shaved around for twelve years. He noted the trademark brush of her Air, ready to step in if he needed help.

The repair complete, he eyed his mother. "You're stronger than Dad was."

"Technically, yes, but what mattered is we shared an equal, fierce love." Her smile turned wistful.

"But you lost your family when you married him."

She'd fallen for a Cajun Fire and left behind a life of mansions and money and power.

"My parents have come around. Emeric's a Fire, a strong one like your dad. The twins are…Goddess, help us." She shook her head. "They're Dual Fire and Airs, double trouble, and they have raised absolute gusty hell with your grandfather. I don't even recognize the man anymore, and my mother invites Emeric for tea."

"The twins are worse than when they were younger?" Little nut punchers, both of them.

"I made them promise to wait a few days before they come to see you. You'll need to be at your best when they show up. They're twenty-two going on eight."

Hope threatened to rise at seeing bookish Emeric and his fire-whirl brothers. Duals. The Goddess must have had one too many the day they were born.

She nodded toward his chain. "I'm glad you still have the vessel ring. It should have disintegrated after use, so it must have some lives left, which is unusual. The Goddess likes to keep us on our toes." She stood, getting that I-have-an-idea gleam in her eye. "I've been rather busy since the day your father passed. I believe I can gain the Lennoxes some support, but you know the situation better than I do. Would you mind if I make a few calls?"

"Sure. They need backers."

"I agree the Lennoxes need allies, and you might be surprised at the pull of Ada Foussé."

"I don't remember you ever being involved in politics."

"A lot has changed in twelve years." She cut her gaze toward the kitchen before locking those steel-blue eyes on him. "Don't you dare let her go unless you *want* to."

"I don't have what she needs."

"I'll be back as soon as I can. And, Aleron?" She moved to the door, then turned and glared down her nose. "If you love her, that's enough."

CHAPTER
TWENTY-SEVEN

E lspeth stirred the bone broth, adding sliced ginger to help settle Aleron's stomach. She should have called his mother sooner, back when she'd read Seanair's diary and learned how Bill Foussé had been murdered, but so much had happened, so un-Goddessly fast. Exhaustion draped across her shoulders. She needed to sleep for a month, tucked against Aleron's warm, firm body.

But then she'd never get caught up.

She still had a treatment to find, a rescheduled sit-down to attend, and a shiny new job as Judex. Oh, and a memorial service to plan, a replacement to hire for her at Kindred—who couldn't be Ross because he'd been tapped as Graham's right hand—and a power-transition plan to put together for her family. She braced her hands on the counter and tried to convince herself she'd be fine. She'd survive, sure. Keep calm, carry on, and all that BS.

But without Aleron, she'd remain forever far from fine. She'd breathe. And work. Exist. Support the family. Do what had to be done.

Like always.

Flora walked into the kitchen, plopped her hemp bag on the breakfast table alongside a takeout container, and dug around inside her purse. Elspeth wouldn't have been surprised if her Earth cousin had started pulling out rosebushes and garden hoes like the satchel was magical.

"Sorry I'm so late. I picked up some freshly roasted chicken for Maylene."

"She's hiding out in my closet. That dog is just as persnickety as Lach. She's sworn her allegiance to Aleron, and she only comes to me when she's sulky or hungry." She pulled a bowl from the cabinet and set it on the counter.

"I'm not surprised she's sulky. Animals experience loss and stress, and she's missing her adoring master." Flora dumped the pre-cut chicken into the bowl, placing it beside Maylene's water on the floor. "You still haven't heard anything from him?"

"Not since right after I got my powers. He likely knows about Seanair, but he hasn't texted or called to check in."

Flora went back to rummaging in her purse. "Isidora's Water may be good for Lach. She has a potent sexual energy unlike anything I've ever felt."

"You've been with her?"

How had she missed that news?

"My first communion and regeneration was with her." Flora put three little baggies on the counter as a peaceful reminiscence softened her expression. "Orgasm's the gate to energy transfer, and she made sure my first experience was sacred and whole. I heard about Seanair, and some of his behavior makes sense now. Desperate men do terrible things." She picked up the baggies. "Good men, however, like Aleron, need adaptogens. Add a pinch of tulsi and maca powder. Turmeric, too, for reducing inflammation."

"You're a walking apothecary."

"I've got oils and tinctures, too, but we don't want to overwhelm his system. Elements are quite good at healing themselves if given time and the right supports." Flora whipped her hair to one side, her fingers quickly plaiting a long braid. "I have something for you as well." She pulled out a glass vial, the liquid inside inky and sparkly.

"What *is* that?" She shuddered at the sensations coming from the small container. The good kind of ahh. Hands. No, stones. Pressing firm and warm all over her body.

"It's called Black Gold, and it's a Freddy special, just for you."

She took the container. So Freddy was more than just a purveyor of Natura moonshine. Earth power, like nothing she'd ever experienced, surrounded her like she'd dropped deep into a well. "What's in it?"

"That's as close to pure Earth energy as you can get. Freddy never gives up his recipes, so I have no idea what's in the base. The gold flecks are samples of the earth's crust from the world's deepest borehole, almost forty thousand feet, in Russia." Flora nodded at the tiny bottle. "Drink it. It'll fortify your Earth energy until you can get a proper regen."

"I won't have to have sex with anyone else?"

Please, Goddess, I just want Aleron.

"Normally, I'd say you would, but I have no idea of the refueling requirements of a Nexus, and they may be different. Who knows? You keep the Fire and Air fed, you might prop up the Earth and Water. Sometimes, a rising tide does lift all boats."

She wanted to pull the cork and down the whole thing. "You trust Freddy?"

Flora's expression darkened. "Freddy's an Earth ace forever in your back pocket. He's brilliant and eccentric, but I honestly believe he is literally the salt of the earth. No shit."

"Down the hatch." She tipped back the vial. Her gag reflex kicked in at the thick, gelatinous glob of wet soil, rock, and the tang of metal clogging her nose and stinging her eyes.

"Freddy said it's like scotch. No one likes it the first time." Flora's bright smile put her clearly on Team Freddy. "He is so… A night with that man will change your life."

A stillness dredged through her. An oil slathering her insides. Something tugged at the soles of her feet, pulling her down, as if towing and tightening her to the planet's surface. Her Earth energy strained and stretched as if waking from a deep sleep.

"I won't be seeking Freddy out for sex, but that tonic—" Holy rollin' Mother, her Earth energy felt…well, solid, with Water skipping along happily beside it.

"Freddy's perfection." Flora's nose wrinkled with her self-assured grin. "I can't believe he makes it in an aluminum pail and stirs it with a stick. By the way, he said you still need a commune. The Great Mother loves to interact with her children."

"I need to have a serious talk with Her." She tried to lighten the mood, mainly to give herself a moment's break.

"I'm sorry," Flora said, taking the empty container and shoving it back in her bag. "In all my Freddy fandom, I didn't think to ask how you're handling all of this."

"We need help." She turned off the burner, moving the pot of bone broth to cool. "Graham's spent the last twelve years out in California. The rumors are rampant that he wants nothing to do with his elements, that he doesn't commune, that he's devoted his life to human science to try to divorce himself from his power."

No one knew the real Graham, but despite his reluctance, she was confident he'd take the leadership role and finesse every detail. As a kid, he'd kept a planner, made exhaustive lists. Behind the scenes, where he thrived, he'd be fabulous as the brains behind their leadership. Given his hatred for protocol? Well…he might not make the best public face for their family.

"When it counts, Graham always gets it right," she added. "But I think you and I should handle the details for the memorial service. He's not one for societal protocol, and I know what's expected."

"Aleron loves you. You know that, right? Tell me you know that."

"We love each other, but it doesn't change anything."

Flora's blond brows whipped up. "It changes everything."

"I need an alliance with power."

"That won't be a problem. People will bend over backward to get in your good graces. Having the support of someone who truly loves you will take you farther than power ever will. You need to be with someone you trust. True love has changed the fate of the world many times, and we're on the cusp of requiring Goddess-level intervention. You're the star we've been needing."

She almost laughed. A shooting star—or the lack of one on her twelfth birthday—had started this whole thing.

"You don't understand. A warlock wants to take down this family, maybe even all Naturas. He's reckless and doesn't care if he outs us to the humans. I can't think of a bigger Rome than that, in Natura terms. In fact, I think he wants our secret known."

"A warlock's the big emergency? I abandoned my group cleaning up an old arsenic mine in Kent for a warlock? Put Kerr on it. He's taken some kind of special interest in the covens. I've caught him reeking of their scent a few times. He may be sleeping with one. I hear their sex charms are the ultimate high."

"That's what I wanted to talk to you about." She took down a bowl from the cabinet and filled it with soup, wondering how Aleron's discussion with his mom was going. "You need to be careful. The warlock who attacked us mentioned you."

She put the empty pot in the sink.

"He'd charmed Earth and nothing else, right?"

"That's the only energy I read." And Goddess, part of her wanted a second read and a third. The allure of Samael had been— what was wrong with her? How could she even go there about a man who'd almost killed Aleron? "He's...enthralling."

"I'm sure he is. His energy's still in your hair, and it reeks of the eroticism Earths are known for. I know what he wants." She waved a *whatever* hand. "Do you know the difference between us and the coven classes?"

Embarrassment stole up the back of her neck. She was doomed to wear the Miss Ignorant crown forever. "Witches and warlocks have to call power to them, but our power lives within us."

There. The sum of her knowledge.

"The difference is in the details." Flora pulled out a chair from the breakfast table. "The elemental seed we're born with has two parts: a shell and the power. It's like candy with a crispy outer shell and the gooey inside. Alphas and Betas get both parts, though the Betas' elements are less strong. The Gammas and Deltas—the coven classes—only get the shell. When they call power, the 'goo' fills up the empty vessel, but they can't hold the energy for long."

"Right. Innate power versus called power. Seanair looked down on anyone who wasn't born preloaded with Alpha-level power, which is so weird, because it's not like Alphas can't have a Beta child. I've heard, too, that coven members can have Alpha-level children, and Alphas can have witches and warlocks. The *scandal.*" She air-quoted the word.

People should love their children. Period. No matter whether they had power or not.

"Being so prejudiced topped his sin list. Now, what did the warlock say exactly?" Flora's eyes narrowed in concentration.

She fought through the haze of the attack, her mind already fuzzing the details to help her cope.

"He said, 'Give me Flora.'" She recalled his voice, how it'd taken on a low, erotic, echo-y tone. "That you were to come to him in two days. You had to be alone. And he'd give you back when he was ready." Aleron's near-death chokes and gasps replayed. She clasped her hands and squeezed, refusing to panic. "I agreed just to get him to stop crushing Aleron's body, suffocating him. But I would never let him take you. I'd die first."

A thought dawned. She knew Samael's signature. Maybe she could track him. Find him. Kill—

I won't be that kind of Judex. I won't be like Seanair.

"Did you literally say the word 'yes' when he made his demands?" Flora put a finger to her mouth.

"I don't remember exactly what I said, but he stopped killing Aleron, so I must have, or at least something similar." Who cared what she said? No way was Flora going anywhere near Samael.

"That explains it." Flora's gaze went long. "I've been summoned before, and it pisses me off."

"Summoned?"

"A Natura-issued warrant for when a binding covenant's been made." Flora stood and hiked her purse straps up her shoulder. "I have to go to him. The longer I wait, the more painful it'll become. Right now, it's occasional stomach cramps."

What the hell?

"You're not going to him."

"He made a demand, gave three terms, and it was accepted by a blood relative."

"No. *No.*" She glared up at her six-foot-tall cousin. "I didn't sign anything. You act like there's a contract."

"There is. You made a deal with a warlock. Did he say anything about killing me?" Her tone held hope, like there'd be some shiny silver lining to this asinine discussion.

"No, he said he'd return you, like he was borrowing a car. You are not—"

She flipped up a listen-to-me hand. "For a warlock to keep an element inside himself for an extended period of time, he'd either have to conjure and call it repeatedly, which is exhausting, and it'd take more and more element energy every time." A tight-lipped smile pulled across her face. "Or he can regen with a Natura, preferably an Alpha. Some say that if a witch or warlock regens enough, they can permanently seal the energy inside their shells. I'm the strongest Earth in the United States. This is about sex."

The high cost of her ignorance hit her. She could have studied their ways on her own, could have borrowed Kazumi's textbooks. But she'd been so determined to prove her worth to a man who'd never seen it that she'd poured every bit of herself into Kindred. Days. Nights. Weekends.

She knew more about humans than she did her own people.

"I didn't know." Oh, Goddess, what had she done? "I'm *sorry.*" She tugged Flora against her, hugged her tight. "I'm so sorry."

"It's not your fault."

"Yes, it is."

How could she have been so clueless? She'd heard the charm in Samael's voice, had fallen into the hypnotic beauty of his gray eyes, but that was no excuse.

Flora should be angry, or scared, or a thousand other emotions. She shouldn't be standing there, seeming more exasperated than anything.

"We are reaping what our grandfather sowed, and this is not the last of the sins we'll have to bear. The Goddess always has a plan."

Flora gave a dismissive flick of her fingers. "Samael said he'd release me, which means he can't kill me—or try to—no matter what I do. I almost wish he'd put that on the table so I could bury his arrogant ass, but I'll go to him and give him what he wants. I'm quite skilled at cycling power."

There had to be another way.

"I won't let you do this."

"You can't stop what you've put in motion." Grass-green light swirled in Flora's eyes. "The lesson, though, is understanding from now on that everything you say matters. Especially with witches."

She gripped Flora's forearms at a wave of dizziness.

"Listen, E," Flora went on before Elspeth could speak. "Samael killed our grandfather, gravely injured the man you love, and threatened you." Her smooth expression sharpened. "I think he needs to get a load of me. Besides, what better way to figure out what he's up to than to be in his bed?"

Hitching her satchel higher on her shoulder, she placed a kiss on Elspeth's forehead. "I've gotta run. The summons was enacted yesterday, so I have until tomorrow. I'll handle it."

She couldn't believe Flora was being so…blasé. "Please don't go. Samael…he's evil."

"He won't be evil to me. He needs me at my best, which means he'll likely be quite charming, so I'll cycle my strongest energy. You don't believe me, but this is a good thing. Something's up with the covens, and I'm going to figure out what."

"Flora…" She'd call Graham. Or Kerr. Kerr would know how to stop his twin.

"I'll be fine." Flora gave her a peck on the cheek. "Trust me, this situation's been brewing for years. Any game with the witches is chess." Green flashed dark and deep in her eyes. "And they've made the mistake of summoning a queen."

CHAPTER
TWENTY-EIGHT

leron sank into the pillows, his gaze locked on a can light in the ceiling, his power thrumming with regenned glee. The sound of Elspeth's shower acted as a soothing white noise. A primal part of him longed to pull her from the water washing him from her skin and body. She'd already hidden his element signature, which was essentially like dusting a piece of furniture and using your own power to remove your partner's essence. He had to do the same with hers. Didn't want to, but they had a ruse to maintain.

He focused on his Fire and carefully baked the essence of her energy into his. His Air next, he funneled and spun her energy, whipping them together until his element overpowered hers. He supposed the elimination resembled cooking, where individual ingredients blended to create a unique whole. The longer he slept with her, his base signature would shift, but her energy would remain indistinguishable.

His elements would run hotter, faster, better, and no one would know the source of the premier fuel. He couldn't help but wonder if she got as much from him as he did from her. He'd pushed a tremendous amount of power into her and had pulled so much in return his eyes had damn near crossed.

He settled into post-sex perfection. His head lolled toward the windows with the gift of her energy now safely tucked away.

His favorite secret. His dream, real for the moment.

Elspeth's scent floated around him, the mix of her, him—the perfumed twist of them—soothing something deep and scarred inside him. Outside the windows, the day brightened, the sun lighting the sky a pale blue. His pulse had returned to normal, his body lax, sated, his power strong.

He hadn't known how different sex could be with someone you cared for. Hot, sweet, slow. *Slow.* He'd taken his time exploring her body, studying her responses, learning how the tip of his tongue brought her to breathlessness, how his hands could have her arching against him, the two of them sliding in sweet friction against each other.

A slow burn.

His body, soul, and power had been healed by a gradual, dreamy, delicious burn.

"You'd better grab a shower fast, or I'll have to bodyguard myself." She stood in the doorway, a white towel knotted over her breasts, covering the curves he'd kneaded and gripped.

Bodyguard herself. Only if he was dead.

"No chance, Ms. Nexus." He took her in, a leisurely study of her skin's flush from the water's heat. "I'd rather you get back in this bed with me." He stretched, grunted, yawned.

"You promised you wouldn't." Her eyes rounded with *please, don't.* "We agreed."

They'd settled on a bodyguard-with-benefits relationship, but he'd lied to himself. A flat-out, willful lie. He could in no way distance himself from her. Not physically. Not mentally. Not lovingly.

He couldn't go ostrich anymore and bury his head in reality's cruel sand. If he wanted her for now, erasing scents and role-playing in public would be their terms. He needed to suck it up, quit dreaming of forever.

"You're right. I'll be out in fifteen minutes." He threw back the comforter and walked his nude body past her and into the guest room. A two-minute shower, sixty-second toothbrushing, and a zig with the razor later, and he was dressed and making one last inspection of his scar-free face.

"Ready?" Her voice invaded the small bath.

Yes, he was. Ready to teach her every Fire and Air trick. Ready to defend her until his elements returned to their source. Ready to love her until his last breath.

In an hour, the meeting at the Roxy would squash the inner voices blasting him about shoving the truth of her situation aside and just loving her.

He wasn't ready. He'd never be ready to let her go, watch her marry another man, or think about someone else regenning with her.

With her, he wanted fast and slow, raunchy and sweet, every kind of sex.

He wanted love and lovemaking and hope of living his dream—with her.

"Be right there," he called out, the irony not lost on him. He would be right there, forever right there.

For her.

He heard the jangling first. A drooling four-legged princess bounded into his room. Maylene plopped her fancy-collared butt right in front of him, her tongue hanging out, her expression *you may worship me now*. The dog had crowned him as her stand-in king, following him to the bathroom, the kitchen, pretty much anywhere. He felt sorry for the poor girl who sulked most days, which was why he'd defied the fresh-chicken-only rule and slipped Maylene a bit of bacon last night in her dinner bowl.

"I'll be back, Miss May." He took a knee, nearly losing his balance as the fifty-pound princess planted her front paws on his chest.

"You are just as bad as Lach." Elspeth leaned against the dresser. "Even the guards are arguing over who gets to walk her next."

The persnickety pooch was a constant reminder of her brother. He shouldn't try to cheer her up with something he couldn't deliver, although his gut told him they hadn't seen the last of Lach.

"He'll be back."

"I hope you're right." She picked a stray hair off the sleeve of her deep-plum suit. "We should go. There is no fashionably late when you're the host."

"You're ready. You'll do great."

"My power's nowhere near as trained as it should be. I don't want my signature to read as Nexus Lite."

Her perfectionist tendencies were going to drive her bonkers. Bonkers? Goddess, he had it bad.

"You can't jam six years of training into a week, and they'd probably fear you if you could. You're already ahead of where you should be. Your goal's to offer them hope, to promise a different approach to justice." He wished she could see what he saw. "A fair Judex who offers something other than punishment has been a pipe dream. You will screw up, but the difference is you'll own your mistakes. That kind of honesty will reach people."

"I hope you're right. I need to be at my best to support Graham. He's got an even bigger sell than I do."

He went to her because he couldn't stop himself. He slid his arm across her shoulders, kissed her hair. "I believe in you."

"Looks like it's you and me against the Natura world, then. Let's get going. I need to talk some sense into my cousin before she hands herself over to a madman."

Elspeth had filled him in on the Flora situation. How that Earth could agree to give herself over to a warlock baffled the hell out of him. Elite One had little information on Samael, especially with not knowing his last name, though they had linked him to a shadow warlock group. The city had been quiet since their attack, leading Aleron to believe Samael would lie low unless Flora didn't answer the summons.

They made the trip in the Mini Cooper in silence and had the good fortune of catching a pocket of faster-moving traffic on the FDR. As they pulled up on the Sixth Avenue side of Radio City Music Hall, two Beta Airs met them, one valeting the vehicle, the other ushering them through the main doors and then through a VIP entrance.

"Who's your mom bringing with her?" Elspeth asked.

He held the door as she stepped into a waiting elevator.

"I have no idea. Her text this morning read, 'See you at ten with reinforcements."' He wished she'd given him more, but he couldn't push. Not at this early stage. His mom might come to her senses, realize she'd made a monumental mistake, and disown him a second time.

The five lit up on the display, and the doors opened.

"Here goes everything." Elspeth straightened, poised and regal and as intoxicating as a finely carved statue of a goddess.

Great Mother N, the woman cut a picture of pure power. Shoulders back, head held high, she walked straight through the reception room into the lounge, her gait smooth and commanding as hell in high-ass heels.

He followed at a respectful distance, picking a spot in the middle of the lounge, assuming the position that had initially been beaten into him, folding his hands behind his back. Keeping close to her. Forever close to her.

Of course, Half Gallon shot from the corner where the Water contingent camped, and he did a double take. Kazumi, or Zum, as he thought of her now since the woman was a serious Water jet, exuded colossal, oceanic potential. Her black hair slicked back, she had on a killer navy jumpsuit and chunky-heeled space boots, like she was an undersea commander straight out of a sci-fi flick.

A veil of tension enshrouded the elegant room. Twenty-foot ceilings decked out in gold. Cherry-paneled walls. He'd been to enough of these gigs with Seanair to recognize custom draperies and furniture.

He took in the groups staked out in tight camps.

Graham, Kerr, Ross, and Flora stood in one corner. Flora was nose to nose with Kerr, chin jutting, lips moving, laying down some serious law with her twin. Graham held up a hand, leaning in, while Ross put a hand on Kerr's shoulder, achieving a moment's détente.

Jon Costa stood at the fireplace with the Fire contingent. His daughter, Liz, looked lost, her gaze somewhere far from the conversation he was having with two other women.

The Earth Magnus would join from Germany via videoconference, which would likely be the shortest speech at today's meeting. The Germans were short on words and long on impact.

A three-toned chime sounded, and a panel slid back into the wall. Aleron's mother emerged in a dark blue dress, her hair swept back in an elegant, tight twist. Not the maker of lemon cakes he remembered. Two others he didn't know followed closely behind her, along with a tall, blond, young man with round glasses, whose dark suit did little to hide his lanky frame.

Pressure shoved at the back of his eyes. His breath slowed. Time stopped, flashed back, spearing him with the youthful intelligence that remained rooted in his brother's eyes.

Emeric crossed the room, threw his spindly arms around Aleron, and squeezed.

"Big bro. Brawn of the family."

The heat of the words pushed through the sweater into his shoulder. He folded his arms, awkward and leery, around Emeric, sure his brother would recover from this temporary madness.

"You're not a little nerd anymore."

"Almost as tall as your bulked-up ass." Em stepped out of the hug and mirrored Aleron's pose, standing shoulder to shoulder, his hands behind him.

His mother looked to Graham, who gave a nod and stepped forward.

"Good morning, everyone." Silence filled the room, everyone waiting to see if Graham could command the space like Seanair had. "Thank you for coming. We'll adjourn to the dining room for business in a moment, but first I'd like to cede the floor to Ada Foussé, lieutenant-elect of the US southern region for Air."

What? That tidbit hadn't been included in any Elite One intel Aleron had seen.

Or maybe Seanair had ensured it hadn't.

"Good morning," his mother said. "I'll be brief and direct. Many of you know my son Emeric, who's recently taken on the role of chief data scientist at the Global Natura Archives." She gestured to Em, who gave a slight bow. "You may not be aware of my firstborn son, the one I denounced twelve years ago." She took a step forward, her gaze locked on Aleron. "I disowned him to save his life from the tyrant who is no more. I love Aleron with all my heart. I never stopped loving him, and I'm humbled to the foundation of who I am at the horrific sacrifices he has made for the safety of our family. I am honored to be his mother and am proud of the man he's become. I'm absolutely certain his father, Goddess bless his departed Fire, feels the same."

His heart had to be beating. His lungs inflating. He still stood, though his leg muscles threatened to revolt. He cut a cautious gaze over the room and locked on Elspeth, whose eyes glistened.

"I request my son's name be reinstated in the family's archive and that he be listed as executor of the Foussé estate and holdings." She placed a hand over her heart and looked to Graham.

"By the Mother, make it so." Graham bowed.

They bent forward in sync, the rest of the room following suit. A symbol of acknowledgment, admiration, and respect.

"Please adjourn to the dining room," Graham invited, and the crowd made their way to a massive round table through a square archway.

"Welcome back to the fold." Em hung back with Aleron and nudged his arm. "We prayed for your safety every night. Mom's become quite the mover and shaker in American Air politics. She's even gaining ground with the Canadians, which is something Seanair never achieved."

"I don't know what to say. I can't think."

"Job security for me as the family's brain." Em's face grew serious. "You were never far from our hearts. Never. I missed you more than you'll ever know."

Em reached into his jacket and pulled out a flash drive. "I've been in my new position for only a few weeks, but I pulled everything I could find in the database on a Nexus. There's not much digitized information, but I'm sure, somewhere in the world, there's a book in someone's library. Someone knows something. We'll just have to figure out who."

As Aleron listened, he cast out his power, making sure Elspeth was fine. He sensed her beside Kazumi, and his worry disappeared.

"You don't hate me?" He couldn't tear his gaze from the drive, afraid of what he'd see in his brother's eyes.

"By totally focusing on Elite One and rising through the ranks, you saved us. There's a whole lot more to this situation than you know. Next time you're home, you need to read Dad's journals."

"I never imagined Dad as much of a write-it-down kinda guy."

"There's a lot you haven't had the chance to learn. He took the one shot he had to try and fix Fire, but sadly he failed. That left you to earn Seanair's trust and keep the rest of us off that bastard's radar."

"I didn't think you knew, or could know."

"Dude, you're counting Mom short. Me, I understand, but wait until you get a load of Mom."

He looked at the woman sitting coolly in her place at the table, neither overly confident nor remotely arrogant.

"My memories of her are more dessert maker than ass kicker."

"Just hang on. She's totally dialed in to our people, and her radar's all over the place with this witch thing. She's sure proud you're protecting our Nexus."

"This sounds suspiciously like you're not planning to double down on disowning me."

Emeric's genius must have shorted out his common sense.

"One and done, bro. My goal's to make sure you have all the information you need to be successful. We'd better go in." Em nodded toward where the Earth Magnus's image appeared on a large flat-screen. "Word of warning. Guard your nads when you see the twins. I'm sure they'll tackle you."

He followed Em and stood just inside the room, facing Elspeth, who spoke with Kazumi and another Water he didn't know. Masako Fukada eyed him with reservation, as if measuring his worth. Her gaze shifted to Elspeth, to him, and the smallest of smiles curled the corners of her mouth. She gave a barely perceptible nod. A gentle wave of Water washed over him.

He returned the nod, not quite believing what he'd seen and felt.

Had the global Water Magnus seriously just visually shipped him and Elspeth and given an elemental thumbs-up?

An image flickered to life on a second television monitor. The Air Magnus. Trace Lima.

Graham stood at the head of the filled sixteen-seat table. "My apologies for the technical difficulties. I've asked everyone here today to assure you of the stability of the North American continent presidency and the Fire element."

As if it'd heard its name called, the cuff heated beneath the sleeve of Aleron's shirt.

"I realize many of you don't know me," Graham continued, "but several weeks ago, my grandfather commenced succession plans with me. He also entrusted Jon Costa with his vision for my ascension."

Jon stood. "I bore witness to Seanair's decision to choose Graham Lennox as his successor. I motion to accept." He retook his seat.

Hildegard Hoffman's face enlarged on the monitor. The Earth Magnus had one green eye and one brown, denoting the ground-to-garden magnitude of her power. "You, Graham Lennox, have no leadership experience, and it's common knowledge both your physical and spiritual commitments to your Fire and Air are lacking. This is no time for placing the world's most powerful economy or an element known for its instability in the hands of an academic. At the next Continental Congress, in one year's time, Earth will move to launch a search for your replacement."

The monitor went black.

Shit. If Graham were actually wearing the Fire cuff, taking the presidency and Fire Magnus role from him would be a death sentence. Once a cuff passed from emissary to its bearer, it had to be worn for life.

Masako Fukada stood and waited for the murmurs to silence. "I respect Earth's conservatism; however, Water hopes for young leadership. With a willingness to learn and a respected mentor, Graham Lennox may be the fresh approach Fire and North America so desperately need. Moreover, with proper training and patience, Elspeth Lennox may put the 'just' back in our justice system." She scanned the table, and an undercurrent of power rolled through the room.

"Until you prove me wrong, both Elspeth and Graham have the full global support of Water."

A spark of hope ignited deep in his gut. Waters around the world had megarespect for Ms. Fukada. Holy shit. This was huge. He cut his gaze to Elspeth, who clearly recognized the enormity of that level of backing.

His mother stood.

"I speak today with the blessing of Trace Lima, global Air Magnus. Air will take a cautionary step and lend the full support of the United States only. At the Continental Congress, we will determine whether to pledge our full support or withdraw it." His mother's gaze shifted between Graham and Elspeth. "I will assume my regional role in six months. During that time, I will lend you my full assistance, along with my staff's." She indicated the two people sitting to Emeric's right.

"Very well. Good luck and Goddess-speed to you both." Trace's screen went black.

Jon Costa rose from his seat, the strain of Rob's loss still lining his face. "If I may, I wish to make a personal statement. I have known Elspeth and Graham since they were babies. You may be surprised that I didn't always agree with Seanair, but when Elspeth and Graham's parents were killed, Seanair called me. He said he hadn't been a good father to his own boys, that he'd neglected his duties. Seanair asked me how to be a good father, and my answer was simple. Love them. Support them when they need it. And do something with each of them that they enjoy. Seanair supported Lach's work as a painter, continued to buy Graham chemistry sets even after he blew up the garage, and he read to Elspeth nightly." Jon turned to Elspeth. "I know he changed after your Mathair's death, but when he discovered you were Passive, he worried for your safety. He always loved you, even when it seemed he didn't. You have my love as well. What you did for my family, I will never forget." He took a moment and looked to Graham. "You will have the support of every lieutenant in North America. We will see to your success. You have my word."

Aleron's gaze locked with his mother's. A slow, tight smile pulled across her face, and she winked.

Her go-ahead. Do it. Get the girl.

Elspeth didn't need more alliances than the several she had in this room.

The spark of hope ignited into flame. They could be together. It'd still have to be secret for a while. Young, inexperienced leadership would be all the Natura world could handle. A high-profile pairing between two different social classes would be too much. For a while. Then things had to change.

All he cared about was that when they closed her apartment door at the end of the day, or wherever they ended up living, she wouldn't be the Judex, and he wouldn't be her bodyguard.

She'd be his Elspeth. His everything. His sweet tastier than lemon.

And he'd be a man in love.

The meeting adjourned. Everyone made their way into the lounge and toward the elevator.

Kazumi strode toward him, all Ms. Business in her power jumpsuit.

He gave her a what-up chin thrust. "Good news, Half Gallon. I'm calling you Zum now."

Man, she sure could knit those brows down tight. He'd never had a sister, but that look sure seemed satisfying for a brother.

"Careful, or you can refer to me as Your Future Excellency of Water. Only E calls me—" Her expression softened, her smile pulling into a smirk. "Easy-B, I'm glad that Bic brain of yours is finally flicking. If anyone deserves to live out a bodyguard fantasy, it's her."

"Please. Bodyguard extraordinaire is the least of my best skills."

An eye roll. Yep. Her frustration equaled total brother satisfaction. He might have to adopt her.

"She is my best friend in the whole wide world. I love her."

He looked to the elevator, where Elspeth was waving at him to join her and Graham.

"I do too." He gave the kickass Water a nod, then headed toward his love, ready to take her home and see if she was up for taking a chance on forever with him.

CHAPTER
TWENTY-NINE

"**M**y family has pulled together in a way I hadn't expected." Elspeth stretched out on the sofa, her feet in Aleron's lap as he kneaded away the pain of four-inch heels. "Kerr stopped being an ass long enough to grab every book he could out of Seanair's library to see if he can find something on being a Nexus. He's not convinced Seanair didn't know anything. Graham and Ross are holding videoconferences to reassure the other continent presidents we have things under control, and it made me realize how much my grandfather depended on Ross. He's giving Graham the credibility he needs right now." She looked down at her hands. "Flora's...well, no one could change her mind. Not even Kerr."

Aleron's thumbs pressed at the squishy base of her toes, and she knew, for sure, she was about to melt into the couch.

"We don't deal with witches at Elite One. They police themselves, and when it comes to oaths, if a witch breaks the moral code they've made with the Goddess, they're held accountable. If Samael didn't vow to kill Flora, he won't without paying an extreme price. He wants something. Maybe Flora can figure out what it is."

She pulled her feet from his lap and sat up. "Why are you making light of this? Flora's in real danger going to Samael as a spy for us."

His mouth pinched together. "The man damn near killed me, so I *don't* underestimate the risk Flora's taking." His warm hand rubbed her knee. "We can't make people do what we want, even when we feel we know what's best for them. It's the same for Lach. He's handling the situation he's been dealt in the way he thinks best." His hand stilled, his grip gentle but firm. "Your devotion to your family is one of the things I love about you. Have a little faith. If they need your help, they'll ask because they know they can count on you."

Family issues were the worst. How could she love someone so much and want to throttle them in the same breath?

"I texted Lach one more time, even though I should know better. Flora promised this Isidora will take care of him."

A lazy growl sounded from beside the fireplace, where the guards had placed the custom purple velvet chaise lounge they'd retrieved from Lach's apartment.

"That dog," Elspeth said. "She's sweet and loyal, but I feel like I've been overthrown in my own apartment." She moved beside Aleron, resting her head on his shoulder.

His Fire and Air circled around her, and hers did the same with him, as if both their energies functioned best when guarding the other. Cocooned in peace, she reflected on the morning and on the pledges of support.

"I can't believe today went that well."

"I can. People want change, and they see opportunity—and hope—with you."

Her phone vibrated on the coffee table, the song "Killer Queen" a loud slash through the calm. Kazumi. Goddess, it'd taken everything she had not to pick up Zum's mother and hug the Magnus at today's meeting. She read the screen.

No French treatment. Mom says S. Korea has new approach and is open to discuss research collab.

"Is everything okay with Zum?" Aleron leaned forward, shifting toward her. "I got nothing through our friendship thing." He gestured to his wrist.

She showed him the text. "Zum's mom is making some progress. I wish I could get out there and do more."

"Look at it this way. South Korea's offering to work with us. You're already showing the world you're a uniter."

She met his beautiful brown eyes, the concern there such a comfort. He always had her back. Always. "I'm going to have to get used to having help. Having people want to help me. That's totally new."

Aleron moved to his knees on the floor, pushing out the coffee table to make space for his big body. His hands rested on her thighs, and his usually stern expression sobered.

"Do you trust me?"

"Absolutely." She didn't hesitate. She cradled his jaw where the scar had been. The internal one would remain, but she would work to soothe it when it flared. A thought occurred to her, the slap of truth sharp, like her heart had smacked her brain with *wake up, girl.*

She could have him. She could have her dream. The man in front of her, on his knees with love in his gaze, could be hers.

"We can do this." She put her hands over his and squeezed. "We can be together."

"No one can know. Not yet." Strain deepened the line between his brows. "But we can. I want to. I've somehow got my family back. The only thing missing is knowing that I'll have you with me forever. I love you, Elspeth, and I want to be with you no matter how we have to make it work. It'll be hard enough for our people to grapple with so much change in leadership. I won't be a liability to either you or your family."

A blowtorch of anger scorched her insides.

"The best Nexus is a happy Nexus." No one would take him from her.

No. One.

His smile turned devious. "I love it when your Fire gets all smelty for me."

She leaned forward, her mouth inches from his. "No one's going to tell me who I can or can't love. I love you, Aleron." She kissed him, a slow, firm press that she felt the flames of all the way to her toes. "I'm all for keeping us secret for now. It's no one's business anyway. I'm not about to share you."

Fire, Air, Water, and Earth charged like warring soldiers at the notion of him regenning with someone else.

"Speaking of sharing, I took an Earth tonic Flora gave me, and for now, my Earth and Water energy are on par with the other two. The regen thing may not be an issue."

"I'll never be comfortable with you being with someone else, but we'll figure it out. What kind of tonic?"

"Apparently, a Freddy special."

He moved over her and her back met the sofa, her neck bent back over the edge, Aleron's gaze hot and wild above her, her body pinned by his. "The man knows his swill. We'll see what happens. Now, about getting all bossy and not sharing me. Be careful, baby. Your power can't talk to mine that way and not expect one helluva refuel." He blew out a steadying breath. "I have a proposition."

Her elements strained toward his, even the Earth and Water. If she hadn't known the rules, she'd swear her Fire and Air had somehow tossed a few scraps of energy to the other two.

"I'll take all suggestions under advisement," she teased, desire swirling in her at the fierceness of his love.

"When we're outside this apartment, you're the Judex, and I'm your bodyguard. When we're home? Here? It's just us." He pulled the chain from beneath his shirt. "Normally, after a relic's used, it destroys itself. I believe it still has value. Whether you agree to my terms or not, the ring saved me once, and I want you to have it." His gaze wandered sweetly over her face. "One day, when everything calms down for you, and you're ready, I want to marry you. I love you, and I can't imagine truly living without you. Unhook the clasp."

Her hands shook, the moment so private and real. Her dream was there, right there, in the warm space between them. She wanted to catch it, live it, ride it until her last breath.

The chain fell to the couch, the ring in his hand. He shifted his weight, the bulk of him, she realized, being taken by his knees as he straddled her. He took her left hand gently, his thumb gliding down her finger, and slid the band on, his gaze locked on her hand the entire time.

The metal heated, the stones backlit by an eerie glow, and the loose band shrank to a snug, but perfect, fit.

"Wasn't expecting that, but I'm fine with you not being able to take off my ring." His brows lowered, and his mouth pulled to one side. "I do recall many occasions where my mother wanted to blast my father into the backyard. Foussés can get a little…overheated at times."

She put her hand to her chest. "I had no idea you had a temper. No clue at all."

"One day, we'll make it official, when you feel the time is right. You're the one with something to lose."

"The only blessing I want for our relationship is from the Goddess. We could join spiritually now, in communion, if you want."

His head moved in a slow, steady nod. "I want."

He stood and offered his hand, pulling her from the couch and guiding her to the hearth and facing her.

"Together." He took her hand closest to the fireplace.

Her Fire reached out and coiled around his, and their combined energies erupted in a flame beneath the logs.

He took a step back, his gaze trailing down her body. "Are you partial to these clothes?"

"No."

His eyes glowed a warm orange. Her pulse went thready at the slight sizzle over her skin. She watched the ashes of her suit sweep over the hearth and then looked down at her nude body.

She met the heat in his eyes with fire of her own and pledged to buy an entirely disposable wardrobe if this was the prize.

"Your turn. Trust yourself. You won't burn me. Turn the heat up slow."

She opened her Fire, letting it out slowly, inching it forward but keeping it firmly leashed.

"There you go. Clean up your mess, young lady."

She channeled a small breeze at the clumps of ash and sent his clothes the way of hers.

The air glimmered. The cuff appeared on his arm, gold and glimmering with power, as if their sole wedding guest.

She took his hands, drawing them up between them to rest above her breasts.

The vow whispered inside her mind, the words fused into her flesh. She would love him forever. In this life and the next one. He was hers, now and into the ever after. Blessed be the Mother.

She blanched at the vivid fire in his eyes. "The words are 'habeo omnia do tibi.' I give you everything. Once you say it back, we'll be bound until death."

She studied his face, tracing her gaze over his deep-brown eyes, the tight knit of his dark brows. His mouth was the only soft feature on his face. Her life flashed before her, every bad thing falling away with every slow sweep of her gaze.

"Habeo omnia do tibi, Aleron."

"Habeo omnia do tibi, Elspeth." He brought up their joined hands and kissed each one. "I love you, always and forever."

She rose up on her toes and kissed him, curling her fingers in his thick hair, realizing she'd met and found and married the love of her life. Her dream. Made real.

"Let's seal the bond." He took her slowly to the carpet, pressing her gently to the floor, his knee parting hers. Reaching between them, he positioned himself and pushed in. "I. Love. You." He punctuated the words with three slow thrusts.

"I love you too." Her heart threatened to melt as he began to move faster.

She canted her hips in their rise from slow to delicious fury. Warmth sizzled over her skin. Air lashed at their joined bodies. He stilled and dug his fingers into her hips as he came.

Her name came on a shout, and the bright light behind her eyelids burst into a thousand perfect suns. Her muscles pulsed around him, and she was Earth and Water and Fire and Air and Love.

She opened her eyes, meeting his, and gaped at their brilliant, jeweled green.

"Your eyes," she gasped.

"They're green?" A flicker of awe burned through the fear in his voice. "I didn't think. Goddess, this is my fault."

She took his face in her hands. "If it happens, it's made of love. I want a family, if it's now or later."

"If it happens, it'll be tough to keep our relationship a secret. Gestation's only six months."

"Do you want to be a dad?" She held her breath.

He bit his lip, his head lowered, his nods fast and short. "Family means everything to me." He moved down her body and placed the gentlest kiss at the top of her sex, teasing his nose over her lower belly and worshipping at her breasts. "I will make as many babies with you as you want. When you're ready." His nose drew up the side of her face and nuzzled her hair.

She felt him firm and hard against her belly. Was she ready to be a mother? With everything else going on in her life and her new responsibilities? She sensed being a mother was one of those things you never truly understood until you were one, and she had a duty to her people, but...she had a responsibility to herself. To pursue what she wanted. To be true to Elspeth. The woman who'd put others' needs ahead of her own for most of her life.

"No more condoms between us. It'll happen when it's meant to happen."

His body stilled above her, and his cock pressed hot and thick against her belly. Flame snaked from the gas logs, a touch of air kissing the orange ribbon. The swath of energy circling them slid into his mouth. A spear of warmth shot down her throat and bloomed in her stomach and between her legs.

His eyes glowed a fervent, lush green. The decision all hers.

For hours, they gave and received from each other, lost in the ecstasy of sensuality and erotic renewal, Fire and Air pushing and pulling from both of them, their voices hoarse, their bodies beautifully exhausted. They'd eventually moved to the bed, and as she fell asleep with his arm and leg draped across her, she sensed a peaceful intrusion inside her, something new and sacred.

She felt herself smile as she succumbed to the steady rise and fall of his chest, her dream alive and well beside her.

EPILOGUE

*N*ew York One is on the scene of a four-alarm blaze in Hell's
Kitchen. Crews continue to struggle against the intense heat,
but the fire remains isolated in a building recently sold by
Seanair Lennox, the now-deceased chairman of the Fotiá Consortium,
to the Hudson Yards Redevelopment Group. We're also receiving un-
confirmed reports of a house fire in the Hudson Valley area, near where
Lennox is reported to have lived…

Samael swirled the last of his Old Pulteney, the whisky's burn
warm and smooth. Such an odd custom, the taking of a flammable
liquid inside their bag-of-blood-and-tissue bodies until their senses
were dulled. He didn't enjoy the perspiration forming along his hair-
line, but he did, indeed, appreciate the woodsy, loamy scent of the
liquor.

He particularly savored the respite from his pain, which would
arrive sometime between glasses three and four. He held up his
tumbler and gained the bartender's attention before swallowing the
last of his second scotch, closing his eyes, waiting for the face of his
missing wife to dim.

He returned his stare to the TV reporter, impressed Elspeth
had used the media so expertly to her advantage. She was clearly
beautiful, and one day soon she'd be immensely powerful, but he
hadn't imagined she'd be so…clever. He rather liked a worthy oppo-
nent, and it'd been years since he'd had one. His elbow propped atop

the long bar, he absently touched his lips, his nostrils flaring at the recollection of what it was like to kiss someone.

He'd been faithful to Ursula in the two years she'd been lost. Not once had he strayed in order to bind Earth energy to him. He called the energy two solid hours each day, chained to the ground and bound naked in his circle, gritting his teeth against the agony of overfilling his vessel to near bursting so he could wield more power.

He glanced down the bar at the two women sitting at the end and willed his dick to respond. Goddess, what would he do if he couldn't get it up with the Lennox Earth?

What are you going to do if you can?

The bartender nodded toward the bottle in his hand. "This'll be the last one I can serve you unless you order food."

No food. He wanted numbness. The kind of bravery derived from liquid courage. The kind of backbone needed to be unfaithful to the love of his life.

He had no choice. He had to screw that Alpha-level Earth and grow stronger so he could free Ursula from wherever those Naturas had taken her. Seanair Lennox had known where she was, and he couldn't be the only Lennox who did.

He sipped steadily and silently thanked Mother Nature for the poor young woman who'd escaped from the Naturas. She'd been able to share the information he and his kind had desperately needed, telling them before she died that fifty witches were being held captive.

At a lab.

More than two hundred witches and warlocks had disappeared in the past twelve years.

Seanair hadn't even blinked at any of Samael's threats to expose his involvement in the covens' missing brethren. He'd considered the coven classes weak and not worthy of his concern.

But now the Lennoxes had a scientist who'd ascended to Seanair's position. And if Graham didn't know now what his grandfather had been up to, he would soon.

And Samael wouldn't bother with threats this time.

The stool beside him slid back. A rush of air escaped the leather cushion as his ingenious son sat down.

"I'll take a beer, whatever's easiest to pour," his son told the bartender, who headed down to the far end to fetch a fresh glass.

"What do you have for me, Egan?"

His heart damn near burst with pride. His blessed honorable, loyal, dependable son had walked away from his dream of being a doctor.

"I've combed through all forty-five hundred families in the database and pulled the ones with a net worth over ten million dollars. That's two thousand Alpha families. Most of the Betas are worth less than a quarter mil. I was sure we'd find a clear money trail, but the field's crowded." Egan picked up the pint glass the bartender had placed before him. "What do you want me to do?"

He nodded toward the television at the headline splashed across the bottom of the screen. "It was smart of them to destroy their element signatures so we can't easily charm them. They're leaving town. You need to make sure you go with them. Do you know their plans?" Samael caught the bartender's attention and and raised his empty glass. "I'll take the basket of sourdough with the herb butter."

The guy had said he'd have to order food. Didn't mean he had to eat it.

"They're heading to Seanair's primary estate in Savannah. He has a house in town and a four-hundred-acre farm an hour west."

"I don't care what you have to do. Get to Savannah and insert yourself into their day-to-day operations." He picked up drink four, his body warm, his vision swimmy.

"Should be easy enough. Ross thinks I'm a rock star. I'll call you when I'm in place." Egan tossed back the last of the lager, then smacked the glass on the bar.

"We'll find your mother, son. I promise. I won't rest until we do. We're getting close, and I have something in play that'll allow us to level up our game."

"I'm not giving up. Any word from our other plant?"

"She's working a new angle too. She has an in." He swiveled his head toward his son, his troubles feeling lighter as he gazed at the thoughtful boy who looked just like his mother. "I'll call you."

"Be safe, Dad. I think this thing's a lot bigger than we realize."

"I think you're right." He bumped fists with his son and watched him walk through the revolving door before returning to his drink.

Ursula's long, dark hair and red mouth faded with every sip. He replaced the fading memory of her features with a new target. Graham Lennox was a man of science. A boring man, based on his early assessments, who spent nearly every moment in a laboratory.

Samael wouldn't attack this time. Instead, he'd sit back and learn everything he could about Graham's work. The young witch who'd escaped had stressed two things—lab and experiments.

Seanair had likely been the money behind whatever'd happened to those witches, and if one thing held about the late leader? He kept his business in the family, so all signs pointed to Graham as the brain behind the operation.

He heard the click of heels first, the timing and solidity of the steps indicative of long, long legs. She stopped just to his right, and the moment held. Freshly turned dirt and grass brushed under his nose, and a web of spider's silk teased over his skin.

Pure. Luscious. Fertile. Earth.

He turned, and his heart knocked hard in his chest.

She slid off a long, thick wool duster, folding it over her arm. Her blond hair cascaded in waves over her bare shoulders, and the long, gauzy dress did little to hide her full breasts and bare sex, no lingerie in sight. No makeup either, but she didn't need any. Swear to the Goddess, if Mother Nature had had a clone, she would be Flora Lennox. Her hot gaze foreshadowed legendary sex, the kind that made men promise a woman anything she wanted, the kind that made a man weak.

She poured on a smile, the bar lights glinting in her green, green eyes. An invisible slide of pressure pushed up his inner thigh, her grin shifting from wanton to wicked as he firmed. "I heard you were looking for me."

Want to read the prequels that put Elspeth and Aleron on a crash course with each other and true love? Download *The Mistake* and *The Birthday* novellas, both available on Amazon.

———•———

For the latest news on upcoming releases, join my newsletter at www.SloaneCalder.com.

About the Author

Sloane Calder has been an accountant for transformers, paint ovens, and lingerie and went on to become a marketer for baked goods, mincemeat, soft drinks, and lawn care products.

An avid reader all her life, she still thinks there's no better escape than a good book, especially if hot heroes and superpowers are involved.

For more books and the latest updates:
www.sloanecalder.com

Facebook: www.facebook.com/sloanecalder

Twitter: www.twitter.com/sloanecalder

Instagram: www.instagram.com/sloanecalder

Bookbub: www.bookbub.com/authors/sloane-calder

Printed in Great Britain
by Amazon

74058257R10208